THE
HIVE

A MESSAGE FROM CHICKEN HOUSE

In a strange, ruthless world set in a human hive, a murder takes place. Not any common murder, but a royal killing. Apparently impossible, the crime sows discord amongst the hierarchy – can order be restored before the next Winnowing decimates the community afresh? Brilliant, intricately plotted and totally fascinating, this will keep you questioning – not only about the murder, but about what the future holds for all of us . . .

BARRY CUNNINGHAM
Publisher
Chicken House

A FUTURE QUEEN LIES
MURDERED...

THE

HIVE

ANNA FEBRUARY

Chicken
House

2 Palmer Street, Frome, Somerset BA11 1DS
www.chickenhousebooks.com

First published in Great Britain in 2025
Chicken House
2 Palmer Street
Frome, Somerset BA11 1DS
United Kingdom
www.chickenhousebooks.com

Text © Anna February 2025
Illustrations © Micaela Alcaino 2025

For safety or quality concerns:
UK: www.chickenhousebooks.com/productinformation
EU: www.scholastic.ie/productinformation

Cover design by Micaela Alcaino
Typeset by Dorchester Typesetting Group Ltd
Printed in the UK by Clays, Elcograf S.p.A

FSC
www.fsc.org
MIX
Paper | Supporting
responsible forestry
FSC® C018072

1 3 5 7 9 10 8 6 4 2

A CIP catalogue record for this book is available from the British Library.

PB ISBN 978-1-915947-27-7
eISBN 978-1-917171-05-2

For H and R.
Keep asking questions.

We're not always selfish hypocrites.
We also have the ability, under special circumstances,
to shut down our petty selves and become like
cells in a larger body, or like bees in a hive,
working for the good of the group . . .
Our bee-like nature facilitates altruism,
heroism, war, and genocide.

Jonathan Haidt, *The Righteous Mind*

THE ROYAL FAMILY

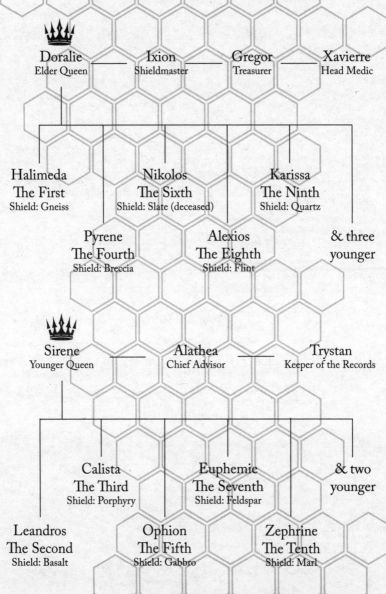

Doralie
Elder Queen

Ixion
Shieldmaster

Gregor
Treasurer

Xavierre
Head Medic

Halimeda
The First
Shield: Gneiss

Nikolos
The Sixth
Shield: Slate (deceased)

Karissa
The Ninth
Shield: Quartz

Pyrene
The Fourth
Shield: Breccia

Alexios
The Eighth
Shield: Flint

& three
younger

Sirene
Younger Queen

Alathea
Chief Advisor

Trystan
Keeper of the Records

Calista
The Third
Shield: Porphyry

Euphemie
The Seventh
Shield: Feldspar

& two
younger

Leandros
The Second
Shield: Basalt

Ophion
The Fifth
Shield: Gabbro

Zephrine
The Tenth
Shield: Marl

FIRST MURDER

Wherever you are in the Hive, you can hear the hum of electricity. I'm not sure why it hums. Most of the time, it's just background noise, something so common that it doesn't even register – like the earthy damp scent of the passageways. Like breathing. But at least once a day, as it has this morning, the hum changes to a more urgent pitch, and that's when I know a storm is coming.

I touch the cool stone wall behind me for reassurance, then catch myself doing it and drop my hand. I'm a shield, raised with a single purpose: to protect my charge. I shouldn't be afraid of lightning. I shouldn't be afraid of *anything*.

'Feldspar!' Euphemie calls me, voice high and imperious. She's in front of the mirror, her handmaiden arranging her braided hair in a complicated crown, stormglow from the wall panels bathing their faces in yellow light. I move smoothly to her side, bowing my head.

'Seventh.'

'Oh, stop that. You know I hate it.'

I look up, meeting her reflected gaze, but say nothing. She knows I have to call her by her title when anyone else is present. Alone is a different matter.

'Fine, have it your way.' She sticks her tongue out at me, and I do everything I can to remain impassive, despite my silly urge to giggle. When we were little, our second-nurse used to say that Euphemie and I were mirror images of each other: warm brown eyes and quick, mischievous grins, whispers and private jokes filling the air between us like electricity. But that was before I grew tall and broad-shouldered and serious, while she stayed small and dainty and full of fun.

'Well?' she asks, turning so I can see the full effect of the golden threads woven into her hair, matching the thick make-up that lines her eyes. 'How do I look?'

Beautiful. But I say stolidly, 'The new style suits you.'

She dismisses the handmaiden with a wave of her fingers, then looks at me expectantly.

'It suits you, *Euphemie.*'

'So it should,' she says, rolling her eyes. 'It took long enough. You're lucky you don't have to bother with all this nonsense.' Dancing across the room to pick up a scarf, she throws over her shoulder, 'Read me today's messages, would you?'

I begin working through the small pile, brought by the courier at sunup. 'Umber thanks you for the invitation, and will

4

gladly attend your party in ten days' time. Sienna too. The Second is sadly otherwise engaged with . . .'

But I lose the thread of that third message, because I've glimpsed the fourth and final one below it. Thick paper, unlike the flimsy green slips of the others. Addressed to *Euphemie, Seventh Ascendant* in forceful black characters. And on the back . . . I turn it over, my throat dry. A pointed oval with five alternating horizontal stripes and six equally spaced lines radiating from it. The royal emblem.

I break the seal and unfold the expensive paper, but I know what it says without having to read it. A message from the Apex – the Hive's royal council – can only mean one thing. My pulse accelerates, the two queens' signatures blurring in front of my eyes. But this is Euphemie's duty, and mine, and I should be glad of it.

'There's to be another Winnowing,' I say. 'The day after your party.'

In the answering silence, I lift my head and am caught by her frozen gaze. Beneath the make-up, her face is stiff, her lips dry. There have only been two previous Winnowings since she came of age a year ago. Perhaps she was able to forget there would be more – or, at least, allow everyday concerns to push the knowledge to the back of her mind, the way I try to.

'Euphemie,' I begin, unsure exactly what the rest of the sentence will be.

I promise I'll protect you.

The cutter soldiers will do most of the work.

There's no need to be afraid.

But before I can get any further than her name, she's taking the Apex's message from me and scanning it with a careless shrug.

'Drones over the age of forty to be reduced by three-quarters,' she says. 'That includes both Sienna's parents. At least she can enjoy the party first.'

'Euphemie . . .'

She drops the paper back on to the dressing table. The fear has melted from her eyes, to be replaced by feverish excitement. 'This is my chance to start proving myself. To show everyone how good a queen I'd be. And this time, you're not going to spoil it.'

It's an unexpected accusation. Faintly, I echo, 'Spoil it?'

'Last time, you didn't let me *do* anything.'

Last time, she barricaded herself into a corner with her face hidden against her folded knees and cried until it was over. Not that I blamed her. A Winnowing is meant to be an orderly exodus of those identified as surplus to the requirements of the Hive, not the massacre it turned out to be.

We'd seen people killed in the first Winnowing we were in, but not many. That matched what we'd been taught: that the chosen exiles would be reluctant to leave, but most of them would rather accept the merciful gift of a chance at life outside than resist and die. So when, in the most recent Winnowing, the surplus fought back as a group, it took everyone by surprise. Not that they stood any chance against fully armed ascendants and shields and soldiers. By the time it was over, the sloping rock leading out from the winnowing gate to the causeway was scarlet with blood.

And maybe Euphemie is right: watching them scream and bleed and die, maybe I was at least a little glad that her fear had given us a legitimate reason to stay on the periphery of the action. I'm always so afraid of losing her, of letting her down, that maybe I let my own anxiety hold her back.

'I'm sorry, Seventh,' I mumble.

She doesn't correct me over the use of her title this time. 'It isn't as if there'll be many more opportunities to impress the queens. I have to make the most of every one.'

I nod. Though the primary purpose of the Winnowings is to prevent us from exceeding our population limit, they also give the ascendants who have come of age a way to demonstrate their fitness to rule the Hive as one of the seven people who will make up the next Apex. That's even more important for Euphemie and the other girls, because they have a chance at the throne. Although each of them is given time with our current queens every week, the Winnowings are by far the best test of their strength, teamwork and good judgement – culminating, once the youngest ascendant turns sixteen, in one final Winnowing in which the current Elder and Younger Queens will choose their successors.

Euphemie is good at the first part of each Winnowing, where the ascendants hear each person from the chosen section of the population make their case, before deciding who can stay in the Hive and who is no longer needed. She enjoys listening to the pleas, arguing for her favourites, delivering the judgement. But that isn't enough for her to become a queen. Not without proving herself in the second part as well.

'*And*,' she adds, clearly determined to work through my full list of faults, 'I wish you hadn't lost my royal brooch. How is anyone supposed to know who I am?'

I've scoured our chambers, but it isn't here. I'm almost certain she dropped it down the drain.

'You don't need a gold brooch for everyone to know who you are,' I say truthfully, which seems to mollify her somewhat. She takes a final glance in the mirror, before spinning on her heel and heading for the door.

'Fetch your boots, Feldspar. I want to walk to the sunroom.'

I follow her out into the exochamber, tasting the sharpness of the air. These chambers are as close to the outer walls as it's possible to live without being rendered permanently cold and damp by the vents, so the circulated breeze is still fresh. It makes me question what it would be like to feel it on my face directly, unfiltered by turbines and pipes. But every way out of the Hive is dangerous. There's the causeway that leads from the winnowing gate: a line of rocks above the surface of the ocean, slippery and wreathed in seaweed. That's visible only at low tide, which is when the Winnowings always take place. And there are the tunnels deep underground, leading who knows where and infested with the same lawless people who try to raid our colony for its resources.

Small wonder that no one leaves the Hive unless they're forced to. We live our whole lives underground, within the hollow veins of this island, because it's our one refuge from the merciless sky above and the raging sea all around.

Euphemie's embroidered slippers are already on her feet. She stands by the outer door, watching me tug my boots on.

'You love me, don't you?' she asks. Her irritation has faded, to be replaced by something more wistful.

'Of course.'

'Good. At least someone does.'

Would you care so much if my death didn't mean yours? she asked me once, in one of her darker moods. I told her that I'd love her even without the shield-bond, but I could see she didn't believe me. Her life isn't built around mine as mine is around hers; she doesn't realize that a shield is only ever thinking about keeping her charge alive. The fact that her survival also keeps me alive is immaterial.

'Everyone loves you,' I add, and a little smile touches her lips.

'You think so?'

'I know so. Euphemie—'

'Hurry up, Feldspar.' The fleeting shadow has passed, as it always does. 'Let's go.'

9

I check I have my knives, though I always have my knives. Already, I'm tense. Night-time means that Euphemie is safe, or as safe as she can be. At sunup, when the stormglow first begins to brighten from the dim orange of night, and I unlock this door to let in the handmaidens and couriers and whoever else has business with her first thing in the morning, a weight of fear and responsibility settles on my shoulders. And when we leave our chambers, it bears heavy upon me until we're back. Because there are always additional people in the royal levels – drones attending their chosen ascendants, cutters doing their jobs as guards and cooks and medics – and people mean danger. It's always been impressed on me that no one in the Hive can ever really be trusted except the royal family themselves.

Now there's to be another Winnowing. The knowledge trickles down my spine like ice water. *And this time, she wants to prove herself.*

'There's going to be a storm,' I blurt out. 'Are you sure it's safe to—'

But Euphemie has already left our chambers, and I have no choice but to follow.

The royal family occupy the uppermost levels of the Hive. Euphemie spends a lot of time on her own level, with the aim of forming alliances; whichever girls become queens, they're the ones who'll decide who takes the other five roles in their new Apex, so it's important for her to be liked by her fellow ascendants. Each set of chambers is some distance from its neighbours, but I could find my way to any of them with my eyes closed . . . except the Sixth's, maybe. We pass the turning to his chambers every day, but we never see him. Not that I want to. *If you annoy me too much*, Euphemie says sometimes – half a joke and half a threat – *I'll hand you over to Nikolos. He spends most of his time inventing new ways to torture people with the dark arts. And he despises shields. I'm sure he'd love the chance to experiment on you.*

From here, we have three flights of steps to climb – all guarded, though with Euphemie present, the soldiers just bow their heads and let us through. The first flight takes us up to the communal level, which houses the salon, theatre and baths, as well as important places like the medical centre, treasury and royal kitchens. The next leads up to the Apex's quarters, and the third goes from there to the sunroom itself. Through the centre of every ring-shaped level runs the Spire: the vast metallic rod that rises out of the top of the Hive, ready to be struck by lightning and supply us with power.

The sunroom is the only level that's built on the surface of the rock instead of inside it. Three of its walls and its sloping roof are made of thick glass panes, making it the only place that anyone in the Hive can see the whole sky. The fourth wall is the rocky peak of the island itself, etched with an enormous royal emblem in golden lines. More gold gleams in the filigree design of loops and swirls covering the lower half of each vertical pane.

I can never be comfortable here. I'm always waiting for lightning to strike the Spire. Yet Euphemie loves it. She can usually be sure of plenty of people to talk to; failing that, she can watch for gulls flying overhead, which are the subject of many of her paintings. And she always imagines she'll catch the sky at the perfect moment between storm and sun. Today, though, I can tell she's disappointed. Thick black clouds have already gathered overhead, leaving the room gloomy – not that it's much better at any other time. Despite its name, the sunroom is completely uninhabitable when the sun comes out; no one can stand for long beneath that merciless glare without burning.

I glance around the room, checking who else is present. Several drones, none of them Euphemie's followers. Two members of the Apex: Gregor, the treasurer, with his distinctive tufty hair, looking tall and gangly next to Alathea, the chief advisor, who's slight and sandy-skinned and has a warm tone to her voice that carries even amid the hubbub. And three ascendants: Alexios, Leandros, Calista. Behind each of them stands a shield, their shaven heads easy to pick out among the elaborate hairstyles of the royal family and the ostentatious adornment of the drones.

The other shields are my kind – and I spent years training with some of them – but none of them could ever matter more to me than Euphemie. She and I have been together for as long as I can remember: when we cut our first teeth, took our first steps, learnt to read and write. Even during those years of training, when our lessons diverged to allow her to learn the business of the Hive while I learnt the business of keeping her alive, we always returned to each other at the end of the day. The two halves of an oyster, aligning perfectly.

She's greeted by Alexios, next to her in age, wearing a bright yellow embroidered jacket that contrasts with his dark skin. As the two of them fall into easy conversation, I exchange nods with his pale-skinned shield, Flint, but we don't speak. Our job is to listen and observe.

'You look well,' Alexios is saying. 'Is that a new scarf?'

Euphemie smiles at him. 'Clever of you to notice.'

'I hear the Apex have announced the result of their most recent vote. More cutter women to be granted permission to bear children who'll be trained as soldiers.' His lip curls. 'No doubt that explains the forthcoming Winnowing.'

A renewed chill creeps over my skin. I might die with Euphemie, or in her defence, but at least I'll never be winnowed. Whereas the drones can be winnowed at any time: to make room for new lives, as in this case; because a particular family has been identified as a poor genetic match for future queens; because an individual supported an unsuccessful candidate for the throne. I'd have expected that uncertainty to make them cautious and careful, like shields. Instead, most of the younger ones spend their lives in a frivolous blur, drinking and partying and throwing themselves after their chosen ascendants in a blatant grab for power.

'Plus, there's to be a cut in rations for the carders,' Alexios adds, and the chill sinks into the pit of my stomach to settle there. Unlike the cutters, who have the privilege of living alongside and serving the royal family, the carders live and work separately from the rest of us, in the depths of the lower levels – the Honeycomb. They're smaller and weaker than us, meaning they don't need as much sustenance, so they're usually the first to be affected when the queens want to conserve resources. More soldiers and less food must mean that raids through the tunnels at the very bottom of the Hive are increasing again. Still, I can tell Euphemie isn't really paying attention.

'What are they talking about?' Her head tilts towards Leandros and Calista, deep in conversation with the chief advisor, Alathea.

Alexios follows her gaze. 'Oh, Leandros is claiming that instead of going to the trouble of winnowing an unneeded demographic, we might as well kill the surplus and have done with it. Calista is becoming quite vehement in response. Sometimes I think his greatest pleasure in life is riling up other people for his own entertainment.'

'That's Leandros for you,' Euphemie says, shrugging, but her voice is warm with amusement. 'So, are you going to introduce me . . . ?'

She gestures to the drone boy standing nearby. I don't know his name, but I recognize him – we've seen him with Alexios several times in the past few weeks, and Euphemie has whispered to me on more than one occasion about their potential romance.

As Alexios makes the introductions, I watch him carefully, but I already know he's no threat. He's a healer through and through, to the point where he's willing to show overt disgust at the idea of a few drones dying for the benefit of the Hive. And he's always taken an interest in Euphemie.

I relax slightly, allowing my gaze to wander around the room in search of wider threats. Yet it always comes back to her, like a needle pointing north.

The sky whites out, briefly, making me jump even before the growl of thunder that follows. *I knew it*. Fat drops of water begin to hit the glass above us, clattering like stones. Euphemie's only acknowledgement that the storm has begun is to raise her voice; this weather is too common to be worth any attention. Yet I can no longer concentrate. I'm too busy counting the seconds after each lightning strike. It's almost overhead. Almost at the Spire. And what if it misses? What if it breaks through the roof and Euphemie is right underneath and—

I shake off the unreasonable panic, because someone is approaching us. But when I recognize Leandros – eldest royal son, lethal with a blade, intends to be shieldmaster one day – I tense further still. Even though the ascendants work together for the good of the Hive, making them less of a threat to Euphemie than anyone, I can't help but feel instinctive alarm at the proximity of someone I've seen decapitating a carder with a single stroke. When he walks straight past her and flings an arm around my shoulders, I should be relieved. Instead, I freeze, pulse pounding in my ears.

'You agree with me, don't you?' he asks. He and Euphemie are both the Younger Queen's children, though it's impossible to tell. Each ascendant has unique drone parentage on one side, making their lineage hard to trace just by looking. 'That it would be far better simply to kill a surplus group and save everyone the pain of winnowing?'

I turn my face away from him, back to Euphemie. 'It's not my place to say, Second.'

'Look at me.' His fingers touch my cheek, wrenching my head round. 'She's not going to die if you stop watching her for one moment.'

He isn't supposed to be touching me. I doubt he even knows my name. I dart a glance around the room, before reluctantly returning my gaze to his. 'It's my job to guard the Seventh.'

'Hmm. You know, once I'm part of the Apex, I intend to have a little *fun*. And who better to have fun with than the shields of my surviving sisters, right?'

His hand squeezes my shoulder. Another flash of lightning illuminates the room, thunder hard on its heels. *So close.* Suppressing a shiver, I force out, 'Yes, Second.'

'It was lovely talking to you,' Euphemie's voice says, a little too brightly. 'But I'm afraid I really must go.'

Leandros lets go of me. I look from him to her. For a fleeting instant, I see the family resemblance between the two of them – something around the eyes – and am unsettled by a tiny squirm of fear.

'It's Feldspar's fault,' Euphemie goes on. 'She always becomes unreasonably anxious if I'm out of my chambers during a storm.'

She laughs, and Leandros laughs with her. Alexios glances between us, but says only, 'It's kind of you to be concerned about your shield, Euphemie.'

'But of course,' she replies. 'I love Feldspar.'

That makes her and Leandros laugh again, though I don't know why. She blows him a kiss. Then she heads for the door, and I hurry to take my place at her side. My hands are shaking. Probably just the lightning. Anything else would be silly.

We follow our usual route, a longer path along some of the lesser-frequented passageways of the upper levels. Euphemie is always in a hurry to get to the sunroom, but she's never as keen to leave again. Typically, she chats to me on our slow meander home, telling me everything she said to everyone we met, asking my opinion of what this or that person did. Today, however, we walk in silence. From time to time, I steal a glance at her; she's looking resolutely ahead, her lips pressed together. She feels . . . cold. Distant. And it makes my stomach hurt.

'Seventh,' I venture finally. 'Are you angry with me?'

She doesn't look at me. 'Why should I be?'

I don't know. That's the trouble. I'm not sure what I did wrong. After a while, I say tentatively, 'We could have stayed. The sunroom is safe in a storm, despite my . . . I'm sorry if my fear made you cut short your visit.'

She shrugs. We keep walking.

'Leandros is an ascendant,' she says, two corridors later. 'And my brother. It isn't appropriate for you to flirt with him.'

What? I stumble over my own feet. 'Seventh, that wasn't how it—'

'Don't answer back,' she snaps. 'In fact, I'd really rather you didn't speak to me at all. Or look at me.'

I'm familiar with this mood. Though I try to be careful, sometimes I end up offending her. I suppose it's inevitable, when two people live so close together. All the same, my stomach hurts worse than ever, a nagging dull pain – and I know from experience that it will keep on hurting until she's forgiven me.

We turn a corner into another empty corridor, past a sign bearing the royal emblem and the words *Our lives for the Hive*. Our footfalls strike a muffled echo from the rock. Then Euphemie says crossly, 'You know, Feldspar . . .'

I hear a soft sound, like a sigh.

'. . . I really hate it when—'

A dull thud. Her voice rises to a wordless cry. I turn: she's wavering on her feet, left hand clutching her right shoulder. Between her fingers protrudes a slender bone arrow.

I spin on my heel, my knives in my hands. Yet nothing stirs in the passageway ahead of us. It's striped with stormglow and shadow, like every other route through the Hive.

'Feldspar?' Euphemie's voice is a croak.

Dropping the blades, I hurry to her side. She sags against me, hand falling away to reveal the merest smear of blood on her fingers. The arrow hasn't hit her in any vital organ. It's a small, fragile thing. Yet her arms are twitching, and her lips are turning blue.

Poison.

Her weight becomes too much; the two of us crumple to the floor. I'm fumbling to get a grip on the arrow, slick and smooth with a little blood and my own sweat. Finally, I pull it out of her, throw it on the floor beside us. More blood trickles from the wound, but it's still not much. As an arrow, it would barely have scarred her. But with poison . . .

They taught us battle medicine, the way they taught us anything else that might help us keep our charges alive. Yet they didn't teach us this.

No one uses poison to kill other people in the Hive. The knowledge runs through my head, spinning in useless circles in the face of reality. *It's forbidden*.

The sound of running footsteps, light and quick, makes me look up sharply. A plea for help forms on my lips, then dies as a figure in black races past us, stooping to collect the arrow as it goes. *The attacker*. I snatch up one of my knives, hurling it wildly after the retreating figure. The weapon strikes its arm before clattering to the floor. The figure stumbles but doesn't stop, vanishing into the shadows once more. There's something glinting on the floor beside us, something that wasn't there before. Automatically my hand closes around it.

'Euphemie,' I whisper, barely knowing what I'm saying. 'I found your brooch.'

She takes a painful, rattling breath, and I lean back over her. Her skin is the colour of ash; her limbs no longer twitch, but lie unnaturally still against the stone. A film covers her eyes. She's seeing not this world, but the one beyond.

'Feldspar . . .' Her voice is a breath. Then her head drops against my arm, and she's gone.

Dead.

My charge is dead.

My charge is dead, and I'm still alive.

And that's impossible.

SECOND MURDER

SAME DAY

I must have been in shock. It's the only explanation for the huge chunk of missing time between Euphemie dying in my arms and *this*. Sitting on a narrow cot in a prison cell, stomach churning and throat raw, as if I've been screaming. Or vomiting. Maybe both. There's dirt beneath my nails, except that when I look at it closely, I can see it's blood. Then I have to look away, because if I let myself keep thinking about it, the screaming will start again. And maybe this time, no one will be able to stop it.

She said my name when—No.

Her eyes looked through mine as she—No. No.

The stormglow is dim here, but enough to see the cell by: a few paces in each direction, bare of everything except a bucket in the corner and the cot I'm on. Nothing to occupy my mind. Nothing to stop the flashes of memory.

I cradled her in my arms—

No.

I count the fastenings that hold the stormglow panel in place on the wall beside me. Then I count them in twos. I multiply the rows by the columns. The answer comes out different every time, but that's good. It means I have to keep trying.

'Feldspar.'

At the sound of the voice, I scramble to my feet, reaching for my knives. I didn't hear anyone coming. I have to protect Euphemie from my negligence—

But I have no knives, and Euphemie isn't here.

Letting my arms fall to my sides, I turn my head. A woman is standing just inside the door to my cell: tall and imperious and bronze-skinned, with a sharp nose and cheekbones that look as though they were sketched by a stern hand. Sirene, the Younger Queen. She must be here for answers. And more than answers – her expression is fierce with grief. Likely heir or not, Euphemie was her child . . . *Was.* My stomach heaves.

'Ma'am,' I say, all scratchy. I sound sad, broken, and that's wrong. A shield must always be strong; that's why we're named after the rocks that make up the Hive around us, keeping everyone safe. I force myself to speak with more vigour. 'You've come for my account?'

She doesn't answer, but glances to the side and tilts her head in my direction. Another woman emerges from the shadows: her shield, Ganister, broad-shouldered and dull-eyed. Responding to her curt gesture, I submit to being patted down – though surely they know I have no weapons, given that whoever first arrested me must have confiscated them, during the time I don't remember. Once she's finished, Ganister turns and bows to the queen, before taking up a position at the side of the room.

'Sit down,' Sirene tells me, eyeing my trembling knees. She waits for me to obey before taking a seat at the other end of the cot, regarding me warily – as if she still thinks I could be a danger to her, despite the search. On another day, I might have found that funny. I may be a shield, but she's a *queen*. She wouldn't be that if she didn't have skills far beyond anything I have to offer.

'This evening, as the sun goes down, I will return my daughter to the sea,' she says, every word hard-edged with sorrow and rage. 'She died before she had the chance to live.'

I flinch. There hasn't been another royal death in my life-time, but I know their bodies are sent out through the winnowing gate – the very same place where Euphemie cowered and cried as that last Winnowing became a massacre. She wouldn't have wanted that. I imagine them standing there in their funeral clothes, the queens and the rest of the Apex and all the ascendants, on that sloping bloodstained rock now washed clean by the tides. Watching Euphemie's weighted body sink beneath the surface as a seabird cries overhead. I should be there too. I need to say goodbye . . .

But that could never have happened. Even if I'd died along-side her, we wouldn't have been together in death. Only the royal family are given to the sea; the rest of us are burnt to fuel the generators. Anything else would be too much of a waste.

'Well?' Sirene demands. 'I need you to tell me what happened.'

'The Seventh . . .' I can't put the words together. I can still see it. With what feels like immense physical effort, I get out, 'She was murdered. It – it was poison. Someone shot her with an arrow. I'm sorry, ma'am, but I couldn't see who it was. They were dressed in black, and—'

She raises a hand. 'You misunderstand me, Feldspar. I've already been given an account of the nonsense you were babbling when you were brought down here. I need you to tell me how you survived.'

I failed her. The knowledge I've been trying to ignore is there, seeping through every crack in my defences. *I failed her, and yet I didn't die.*

'I don't know,' I tell Sirene. Perhaps it's unwise, to be so honest, but I can't bring myself to care. 'The bond should have taken me. I don't know why it didn't.'

She says nothing.

'Will I be executed?' I ask dully.

'Not yet.'

That's a surprise. I wait for her to explain, but instead, she gestures Ganister to my side with another of those subtle head movements. This time, there's a small syringe in Ganister's hand. It contains a tiny metallic speck suspended in blue liquid.

'A tracker,' the queen says. 'So we can always find you.'

The threat is overt, but I don't understand it. I'm in prison. It's not as if I'm going anywhere. Still, I'm used to being injected with all manner of things on the Apex's orders, so I extend my arm to Ganister without question.

'Don't try to cut it out,' the queen adds, as the needle pierces the webbing between my thumb and forefinger. 'Without the proper tools, you'll only release it into your bloodstream, where it will eventually stop your heart.'

I wouldn't have thought to try. I mumble agreement, and watch the plunger depress.

When it's done, Sirene nods at Ganister, who opens the cell door for her. In the doorway, she turns.

'Doralie and I will not put you to death,' she says, 'until we find out how you broke an unbreakable bond. And until we have your full confession of how you murdered your charge, against everything that is natural and right.'

My brain is slow, my thoughts viscous; she's already out of the cell by the time I understand the gravity of the accusation.

'No,' I say, scrambling to my feet, wobbling as the blood rushes to my head. 'I would never have hurt her. *Never.*'

Sirene's glance is dismissive. 'Why else would you break the bond?'

Without waiting for an answer, she leaves, and Ganister locks the door behind them.

I'm weary beyond anything I've felt before, with an ache that seems to have penetrated through flesh and bone to my very marrow – but every time I close my eyes, I see twitching arms. I see blue lips. So I start to pace.

I was right: it's barely four steps from one side of the cell to the other. I count them, moving quicker and quicker, slamming my palm against the wall each time I reach it until the skin glows hot. And I do not – *forty* – think about – *forty-four* – Euphemie. *Forty-eight*.

'I saw a bird trapped in the Hive, once,' someone says. 'It dashed itself against the walls until it died.'

I spin on my heel, fists lifting defensively, to find a stranger standing by my cot. It's impossible for him to have entered and crossed such a small room without me seeing him, yet here he is. That's twice I've been caught unawares since I got here. No wonder Euphemie died, with only me to protect her . . . My hands loosen, and I press the back of one of them to my mouth to stifle whatever sob or shout or scream is trying to emerge. *Pull yourself together, Feldspar*.

'I'm Nikolos,' the stranger says, looking past me as if I'm not significant enough to focus on. 'They sent me to investigate your crime.'

So *this* is the Sixth, master of the dark arts. I stare at him. I should be focused on denying the word *crime*, yet curiosity wins. Scarcely anyone has seen the Sixth since he came of age two years ago – not even in the Winnowings, which are meant to be compulsory for all ascendants aged sixteen or above. He exists more in rumour than in fact. And rumour painted a sinister, cloaked and hooded figure out of a children's tale, not a slender boy with tousled black hair and a vague expression.

As pale as a wraith, Euphemie once told me. *I heard the stormglow dims whenever he enters a room. As if his mere presence sucks all the light out of the air.* I can almost hear her saying it, with that combination of fear and glee that accompanied all our best ghost stories. Yet although this boy's coat – high-collared, buttoned to the throat and billowing almost to his ankles – is as dark as his hair, which does make his face look paler in contrast, he's hardly wraithlike. More a kind of light tawny. And Euphemie will be disappointed when I tell her that the stormglow didn't so much as flicker …

Wrong. You can't tell her anything, ever again.

'Sixth,' I choke out over the lump in my throat. 'I am—'

'I know who you are, Feldspar.'

Of course he does. He's investigating Euphemie's death, and it seems I'm the only suspect. I glance to either side of him, but find nothing but empty space … right. The Sixth doesn't have a shield. He's the only ascendant without one. Slate, his original shield, died before they came of age, and he refused to take another. I'm so used to seeing people in pairs

27

that the absence in itself strikes me as unnatural.

'So,' he says. 'How did you kill her?'

'I didn't. I swear.' The denial comes more quickly than I managed with Queen Sirene, but it doesn't make any difference.

'They've given me three days to find out,' he says, as if I haven't spoken. 'After which you will be executed. But you might earn yourself a less painful death if you were to offer a free and full confession straight away.'

I shiver at the prospect – not of my execution, which is inevitable, but of being trapped in this cell for three days beforehand. Maybe I should lie and get it over with . . . *No. Stop it.* I shake my head. 'I'm sorry, Sixth, but I can't confess to something I didn't do.'

'I could make you, you know.' For the first time, he focuses on me. Now that they're looking at me directly, his eyes are very black, very bright and very alive. They seem to pull far more understanding from my face than I could glean from his. 'Haven't you heard? I am a master of the dark arts. I can send nightmares screaming through your mind until nothing remains but the desperate need to make them stop.'

'I know.' My lips are dry. Now I'm thinking about everything Euphemie ever told me about the Sixth's skill in the dark arts, all bloody experiments and unnatural powers. Stories I listened to with a shiver that was half fear and half enjoyment, believing I'd never have to face him.

I drag my gaze away from his, fixing it on the floor. The

relief is instant: like moving from uncomfortably hot sunlight into the shade. He might not be cloaked and hooded, but all the same, rumour didn't lie.

Quietly, I repeat, 'I know.'

'Then tell me the truth. Or I'll have no choice but to spend the next three days getting it out of you.'

I have no desire to find out what that involves. But since there isn't anything I can say that I haven't already said, I don't reply.

'Euphemie's death is a threat to the entire Hive, surely you realize that. If one shield can find a way to break her bond, others can follow. They won't let you meet your own end without telling them how you did it – because no one has ever broken a shield-bond before.' He makes a noise that I'd take for a laugh, were it not for the complete lack of amusement in it. 'Though people have tried.'

The words hold a prickly undercurrent of something that could be either sorrow or rage. My nails dig into my palms, a new sense of futility washing over me. Nikolos might not have been related to Euphemie – his mother is the Elder Queen – but he's still part of the royal family. He must hate me for her death. Which means there's no chance he'll listen.

But I have two choices: give up or keep trying. And if I knew how to give up, I wouldn't be a shield.

'I didn't break it,' I insist, though I don't quite dare to look at him. 'How could I?'

'I don't know. Yet. But it's either that, or the bond was weak and you took advantage of the opportunity that presented itself. And if I can't find out which, I—'

He stops. It's as if he veered too close to the edge of a cliff and caught himself just before falling.

'I'll be made to take another shield so I can winnow with the rest,' he says at last, in a voice like sunlight on the ocean: all glinting surface, concealing unfathomable depths. 'We must all play our role in maintaining the Hive, after all. But that's one role I've no desire to play, so it'll save us both a lot of trouble if you just *confess*.'

I'd assumed the Apex chose him to investigate Euphemie's death because of his skill in the dark arts, and perhaps that's true. Yet not the whole truth – they also want him to take his proper place in the Hive. And why not? Winnowing is the ascendants' ordained task, the way they prove their fitness to rule; it doesn't make sense that he'd refuse to do it. Unless he really does despise shields that much.

'The queens can conceive of no possible explanation for these events that does not make you a murderer,' he adds. 'And neither can I.'

Murderer. Part of me wants to accept that label. I didn't save Euphemie from death, so what difference does it make whether I wielded the fatal weapon?

But I would never have hurt her.

I straighten, turning to look Nikolos in the eye even though

I half expect him to punish me for that presumption alone.

'I failed the Seventh,' I tell him. 'To the greatest possible depths of failure. But I didn't break the bond, and I didn't kill her.'

Then I grit my teeth, waiting for him to do something horrible to me. Instead, he regards me with his black brows knotted in a frown, as if I'm a problem that's proving trickier to solve than he'd expected.

'You're not afraid,' he says finally.

A laugh bursts out of me before I can stop it. I close my eyes, covering my mouth with both hands this time, not sure if the sound was hysterical or agonized or both. Nothing about this is funny, but he doesn't seem to understand . . . 'With the greatest of respect, Sixth, the worst has already happened. What is there left to fear?'

'Interrogation with the dark arts followed by execution would do it for most people.'

'But why should I expect anything else? The Seventh is dead. And I'm alive, when it was my place to die for her – or, if not that, to die with her. Without her, I can't – I shouldn't be . . .' The words won't come. Roughly, over the renewed lump in my throat, I repeat, 'The Seventh is *dead*.'

'What makes you think that means she'd want you to die too?' For the first time, his voice is sharp. It reminds me of everything that was whispered about him, after Slate died. That he laughed at the offer of a replacement. That he curled his lip, and asked what could possibly make him want another fallible human to protect him when the dark arts could do a far better job. That he killed his shield himself, in some arcane ceremony, to increase his power. From the tone of his voice, I can believe it, but the words . . . the words don't fit.

'All right,' he says, when I don't answer his question. 'So you're telling me you didn't kill Euphemie, but you want people to believe you did.'

'Of course I don't!'

'Then you should help me.'

'*Help* you?'

'Yes. You're the only witness. So if you're going to insist on drawing this out, you can at least be useful in the meantime.'

I look at him blankly. He sighs.

'If you're claiming you didn't do it, you must also be claiming that someone else did. Either way, it seems I need you if I'm to find out the truth.' His voice takes on a mocking note. 'Who knows? Maybe you'll prove your own innocence.'

He's right. The realization settles on me, another layer of guilt. I've let my own grief blind me to the very obvious fact that *Euphemie's killer got away with it*. Poisoned her, as if she were an animal rather than an ascendant. And though I might have failed her, there is one final duty I can perform before my death: bring her murderer to justice. No more self-pity. I was trained to fight on through loss of limb and fatal injury, and this wound is no different.

'All right,' I say. 'I'll do everything I can to help you. I swear on the Spire.'

'Good. Then I'll be back in the morning.'

I want to ask why we can't start straight away, but the ever-dimming stormglow tells me the answer. It's close to sundown. They're about to give Euphemie's body to the sea.

'Sixth,' I whisper. 'Will you . . . ? Could you . . . ?' But I don't know what I'm trying to ask, or why. It's not as if he owes me any favours. In the end, I choke out, 'Tell her I'm sorry.'

Too late, I realize that could be interpreted as a confession, but he doesn't haul me off to be executed. Instead, his expression softens by a fraction.

'Tell her yourself,' he says. 'She's just as likely to hear you here as she is at the winnowing gate.'

With that, he leaves. As the key turns in the lock, I wrap my arms around my knees and scream soundlessly into the void. No one is going to accept what really happened. I'm on my own. But I can't let that stop me.

'I'll find out who did this to you, Euphemie,' I tell her memory. 'I promise.'

ONE DAY AFTER

I don't sleep. I seem to have forgotten how. When the storm-glow is so dark that I can barely see my hand in front of my face, I know it's midnight. After that, it slowly brightens from dim orange to the yellow of sunup. A new day. My first without Euphemie.

She's my earliest memory. Her face close to mine, breath ghosting against my cheeks. The two of us wrapped in the blankets of our single bed, limbs intertwined as if we'd grown together in the womb. Like twins, yet not like. Because I knew, even then – aged two? three? – that my job was to love her more than myself. That knowledge was in my blood, in my bones, before I was old enough to put it into words.

You love me, don't you?

Of course.

That was it. That was us. Our entire relationship in a hand-ful of words. And without her to love, I don't know who I am.

My eyes sting, but no tears come out. Eight years of training crushed my ability to cry. Or maybe I'm dehydrated. I haven't eaten or drunk anything since the morning I lost Euphemie, which I assume was only yesterday, though I can't be sure. I'm not hungry or thirsty; it's as if my body knows I should be dead and has shut down all its functions accordingly. But I'll have to consume *something*, sooner or later. The lack of sleep is bad enough. And my hand hurts . . .

I look at my palm. It's marked with six evenly spaced red dents, in a circle, as if I gripped something with many points so hard that it came close to breaking the skin – *yes*. That's right. I found Euphemie's brooch. Or so I thought, in my panic and distress. But it couldn't have been Euphemie's, could it? She'd lost hers. And besides, it hadn't been there on the floor until her attacker ran past us. Which means her attacker must have dropped it.

Desperately, I hunt through my pockets, but they're empty. Of course they are. Ganister would have found a brooch if it had been there when she searched me; a pin is sharp enough to do damage, and therefore counts as a weapon. Maybe they took it off me before I even got to prison. But then, wouldn't Queen Sirene have asked me about it? In which case . . .

Head swimming, I sit up. Amid the unbroken grey of this cell, anything golden would have been spotted long ago – unless it fell under the cot I'm sitting on. I drop to the floor and scrabble in the dark, dusty recesses at the very back until my hand closes around it. A small, cold object, the six points of the radial lines fitting perfectly into the dents they left. I must have carried it here, unnoticed by anyone else, and at some point I let it go again.

This is evidence. Proof that someone else killed Euphemie. And no one knows about it but me.

A tap sounds at the door, followed by the scratch of the key. Shoving the brooch into my pocket, I scramble back into my previous position on the cot. When the Sixth walks into the room, I blurt out, 'You knocked on the door of my prison cell?'

He sits down beside me – not at a careful distance, like Sirene did, but with casual serenity, as if he doesn't consider me dangerous at all. I'm not sure which is worse.

'You seemed alarmed when I turned up yesterday,' he says, fishing a large cloth-wrapped package out of one of his capacious pockets and dropping it between us. 'I thought this would be politer.'

Turned up is a distinctly understated euphemism for *appeared out of nowhere*, but I say nothing, concentrating on opening the package. It contains a bottle of water and a portion of fish, biscuits and greens – the same briny food I've been eating my whole life. Most of the Hive's resources come from the sea: fish and shellfish, for meat and glue; seals, which are harder to catch but offer useful skins as well as flesh and bone; seaweed, seagrass and algae for all kinds of purposes, from fabric to medicine. What the carders can't harvest, they produce using the technology of the Honeycomb. That includes fresh water; we might be surrounded by water, but neither the rain nor the sea is safe to drink without being purified first.

The familiarity of the meal means I'm slow to realize its significance. The treasurer keeps careful track of all the Hive's necessities. No one gets more than they need, not even the royal family. Which means Nikolos must have taken this out of his own rations, or used some of the monthly allowance for luxuries that he's given as an ascendant. I stare at him.

'You brought me *food*?'

'I told you. I need your help. I can't have you passing out on me.' He gives me a sidelong look. 'Besides, I doubt anyone else remembered.'

No. They didn't. But that's what I'd expect. An ascendant going out of his way to feed me, on the other hand . . . that's unusual. Even if it is largely down to self-interest.

I take a sip from the bottle, and it's as if that one small trickle of fluid brings me back to life – like dried mushrooms when you add hot water. My stomach grumbles a fervent demand for more. I finish the rest in three quick gulps, then apply myself to the food. It's only once I'm down to crumbs that I remember I'm not alone. 'Please excuse me, Sixth, I was—'

'Hungry,' he finishes for me. I wait for a lecture, but instead he says, 'You can call me Niko. And since we are making introductions, this is Astrapē.'

He gestures to his shoulder. Or rather, to the air above his shoulder. I blink at it, then turn my attention to his face, studying it for clues – but find none. It could be a joke. It could be a test. Cautiously, I ask, 'Astrapē?'

'My familiar,' he says, with a dark smile that I can't interpret. 'Right now, she's in the form of a gull.'

I *hope* it's a joke or a test, because otherwise he's lost his grip on reality. 'Yes, Sixth.'

'You can call me Niko,' he says again. 'Apparently, we're going to spend more time in each other's company than I anticipated, and I'd rather not have my title hurled in my face throughout.'

An order, then, rather than a nicety. I nod, though it's hard to make myself do it. Even with Euphemie, even in private, I would never have dreamt of shortening her name.

'So,' he says. 'Are you ready to begin?'

Yes, Sixth. But I swallow the automatic response. I can't be that person any more. Euphemie is relying on me. 'I . . . Actually, no.'

My head is clearer now than it was yesterday; funny, how much the brain relies on the stomach. It occurred to me somewhere between the biscuits and the fish that I only have the Sixth's word that he was sent to investigate Euphemie's death. And given the small weight of the dropped brooch in my pocket, with everything it implies . . .

'How do I know you didn't kill Euphemie yourself?' I ask,

all in a rush, then grimace. That question was a bad idea on a number of levels. One, I used her name instead of her title. I've been thinking about her so much that it slipped out. Two, if he really did it, his response could easily be to dispose of me on the spot.

I tense, ready to do my best to avenge Euphemie even though I'll be fighting a power that's beyond my understanding, but the Sixth only shrugs. 'Still claiming your innocence this morning, I take it.'

'You're more likely to have killed her than I am,' I insist, emboldened by frustration. 'What better explanation could there be for her death and my survival than—'

I break off, face heating. He raises his eyebrows.

'Than?'

'Than the dark arts,' I finish in a small voice.

'Right. Because everyone knows I spend my free time sacrificing carder children and making necklaces from their bones, so what's an ascendant or two to add to that?'

Rumours or no rumours, I'm almost certain he's joking about the children. Apart from anything else, the Apex would never allow such a waste of resources. Carder children are the workers of the future.

'But even if I had the power to kill an ascendant without destroying her shield,' he goes on, 'why would I do it? The whole thing seems nonsensical.'

'What do you mean?'

39

He glances at me with those bright black eyes. 'It's conceivable that someone might want to kill an ascendant. Maybe someone whose loved one was banished or killed in a *Winnowing*.' He gives the word a rather scornful emphasis. 'But in that case, what would be the purpose of your survival? I can't fathom why anyone would want to keep you alive.'

'Thanks.'

He laughs. His laughter is nothing like the vagueness of his usual expression; it's sudden and vivid, like a bolt of lightning. It makes him seem . . . well, not ordinary, exactly. I don't think he could ever be that. But *approachable*.

'You shouldn't thank me,' he says, once he's stopped laughing. 'That's one of the main reasons that no one believes your story. You're the only one who gained something from this.'

'Gained?' I repeat incredulously. 'Gained what?'

'Freedom. Perhaps Euphemie was cruel to you. Perhaps you were tired of being treated as expendable—'

'No. *No*. Stop it.' That isn't true at all. I loved Euphemie, and she loved me. No matter how she enjoyed the company of her followers among the drones, she always knew their regard was dependent on what she could do for them; no matter how close she was to the other ascendants, those alliances always held an element of politics. All we really had in the world was each other.

And now, all over again, I'm missing her smile. The way she used to tease me. The way she'd whisper secrets to me at night.

Her absence is like a near-fatal wound: it hurts all the time, but it doesn't take much to make it hurt *more*.

Nikolos glances sideways at me, taking in my tightly crossed arms, my balled fists. He nods to himself, though what thought or suspicion I've confirmed for him I have no idea. Then he asks abruptly, 'Do you have any friends, Feldspar?'

'Shields don't have friends.'

'But you're not a shield any more.'

Something inside me snaps. 'I *know* that. I *know* I failed. You don't have to keep *needling*—'

With a gasp, I catch myself. I've gone too far. Too angry, too vocal, not nearly polite enough. And though my stomach clenches with the knowledge that the Sixth's punishments are bound to be far crueller than Euphemie's, what really matters is that he might decide my help isn't worth the trouble – and then I won't be able to fulfil my last duty to my charge.

'Forgive me, Six—I mean, Niko,' I mumble. It feels un-bearably overfamiliar to use his name – and a short form, at that – but he *told* me to use it. I can't afford to antagonize him any further. 'I didn't mean to be rude.'

'And I didn't mean to hurt you.' He looks away. One hand drifts up to his shoulder, only to be snatched away again. 'Electric eel,' he murmurs.

Don't panic, Feldspar. That wasn't some kind of obscure threat but a reference to Astrapē. His *familiar*, whatever that means. Then my stomach plunges again, because if he electrocuted me and said an invisible eel did it, who would argue with him?

It takes all my self-control to sit still, but no retribution is forthcoming. Maybe he's the kind to hold on to a grudge until I've forgotten I did anything wrong, then spring it on me. Which is worse, but there's nothing I can do about it.

'I was only trying to point out that now you have options,' he adds.

Bitter terror fills my throat, far greater than any fear of punishment, as I'm overwhelmed by the sheer vastness of a world where I'm not what I was born to be.

'Options?' I choke out. 'What options? I'm going to be executed.'

'But you claim to be innocent. If that were really true, you wouldn't deserve execution.' Noting my shiver, he asks, 'Why does that scare you, when the execution itself doesn't?'

'I'm not scared, exactly. I just . . .' It's a struggle to explain. 'This is *wrong*. Me, being alive now. It goes against the order of things. How could you understand? I may not be a shield any more, but you were never one.'

'The order of things,' he repeats. 'Do you really believe that?'

'What? Yes. Of course.'

'Hmm.'

'What does that mean?'

'Someone who thinks the way you seem to think, Feldspar, would never murder an ascendant, and would *certainly* never break her own shield-bond,' he says. 'Which is why it would also make a good smokescreen.'

I don't know how to answer that. If his default assumption is deceit, no wonder he views the truth and its opposite as equally likely. Nothing I can say will prove the difference.

In the silence, Nikolos – *Niko*, I have to call him Niko – gets to his feet. I guess my interrogation is over, for now. But in the doorway, he turns and looks at me expectantly. 'Well? We'd better get started.'

I'd assumed we already *had* started – that this odd, oblique conversation was his way of determining my innocence or guilt. It's not as if I have any concept of how to investigate a crime using the dark arts. 'What do you want me to do?'

'Show me where it happened.'

'You're letting me out? Does Queen Sirene know?'

He shrugs. 'How else would I go about this?'

I hate it when people answer a question with a question. It's meant to be a private remark, safe inside my own head, but he laughs. I said it aloud. Muttering another apology, I follow him from the cells.

It's only once we've climbed all the way through the drones' levels and back up to the royal quarters that I realize he didn't answer my second question at all, and by then I have more important things to worry about. I thought it would be easy to find the place where Euphemie died. Every moment of her death is etched on my memory; I only have to close my eyes to see it. Yet all the corridors of the Hive look the same, and after we've walked around a bit, I'm forced to admit defeat. It's as if I've been in prison for far longer than a day, and forgotten everything I ever knew.

'I'm sorry. I can't—'

'Retrace your steps,' Niko says. 'Walk me through what happened that day.'

So I take him to the sunroom. It's that time between storm and sun, when a few bright rays are beginning to spill through the fading clouds. It won't be long before the sky clears completely and the sun blazes too hot again, but for now, the weather is as good as it ever gets. Euphemie would have liked it. I wish—

'Ignore them,' Niko's voice says softly at my ear. I don't know what he's talking about. Blinking, I glance around and see that a couple of other ascendants are up here too. Halimeda, Pyrene, both escorted by their shields. I'd never have missed their presence when Euphemie was alive, particularly not with all four of them watching us. Yet there's no hatred in their eyes – which is what I would have expected, if I'd thought about it at all. No, they're looking through me as if I'm not even here. As if I'm a dead girl walking.

I suppose that's what I am.

'You and Euphemie came here,' Niko prompts me. 'Who else was present?'

'Some drones – I don't remember which. The treasurer and the chief advisor. The Third and the Eighth, and – and the Second.'

If he notices my brief hesitation over Leandros, he doesn't remark on it. 'Along with their shields?'

Doesn't that go without saying? But he's waiting for an answer, so I nod.

'And then?'

I lead him along the route we took, the long way down, the deserted passageways. I say nothing, and he asks me no questions. Until—

My breath catches in my throat. We've rounded the corner into another corridor, an ordinary straight corridor like all the rest. Dim stormglow on dull stone walls, a floor worn smooth by generations of feet. Air that smells of saltwater and the familiar musty undertone of ancient rock. But suddenly my chest is tight. *Our lives for the Hive.*

'Here,' I whisper. 'This is where it happened.'

Niko glances around. 'You're sure?'

I stumble forward, my fingertips trailing over the rough wall. My lungs ache as if I'm drowning.

'There.' I indicate the floor. Niko crouches to examine the small bloodstain near one side of the passageway.

'According to the queens, you claim Euphemie was shot with a poison arrow. That's why there was so little blood?'

'I couldn't hold her. She fell. I pulled out the arrow.' I'm not

45

telling it right. These stilted, cold words don't come close to what happened. But it's all I can do to hold myself here instead of fleeing.

'Where did the arrow come from?'

'It . . . I . . .' The sentence won't form. I'm shaking. I let my forehead fall against the wall, pressing hard enough to hurt. 'I'm sorry.'

He's quiet a moment. Then he touches me lightly between the shoulder blades and says, in a different sort of voice, 'Take a deep breath, Feldspar. Hold it . . . and release. Now another.'

I obey him. A soft warmth spreads through my body, originating from somewhere beneath his fingers. I concentrate on breathing, following his orders, until finally, I have sufficient control of myself to turn and face him.

'I didn't know the dark arts could do that.' There are a hundred things I imagine the dark arts *can* do. Kill without weapons. Protect without a loyal shield. But making someone feel less cold and afraid wasn't on my list.

'That wasn't the dark arts,' Niko says. 'That was Astrapē.'

'Gull or eel?' I ask, to humour him – because he did just do something nice for me, even if it was because he wants me to answer his questions.

'Neither,' he says absently. 'You needed comforting. She's currently something soft and fluffy. So, where did the arrow come from?'

Right, then. Still, I do feel less shaky. Straightening my shoulders, I tell him, 'It came from ahead of us. It struck the front of her body, the right shoulder. But I couldn't see anyone there.'

'Queen Sirene told me you claim to have seen the killer.'

'That was later. After Euphemie had fallen. I'd pulled out the arrow, but I couldn't—' For a heartbeat, the shivers threaten to consume me again. I take another deep breath and say quickly, 'The attacker ran past us and retrieved the arrow, before disappearing the way we'd come.'

'So,' Niko drawls. 'Euphemie was killed by an unknown person who left no trace of themselves or their weapon behind.'

'No! They did leave a trace. Look.' I pull the royal brooch out of my pocket.

'Surely that was Euphemie's?'

I shake my head. 'She lost hers. No, the killer dropped it as they fled.'

'Are you saying that Euphemie was killed by someone in my family?'

'I . . .' That isn't a thought I'd allowed myself to have. It's too big, and too terrifying. But I can't run away from it, not if I want to find out the truth, so I lift my chin and repeat, 'All I know is that the killer dropped it.'

'You're the only one who can vouch for it not belonging to Euphemie,' Niko points out. 'Just as you're the only witness to the crime itself.'

So much for my evidence. I stare at him. 'You don't believe me.'

'The simpler explanation is by far the more likely. And the simpler explanation is that you stabbed Euphemie and lied about it.'

Without waiting for a reply, he walks off down the corridor, examining the walls to either side as he goes.

'How often did you and Euphemie take this route?' he calls back over his shoulder.

'Quite often.' I hurry to catch up with him. 'Euphemie was . . . restless, I suppose. She wanted to be outside, but since that could never be, the sunroom was her closest option. And going home, we always took the long way round. Maybe . . .' My throat dries as the thought forms. 'Maybe she didn't want to be alone with me more than she could help.'

'Not you, specifically,' Niko says, still scanning the walls. 'Some people just don't enjoy solitude. And being alone with someone who's trained to obey you without thinking can feel very much like solitude.'

Whether he intended that as a criticism or not, it lands like one.

'What are you looking for?' I ask in a small voice.

'Something to . . . Ah.' He stops in front of a stormglow panel that isn't working, resulting in a stripe of shadow that's wider than usual, and pulls a screwdriver out of one of his pockets. 'I'm dressed in black. Return to that bloodstain, will you?'

When I get there, I turn and look back at him. 'Now what?'

'Pretend my face is covered. Can you see me?'

Oh . . . he's trying to work out where the attacker could have hidden. I'd love to say he's completely invisible, because it would give more weight to my story; yet although at this distance he's in shadow, I can distinctly make out his full shape.

'Yes,' I answer him. 'I would have seen a person standing there, even covered head to foot.'

He turns and applies the screwdriver to something on the wall. And then, like magic, he disappears.

'You've gone,' I call, starting to jog back towards him. 'How did you . . . ?'

But as I get closer, I can see for myself. He's swung the malfunctioning panel right out from the wall and concealed himself behind it. The matte, uniform grey of an unlit panel blends perfectly into the shadows in a way that the figure of a person doesn't.

'This is close enough to where you were standing to be within reach of someone armed with a blowpipe,' Niko says. 'And there are a few scratches around the fastenings on one side of this panel. It's possible that someone tampered with it in order to create themselves a hiding place.'

'Then that proves I'm telling the truth.'

He looks at me, frowning – as if, for the first time, he's giving genuine consideration to the possibility.

'It doesn't prove you're not,' he corrects me finally. 'Someone could have watched you and Euphemie carefully enough to know your habitual routes. We've demonstrated that you could have been ambushed in the way you claim. But that does nothing to discount the other, more likely explanation . . . and if you're a clever killer, you would have made sure this was here for me to find.'

I suppress a sigh. As far as I can see, the dark arts are at least fifty per cent not believing anything that anyone ever says. It's only doubt over the other fifty per cent that keeps me from pressing my case.

'It's a shame they didn't let me examine her body,' Niko adds, half to himself. 'Death by poisoning looks very different from death by stabbing. Though even then, it wouldn't prove you didn't murder her.'

Now I know he's just being provocative. Euphemie's body has already been given to the sea, as is right. Her chambers will have been declared out of bounds for seven days, left untouched until the period of mourning has passed. No one would dare challenge that. So instead of arguing, I ask suspiciously, 'How do you know what death by poisoning looks like?'

'Poison might not be allowed in the Hive as a way of killing *people*, but there are always pests to be disposed of. That's why the carders are permitted to make a few carefully chosen poisons.' Seeming to sense that I don't find that an illuminating answer, he adds, 'One of their children ate some by mistake once. I saw the body. It wasn't pretty.'

I see a flash of blue lips, rigid limbs, but blink it away. He's right: poison isn't pretty. And I still don't understand what he was doing among the carders in the first place. They keep the machinery running and supply us with food, but there's no reason an ascendant would ever need to seek out their quarters in the Honeycomb. Not that anyone would have stopped him; the royal family can go where they please. But typically, the soldiers and couriers form the only connection between the upper levels and the lower – and the role of courier exists purely *because* some long-ago queen decided that no one from the upper levels should have any more to do with the carders than was necessary.

'You're full of questions,' he says. 'Pick one.'

Perhaps that was another criticism, but the tone was almost complimentary. And he anticipated me again. Still, I manage to stop myself asking whether part of the dark arts is the ability to read minds. There are more important questions, and I'm only allowed one.

'All right. Then assume, for a moment, I'm telling the truth and Euphemie was poisoned. Do you think the poison would have come from the Honeycomb?'

'That's a good question,' Niko says, staring abstractedly at the faulty panel. 'If you wanted to use poison on someone, you'd need to get it from somewhere. And if you couldn't brew it yourself, you'd have to send a courier to the carders who work with chemicals. They don't come up here.'

That implies there might be people in the upper levels who do have the ability to brew poisons. But since Niko himself is the most likely to have that knowledge – surely poison is part of the dark arts? – I don't mention it. Instead, I venture, 'I know you said it's conceivable that someone who bore a grudge for a previous Winnowing might have killed Euphemie, but I'm not sure I agree.'

He turns to face me. 'What makes you say that?'

I falter under the impact of his suddenly sharpened focus. 'Well, I – she only ever took part in two Winnowings, and she didn't hurt anyone. She was scared, she . . .' *This time, you're not going to spoil it.* Swallowing over the ache in my throat, I force myself to go on. 'I didn't have to do much to defend her. People barely noticed she was there. There are far more likely ascendants to be the object of a grudge.'

'There are two possible answers to that,' Niko says. 'One being that if *you* killed her, none of what you just said is a consideration.'

'And the other?' I ask hopefully.

'The other is that you're right: Euphemie wasn't a warrior. She wouldn't have been the obvious target of a revenge plot. But perhaps that was the point. Perhaps they went after someone who was as ill-equipped to defend herself as they were themselves. Not the most *suitable* target, but the *easiest*.'

'But there's no reason a carder assassin would have dropped a royal brooch,' I say stubbornly. 'So, assuming I'm telling the truth about that as well, what would that mean?'

He gives me a sceptical look. 'If I'm to believe every one of your implausible claims, Feldspar, the only logical explanation is that Euphemie was poisoned by someone in her own family. Presumably a fellow ascendant, since they at least might have some reason to want her out of the way – a rival for the throne, say, or another position in the Apex. But none of these other theories explain your survival, so they remain the less probable option.'

Yet, I realize with terror yawning like a black pit inside me, what he just said must be the truth. Though the ascendants are meant to trust each other implicitly, working together to winnow the population for the good of the Hive, an ascendant *must* have murdered her. Poisoned her, like a coward. And since anyone who was found to have done such a thing would be instantly disqualified from a place in the Apex, *that* must mean that if they took the risk anyway, it was because they were certain they'd never be caught.

'All right,' Niko says. 'We'd better get you back to your cell.'

I should have known this was coming. He has my account of what happened and where, which means I'm no further use to him. All that's left is to wait in my cage for two more days while he concludes his inquiry, and that's not good enough.

'I want to do more,' I say hurriedly. 'Can't I come with you, when you talk to other people? Be a part of the investigation?'

'How? You're the main suspect.'

'But I—'

'You know, the queens want this dealt with as soon as possible,' he says. 'Prove to everyone that it was a singular event, a never-to-be-repeated aberration, the act of a traitor who was swiftly dealt with. Because what do you think will happen if ascendants can no longer trust their shields? If word of Euphemie's death spreads, and other people in the Hive start thinking they can attack a member of the royal family without consequence?' He glances at me, before answering his own question. 'Panic. Chaos. Everything the Apex most fear.'

'What are you saying?' I whisper.

'That since the queens are pressing me for answers, by far the easiest course of action for me would be to make something up. None of the Apex know anything about the dark arts! I could tell them I've confirmed you broke the bond, invent a few plausible details, and go back to my normal life. No shield. No Winnowings.'

It hadn't even occurred to me that he might lie. That my life is in his hands – and, more importantly, so is justice for Euphemie. 'Then why don't you?'

'Because the truth matters.' His response is swift and fierce. 'If I can't give them that, I'll give them nothing.'

The nearest working stormglow panel has started to flicker, dimming and brightening in an erratic rhythm like a frightened person's pulse. He watches until it steadies again.

'Maybe I'd do it, if I were sure you're guilty,' he adds lightly, as if he regrets revealing so much emotion. 'But there's no certainty in any of this. Not to a satisfactory standard of proof.'

So he thinks there's at least a small chance I'm innocent. That's better than anything else I've heard since Euphemie died.

'Then let me help you,' I say. 'Please, Niko. I can't just sit and wait. I promised myself I'd bring Euphemie's murderer to justice. And – and if I'm guilty, then you're far more likely to discover that with me there, right?'

Now his expression has turned blank. But after an agonizing moment, he shrugs. 'Fine. I'll come and fetch you tomorrow morning.'

TWO DAYS AFTER

I sit on the edge of my cot and run a hand over my scalp. Without the morning ritual of razor and basin, it's exhibiting the faintest growth, like the soft fuzz on the head of a newborn. My second day without Euphemie, and already I'm not who I used to be.

'It's just hair,' I say aloud. 'It doesn't matter.' But it does. The small everyday tasks of life might seem insignificant, but they're the glue that holds everything else together.

In the past, when the walls closed in on me, I used to exercise. Euphemie would grumble, because it meant she had to come with me to the training floor, but she knew I needed it. For me, an active body has always meant a quiet mind. But I'm not going to let Niko catch me pacing again and compare me to a *trapped bird*. Instead, I drop to the floor between cot and wall, and start doing push-ups.

At thirty, it occurs to me that Niko might not be coming –

and if he doesn't keep his word, I'll have nothing to do but wait to find out how I'll die. Executions are rare nowadays, but that's because everyone in the Hive is taught about the methods in gruesome detail; no one would willingly do anything to bring one of those four cruel punishments on themselves. Trapped in one of the fishing tunnels, below sea level, to be drowned when the water rushes in. Walled in a lightless cell to starve. Chained to the Spire, so that lightning courses through the body and fries it from the inside out. Or left in the sunroom to burn to death in the full, merciless heat of the sun. Sea and stone, storm and sun: the four forces that control our lives. And one of them will destroy me.

My arms buckle, but I catch myself. I keep going. I focus on breathing, and on not panicking. At fifty, I hear footsteps and collapse with relief. Whoever is coming, and whatever they're going to say, it's better than being left alone with my thoughts.

Niko enters the cell and looks down at me quizzically. He's wearing the same coat as on the previous two days. Euphemie used to say he never sleeps, and maybe the shadows under his eyes are evidence of that – but to me, it's more as if he tried to sleep and didn't do a very good job of it.

'What are you doing?' he asks.

'Push-ups.'

'Before *breakfast*?' He steps over me to sit in the exact same spot as before, emptying one pocket of a package similar to yesterday's as he does so. 'Is that usually how you start your day?'

I sit up, wiping the sweat off my forehead with the back of one wrist. 'Usually I shave my head.'

His gaze drifts over my scalp. I wait for him to say something indifferent – *everyone has hair* – at which point I will either cry or punch something. But instead, he reaches into another pocket and produces a razor.

'It will have to be dry,' he says. 'And I'll need it back afterwards. The queens don't want you to have any weapons.'

I don't know what to say. I'm genuinely afraid that I might cry in earnest, which would shame me so much that I'd never be able to look him in the face again. Finally, taking it from him, I manage, 'Do you always carry a razor around with you?'

He shrugs. 'You never know what might be useful.'

Once I've shaved and eaten, Niko packs everything back away. I watch in fascination. I'm beginning to think that when he selected the coat, the sinister effect of all that voluminous black was very much secondary to the capacity of its pockets to hold random objects.

'Thank you for coming,' I say when he's finished. 'I wasn't sure you would.'

'I said I would, didn't I? Though I might not have,' he adds reflectively, 'except for the fact that I need to at least try and follow the queens' orders. They told me to find out how you broke the shield-bond. If I uncover any proof you did it, that would also be fairly conclusive proof that you murdered Euphemie, knowing you were safe.'

'And if you don't, it proves I didn't?' I suggest, though I know perfectly well it isn't that simple. I just need to hear *someone* say I'm not guilty, even if it's only me. Niko doesn't dignify the question with a response.

'We'll talk to Ixion,' he says. 'If there's anything wrong with your bond, he should be able to tell us.'

Ixion is the shieldmaster. He's responsible for training all the shields and soldiers. He's also the one who created the bonds between each of the current ascendants and their shields. I don't know if I'm still allowed to ask questions, but if I'm to continue protecting Euphemie, even after her death, I have no choice.

'Wrong?' I echo. 'In what way?'

'I don't know. Maybe you did something to weaken it. Maybe Ixion failed to set it up properly to begin with, but was afraid to reveal his mistake. Maybe you were never bonded with Euphemie at all. We'll find out, won't we?'

'Surely you don't think the shieldmaster would have done his job incorrectly.'

'Would you rather I thought it was you?' Niko shakes his head. 'It's almost as if you don't *want* to be proved innocent, Feldspar.'

'I do,' I say quietly. 'But even more than that, I want the world to make sense again.'

He pulls a face. 'When did it ever?'

We find Ixion in the armoury, on the same level as my cell. Like the rest of the Apex, he has rooms at the top of the Hive, but he spends the vast majority of his time down here: training soldiers and overseeing their deployment to different posts, as well as teaching any shields between the ages of eight and fifteen. When I was that age, I spent half my life here too, flitting between the training floor and Euphemie's chambers. Ixion and his shield, Rhyolite, almost felt like parents to me – or, at least, what I imagine having parents would be like. Someone to look up to.

Rhyolite is also in the armoury, making notes while Ixion checks each sword for notches and other damage. He goes from sitting to standing in an instant when Niko and I enter, setting himself between us and the shieldmaster. It isn't as if a shield loses their protective instincts once their charge reaches the Apex, and Rhyolite is one of the best; he attended all our training sessions alongside Ixion and helped him to demonstrate a great many of the techniques we were taught. I always used to admire his hairstyle – still mostly shaved but with a longer spiky strip down the centre, which he colours green or black or silver to suit his mood. As long as the shields of the Apex keep at least part of their head shaved, they're permitted to choose a more individual style than we are. *When I'm a queen*, Euphemie used to say, sketching one outlandish design after another, *you can have hair like this*.

But that will never happen now.

I take a deep breath, drawing in the familiar scents: metal and polish and, underlying it all, the faint tang of blood. Then, trying to seem normal and unaffected, I lift a hand in greeting. But Rhyolite doesn't respond. He steps to one side, bowing his head, and now Ixion himself is in front of us.

Ixion's face has always reminded me of a piece of driftwood that Euphemie had in our chambers: a light, weathered brown, lined with age yet somehow smooth, as though scoured by storm and sea. His head is completely bald, like a younger shield's. He nods at Niko, uncle to nephew, but he doesn't even acknowledge my existence. His gaze slides off me like rain off the sunroom roof, and a sharp pain twinges beneath my ribcage. If there's anyone in the Hive whom I failed most grievously, other than Euphemie herself, it is the shieldmaster.

I remember, once, he was teaching a small group of us. It must have been me, Flint and Quartz – shields of the Seventh, Eighth and Ninth. Near the start of our training, when I was nine and the others were eight, scarcely out of the nursery. Shields might not have friends, but those two were the closest I had to it: around the same age, always being taught together. Ixion asked us what we would do if someone attacked our charges. Our voices stumbled over each other as we rushed to answer: throw ourselves in front of the blade, draw the attacker's focus, make a heroic stand. A hundred different suggestions, but underneath, they were all the same: *I would die for her. For him. I would give my life.*

When we ran out of ideas, the shieldmaster looked at us for a long while without speaking. Then he said, *Unlike the older ones, your ascendants cannot defend themselves. They are gentle. Soft. Weak. I've yet to see any one of them acquit themselves even passably in their weaponry classes, and I've no real hope of that changing.*

We stared at him, not sure where this was going. His tone held a warning, as if we'd given the wrong answer – yet we knew our ascendants weren't skilled at fighting. Why else would we be so willing to die for them?

If your charge is attacked, and you are killed, what will happen next? he asked. *The attacker will kill your charge. And you won't be there to prevent it. By dying for your ascendant, you would condemn her to death.*

We looked at each other, fear in our eyes. We hadn't thought of that.

Your task is not to sacrifice yourself, Ixion said. *That might work for the shields of the older ascendants, but not for you. If your charge is attacked, your task is to get her to safety, or kill the attacker. Nothing else will suffice.*

Perhaps that's why I reacted so badly when Niko suggested that I was tired of being treated as expendable. Because Ixion never said we were expendable. On the contrary: he always said how vital it was for us to stay alive, so that in turn we could continue to keep our charges alive. Now here I am, living when she is dead, and I can no longer look at him for shame.

'I was told to expect you,' he says to Niko. 'I was against this investigation, you know. Put the girl to death and have done with it. But I was outvoted.'

For eight years, this man taught me, and now he wants to see me dead. The pain beneath my ribcage squeezes harder.

'The queens want me to find out how the bond between Euphemie and Feldspar was broken,' Niko says, and the pain eases slightly – because he said *how it was broken*. Not *how Feldspar broke it*. 'Ascendant–shield pairs are bonded before birth, right?'

'In the womb,' Ixion confirms. 'As soon as a royal baby is confirmed, we grant a cutter woman permission to bear a child of the same biological sex. The pregnant woman will become first-nurse to both ascendant and shield, and attends the royal birth either before or after the birth of her own child. The bond is checked as soon as both babies are safely delivered to the world.'

Aren't you glad you were created to be bonded to me? Euphemie asked me once. *What else is there for cutter girls? Soldier, cook, nurse, medic, teacher, courier, handmaiden . . . I can't imagine you as a handmaiden, Feldspar.*

'So if there was a problem with a shield-bond,' Niko presses, 'you would notice it straight away?'

'Yes.'

'And Euphemie and Feldspar's was normal?'

'Yes.'

'Is there any way it could have weakened over time?'

'No.'

I sense Niko's frustration. This mood of Ixion's is familiar to me: like the walls of the Hive, immovable and impermeable. He would often fall into it when he felt we were asking particularly obtuse questions or failing to grasp the point he was making. Yet underneath it, he appears on edge in a way I've rarely seen. Perhaps that's not surprising. He's almost certainly followed the same logic as Niko and realized that if there was a problem with the bond, even if he didn't cause it, he'll be the one who gets the blame.

'Can you tell anything about how the bond failed from Feldspar herself?' Niko persists, and a scathing smile appears on Ixion's face. I used to be terrified of that smile, in training.

'The shield-bond isn't a piece of rope, Nikolos,' he says. 'When it is broken by death, it disappears as if it were never there. Just as no trace of your bond with Slate remains in you, no trace of Euphemie's bond remains in Feldspar.'

'But this has never happened before,' Niko says. 'It's never been the ascendant who died and the shield who lived. So couldn't you—'

'No.'

'Then how can we possibly find out who broke the bond?'

'As I have already told the Younger Queen,' Ixion says

impatiently, 'there is no mystery here. No outside agency has the power to destroy a shield-bond formed in the womb. The *only* possibility is that one of the two parties to the bond broke it.' His gaze meets mine for an instant; the sheer force of his antipathy takes my breath away. 'And since Euphemie would have had no reason to do so, it must have been Feldspar. *How* she did it is a question for her to answer. Under torture, if necessary.'

Well done, Feldspar, he said, before I left his tutelage. *You're a credit to me. Euphemie is lucky to have you.* My hands are shaking. I clamp them under my armpits.

'So it's your considered opinion, as Feldspar's former teacher,' Niko says, 'that she broke the bond deliberately in order to murder Euphemie?'

'Yes.'

I should be worrying that this doesn't look good for me, but I'm too focused on trying not to betray my emotional turmoil. The shieldmaster really believes I'm a murderer. I thought he knew me better than that.

'But how is that possible?' Niko asks. 'I thought the bond itself was meant to prevent her from turning against her own charge. In which case, she could only break the bond if the bond was already weak . . .'

I close my eyes. Now I understand why, at certain points in this conversation, Niko has seemed to be on my side: he doesn't fully understand how shield-bonds work. Which means that as soon as it's explained to him, he'll go back to believing me guilty.

'The bond can't control human behaviour,' I hear Ixion say. 'It's no more than simple cause and effect: if this person dies, that person dies. We do the rest with conditioning.'

'Conditioning?'

'The shields are raised from birth to internalize the rules. Protect your ascendant. Protect all other members of the royal family, unless that conflicts with the first rule. And so on. They know that if they fail the first rule, they will die. It makes the rest stick more easily. The end result is that although they can fight for training purposes, the intent to kill can come only when they are protecting their charges. Our soldiers have slightly different conditioning, but the basic principle remains the same.'

'But . . . wait. If a shield can only defend herself if her charge is under threat, what's to stop someone attacking the shield first, and only turning on the ascendant once the shield is dead?'

I open my eyes in time to see Ixion's scathing smile return. 'This system has existed for far longer than you have been alive, Nikolos. Do you think your ancestors failed to consider these things? Once they come of age, an ascendant and her shield are always together. A threat to one *is* a threat to the other.'

'But it means that without Euphemie, Feldspar is essentially powerless to keep herself alive.'

'Which wouldn't have mattered, if she had died as she was meant to!'

That hurts, but he isn't wrong. I watch his feet as he paces back and forth, fighting his temper. When Niko speaks again, his tone is conciliatory.

'All right. I take the point. Still, for Feldspar to have murdered Euphemie, she would have to have broken her conditioning as well as her own shield-bond. Correct? And I can't believe that would have been easy to do. The conditioning must be extremely strong, if it's what we all rely on to keep our shields from turning against us.'

Why does Niko still sound like he's on my side? Surely he'll only make Ixion angrier. I risk a glance at the shieldmaster, anticipating one of his famous explosions, but whatever irritation he's feeling is now concealed behind an impassive façade. Even more dangerous.

'Correct,' he says. 'Indeed, I would have thought it almost impossible for any shield to overcome their conditioning. Nevertheless, Feldspar must have done so.'

'Can you test it?'

Ixion hesitates.

'We could try a test,' he says at last. 'The second test I give all shields and soldiers just before they turn sixteen, after they've passed the first by proving themselves in combat. It's the safety check, if you like. The limitation on their fighting abilities. It ensures that the conditioning has held and that the shields are fully ready to protect their ascendants without putting our wider community at risk. But if she has broken the bond, she may be clever enough to fake the conditioning.'

'Surely not,' Niko says. 'If it's as good as you say it is.'

I thought I heard a trace of sarcasm in that, yet his expression is polite and vague.

'Come here, Feldspar,' the shieldmaster orders. He holds out a knife, hilt first. That's part of the test: I have to be given the ability to defend myself. It wouldn't prove anything unless it came with some very real risk on Ixion's part. And it says something about the effectiveness of his training, of the conditioning, that he's never once been hurt as a result.

Tentatively, I reach out and take it. The hilt sits strangely in my hand. It's only been two days since I last held a knife, but it feels like forever.

As soon as my fingers have tightened around the weapon, he hits me. Not a punch, but a slap, almost playful. It stings, but I stand my ground. He would expect nothing less.

The second hit is harder, enough to wrench my head around and send me back a step. It hurts. And now, all the memories of the first time I took this test are pouring out from whatever dark corner I locked them away in. It's intended to try and break you, the test. Because if it does, then you never would have been strong enough to protect your charge. It was bad enough the first time, when I didn't know what to expect;

standing at the start of it and *knowing* makes it a thousand times worse.

Fight back, a little voice insists. *As Niko likes to tell you, you're not a shield any more.* But the wave of revulsion that floods me at the idea of hurting the shieldmaster, a member of the Apex and my old teacher besides, is more than enough to quench the tiny spark of rebellion. I can't. I'm not allowed. Euphemie is gone – there's no one left to protect – and that means if I hurt Ixion, something terrible will happen.

'I'm not surprised you murdered her,' he says conversationally. 'She didn't treat you very well, did she?'

That's not true. I start to stammer out a contradiction, the nails of my free hand digging into my palm. He responds by shoving me, hard enough that I fall down.

'Euphemie was shallow and envious and thought only of herself,' Ixion says. 'And that's why you killed her.'

I try to get up, but he knocks me down again. I want to make him stop. I want to punch him until he stops talking. The knife is still in my hand – I could . . .

But the thought makes me feel sick again, a pulsing twist to my stomach that matches the ringing in my ears.

'Get up,' he says. I obey, though my head is pounding. He pushes me again, not hard this time, but repeatedly. An aggravating little prod. His expression is mocking.

'She hated you, you know that?' he says. 'She begged me to bond her to someone else, but . . .'

He keeps talking, and prodding me, but I can't hear it any more. The ringing in my ears is too loud. He's right there in front of me, and the knife is in my hand, and all I have to do is stab him. That would be the end of it. The storm inside me would break, instead of building and building with nowhere to go—

But I can't. I can't. I can't.

'Stop it,' Niko says loudly. Ixion turns to look at him, and it's as if a spell is broken. I step back, shaking all over. The knife falls to the floor. My face is drenched with sweat; I wipe it quickly on my sleeve.

'You think she's faking *that*?' Niko demands.

'You cut the test short.' With a shrug, Ixion bends to retrieve the knife from near my feet. 'So really, it proves nothing. I'm not saying it would be easy for her to have broken her conditioning. As you saw, it would have put her under a good deal of mental stress. But that doesn't mean she couldn't have done it.'

Niko looks at him for a long moment. I can't tell what he's thinking. In all honesty, I can't tell much of anything at all.

'Thank you for your time,' he says finally, still polite and distant. Then he's at my side, somehow guiding me towards the door without touching me – which is good, because I couldn't bear to be touched right now – and leaving the shield-master behind us.

*

The test must have taken far more out of me than I realized. The next thing I'm aware of is the light pressure of a hand on my shoulder, causing my knees to bend automatically. When I lift my head, I find that Niko hasn't brought me very far. I'm sitting on a bench in a small storage room near the barracks, surrounded by threadbare blankets and uniforms waiting to be mended.

I look up at Niko. I don't understand him in the slightest. He doesn't believe anything I say. He doesn't want any more to do with me than he can help. Yet he brings me food, and he let me shave my head, and he hasn't shown any sign of using the dark arts against me. And the way he's watching me now, with a frown that's neither vague nor menacing but something softer . . . it's almost like he feels bad for me.

'I didn't intend for that to happen,' he says, confirming that impression. 'I shouldn't have brought you with me after all.'

The last thing I want is for him to decide I'm not resilient enough to help with the investigation. I lift my chin, breathing deeply to suppress my nausea. 'Why not?'

'Surely you aren't going to tell me that didn't hurt.'

'It was no worse than training.'

'All right, but . . .' For the first time since I met him, he appears to be struggling for words. 'Do you think it's fair? For them to have made it so you can't defend yourself at *all*?'

'That's not true. I can still defend myself against ordinary people. Just not against . . .' I make a broad gesture. 'You. Your family.'

71

'Not against us,' he repeats. 'And you're *happy* with that?'

As is often the case with Niko, I don't know how he wants me to answer. Finally, I say, 'I owe my entire existence to the royal family. What do I have to be unhappy about?'

It's no more than the truth. Cutters are designed to serve; their children are grown with the Apex's permission and genetic intervention, enhanced as required to fulfil specific purposes for the good of the Hive. And it isn't just us – the entire population owes the same debt to the royal family. Most people in the colony are unable to have children without help. The royals alone have the gift that's been passed down through their line since their revered ancestor Melissa founded the Hive, centuries ago: the ability to conceive children freely, and to use the arts of medicine and genetics to grant others children as well. Without that gift, we would have died out long ago. It's so precious, and so important, that only the queens are allowed to use it. That's why all ascendants are given a contraceptive implant; it's removed from those girls who are selected as queens, but the rest retain theirs forever.

Of course, when deciding who gets to benefit from the royal gift, different considerations have to be taken into account for the different levels of society. Among the carders, it's usually a simple matter of numbers – when some of them die of natural causes, or grow too old or infirm to work and are exiled in a Winnowing, more can be born in their place. As for the drones, their children are granted based on both politics and genetics: who is in favour, but also who might provide a good mate for a future queen. With the Apex able to assess everyone's genes and analyse the outcome of every possible combination, the two factors often go hand in hand.

I've understood all that since I was old enough to have formed memories. I feel nothing but gratitude for the gift of my life. If anything, *Niko* must be the one who's unhappy, the way he constantly questions everything. His questions make me unhappy too, but not for the reasons he seems to think. I just wish he would stop.

'What did they teach you was the purpose of our involvement in the Winnowings?' he asks, because it's not as if an ascendant has ever stopped anything as a result of my wishing. Still, at least this question is an easy one. I learnt the answer before I left the nursery.

'It allows the ascendants to play an important part in the maintenance of the Hive and, at the same time, gives them the opportunity to demonstrate which of them would be best suited to lead us in the future.'

'*The maintenance of the Hive*,' Niko echoes. 'That's an impressively euphemistic way of describing it. So do you think it works?'

The easy questions didn't last long. 'I . . . What do you mean?'

'Do you think the ability and willingness to remove those who are no longer considered useful are the best criteria on which to select our rulers?'

'The queens and the Apex have to be ruthless enough to control our finite resources,' I venture, falling back on what I was taught. 'Send the soldiers against raiders. Decide who should be born and who is superfluous. And everyone in the Hive needs to *know* their rulers are that ruthless so they don't step out of line. It's for the good of us all.'

'Right,' Niko says. 'Turning repeated mass slaughter into a political campaign is for the good of us all.'

That sounded sarcastic, but I go on doggedly. 'Winnowing isn't slaughter. The only people who die are the people who refuse to leave when the time comes.'

'Oh, really? You think the exiles all live happily ever after, out there somewhere in the middle of the ocean?'

Since I've wondered about that myself, I can't pretend otherwise. Still, I cling to what I know. 'At the end of the Dark Ages, before the Hive was established, there was fighting every day. People killing each other for food, access to technology, the little land that was left after the seas rose. We can't go back to that.'

'No. I'm just not convinced that *better than terrible* is the best we can do.'

By now, I'm really not sure what he wants of me. I don't answer.

'Did Euphemie never talk to you about any of this?' he asks, and I shake my head. 'Then what did she talk to you about?'

Herself. The answer pops into my mind, and it's the truth. Mostly, we talked about her: her dreams, her frustrations, her plans. Whether her make-up suited her, whether a particular pattern of fabric would make a pretty shawl. Her talent for art and conversation. Yet it feels disloyal to say so – because although I don't think Euphemie herself would have seen anything wrong with it, somehow I suspect Niko will.

'Are you telling me you did talk about it with Slate?' I ask, hoping to deflect the question. 'Before—'

The stormglow in the little room flares, then darkens, plunging us briefly into night before returning to normal. It's flickered around him before, I remember now – when he declared his commitment to the truth or nothing. Maybe that part of what Euphemie told me about the dark arts is correct: he's so powerful, his emotions are enough to block out the light. That isn't the most comfortable thought. Still, at least the confusing discussion is over.

'What now?' I venture.

'You'll go back to your cell, while I learn everything I can about shield-bonds. Because Ixion wasn't very helpful. Either he's lying or the bond was normal.'

'The shieldmaster is the Elder Queen's brother. Surely he'd tell you if he knew anything.'

'Not if it would incriminate him. Maybe he's holding a grudge. Maybe he longed for the children that he'd never be allowed to have, and resented having to train the shields of his nieces and nephews instead.'

I frown. 'Then . . . you're suggesting more than a failed bond. You're suggesting deliberate sabotage.'

'I'm merely proposing a theory. After all, you claim Euphemie's killer dropped a royal brooch. And Ixion wasn't wearing his today, I noticed.'

Nor is Niko himself, for that matter. He hasn't worn his golden pin on any of the days I've seen him.

'But the shieldmaster is bound to the queens,' I say, 'just like . . .'

Like I was bound to Euphemie.

Niko throws me a glance, but doesn't comment; we both know where that sentence was going. Yes, all the ascendants in each generation who aren't chosen to be queens are bound to those who are, using a bond similar to that which binds shields to their charges. But I'm living proof that such bonds can fail – or be broken.

'It's not as if being bound to them would even stop him from hurting their children,' Niko says. 'As long as the queens themselves remained unhurt, he would also.'

'The shieldmaster is a big man. The killer wasn't as tall as him, or as broad. Though I only caught a glimpse, I can tell you that.'

Silence falls between us, deep enough for the faint scurry of a nearby cockroach to be audible. He's about to return me to prison. Maybe that's what spurs me to confess, 'The words hurt more.'

'Mmm?'

'Punches, I can handle. I've taken plenty of them. But when he said cruel things about Euphemie and me . . . it was like that before, in the test, and I hated it then too. If anything could make me break my conditioning, I think it would be that.'

'Although it didn't.'

'No.'

He nods. After a while, he says, 'Maybe it would help if you remembered that Euphemie wasn't perfect.'

I shrug. Although Niko is very clever about a lot of things, he's completely missed the mark on that one. Because it wasn't the lies the shieldmaster told that hurt the most. It was the things that were true.

THREE DAYS AFTER

On the third day – my last day – sunup comes and goes, but Niko doesn't arrive. What was it he said yesterday? He only showed up because he thought I could be useful. So if he's not here now, he obviously thinks my usefulness has run out.

Maybe he's abandoned the investigation entirely, a mean little voice whispers in my ear. *He got bored, or yesterday convinced him you're guilty, and he's leaving you to die. And there's nothing you can do about it . . .*

But I can't think like that. The Apex gave him three days to solve an impossible crime. He doesn't have any time to waste on sparing my feelings. After all, he must always have been questioning people without me too. Maybe the fact that he's not here means he believes me – at least enough to make it worth pursuing other lines of inquiry.

Maybe. Or maybe he's telling the queens at this very moment how you broke the bond and killed Euphemie.

I try to fight my anxiety the only way I know how: constant physical activity. But as the stormglow whitens towards noon, it only gets worse. *You're powerless. You failed to protect her in life, and you're failing to protect her in death. Soon you'll be executed, and you'll never know who killed her.*

Euphemie wasn't perfect. I know that, despite what Niko might insinuate. I lived alongside her for seventeen years, which means I saw both her best days and her very worst. True, since she died, the memories that have haunted me are of all the times I loved her most. When we were fourteen, and skipped school and training to spend the afternoon lying on the floor in a blanket cave, eating snacks and telling each other stories like we used to when we were little. My sixteenth birthday, when she gave me my knives: the way she stretched up on tiptoes to cover my eyes, laughing that it was a surprise; the way she watched my face to see if I was pleased with the gift, then danced around the room in glee at whatever she read there. The time she used her make-up on me, frowning in careful concentration as she painted my face. I was afraid I'd look foolish, but she didn't use the bolder palette she preferred for herself. The reflection she showed me in the mirror was more subtle than that: me, but not me – the same eyes and cheeks and lips I'd always had, only *more*, somehow. And when she told me how beautiful I looked, I could hear in her voice that she meant it.

But that doesn't mean I've forgotten the other days. Days when she'd ask me, over and over, to tell her I loved her – that everyone loved her. Days when she refused to get out of bed, when she said she was fed up with the same old walls and the same old faces and everything was pointless, and I had to tell her handmaidens she was sick. Days when she threw things at me and called me names. And, yes, sometimes I resented her for it. Not because I thought she shouldn't feel those things, but because I felt them too. Doesn't everyone, from time to time? The mean little voice that told Euphemie she was running in circles is the same one now whispering that Niko has given up on me. Yet the difference is that Euphemie was allowed to submerge herself in her dark moods, to sink right under the surface and come up only when she was ready, whereas I . . . I had to swallow mine. Like poison.

But this time, if I'm going to die anyway, maybe I should let it out.

'It's not fair,' I try. My voice falls softly and awkwardly into the small room. So I say again, more loudly, 'It's not fair! She didn't deserve to die!'

That's true. But it's not enough.

'*I* don't deserve to die!'

Better.

'I didn't kill her. Someone else did. Someone is getting away with murder. And I can't do anything about it, no matter how much I want to, and it's not *fair*!'

Anger burns through my body, down to the tips of my fingers and toes: as if I'm full of lightning, hot and glowing, making my skin feel a size too small. The next thing that emerges from my mouth isn't words but a formless shout. I let it carry me forward, to pivot on the ball of one foot and drive my fist, hard, into the nearest stormglow panel.

Pain jars through my knuckles and up my arm, and in an instant the anger is gone. I stare at the cracked panel, already regretting it. There's a reason we are taught to control our emotions in a way the ascendants aren't. Strong emotion leads to recklessness. It prevents us from putting our charges before ourselves. I can almost hear the shieldmaster saying it: *You've let her down, Feldspar.* As a result of my indulgent display of temper, I may have damaged my hand, and that makes me less than fully useful. I shouldn't have done it.

All the same, alongside the guilt, I feel relief. It's like the aftermath of a storm: the unbearable tension discharged in a single cathartic crack of heat and power and rage, leaving behind a sky washed clean.

Tucking my right hand under my left armpit, I sit back down and wait. Mere moments later, the door is unlocked and Niko walks in, his hair even more tousled than usual, the shadows under his eyes deeper. He's calm, but it's that very controlled sort of calm that's all the more alarming for what it's holding in check. It brings me to my feet.

'Niko? What—'

'Another death.' That's all he has time to say before the Younger Queen strides into the room, and Niko drifts unobtrusively backwards to stand by the wall.

'Well?' the queen demands of me. Behind her, Ganister looms in the doorway. I flick a quick glance in Niko's direction before returning my gaze to Sirene. Not her face – I was taught never to look a queen in the eye – but somewhere in the region of her chin.

'Your pardon, ma'am. I don't understand.'

'Leandros was murdered last night,' she says, in a tone that suggests she holds me personally responsible. 'His shield found dead but unmarked. We can only conclude that Basalt stabbed Leandros before succumbing to the bond.'

I can't speak. Euphemie's death and my survival were inexplicable enough, but *this* . . . it goes beyond all my understanding of the world. No shield should be able to raise a weapon to his charge; Niko and I proved that yesterday. And besides, Leandros is – was – the *Second*. Most people wouldn't have stood a chance against him.

Most people wouldn't . . . but his own shield might.

'How is this possible, Feldspar?' Sirene takes a threatening step towards me. 'I will have answers, and I will have them *now*.'

'I d-don't know how to answer,' I stammer. 'I was locked in here last night. I don't know anything about what happened.'

She dismisses that with a vicious gesture. 'Leandros's shield turned on him, exactly as you did on Euphemie. *How did you break your conditioning?*'

'I didn't. I swear. Someone else killed her. Not me.'

'So you say. There were no witnesses. No trace of this supposed poison arrow. Only Euphemie, and you, and your bloodstained knives.'

Then I did wound Euphemie's killer, with that wild throw. There's no other reason for them to have found blood on my blades. Though it's not my place to argue with a queen, I find myself saying, 'The Seventh's wound was too small to have killed her. It must have been poison. I am deeply sorry for the Second's death, but hers was not at all the same.'

Sirene snorts. 'The only difference is that you didn't have the decency to die for your treachery. But that will change, today.'

'Ma'am,' Niko says softly from his position by the wall. 'I must respectfully request that Feldspar's execution be delayed.'

'And I must respectfully decline. Two of my children have been murdered by their *shields*, Nikolos!'

'She is the only living witness.'

Sirene pivots to face him. 'You've had your chance to interrogate her. You've given us nothing. Her execution stands.'

'But everything has changed with Leandros's death. We're no longer dealing with an isolated incident. Two ascendants dead. Two shields failed . . . What if there are more deaths to come?'

'Do you think it likely?'

'The existence of a second murder makes it considerably more probable,' Niko says. 'And Feldspar is the key to this, I'm sure. Our only way to find out how the shields are breaking their conditioning. If she is executed, we lose our chance of discovering the truth before more of the royal family die at their shields' hands.'

My stomach churns with a confused mixture of alarm and hope. Now I've come to it, I don't want to die. Not until I've achieved justice for Euphemie. But by describing me as *the key to this*, Niko is placing a heavy weight of importance on my shoulders. I don't know any more than what I've already told him. I don't know how to give him what he wants.

'Very well,' Sirene snaps finally. 'If Doralie agrees, her execution will be delayed. But not for long, Nikolos. This is borrowed time.'

She stalks to the door. I bow my head, weak with grateful relief.

'One more thing,' Niko adds. 'I need to see his chambers.'

Sirene turns on her heel. 'What?'

'Leandros. I need to see his chambers.'

'I heard what you said. My question was intended to express my utter disbelief that you would think it an appropriate request.'

'Ma'am, we know nothing of these deaths,' Niko says. 'Down to whether shields are turning on their charges of their own accord, or whether someone else is involved. The scene of

84

the crime may give us answers. I don't see anything inappropriate in that.'

Sirene glares at him. When she speaks, disdain drips from
every word. 'You're the master of the dark arts. Do whatever it
takes.'

The door slams behind her. As her footsteps recede, Niko
looks at me meaningfully. '*Leandros* is dead.'

'Yes . . .' Something in his tone makes me nervous. 'Do you
see a connection between his death and Euphemie's?'

His gaze never wavers. 'I've asked both Calista and Alexios
about the morning Euphemie died. Alexios, in particular,
seemed to think that you and Euphemie left the sunroom
when you did because Euphemie was jealous of the attention
Leandros paid you. So I wonder if perhaps you had reason to
dislike him?'

I suppress a shiver. 'It's not my place to have any feelings
about him at all.'

'Never mind your place!' Niko moves closer. 'Feldspar, some
of the Apex are ready to accuse you of this second murder,
whether it's physically possible or not. They won't let a locked
cell get in the way of a convenient explanation. And if it occurs
to them that how Leandros behaved towards you might have
given you a reason to want him dead, that will only lend
credence to the accusation. Which is why I have to ask, and
you *have* to answer.'

'It wasn't just me,' I mumble. 'The Second was that way

with all the female shields. It made me uncomfortable. But it hardly warranted murdering him.' Though I know it's not the point, I can't help adding, 'And of course Euphemie wasn't jealous. He was her brother.'

'Yes,' Niko agrees. 'But Euphemie liked to be the centre of attention, didn't she?' Without waiting for an answer – which is good, because I wouldn't have known what answer to give him – he adds, 'I'm sorry.'

Now I'm even more confused. I'm usually the one apologizing. A shield has to be careful not to offend anyone: either their own ascendant, who can punish them as they see fit, or any other member of the royal family, for fear of damaging their charge's prospects when roles in the Apex are allocated. I don't think an ascendant has ever apologized to me before. Cautiously, I ask, 'For what?'

'That Leandros was . . . what he was. That you felt you had no choice but to put up with it.'

I *didn't* have a choice. But all I say is, 'He never did anything wrong, exactly. He was just . . .'

I can't find the right word, any more than Niko could a moment ago, but he nods at me as if he understands. Sitting down in his customary spot on my bed, he produces the usual package from his coat pocket.

'Breakfast. Sorry it's so much later than usual. This morning has been . . . difficult.'

Sorry again. Bewildered, I take the food. 'What happened?'

'From what I can gather, when Leandros and his shield – Basalt – were discovered, no one understood what had happened at first. It was obvious from the blood that Leandros had been attacked by someone, but they couldn't work out why his shield showed no sign of any injury in his defence. Until, that is, it was determined that *Basalt* murdered Leandros.'

The biscuit turns to ashes in my mouth; I swallow it with an effort. 'No doubt that's when they thought of me.'

'Well, yes. There is a clear similarity between Euphemie's death and Leandros's. Some people claimed that Ixion's conditioning of the shields must have been faulty. Others suggested that since you survived and Basalt didn't, it was more likely that you were behind both.' Niko sighs. 'I didn't know about any of it until Queen Sirene stormed into my chambers to interrogate me about everything I've done since Euphemie died. She was ... let's say, *unimpressed* that I couldn't yet tell her how your bond was broken. That's when she decided to come down here and ask you herself.'

I almost don't want the answer to my next question, but it's better to face the worst head-on. 'When we spoke to Ixion yesterday, he mentioned torture. Is that something the Apex—'

'I don't think so.' Niko pushes the last biscuit into my uninjured hand. I know he's right – I'll need the fuel to get me through the day – but my stomach is still churning. 'It's been generations since the Apex included a chief inquisitor. I doubt they'd know how to go about torturing you.'

'But you said . . . Isn't that why they sent you? Because you have the ability to – to force a confession out of me, true or not?'

He doesn't reply. When I look at him, he's watching me with something very like guilt.

'I did say that,' he agrees. 'But I shouldn't have let you think . . . I wouldn't, Feldspar. Even if I could.'

Surprisingly, I find that I believe him. Or maybe it's not so surprising. He might project an aura of dark power and be surrounded by a swirl of sinister rumours, but he's also the least violent person I've met. I smile at him, very tentatively, and one side of his mouth twists up in response. But then his expression turns vague again, and he looks away.

'They're far more likely to wash their hands of the whole thing and have you executed,' he adds. 'As you could probably tell, from what the queen said.'

'Yes.' I force myself to take another bite of food. 'Thank you for intervening.'

'You're not still eagerly awaiting it, then?'

'Not until we find out who killed Euphemie.'

'That'll do for now.' Before I can ask what he means, he tilts his head in the direction of the cracked stormglow panel. 'So how did that happen?'

'I – um. I punched it.'

I'm not sure what kind of reaction I expected, but he just shrugs as though it's perfectly normal for me to have punched a wall. 'If you cracked the panel, you must have split your knuckles as well. Want me to take a look?'

'You can fix it with – with the dark arts?'

'Perhaps.'

I hesitate. But my hand is throbbing, and I need it to be functional, so I extend it to him. As he said, the knuckles are bleeding, and I can tell it's going to bruise, but I'm lucky: I haven't broken any bones.

'I don't think you need the dark arts,' Niko says, smiling slightly. 'But maybe a bandage.'

When he touches me, I tense. Ascendants aren't meant to touch each other's shields; when that rule has been broken in the past, it's been by someone like Leandros with no regard for personal boundaries. So my instinct is to assume danger. Yet there's more to it than that. There's the warmth of it, an un-familiar spark of contact that leaves me strangely aware of his hand on mine. There's also the literal spark that stings my skin.

'Astrapē is restless,' Niko says, catching my wince. 'She tends to get that way when I'm stressed.'

'What form is she in today?'

'A piranha, I think. Looks dangerous, anyway.'

He bends his head, concentrating on wrapping the bandage around my hand. After a while, he says in a deceptively abstracted voice, 'The queens said there was blood on your knives, after Euphemie's death. Why?'

I explain about my futile attempt to stop the attacker.

'Good,' he says. 'If there was blood, you must have left a mark. Which arm?'

'Left. The cut would have been deep enough to need stitches, I think.'

'Then we have something to look for.'

I dart a glance at his face. 'You believe me. Not just about Leandros, but Euphemie too. That's why you asked Queen Sirene to delay my execution.'

'Put it this way,' he says. 'I think it would be foolish not to allow for the possibility, at least until I'm presented with definitive proof of your guilt.'

'Then ... that's a yes?'

He laughs – one of those quick, sharp flashes of laughter that light up his whole face. 'It's a reservation of the right to withhold judgement. Even though investigating alternative explanations will make the rest of the family dislike me even more than they already do, I can't let that stop me.'

'Why should they dislike you for trying to find out what happened?'

Niko tucks the ends of the bandage into place and sits back. 'Because if you're telling the truth, that includes the brooch, which means Euphemie's killer was a royal. More specifically, an ascendant – though she wasn't the obvious choice to remove as a rival, I can't see any other likely motive. So believing *you* means accusing *them*. And no one wants to be accused of murdering their family.'

Not the obvious choice to remove as a rival. He said that as if it were undeniable that Euphemie would never have been chosen as a queen. It goads me into saying, 'You're not wearing *your* brooch.'

'You noticed,' he shoots back.

'Then where is it?'

'Did you miss the part where I said no one wants to be accused of murdering their family?'

My heart is racing, but I go on stubbornly. 'You didn't answer me before, when I said you could have killed Euphemie. Not properly. And you are Queen Doralie's child, which means you're not related to either of the dead ascendants. It isn't implausible that you might want to clear the way for you and your side of the family to control the Apex.'

Niko snorts. 'I can reassure you on that point, at least. When I relinquished the right to another shield, I also relinquished the right to a place in the Apex. That's why I get away with not attending the Winnowings. Or did, until they decided to hold it over my head as encouragement to bring this matter to a swift conclusion.'

Oh. I drop my gaze. I knew, of course, that every ascendant is bonded before birth. I *didn't* know that replacing a dead shield is compulsory for anyone who wants to be considered for a role in the Apex.

'As for the brooch,' he adds, reaching into one of his pockets, 'I don't wear it because I hate what it stands for. But that doesn't mean I killed anyone.'

He shows me the gold emblem before tucking it away again. Full of remorse, I mumble, 'I'm sorry, Sixth. Niko. I shouldn't have—'

'It's fine. If I'm allowed to ask questions, then so are you, right?'

According to everything I know about how the world works, one hundred per cent wrong. But I say nothing.

'Well, then,' he says. 'I'm off to search Leandros's rooms.'

Though nothing ought to surprise me when it comes to the dark arts, still I keep finding myself surprised. 'You're really going? Even though they should be left untouched for seven days?'

'It's in your interests. If I can find something that proves Basalt acted of his own accord, or was influenced by a third party who was present at the time, then it will also prove your innocence. In Leandros's case, at least.'

'Then . . .' I can hardly believe I'm about to say this, but I can't let the opportunity slip. If I'm to bring the killer to justice, then I have to be part of the investigation, no matter how many rules it breaks. 'Can I come too?'

'Aren't you afraid his ghost will walk?'

Of course I am. But I shake my head. 'I owe it to Euphemie.'

'All right,' he says. 'I suppose I have started to get used to your company.'

THIRD MURDER

THREE DAYS AFTER

I've never visited Leandros's chambers before. Euphemie and I passed them every time we took the direct route to the sunroom, but we never had reason to go inside. From what she told me, his social events were wildly decadent, and it was probably for the best that he didn't invite any of the female ascendants. Now I hesitate beside the carved number to the right of the door, my heart beating uncomfortably fast. Talking to Niko in the safety of my cell, it seemed logical that I should do this, but now we're here . . .

'You can go in,' Niko says. 'It's unlocked.'

Yes, for the simple reason that no one would even think of entering. I look at him sideways, remembering the mocking note in his question. *Aren't you afraid his ghost will walk?*

Maybe it's the dark arts again. He must have some reason to be so unconcerned, when everyone knows that if you disturb a person's possessions within a week of their death, the spirit can sense it and might come back to see what's going on. The question is, does whatever protection he has against the dead extend to me? I can't think of much that would make my current situation worse, but being haunted by Leandros is on the list.

'We're in no danger from ghosts,' Niko says. 'And if we are, I'll deal with it. All right?'

Reluctantly, I follow him into the exochamber, which is cold and empty. Not of things: there are chairs and a table and other basic metal furniture much like Euphemie's; a couple of swords hang on the far wall, cups and plates litter the table, and a pair of boots lies discarded by the door. Yet it feels unlived in. A shiver crawls down the back of my neck.

'I take it you haven't returned to your own chambers since Euphemie died,' Niko says.

'Of course not.' The idea is repugnant. He might be willing to take his chances with Leandros, but I want Euphemie to be at peace. Forestalling any further questioning, I add, 'And even if I wanted to, I couldn't. I'm only ever locked up or with you.'

'Then I should fetch you some things.' He raises a hand as I open my mouth to protest. '*Not* from her rooms. I won't inflict that on you. But you must need more clothes, at least.'

It's like he doesn't understand how prison works. 'I don't think you're supposed to—'

'I'll bring you some tomorrow. With breakfast.' He strides off towards the door that in Euphemie's chambers would have

94

led to the bedroom. 'Come on.'

As soon as he opens it, the smell of blood hits me. Instantly I'm back at the winnowing gate, hearing the screams and the wet thuds and Euphemie's terrified sobbing. I take a deep breath, trying to rid myself of the memory, then wish I hadn't. Now the smell is not just in my nose but in my mouth and lungs, so I can taste it on the air. And that, it becomes clear when we step across the threshold, is because a good deal of blood has been spilt here. Not as much as in that disastrous Winnowing, but the bed is dark with it. It shouldn't bother me, because I'm a shield and I've seen worse and I didn't even like Leandros, but it does. It makes me queasy with disgusted horror.

While Niko examines the blood-soaked blankets, I distract myself by gazing around the rest of the room. The closet door is open, revealing clothing in shades of blue and silver; the dressing table holds a pot of pomade and a couple of sticks of make-up. Leandros was determined to appear more serious than the drones, with their painted and powdered faces, but he still had his vanity. I hunt quickly across the top surface and in the drawers, but can't find his royal brooch.

On the opposite side of the room is a lower bed – I guess Basalt didn't sleep between his charge and the door like I used to – and beside that, a table. On it lies an overturned cup, spilling a small puddle of water across a silver tray. To my eye, the liquid has a pinkish tinge. I lean closer to take a cautious sniff.

'Queen Sirene was right,' Niko says. 'Basalt stabbed Leandros before dying himself. I wondered if someone else could have been here – perhaps the same person who you say attacked Euphemie – but it wasn't so.'

How can he tell all that from dried blood? I shake my head. 'If you say so. I don't understand the dark arts.'

'Not the dark arts. Just science.'

I swallow my questions, though I have more than ever. The dark arts might be mysterious and frightening, but they aren't inconsistent with Niko's position as an ascendant. Science, on the other hand, is not fit knowledge for royalty. We all need it – apart from anything else, it's what takes the lightning that hits the Spire and the sunlight that hits the vast panels on the outside of the Hive and turns them into electricity – but it's a matter solely for the carders, just as the royal arts of medicine and genetics are under the Apex's control. I don't see how or why Niko knows anything about science.

'You disapprove,' he observes.

'No! No, I—It isn't my place to . . .' But I trip over myself as I remember his impatience with that, earlier: *Never mind your place!* Gulping, I fall back on my lessons again. 'In the Dark Ages . . .'

'I know. In the Dark Ages, humanity turned the ocean black and the sky to ash.' He gives the words a sing-song sound, like a children's rhyme. 'Pursuing science at the expense of nature, until nature itself rebelled in the form of the Great

Rising. The seas rose, the sun burnt hotter, and storms scoured the surface of the earth until it was wiped clean of all but a fraction of a fraction of human life. It's a wonderfully cautionary tale.'

I say nothing. However contemptuous he may pretend to be of what we were taught, he need only go to the sunroom in either a storm or the merciless heat of a clear sky to know it for truth.

'But that doesn't make science evil,' he goes on. 'It just makes people short-sighted and foolish. And when it comes to solving murders, I don't consider any tool to be off limits.'

I can't argue with that. I don't care myself how we find Euphemie's killer, as long as we do. Humbly, I say, 'I still don't see how it relates to Leandros's death.'

'Look. The bloodstain is in the right place for his throat to have been cut when lying down. He must have been asleep, which means Basalt wouldn't have admitted anyone else. And if there had been a break-in, we'd see signs of it.'

I already knew all that, though I wouldn't have called it science – only common sense. My assumption was that Niko had read some dark and sinister secret from the blood itself. If all he's saying is that we should use logic . . .

'Here's some science for you, then,' I say, gesturing to the overturned cup. 'Basalt was drinking this right before he attacked Leandros.'

'What makes you think so?'

97

'It's strengthening water. All the shields drink it, three times a day: first thing in the morning, at noon, and every night before bed. If Basalt had spilt it at any time before he attacked Leandros, he would have cleaned it up. That means he must have been drinking it at the moment when – when whatever happened, happened. When the urge to kill overcame the constraints of his conditioning.'

'Then you believe something in the water did it?' Niko asks.

'Maybe. It's pinker than usual. And it doesn't smell quite right.'

'In what way?'

'Usually it smells brackish. This is sweeter, like the saltwater candies Euphemie used to eat.' I frown. 'Do you think it could be something like a poison? One that doesn't kill, but makes the person behave differently. Does anything like that exist?'

'I don't know, but if so, the method would make sense. A poison like that, capable of forcing a shield to kill an ascendant . . . you'd administer it at night, when the two of them were shut away together in their chambers. You'd put it in a drink that only the shield would touch.'

He fishes a glass tube with a stopper from one pocket, then a pipette from another. Carefully, he sucks up some of the spilt liquid and drops it into the tube.

'What will you do with it?' I ask him.

'Compare it to regular strengthening water,' he says, replacing the stopper and stowing the tube away. 'See if I can figure out what's in it that shouldn't be.'

'You can do that?'

'Maybe.'

'And if you do,' I press him, 'it will prove I had nothing to do with these deaths. Right?'

'Maybe,' he says again, and I snap.

'You think I poisoned the water from inside a locked cell? And then *told you* it was poisoned – what, to make my own life even harder than it is already? I know you don't believe anything I say, Niko, but that's a little much, even—'

Even for you. With a gasp, I manage to swallow the last two words, though it's far too late to attempt self-control. Surely the damage is done.

'It's not a matter of belief,' Niko says mildly. 'It's a matter of evidence. But I agree, that scenario does sound unlikely.'

I wait, but that's it. My outburst doesn't seem to have bothered him in the slightest. Euphemie would have forbidden me to speak for a day if I'd ever been that disrespectful towards her. Discomfited, I change the subject. 'So what will you do now?'

'Question people again, for a start. I spoke to all the ascendants and shields after Euphemie's death, but at that point, everyone was focused on you. Why you did it. How you did it. Now, they'll have to answer our questions properly.'

'Wait.' I've grown used to asking if I can help. I was already preparing the latest version of the question, making it extra polite because I just yelled at him. As a result, that casual *our*

99

has thrown me. 'You *want* me to come?'

'Isn't that what you want?'

'Yes, but—'

'You're helpful, Feldspar. You see things I don't.' And before I can get over the astonishment of that, he's already moving on. 'So who do you think we should talk to first? I've established that the five youngest ascendants were at school together when Euphemie died, alongside a large number of drone children who can vouch for their whereabouts. Their shields were in training. And I was with Ophion –' the Fifth – 'when Leandros died, which rules him out. Taking the dead into account, that leaves six ascendants we need to consider.'

My mind leaps straight to the three eldest royal daughters: Halimeda, Calista and Pyrene. They're the ones who take charge of the discussion in the first part of each Winnowing, deciding who should leave the Hive. They lead the soldiers in the second part, working together in accordance with the ascendants' credo – *We winnow as one* – to drive out the surplus, no matter how much blood is spilt. I've seen all three of them kill before.

'Not all ascendants would benefit from both Leandros and Euphemie dying,' I explain, when I propose the idea to Niko. 'But those three would. Removing Euphemie gives them one less rival to worry about. And removing Leandros leaves the role of shieldmaster up for grabs too.'

'Why Euphemie, though? If you're one of the three main

contenders for two thrones, why not remove your closest rival?'

Because Euphemie was too ambitious. The thought feels like a betrayal, but it might be true. Many roles in the Apex were unsuitable for her; the rest, she considered boring. She made no secret of the fact that she'd only be content with becoming a queen.

'I'm wondering if there's anything in what you pointed out earlier,' Niko says. 'That only Queen Sirene's children have died. I'm not trying to gain control of the Apex for my side of the family, but someone else might.' He considers that for a moment. 'Perhaps we start with Halimeda and Pyrene? They're my sisters – Queen Doralie's children. That makes them suspects in both our theories.'

He seems genuinely to want my opinion. It's as if I really was executed today, and now I'm at the start of a brand-new life where I no longer understand the rules.

'The three eldest daughters always used to visit the training floor with their shields in the afternoons,' I venture. 'I doubt that will have changed with Leandros gone.'

'And once again, you prove your worth.'

'You didn't know that?'

'I haven't been near the training floor in years,' Niko says tranquilly. 'Let's go.'

THREE DAYS AFTER

The training floor is a vast cavern at the heart of the Hive, illuminated not by stormglow panels on the walls like most of the other corridors and rooms, but by smaller, brighter panels across the ceiling – making it one of the best-lit areas in the entire Hive, despite its distance from the outer walls. With all the physical exertion that goes on in here, it would be a hot, humid place, but it's kept fresh by the ventilation system that sucks in cool air near sea level and expels it up through the central shaft that surrounds the Spire.

As soon as we enter, I relax a little. I've spent so much time here that it feels like home. Even the sound of the room – the whir of the fans and the echoey acoustics, so different from anywhere else in the Hive – calms me on a level deeper than reason, like a childhood lullaby.

As I predicted, the three eldest female ascendants are all here. Halimeda, the First, her hair bound back from her face in a tight knot, is sparring with her shield, their swords flashing back and forth. Calista, the Third, is engaged in target practice with her bow and arrows, while Pyrene, the Fourth, throws knives with her usual fierce intensity into the next target along. Surrounding them, and spilling into the tiered seating to one side of the floor, are a group of drones – their friends and followers. My brief sense of safety melts, to be replaced by a visceral wave of anxiety.

I follow Niko towards the rows of seats, only to stumble as all three ascendants stop what they're doing to sweep me with identical glances of disgust. Throat tightening, I reach for a weapon – but I don't have any weapons. And even if I did, it wouldn't be possible for me to use them against these girls.

Be strong, I tell myself. *Be strong for Euphemie*. Though everyone believes I murdered her, and somehow murdered Leandros as well, I have to be willing to come out here among the ascendants to hunt down the real killer. It doesn't matter what they think of me.

When I reach Niko's side, I lift my chin and return their gaze defiantly. Halimeda looks away, as if I'm beneath her notice; Pyrene scowls; Calista laughs.

'Good afternoon, Karissa,' Niko says. Turning, I see the Ninth a few rows back, sitting apart from the other spectators. A book is in her hand, though it's not one of the approved texts – the treasurer must have lent it to her. Everyone knows that she intends to take his position in the new Apex; she's spent her life studying mathematics, ensuring a position for herself no matter who takes the throne. Grappling with the combined weight of the older girls' disapproval, I barely registered her presence.

Her shield, Quartz, stands at her shoulder: ochre-skinned and solemn-eyed, a little shorter than most shields, radiating nervous energy in everything from her folded arms to her silently tapping toe. Quartz has always been a fidget. Even when the shieldmaster made her practise standing still for entire afternoons at a time, one hand would be moving restlessly out of his sight, running a thumb over her fingernails or picking at the torn hem of her shirt.

'Oh . . . hello, Nikolos.' A blush rises in Karissa's freckled cheeks as she smiles at him. She has the reddest hair I've ever seen on a person. It must have come from her drone father, because Queen Doralie certainly doesn't have hair that colour.

'You're not joining in the training today?' Niko asks.

'Oh, no. Quartz has enough to do without protecting me from my own clumsiness. We're only here so she can practise, once . . .' Her gaze flickers in the direction of the older girls, and I hear her unspoken words. *Once they've gone.* The flip side of the ascendants working together to winnow the Hive is that they have little patience for anyone who fails to play their part. Yet during the one Winnowing in which she's participated so far, Karissa didn't even allow her shield to take an active role, much less join in herself. They remained guarded by soldiers throughout, leaving fewer to help do the work.

Pulling out a notebook, Niko begins to climb the tiers. 'While I have you here, do you mind if I ask you a few questions?'

As they talk, I watch Karissa covertly. She's much shyer than Euphemie, who was able to win the older ascendants round with compliments and conversation. She's tolerated, because *someone* has to be treasurer in the next Apex, but that doesn't mean she's liked. Still, I'm sure Niko won't assume she's harmless just because she seems that way. Aside from anything else, she's another of Doralie's daughters – so if his theory is correct, she has to be considered alongside Halimeda and Pyrene as a possible killer.

Once they've finished, Niko leaves her to her book and rejoins me on the floor. 'Did you hear what she said? Leandros argued with Calista on the day he died.'

'I'm not sure that means anything. They used to argue all the time. Alexios said, that morning in the sunroom . . . He said Leandros liked to make controversial arguments to entertain himself.'

'True enough,' Niko agrees. 'But I doubt Calista would willingly put up with someone entertaining himself at her expense. And Karissa said Calista was angry.'

'But it doesn't match your theory. Calista isn't Queen Doralie's daughter.'

'Having a theory doesn't mean I get to throw away evidence

that doesn't fit it.'

I watch Calista fire one arrow after another into the target, clustering them perfectly in the centre. There's no denying her prowess, or how impressive she looks while demonstrating it. I always thought it was just showing off – the Hive, with its twisty passages and confined spaces, is not generally suited for long-range weapons – until I saw her dealing with the rebellious exiles in the most recent Winnowing. She took down five drones before anyone else could do anything, not her own followers' relatives, but still people she'd exchanged pleasantries with before: aiming into the screaming crowd with focused precision, as if she saw no difference between them and the practice target. The approach to the winnowing gate is a long, straight corridor that transitions smoothly into the sloping rock on the other side, leading down to the start of the causeway. It must be the only place in the Hive where archery becomes not only possible but advantageous.

The bow and arrows are a unique relic of the Dark Ages. Unlike knives and swords and other bladed weapons, which are relatively plentiful and easy to come by, they are made of an unknown material of immense durability and high strength. Even the carders don't have the skill to fix that bow, if it ever gets broken; the best they've figured out is how to supply Calista with spare strings. No wonder she guards it so jealously. She's as competent as the other girls with all kinds of blades, but the bow is hers alone.

Could Calista have fired that poison arrow at Euphemie? I'm sure she has the skill. But if so, she couldn't have used her bow to do it. The poison arrow was small and thin, and the sound I heard before it struck wasn't the snap of a bowstring. It was a vocal sound, an exhale. *Blowpipe* – that was the word Niko used. So a dart, then, rather than an arrow as such. Anyone could make that. But that doesn't mean Calista *didn't* do it, because it's not as if she would be foolish enough to use her own, very distinctive weapon.

On the other hand, now I'm here, my theory that an older girl killed Euphemie and Leandros to get them out of the way feels suddenly shaky. Would Calista, as lethal as she is, really have considered Euphemie a rival? Euphemie admired her, but if I'm honest, I doubt Calista paid her much attention in return. As for Leandros, I stand by what I said: he and Calista argued all the time. They were alike in many ways, tall and attractive and supremely arrogant, and maybe that was part of it. But being angry with someone doesn't have to lead to killing them.

I'm having the same difficulty with Pyrene and Halimeda. Though anything's possible, I can't imagine Halimeda as a poisoner. As the First, she always seems remote: a younger version of Queen Doralie, part of her already inhabiting the role she believes she was born to play. As such, she has a quiet dignity that's even more impressive than Calista's self-assurance. Once again, I'm finding it hard to believe that

Euphemie would have registered with her as a possible rival. Not only that, but she considers it her job to uphold the rules for the younger ascendants. Even when she fights, she does it with detached elegance, as if to prove that it's possible to remain regal while performing unpleasant tasks. Whatever else poison is, it isn't regal.

Pyrene, though . . . If anyone was going to kill out of temper, I would have guessed it to be her. Amber-skinned and curly-haired, she's small and fiery and takes no nonsense. I remember a cutter man, in the previous Winnowing – someone who'd been a courier, until he damaged his knee and could no longer move fast enough to be of use. He'd managed to get hold of a dagger from a soldier's belt and fight his way back into the Hive, away from the winnowing gate. I think he'd have escaped, had he not come up against Pyrene's shield, Breccia. When Pyrene saw them struggling with each other, she hurled a knife at him so hard that the blade pierced his neck and came out the other side . . .

I shake my head, pushing away the memory of the spurting blood. The point is, Pyrene can be driven by anger, and that can make her dangerous. But again, I find it hard to imagine her using poison. She's honest to the point of hurtful; if she wanted to kill someone, she'd look them in the face while she did it.

'What are you thinking?' Niko asks me.

'That I can't make it fit. With any of them. Their chance at the throne is already high. Why would killing Euphemie and Leandros be worth the risk?'

'That's what we're going to find out. As soon as—'

Out of the corner of my eye, I catch movement. I tense, turning in the direction of the potential threat, and Niko stops talking. Calista is crossing the floor towards us. Instinctively my hands drift towards the non-existent knives at my belt. Yet it isn't us she's coming for. She stops in front of Karissa, smiling, one hand on her hip. Somehow her beauty only makes her look more dangerous.

Her shield, Porphyry, stands impassive beside her: dangerous-looking in her own way, with a long scar that runs from her jawline to the corner of one eye, left by a wayward blade. Porphyry has never spoken more than two words to me, but why should she? She can measure her own value by the number of times she's fulfilled her purpose; I saw her save Calista's life more than once in just the two Winnowings I was in. The two of them fight alongside each other with the kind of absolute trust that I could only have dreamt of with Euphemie.

Karissa herself doesn't appear to have noticed their presence, but Quartz is eyeing both of them warily.

'Ninth,' she whispers.

Karissa looks up and blushes again. 'Hello, Calista.'

The Third smiles down at her. 'I thought you might like to come and train with us.'

'Oh, I – I'm not sure.'

'Come on. It'll be fun. Surely you can spare a few moments away from –' she pauses, ostentatiously, to read the title of Karissa's book – '*Euclidean Geometry.*'

'I . . .' It's very obvious that Karissa wants to say no. It's equally obvious that she doesn't know how. Finally, she mumbles, 'All right.'

Leaving her book on her seat, she follows Calista down on to the training floor, stumbling once as she goes. Quartz hurries after her.

'Here.' Calista grabs one of the discarded swords from the floor. Quartz starts forward, then stops when the Third offers it to Karissa hilt-first. 'This one shouldn't be too heavy for you.'

Karissa takes it. She looks unbearably awkward. Though all the shields have been ignoring me since I entered the room – part of their unspoken mutual agreement to continue pretending I don't exist, which in turn I'm pretending I don't care about, because I don't want them to know it feels worse than if they punched me – Quartz breaks that covenant to shoot me a terrified glance.

'Hold it like this,' Calista says. She adjusts Karissa's hold on the hilt of the sword. Almost immediately, Karissa drops it. She fumbles to pick it up, only to drop it again. By now, her cheeks are as red as her hair. One of the drones laughs behind his hand.

'Oh, leave her alone,' Pyrene snaps. She'd been continuing to practise her knife-throwing, paying little attention to Calista or her hangers-on, but now she's turned on her heel with a scowl. 'I'd like to see you try solving an equation without counting on your fingers.'

'I don't need to,' Calista says lazily. 'That's what we have mathematicians for.'

'Then why are you trying to turn this mathematician into a warrior?'

'Because it's fun.'

Pyrene's scowl deepens. 'Fun for you, maybe.'

'She needs to do better in the next Winnowing. Don't you, Karissa? It isn't fair to leave us to do all the work.'

The Ninth looks from one to the other, but says nothing.

'You don't have to train with Calista if you don't want to,' Halimeda puts in, calm and aloof, as if the squabbles of lesser ascendants are beneath her notice but a sense of fairness requires her to intervene. Her unusual blue eyes are the colour of the sea beneath sunlight.

'She needs to learn how to defend herself,' Calista argues. Then, to Karissa, 'Hiding in a ring of soldiers won't do you any good if some rabid cutter breaks through their guard and goes straight for your throat.'

Karissa blinks up at her. 'Isn't that why I have Quartz?'

'You think Quartz is enough? What if two of them band together and kill her first?' A gesture brings Calista's shield rushing to her side. 'Porphyry and I will try and get past her. Let's find out how good a protector she really is.'

The terror clears from Quartz's face, as if now she's confronted with the worst, she doesn't need to be afraid of it any more. She picks up the dropped sword and stands in front of Karissa. 'I'm ready.'

'Quartz, don't.' Now there's genuine fear in Karissa's voice. 'Please stop.'

'Come on, Calista,' Pyrene adds in disgust. 'You can't kill a shield just to prove a point.'

'Karissa has to learn that relying on someone else to protect her is a bad idea.'

'Not if there's more than one of us.' I'm halfway across the floor before I think about what I'm doing, and by then it's too late. I take up a position beside Quartz, reaching for my knives only for my fingers to close on nothing for the *third* time today. This . . . may have been a bad idea.

'You?' Calista laughs, her eyes following my futile attempt to arm myself. 'What can *you* do? With Euphemie gone, you can't so much as touch me.'

'No, Third.' I hesitate. Last chance to back out. But I can't. 'I'll fight Porphyry. The two of you against Quartz . . . it isn't fair.'

'And if I set Porphyry against Quartz, and run you through with my blade before you can blink?'

'That doesn't seem fair either,' Niko says mildly, joining us.

112

'Nikolos . . .' For the first time, a hint of uncertainty enters Calista's eyes. After all, he's a difficult quantity to gauge. He might not be competing for a place in the Apex, but that wouldn't stop him wielding the dark arts to support a favoured ascendant – or, given that his lack of participation in the Winnowings implies a corresponding lack of care for his family, hurt one he dislikes. At least, that's why I'd have urged Euphemie to caution, if she and I had met him before she died. 'This doesn't have anything to do with you.'

'I disagree.'

My heart thumps wildly. She could still escalate the situation, if she wanted to – and I don't reckon much to our chances. Halimeda and Pyrene would probably stay out of it, but a few of Calista's drone followers have some skill with a blade. I suspect their sheer weight of numbers would overwhelm whatever Niko can do. And I don't have any weapons.

'I don't know why you're all taking it so seriously,' Calista says at last. 'I was only trying to teach Karissa a lesson. I would never hurt her, or even her little shield.' She waves a hand at us. 'Go away, all of you, before I execute *that* one –' a nod in my direction – 'for disrespect. It's not as if anyone would miss *her*.'

Karissa and Quartz obey. Automatically I start to follow, before I see Niko shake his head. 'We're not going anywhere until you answer our questions.'

They look at each other: Calista poised ready for action, Niko slender and breakable in the face of her aggression. But then the stormglow overhead flickers, and she backs away a step.

'What do you want to know, Nikolos?' Halimeda asks calmly, as if that small demonstration of power has earned him the right to her attention.

'What you thought of Leandros.'

'He was almost certain to be made shieldmaster, whoever the new queens were.'

'He had a lot of followers among the drones,' Pyrene adds.

'That's not what *you* thought,' Niko points out. 'Those are just facts. Did you like him?'

'He was a skilled warrior.'

'Always very well dressed.'

'Good at making speeches.'

At some point, Niko stops scribbling their answers in his notebook in favour of pushing for more information. I can see he's getting frustrated. Halimeda and Pyrene are saying a lot of complimentary things about Leandros, but none of it really means anything. Which implies that either they hated him or they're remaining superficial for fear of incriminating themselves. Meanwhile, Calista stands in silence with her arms folded, smiling.

'All right,' Niko says finally. 'Then can you tell me what you did last night?'

'I read the notes from the most recent meeting of the Apex,' Halimeda says. 'I like to keep up with matters of governance. And then I walked to the baths.'

'I saw her there,' Pyrene chimes in. 'We walked back together.'

'And before that?' Niko asks.

The Fourth's eyes flicker in the direction of the gathered drones. 'I had a friend over.'

'What about you, Calista?'

The Third gives a scornful laugh. 'What makes you think I'm going to tell you anything?'

'I hate it when people answer a question with a question,' Niko says. His glance at me is so brief that it's almost non-existent, but I have to stifle a smile. Calista catches it too; her lip curls.

'Here's another question for you,' she says. 'Why don't you stop wasting everyone's time with your so-called investigation? Everyone knows *she's* responsible for the deaths.' Once again, her head tilts in my direction. 'That's what happens when you break a shield-bond, Halimeda.'

Her tone of voice made that last sentence sound like the continuation of an old argument, but I don't have the context for it.

'Feldspar is the only person here whose movements last night are fully accounted for,' Niko says. 'She was locked in a cell. So how do you suppose she could have killed Leandros?'

Calista rolls her eyes. 'Now you want me to do your job for you. There's never been a shield who survived her ascendant's death before. Maybe breaking her bond with Euphemie gave her the power to control everyone else's bonds as well. You're the master of the dark arts; torture it out of her if you have to.' She turns, before glancing back over her shoulder. 'As for your questions: I was in my own chambers all night, and Leandros and I disagreed on almost everything. He was an insufferable troublemaker and I don't particularly care that he's dead. But I wouldn't have killed him. Like I said, I don't treat my family that way. We winnow as one.'

After that, there doesn't seem much point in lingering. The female ascendants go back to their weaponry practice, and Niko and I retreat.

'That was ridiculously brave,' he says, once we're outside the room.

'What was?'

'You didn't have to step in for Karissa and Quartz.'

'Neither did you.'

'No . . . but I have far more protection than you have.'

I'm not sure if he means the dark arts or his ascendancy. Maybe both. All the same, I don't think I was being brave. I wanted to protect Karissa because I failed to protect Euphemie. That's all it was. Instincts with nowhere to go.

'Did you learn anything?' I ask.

'Not much. Although Calista seemed the most honest of the lot.'

I nod.

'All four of the ascendants in there were wearing the royal emblem,' Niko adds. 'So by your evidence, that rules them out.'

Right. Find someone who can't produce their golden brooch on request, and we find our killer. That should make our task simple . . . but then I see the problem.

'I didn't spot Leandros's pin in his chambers,' I say. 'Did you?'

'No.'

'Do you know if he was wearing it when he died?'

'I doubt it. Not while he slept.'

'Then I'm not sure the emblem proves anything. Because if Euphemie's killer realized they'd lost their own . . .'

'They could have taken Leandros's,' Niko says softly.

I nod. 'A murderer doesn't care about the sanctity of a dead person's belongings, only about covering their tracks. The dropped brooch was the one thing tying them to Euphemie's death. Replacing it removes that weak point.'

He gives me a long, assessing look.

'Don't tell me,' I say. 'I came up with that story to explain why we'll never find anyone with a missing royal emblem, to hide the fact that I really did kill Euphemie and it's her brooch in my pocket.'

'I wasn't thinking that. No, I was thinking that you have a surprisingly devious mind.'

117

That should be an insult, but his tone of voice suggests the opposite. I suppose if anyone in the Hive would view deviousness as a good thing, it would be Niko.

'Come on,' he says. 'I'll take you back to your cell. We've more to do tomorrow.'

FOUR DAYS AFTER

When Niko arrives at my prison cell the next morning, he looks rounder than usual – as if he's been inflated. He stands in the doorway and proceeds to deflate himself by emptying several of his pockets. Breakfast. A couple of bathing-room bits. One folded garment, followed by another. By the time he's back to his normal size, an entire outfit is stacked neatly on the cot beside me. I'm not sure where he got it. They can't be his own clothes; I'm broader in the shoulders than he is.

'I hope you don't mind,' he says. 'After Slate . . . I kept his things. I don't think he'd object to you having them.'

I stare at the clothes. The food. The razor and toothbrush. All apparently intended to help me feel like myself again, and not just a shadow. Suddenly, I find I can't look at him.

I remember Slate's death. Euphemie and I were fourteen at the time, which means Niko himself must have been fifteen. The rumours started almost straight away; it seemed that every day, Euphemie was coming back from her lessons with something new to tell me. Niko and Slate had been missing on the night it happened, and no one knew where they'd been. Niko had returned dragging Slate's charred corpse behind him. He had refused another shield. He didn't seem to care about Slate's death at all. And from there, it only became wilder: Niko had *killed* Slate. He'd been practising the dark arts in secret for years. He'd found his own uniquely sinister form of protection, far better than any shield.

For the rest of his final year at school, Niko hardly spoke to his classmates. When he turned sixteen, he disappeared from public view, leaving nothing behind but gossip. And I believed it. I accepted everything Euphemie told me about him as unquestionable fact. Maybe it took being the subject of my own rumours to understand that the Hive's collective opinion of someone is not necessarily based in reality.

I bite my lip. I want to apologize, but I'm not sure exactly what for. It isn't as if he ever did anything to contradict what people were saying about him; I don't even know which parts are true. Finally, I blurt out, 'I'm sorry I accused you of killing your family.'

'Hmm?'

'I've done it twice now. Judging you purely on your reputation. But you've been nothing but nice to me.'

'That's a bit of a stretch. I still half suspect you of murdering Euphemie.'

'That only makes it worse!' I say, somewhere between a laugh and a sob. 'You think I might be a murderer, but you bring me breakfast!'

'Even murderers have to eat.' He backs out of the cell. 'I'll be outside with the guard.'

I sit in blank incomprehension before understanding that he's given me privacy to change. There's no denying that I'd love to be rid of what I'm wearing now, which has been on me for four days straight and shows spots of Euphemie's blood. Part of me is worried that Queen Sirene wouldn't approve – that since I didn't have the decency to die when I should have, she'd say the least I can do is remain ragged and half starved. And that part of me agrees with her. Meanwhile, the rest of me insists that the only thing better than fresh clothes would be a bath first, and since that clearly isn't feasible, the clothes are a great deal better than nothing.

Once I've changed, I call softly to Niko and he reappears. When he packs my old clothes into the same pockets, I start to protest – it seems terribly undignified for an ascendant to be dealing with my dirty laundry – before realizing it means the evidence is gone.

'I tested the sample we took from Leandros's rooms,' he tells me as I eat breakfast. 'You were right: it wasn't the same as normal strengthening water. The liquid is denser than usual, and *maybe* a little pinker, though that's hard to discern. But I couldn't detect any known poisons.'

'So what does that mean?'

He shrugs. 'Either it's an unknown poison, or Basalt had simply added something to make it taste better.'

'You couldn't tell what?'

'It's like trying to find a drop of blood in the ocean. Testing for a specific poison is straightforward: add a drop of the water to something the poison is known to react with. But once I'd run out of the usual tests . . .' He spreads his hands. 'I agree with you – it smells sweeter. Maybe Basalt liked dissolving candy in his drinks.'

'Oh.'

'Poison is still my working hypothesis,' Niko says encouragingly. I get the sense that he can read my disappointment and wants to cheer me up.

'Is it?'

'I think it has to be. Setting aside the more . . . *far-fetched* explanations, like the dark arts, or the idea that you have the power to control other people's shield-bonds at a distance, what does that leave us with? *Something* must have caused Basalt to turn on Leandros in the face of all training, conditioning and common sense, and since they were alone at the time, we can only assume that it was something he heard, saw or ingested. The strengthening water is by far the most likely explanation.'

I study his face curiously. 'Did you just call the dark arts far-fetched?'

'I tend to get a bit carried away when I'm reasoning. But I can assure you that if *I* don't know how to make a shield attack an ascendant using the dark arts, no one does.'

'What about Alexios?'

'I never heard that he's a practitioner of the dark arts.'

'No, I mean . . .' I try to gather my thoughts. 'He's a healer. He might know something about unusual poisons.'

'Good idea. We'll visit him this afternoon. I've promised to meet up with Zephrine this morning. She's the only female ascendant we haven't questioned who doesn't have an alibi.'

'But she isn't of age yet. Shouldn't she be in school?'

'She should,' Niko says. 'But from what I hear, she rarely is.'

'Oh, good,' Zephrine says. 'I've been looking forward to this for *days*.'

She's at the long table in the salon, where the more creative ascendants come to draw or sew or try their hand at one of the ancient musical instruments that hang on the walls. Behind her are cabinets full of half-used materials, perhaps left over from ascendants past: old paints, damaged but salvageable fabrics, good paper scraped thin with reuse. The table itself has stormglow panels closely spaced on the wall behind it, for the best light.

As we approach, I see that Zephrine is pushing a needle rather clumsily through an old dress, which she appears to be trying to make into a skirt with the help of various scraps. The ascendants' monthly allowance might provide them with relative luxury, but the products of the Honeycomb are finite, and new fabric is in short supply. It's not rare to find an ascendant patching up their old clothes or – more likely – getting a follower to do it for them.

I also see that despite her flippant words, Zephrine is scared and confused and looks like she might have been crying not so long ago. She's not old enough to have experienced a Winnowing. The shock of losing two of her siblings is the closest she's come to death.

'You shouldn't be here by yourself, Tenth,' I say impulsively. 'It's not safe without Marl. If you don't want to attend lessons, then at least stay in your chambers.'

Zephrine casts me a disparaging glance. She has the same bronze skin and dark hair as her mother, Sirene, but she's far slighter in build, which matches the glimpse I caught of Euphemie's killer. A needle isn't the best weapon, but it could still cause serious damage if wielded by the right person. I hold myself ready, just in case, but she only casts her half-sewn skirt aside.

'Why is *she* here?' she demands of Niko, though I catch a tremor in her hands before she folds her arms across her chest. 'I heard she's the one who did it. I heard she was going to be executed.'

'It sounds like you hear a lot,' Niko says, sitting down beside her. There's no sign of the powerful and sinister master of the dark arts now; his voice is friendly, maybe even admiring.

Zephrine smirks, her unease fading. 'I know more secrets than anyone else in the Hive.'

'Will you tell me your secrets?' Niko asks.

'That depends. What will you give me for them?'

'That depends,' he returns gravely. 'What are they worth?'

'I would think at least . . . spending the rest of the morning with me and giving your opinion on all these fabric combinations.'

That's a lot of time to dedicate to a conversation that might not lead us anywhere. But Niko extends his hand to shake hers, a pretence at formality that seems to delight her. 'You have a deal.'

I watch her show him the various bits of fabric, listening to his comments with rapt attention despite the fact that he only ever seems to wear black, which I wouldn't have thought made him the most obvious source of fashion advice. By the time she starts asking *me* whether I prefer a scrap of blue or a wisp of green, I can no more imagine her killing anyone than I could the older girls. Listening to her chatter with Niko reminds me of Euphemie and her drone followers when they used to put on epic tragedies in the small theatre next door – learning lines, cobbling together scenery and costumes. She tried to make me play a soldier, once, despite my reluctance. *It's basically your job anyway, Feldspar – don't be so boring.* But in the end, she decided my face wasn't expressive enough and got Sienna's cousin to play the part instead.

I close my eyes against the vividness of the memory. I'd stand there all day, covered in paint and clutching a spear that bent in half every time I gripped it too tightly, if she'd only walk through the door right now.

When I drag myself back to the present, Zephrine is explaining what she did on the day of Euphemie's death: a convoluted prank in the cutters' quarters and a stint of drawing on the walls of her old nursery, none of it anywhere near the sunroom. Then she tells us about the night Leandros died, when she was visiting the ascendant next below her in age and didn't get back to her own chambers until past midnight. Finally, the conversation moves on to the topic of her secrets. Not just secrets that obviously relate to murder, Niko reassures her. *All* of them, no matter how unlikely she thinks they are to be helpful.

'Hmm.' She thinks for a bit. 'Did you know Alexios's shield and Karissa's are in *love* with each other? Karissa told me that she and Alexios make sure to visit each other at least once a week so their shields get a chance to spend time together.' She giggles. 'I'd say it was encouraging them to neglect their jobs, if it wasn't so terribly romantic.'

I say nothing, though I've known that so-called secret for years. When we were in training, Flint and Quartz would spar with each other, sit beside each other at the noon meal, find every excuse possible to spend time together. I also know – as do they – that their relationship can never be anything more than a series of stolen moments. Shields don't have room in their lives for another long-term commitment.

Except me. The sole purpose of my life is gone. Without Euphemie, what am I? *Now you have options*, Niko told me, but I can't see how that's a positive. It makes me feel small and frightened and alone, as if I'm falling forever down a bottomless well.

She's still your purpose, I tell myself sternly. I need to stop missing her and concentrate on avenging her.

'Interesting,' Niko says. 'What else?'

'Hmm . . . I heard Leandros argued with Calista on the day he died.'

'That one's not worth much. We heard about it already.'

Zephrine notes the *we*; her expression becomes petulant as she says, 'How about this, then: *I know why Feldspar did it.* She's secretly the daughter of one of the Apex, and feeling that she's been robbed of her rightful position as a member of our family has driven her to murder!'

It's so ridiculous that I don't know whether to be annoyed or amused.

'Why do you think that?' Niko asks her gravely.

'Because of what my second-nurse told me when I was little. She was trying to comfort me when I got upset that I'd probably never be a queen. I hadn't thought about it for years, but now it makes sense of everything!'

127

Her excitement is so infectious that I lean forward to listen, even though this story is supposedly evidence against me.

'My nurse said that when her best friend was granted permission for a pregnancy, she kept talking about how special the baby was. How it was going to be royalty. But then, before the baby was even born, it was bonded as a common *shield*.' Zephrine casts me a sly glance. 'It drove the friend to such despair that she died soon after the child was born. My nurse said that having children can do strange things to a person, and I'd be better off out of it.'

'That doesn't make any sense,' I say grumpily, unable to stay quiet any longer. 'Unless your nurse's friend was a queen – which I *very* much doubt – how could her baby be royalty?'

Zephrine shrugs. 'Fathered by one of my uncles, I presume.'

'But that's impossible.' No male of the royal family is permitted to conceive a child. The royal gift must be kept within the matriline.

'Forbidden, yes,' Niko murmurs, 'but that's not the same thing. A member of the Apex could work out how to achieve it.'

'Without anyone else ever finding out?'

'I agree it's unlikely, but that doesn't make it impossible.'

'Exactly!' Zephrine flings out her hands in my direction, as if expecting me to confess. I shake my head.

'I can assure you, Tenth, I am not the secret daughter of one of the Apex.'

'Oh, but what if you are, and you just don't know it?'

'In that case, I couldn't have been driven to murder by the knowledge,' I point out. Then, seeing how absurdly crestfallen she looks at this destruction of her theory, I add, 'Though I grant you, I don't know who my parents are. No shield does.'

'That's no use as a motive for murder!' Cupping her chin in her hands, she regards me avidly, any wariness long gone. 'Can you think of a better one? Well, I mean, I guess you already did. What was it?'

I can't help but laugh. 'I didn't kill Euphemie, Tenth.'

'You know,' she says thoughtfully, 'I almost believe you. Maybe the chief advisor is right that the shield-bond should be abolished.'

'Wait,' Niko says. 'The chief advisor believes *what*?'

Zephrine turns to him. 'I thought for sure you'd already know that one! With what happened to Slate, I figured you must be in the group.'

'What group?'

'Apparently, there's a group of ascendants who are looking for a way to break the shield-bond and free all the shields. They went to Alathea for advice. I've no idea who's in it, because I wasn't invited.' With a touch of unironic indignation, she adds, 'They don't think I can keep a secret.'

'Would you have gone?' Niko asks softly. 'If you had been invited?'

'I . . .' For the first time since we arrived, Zephrine seems at a loss for words. 'I don't know. I like Marl. I don't want her to die. But . . .'

'But it's her duty to protect you,' I say. 'It wouldn't be fair to leave you to defend yourself, in the Winnowings or outside them, and Marl wouldn't want that either.'

Zephrine nods, looking relieved, but Niko turns to me. 'How would it be any less fair to make ascendants defend themselves than it is to make other people do it?'

'They do defend themselves. If you'd ever turned up to a Winnowing, you'd know . . .' Briefly, the screams of carders dying at the hands of the older ascendants ring in my ears. 'But royal blood is precious. Shields are there to stop it being spilt. Not only that, but without us, the younger ones wouldn't stand any chance of proving themselves in the Winnowings. We put all the ascendants in a more equal position to be selected for a throne or the Apex.'

'At the expense of your own lives.'

'Not many shields die.'

'That's not what I'm talking about!'

By now, we're glaring at each other. *I'm* glaring. At an ascendant. If I'd ever argued with Euphemie like this, I'm not sure she'd have forgiven me. But Niko's frown only relaxes into his usual vague expression, as if arguing is no more disruptive a pastime than walking or painting or taking a bath. He turns back to Zephrine.

'It's easy for us not to change,' he says. 'To look at the world and think, *this is the way things are*. Of course it suits us to believe that, because the way things are is of benefit to us. But maybe, if this group ever do come knocking . . . you might consider listening to what they have to say.'

She stares at him, torn between fascination and fear. But after a moment, she drops her gaze and turns away, bundling her half-finished skirt and all the fabric scraps into a bag.

'I should get to class,' she says brightly, and more or less runs for the door.

Once she's gone, Niko sighs. 'I'm sorry she didn't agree.'

I don't know how to answer that, because why should she have done? He knows I didn't agree with him either.

'What about this secret group of ascendants?' I ask, deciding a subject change is the best way forward. 'Could it be true?' I remember that hint of an ongoing argument between Calista and Halimeda: *That's what happens when you break a shield-bond.*

'I haven't heard anything about it,' Niko says. 'But then, everyone knows I killed my own shield. So I guess they wouldn't have expected me to be sympathetic to the cause.'

I can't tell if that's sarcasm or a genuine admission of guilt. Niko misses Slate – that much is clear by now – but it doesn't mean he didn't kill him.

'I don't believe Euphemie knew about it either,' I reply. 'Or else . . .'

My voice dies, a lump forming in my throat. Euphemie liked having a shield. She liked having someone who was willing to die for her. I force myself to finish the sentence. 'Or else they asked her and she wasn't interested.'

Niko doesn't comment on that, for which I'm grateful.

'We can talk to Alathea,' he says. 'The chief advisor. Zephrine said she's been advising the group. She'll soon tell us if that's true.'

'I suppose it could explain the murders,' I think aloud. 'If . . . I don't know. Euphemie and Leandros both argued against what the group were doing, and were killed for it. Or . . . or the group have already found a way to break the bond, and used it successfully on me and Euphemie, but something went wrong for Leandros and Basalt.'

'Hmm.' Niko runs a thumb over one of the musical instruments on the wall – a curved wooden shape, with lots of metal wires strung across it; I don't know what it is, since Euphemie had little interest in music except as entertainment for her parties – and winces at the discordant sound. Then he adds, 'There was also the story about the nurse.'

'You think that's true? It sounded pretty silly to me.'

'Some of it, yes. I don't suppose anyone ever died of despair.' Absently, he reaches up to caress the empty air above his shoulder. 'But there's a grain of truth in every story.'

FOUR DAYS AFTER

I've been in some awkward situations in my life, but sitting in a soft, squashy armchair is up there with the worst. I've sunk so deep into the cushions that it's going to be a struggle to stand. How am I meant to be ready to meet any threat if I have to get out of a chair first? But Alexios invited me to sit down, and I couldn't think of a polite way to decline.

I glance at Niko, beside me, then across at the Eighth himself. He gives me a friendly smile, as if nothing about this situation is unusual. Flint stands behind him, an angry flush warming his pale skin. I perfected my punches on him; he learnt to disarm an opponent with me. It doesn't take the dark arts to work out that he views everything I've done since Euphemie died as a betrayal – from surviving, right up to sitting in this chair. He didn't even call me by my name when he answered the door to us and let Alexios know who was visiting. He referred to me as *the Seventh's former shield*. And now he's watching me with tension in every muscle, as if he thinks he might need to defend his charge at any moment.

'You said you were here to question me about Leandros,' Alexios prompts, breaking the silence. 'I'm not sure I've much to tell you, but I'll do what I can.'

I force myself to concentrate. As a shield, if I'd been asked to rank the ascendants according to how much of a threat they posed, the Eighth's name would definitely have come last. Yet what I said to Niko is true: he's the most likely to know about poisons. Which means we can't rule him out, however kind he's always been.

'The usual question is what you were doing on the night he died,' Niko says. 'But to be honest, I'm not sure I need to ask.'

Alexios nods. 'I was with Damon.' The drone boy he introduced to Euphemie on the day she was murdered. 'He'd confirm that, if you asked him. But then, you probably think he'd be willing to lie for me if necessary, so it's not much in the way of evidence.'

'It's certainly not definitive.'

'I mean, it's probably more relevant that I've always made it clear I don't approve of murder,' Alexios says. 'But I realize even my core beliefs could be an elaborate lifelong ruse to lull you all into a false sense of security.'

The words were accompanied by a smile, like a joke, but I heard sadness there too. It reminds me of that day in the sunroom, when he talked to Euphemie about the Apex's decisions and she failed to listen.

'You didn't approve of the latest Winnowing,' I say, though I know it's not what we came for. But somehow I want him to know that someone heard, even if it was only me.

'I never do,' he agrees. 'They winnow people to free up enough resources to grow soldiers, who are sent against the raiders to be killed in turn. We're told the royal gift is the creation of life itself, but in truth, the entire Hive is built on death.'

Like me, Alexios has been in two Winnowings. Unlike Euphemie, he played a very active part in both. He didn't wield a sword or a bow or anything else designed for carnage and destruction; only one small, sharp knife, which he used to relieve the suffering of the mortally wounded. Flint followed him round and watched over him, but not one of those desperate cutters or carders tried to harm Alexios. Though he was as bloodstained as the rest of the ascendants, they could see the difference.

All the same, I tell myself, *that proves he knows how to kill. Not only that, but if he believes he has a good enough reason, he'll do it.*

'I've always intended to be head medic in our Apex, if I have to be anything at all,' Alexios adds. 'And I would vote against any decisions that involved people being banished or dying. Does that convince you?'

'It's enough for now,' Niko says. 'The truth is, we're not so

135

much here to question you as because we need your help.'

'Oh?'

Niko pulls a small bottle from one of his pockets. 'This is part of a sample that I took from Leandros's chambers. I can't detect any of the standard poisons in it, but your knowledge of such things is broader than mine.'

'Perhaps.' Alexios takes it. 'What kind of poison are you looking for?'

'Something that could turn a shield against his charge, despite the constraints of his conditioning.'

Alexios shoots a glance over his shoulder at Flint. When he looks back at us, there's something closed in his expression. Yet all he says is, 'I take it this doesn't relate to Euphemie's death.'

'Leandros and Basalt,' Niko agrees. 'Euphemie's death was something else.'

'She was poisoned too,' I put in. 'With an arrow. It made her limbs shake. Turned her lips blue, her skin grey. She couldn't breathe . . .' Tears prick behind my eyes, but I didn't spend a lifetime learning how to control my every vulnerable response for nothing. I squeeze all that emotion into a tight, hard ball and speak matter-of-factly. 'Do you know what poison could cause symptoms like that, Eighth?'

'It sounds like aroura. They make it in the Honeycomb. It's used to kill rats.'

One of their children ate some by mistake once. I saw the body. It wasn't pretty. So Niko was closer than he knew, when he compared his experience to mine.

'Of course, the rats usually ingest it,' Alexios adds. 'In which case, it takes longer to act. That's deliberate; it stops other rats being warned off the bait. But in the blood, it's deadly swift.'

I manage a nod, but I'm shivering too hard to speak. Someone murdered Euphemie with *rat poison*. The sheer cruel indignity of it fills me with bone-deep rage.

Alexios looks at me, his expression no longer closed but full of sorrowful sympathy. I brace myself, fearing to lose control completely in the face of his kindness. But he only turns back to Niko.

'I'll test your sample,' he says. 'I may have to send a courier for a few ingredients first, but I should get it done sometime tomorrow.'

Once again, I sense something hidden. Whatever he was debating with himself before, he's made up his mind. Maybe it was whether or not to help us, but I'm not sure.

'Eighth,' I blurt out. 'If there's anything else you know that could explain these deaths – anything at all . . .'

He meets my gaze with his usual non-judgemental frankness, so open that I'm half convinced I must have imagined it.

'No, Feldspar,' he says. 'There's nothing.'

'What was that about?' Niko asks once we've left the Eighth's chambers.

'It felt like he was hiding something,' I explain.

'Who, Alexios? By far the most decent of the lot of us?' He shrugs. 'Probably.'

'You don't seem to mind.'

'Everyone has secrets. That's what makes it so hard to uncover the truth about anything.'

I frown. 'Surely most people's secrets don't have anything to do with murder?'

'No. But I bet that for every single person we've spoken to, there's some overlap between what they're trying to hide and what it would be useful for us to know. For the killer, the overlap might be one hundred per cent, but even for the nice, honest ones, I expect it's about twenty.'

'And where do you fall on that scale?'

'I'm a master of the dark arts,' Niko says placidly. 'Secrets are expected of me.'

I don't reply. I'm thinking about Alexios again – not so much his secrets, but his description of the Hive as *built on death*. About the raiders, and the soldiers who are sent into battle against them.

It's been the same relentless cycle ever since I can remember. Soldiers are taught a lot of the same skills as shields, so I'd speak to them on the training floor or hear their conversations as I went about my day. I've been there when a new cohort of soldiers was sent to the lowest levels in response to a raider incursion through the tunnels. I've seen the survivors return in far smaller number, noted the disappearance of familiar faces.

The Apex will announce a victory and increased rations for all; then a few months later, there comes a Winnowing, the rations drop back down, more babies are grown to replace the soldiers who are about to die, and the cycle starts again.

People invade the Hive because they want to take our resources for themselves. Elsewhere, in whatever other underground pockets of land survive above the flood line, there's fighting and chaos, as there used to be here before order was established. I've always known that soldiers have to die for the good of the colony, just as people have to leave when they can no longer be supported. Yet Alexios sees all that as something bad. Something wasteful.

'Feldspar?' Niko says, and no wonder. I haven't spoken for a long time. I expect him to ask what I was thinking, but he only says, 'Here.'

He fishes a protein strip out of his pocket and hands it to me. He does this all the time, when I'm traipsing around the Hive with him. It's like he thinks I need constant feeding. When I express that to him, he shrugs.

'You're probably used to regular meals.'

'Aren't you?' I say.

'Mmm . . . I tend to eat when I remember. If I'm very distracted—'

'With science?'

'*Yes*, with science – sometimes, I can get to sundown before I notice I'm hungry.'

I tear the strip in two and hand half of it back to him. 'Sounds like you need this more than I do.'

We munch in silence. Then, abruptly, he asks me, 'Do you know why the Hive is called that?'

I shake my head.

'A long, long time ago – before the chemicals of the Dark Ages destroyed it, before the Rising happened and the weather became too extreme for anything except the hardiest seabirds to thrive above ground – there used to be a creature that made plants grow. As payment, it took the sweet liquid from the flowers to be its food. And it lived in something called a hive.'

I can barely imagine what he's talking about. Plants are grown in the Honeycomb, under glass. Doubtfully, I ask, 'Why would anyone have named the Hive after the home of some mythical creature?'

'They were called bees,' Niko says. 'And they came in three types: workers, drones and a queen. The workers did every-thing needed to protect their home and keep it running. They were the ones who collected the food, storing it in lots of tiny chambers so that the hive would never run out. Mean-while, the drones and the queen thought about nothing but having children and who would become the next queen. Sound familiar?'

'Yes . . .' But I don't know what point he wants me to take from this, so I change the subject. 'Where exactly are we going now, anyway?'

He passes me a fresh bottle of water from a pocket. 'I have to take you back to your cell, I'm afraid. Queens' orders: you always have to be back before sundown.'

'Right.' I don't know why I'm so disappointed. I am meant to be in prison, after all. Niko has to do as he's told. Yet today, he's treated me as if he respects me. As if he believes I'm someone who has a right to exist, despite my failure to protect Euphemie. And it's left me confused. I know I'm going to die – that my final purpose is to find the killer, allowing me to be at peace when I meet my own end. That should be as easy to accept as being a shield was in the first place. Yet Niko makes me feel like the world could hold something more for me than duty and death, and I think . . . I think I like that feeling.

When we reach my cell, I stumble to the cot without looking back. I can feel a storm coming. There must have been other storms, since Euphemie died – while I was sleeping, or busy with Niko, or distracted by other things. We usually have at least one a day. Yet now the Hive's hum has sharpened, and the air is full of the promise of lightning, and my hands are shaking. I didn't want to go to the sunroom, the day it happened. I was afraid. If I'd listened to that feeling – if I'd made her stay – would she be alive now?

You couldn't make her stay, I remind myself. *You had no right to make her do anything.*

But I could have tried.

'All right,' Niko says. 'I'll see you—'

141

'Don't go.' The words are torn from my lips. I turn, realizing too late that my eyes are brimming with tears. 'Sorry. I didn't mean to say that. I—'

'What's wrong?'

I don't know whether I truly believe that something bad will happen to him if he leaves, or whether I'm adding Euphemie's death to my usual dislike of storms and coming up with something greater. Either way, there's no reason for him to listen to me. I sit down slowly, no longer able to look at him.

'I'm afraid of lightning,' I admit, though saying it makes me feel small and foolish. I know he's going to laugh – or worse, ask me how I could ever have called myself a shield when I'm such a coward. Hastily, I go on, 'I try not to be. I know it's silly. The shieldmaster once made me stay by myself in the sunroom during a storm, but it didn't work.'

Head bowed, I brace myself for mockery. I hear his footsteps cross the floor before he sits down next to me. Not quite touching, but close enough that I'm aware of his warmth. I'm suddenly very conscious of myself: my pulse and my breathing and where all my limbs are in relation to his. It's similar to how it feels when I sense danger, only . . . not.

'For me, it's spiders,' he says.

'What is?'

'That I'm scared of.'

I dart a glance at him. 'You're just saying that to make me feel better.'

142

'Why would I need to? No sensible person wants to be struck by lightning.' His mouth twists as if he's acknowledging a private joke. 'Spiders, on the other hand, are perfectly harmless, and therefore *not* a respectable source of fear. But it's the legs. There are so *many* of them.'

Don't laugh, I tell myself sternly. *He didn't laugh at you.*

'I used to have to call Slate to catch them for me,' Niko goes on, gazing at the door to my cell in a kind of horrified trance. 'Even the little ones. Now I make do with a piece of paper and a cup.'

I heard he goes round catching spiders, the memory of Euphemie's voice says. *Do you think he uses them in his creepy experiments? Or worse, eats them?*

Suddenly, I've lost the desire to laugh. I wonder if Euphemie ever visited Niko after Slate died. Neither of them had come of age yet; she could have gone without me knowing about it. But I've a feeling he was worth more to her as a form of entertainment than as family.

'I'm sorry,' I say.

'That I have to catch spiders in a cup?'

'That Slate isn't here to do it for you.'

I expect him to close up, as he did when I mentioned Slate before. For the stormglow to flicker with the force of his rejection of the subject. But instead, he says simply, 'I miss him.'

'I can tell.'

He looks at me, eyebrows raised. 'Can you? No one else

143

seems to be able to. I've heard the rumours. *Oh, the Sixth – isn't he the one who killed his own shield? He hated Slate. He wanted him dead*. And the worst of it is . . .'

I wait, but he says no more. His hand reaches briefly to his shoulder. After a while, he stands up, turns to me and – with what seems a vast effort – smiles.

'I think the storm is passing. Good night, Feldspar.'

FIVE DAYS AFTER

My cell door clangs, jerking me out of a muddled nightmare in which I was trying to pull a poison arrow out
of my own leg. I scrabble upright, heart racing as grogginess
and adrenaline chase each other in cold waves down my spine.
This is it. The end. They've come to fetch me for execution, or
maybe to finish me off right here and now. Someone sits down
on the cot next to me, and I shoot out a hand to grab their
wrist before they can stab me.

'It's me,' Niko's voice says.

'Oh.'

'So you can let go of my arm now.'

I release my death-grip, stomach aching with familiar revulsion at the idea of hurting an ascendant, however accidentally.
'Sorry.'

'My fault,' he says, gingerly rotating his wrist. 'I should have
told you: I convinced the queens to let me keep hold of the

only key to this cell. No one can get at you in here.'

Rubbing my eyes, I look around. By the shade of the storm-glow – dull orange only just beginning to brighten to yellow – it's not yet sunup. Niko never arrives this early.

I focus on his face. He's looking at his knees, one hand moving in a soft curve over an invisible shape. Somehow, from the tension in his shoulders and the frown on his face, I read the news he's brought and say it before he can.

'There's been another death.'

His chin drops. 'Halimeda.'

The First. A perfect warrior, like Leandros. Queen Doralie's daughter . . . and Niko's sister. I think of her, the way she was on the training floor – was it only the day before yesterday? Regal and competent, dismissing the petty squabbles of the other ascendants, wielding a sword with precision. It doesn't seem possible that she could have been killed.

'How did she die?' I ask.

'Same as Leandros. Her shield stabbed her, before dying without a mark – taken by the bond. And two shields breaking their conditioning in exactly the same manner can't be a coincidence.'

'Then – then that proves it. Someone is causing this.'

'They must be. But Halimeda was Queen Doralie's daughter, which disproves my original theory, and Calista and Pyrene were apparently together last night, which disproves yours. We're no further than when we started.' Sighing, Niko lifts an

146

invisible Astrapē back on to his shoulder. 'And there will be more deaths, Feldspar. Unless we can do something about it, there will be more.'

'That's what you said would happen, when we spoke to Queen Sirene.'

'I know. But that was when I thought I could solve it before anyone else had to die. I wasn't quick enough, and now Halimeda's blood is on my hands.'

'Her death isn't your fault,' I tell him. 'None of this is your fault. We're doing the best we can.'

'But no one will answer my questions! Or rather, they answer because I scare them and the dark arts scare them, and they think that if they don't comply, I'll retaliate. But none of the answers are any use. No one can tell me anything I need to know – or if they can, they aren't. And the queens . . .' His fists clench. 'They still think it's you, Feldspar. No matter how many times I tell them that there's no way you could have killed Leandros, all they ever ask me is whether I've worked out how you did it. They won't give me any resources to mount a wider investigation. I'm on my own. And I'm afraid that now, with Halimeda's death . . .'

'They'll decide that enough is enough, and execute me,' I supply softly. No wonder he always looks so tired – and no wonder he agreed to let me help him. Whether I murdered Euphemie or not, I'm all he's got.

*

147

The passages of the Hive are never crowded or lively at the best of times, but now they feel deserted. We pass closed door after closed door, our footsteps echoing in the silence. Sometimes we see couriers and handmaidens, going about their business with their heads down, and occasionally drones, travelling in small groups as if they believe they'll be attacked in the corridors, casting us suspicious glances. But there are no ascendants and shields about. Not surprising, I suppose. Ascendants have always been sure of their shields' protection in the most dangerous of situations, but now the people they rely on are the very people who could turn on them.

'We'll visit Ophion,' Niko murmurs. 'He was with me when Leandros died, but at this point, I don't want to talk to a suspect. I want to talk to someone who's willing to help. And Ophion is the only friend I've got.'

When we get to Ophion's chambers, though, his shield, Gabbro, is outside the door. As soon as he sees us, his expression darkens. Ignoring Niko, he prowls towards me, one hand dropping to the knife at his belt.

'He locked me out,' he says. 'The Fifth locked me out. Said he's safer without me.'

I back up a step, reaching for my own weapon but, of course, finding nothing. His eyes follow the movement.

'You did this, Feldspar,' he accuses. 'Everyone knows it. They should have executed you as soon as the Seventh died.'

'Feldspar isn't responsible for these deaths,' Niko says

sharply. 'The only one she could possibly be blamed for is Euphemie's—'

'And isn't that enough?' The retort is out apparently before Gabbro can stop it. He looks discomfited, but rallies quickly. 'Besides, who knows what she's capable of? With all due respect, Sixth, maybe you're not the only one who has skill in the dark arts.'

That's close to what Calista said: *Maybe breaking her bond with Euphemie gave her the power to control everyone else's bonds as well.* I've let Niko's common sense blind me to the fact that most people in the Hive probably believe I can do all sorts of outlandish things. Suddenly, the fact that the Apex are refusing to look for any other killer doesn't seem so surprising.

'I can assure you,' Niko says, 'that whatever else Feldspar is capable of, she has no skill in the dark arts whatsoever.'

Gabbro's hand falls away from his knife, and Niko relaxes slightly. I don't. The shield's stance is still tense, his intent clear to read. He's remembered, as I had forgotten, that he can't kill me. Not when Ophion is on the other side of a door and clearly in no danger. So bladed weaponry is out, but that won't stop him using his fists.

Be ready, Feldspar. He'll hurt you if he can.

Blocking the first punch, I glance swiftly at Niko, who raises his eyebrows in question. I shake my head. Maybe it would be sensible to let him sort it out. Any kind of intervention from an ascendant, and Gabbro would have to back off, no matter how he feels about me. Yet I don't *want* intervention. For once, this is a problem I can deal with – a situation in which I'm allowed to defend myself – and it feels so good to have control over that one tiny part of my life that I can't bring myself to turn away from it.

I sidestep, assessing my odds. Gabbro is a year older than me. Stockier. We're evenly matched in height and reach, so his obvious move is to use his additional weight against me. Sure enough, he closes in, trying to force me backwards. I struggle to hold my ground. Hot breath hits the side of my face. If he traps me against the wall . . .

I lower my head, driving my fist hard into his guts, and feel my face split in a reckless grin. Much better than a stormglow panel. I didn't realize quite how much I've been longing to hit someone all this time.

My aim was to wind him, but he comes in again fast, his return blow catching my jaw. My head snaps back, eyes watering at the impact. A curse drops from my lips. Yet even the hot throb of pain is welcome in its familiarity.

'Had enough?' he spits at me.

I try another punch, but he catches my fist and spins me round, shoving me against the wall. Though I struggle, his superior weight has me pinned. Rough stone scrapes my cheek. I fight to suck in enough air.

'This is for the Seventh,' he hisses in my ear, twisting my arm up behind me roughly enough to make me cry out. He hits me hard in the lower back, a sharp spike of agony, and now I'm no longer enjoying myself. *I didn't kill her*, I want to cry. *It wasn't my fault.* But I swallow the weakness. I've seen Gabbro pull this move before, on the training floor. I know what's coming next.

When he yanks me off the wall again, spinning me for another punch, I'm ready for it. I use his momentum to carry myself towards him, low and fast, striking as hard as I can beneath his ribcage. This time, my fist lands squarely. He doubles over, wheezing. And I slam the heel of my other hand up into his face.

'I should have been a better protector for her,' I pant. 'But I'm not a traitor.'

We regard each other warily, both breathing hard. I find a grim satisfaction in the thick crimson stream coursing down his upper lip. My jaw is throbbing, my hands sting, and no doubt I'll have a few bruises tomorrow, but I can claim first blood, at least.

'Feeling better?' Niko murmurs. It's too low for Gabbro to hear, but he scowls all the same. That's when, finally, Ophion comes to the door. I haven't spent much time with him before; Euphemie didn't invite him to her parties or hang on his every word, like she used to with Leandros. The most I saw of him was in the Winnowings. He didn't have the skill of the four eldest ascendants, but what he lacked in brute force, he made up for in sneakiness. He used to send Gabbro charging towards people who were resisting exile, then come up behind them while they were distracted and stab them in the back.

'What's going on?' He leans against the frame, a nasty smile glittering on his face as he looks between us. 'Nikolos, why have you let your pet murderer loose on my shield?'

'He attacked Feldspar first,' Niko says. 'Call him off, Ophion. We need to talk to you.'

'Really? I don't think you do.'

'Just let us in, will you? We don't intend you any harm.'

Ophion considers that, then shrugs. 'Why should I?'

'Because you and I are . . .' I feel Niko waver over the word *friends*. But faced with that glittering smile, he changes his mind. 'Allies.'

'Are we?'

'You know we are. Let us in.'

'Queen Sirene told me how you begged for that one's life,' Ophion says, nodding at me without breaking eye contact with Niko. 'As if it mattered more than ours.'

'Not more,' Niko says. 'But not less either.'

'She should be dead!'

'You know how I feel about the shield-bond.'

'As a matter of theory, yes. But you're talking about a traitor who killed her own charge. I think that makes the situation rather different.'

'Come on, Ophi. How many nights have we spent talking about justice? There's no proof that Feldspar is responsible for

Euphemie's death or her own survival. And there can't be any real justice without proof.'

'What more proof do you need? She's alive!'

'I think your arguments are becoming rather circular, my friend,' Niko says, and Ophion's eyes narrow.

'Friend? I was never your friend. I tolerated you because I thought you might be useful. Perhaps help me to gain the role of shieldmaster over Leandros.' Leaning forward, he adds very distinctly, 'But the good you might do me no longer outweighs the embarrassment.'

I wait for Niko to show one of those flashes of dark power I've seen from him ever since we met – the kind that make the stormglow flicker with the force of his emotion. But instead, he repeats softly, 'Let me in, Ophion. I'm not your enemy.'

A harsh laugh catches in Ophion's throat. 'Oh, I know *exactly* what you are, Nikolos, and don't forget it. Now *go away*.'

Curtly, he gestures to Gabbro to stay where he is. Then he retreats into his chambers and slams the door. Niko hesitates, looking at it as if he can make Ophion come back out through sheer force of will. Yet even he can't withstand Gabbro's baleful glare for long; with a barely audible sigh, he turns away.

'Come on, Feldspar. There's no use being here.'

I follow miserably. I wanted so much to be part of this investigation, to help bring Euphemie's killer to justice, yet I'm only making things worse.

'You should leave me behind in future,' I mumble. 'Maybe

then people will talk to you.'

Niko snorts. 'In case you hadn't noticed, I'm not exactly a favourite among the ascendants. They were never going to welcome me with open arms.' Half to himself, he adds, 'Though I really thought Ophion . . .'

'What did he mean, he knows exactly what you are?'

'Oh, nothing. Just the hazards of sharing secrets with friends.' He attempts a wry smile. 'Good thing neither of us has any friends, right?'

I know the difference between a person who's waiting to be encouraged to talk about something and a person who's genuinely trying to avoid it. As Euphemie's shield, I learnt to differentiate between the two to a *very* fine degree. So I don't press him.

'All right, so Ophion's no good,' I say. 'That doesn't mean we give up. What next?'

This time, Niko's smile is more genuine. 'I don't know about you, but I could really use a break. Want to visit my place?'

FIVE DAYS AFTER

If I ever tried to imagine Niko's chambers, back when Euphemie was alive, no doubt I came up with a picture of sinister malice. Walls draped in black, dimming the stormglow. A few skulls lying around. Maybe a cage of rats for his blood-thirsty experiments. Yet now, taking a long, surreptitious look around his exochamber, I can see that my impression of the dark arts sprang fully formed from the ghost stories that Euphemie and I used to whisper to each other on stormy nights as children.

In reality, this living room is very similar to the others I've seen: plain and functional, save for the few touches that put a personal stamp on it. With Euphemie, it was the filmy scarves scattered over the table and chairs, the embroidered slippers discarded on the floor, the vase of sea-coloured stones. Niko's personality, meanwhile, leans towards books. *Hundreds* of them, crammed haphazardly on to the shelves, far outnumbering the handful of approved texts that Euphemie studied in school. I had no idea there were so many books in the world.

Yet more books lie open on the table, interspersed with various metal objects whose uses I can only begin to guess. I sidle close enough that I can confirm, to my own satisfaction, that they don't look like weapons or arcane torture devices. Nor do the books – splayed open by random bookmarks, including rocks and pens and, in one case, a half-eaten biscuit – appear to contain spells or magical incantations. Instead, there's a lot of dense text, interspersed with diagrams of what look like machines: the kind that turn the lightning from the Spire into electricity or extract salt from seawater. I've never seen them myself, but I know they exist. Although I might have been joking when I asked if Niko got distracted with science, he wasn't. These books must have come from the carders.

Silently, I review my ever-changing concept of what the dark arts entail: *scepticism*, *logic*, *books*, *untidiness*. It's not exactly the scariest list. Even science – that dangerous know-ledge which caused the Rising and must be restricted solely to what's necessary to keep us alive – appears in Niko's hands to be more a way of thinking than anything else.

Niko wanders over to the table, where he peers down at several handwritten sheets of notes lying on the nearest chair before picking them up and dumping them haphazardly on an already teetering stack. 'Take a seat, Feldspar.'

I perch on the edge of the chair. He removes a couple of

books from another one before sitting down himself.

'I love the smell of paper,' he says, taking a deep breath through his nose and releasing it slowly. Already, he looks calmer than he did after Ophion's rejection. 'Don't you?'

'Sure.' The honest answer is that it smells like everything else in the Hive: of stone and sea. Paper is made of seaweed, just like our food is fish and brackish greens, and our clothes are woven from seagrass fibres. There's no getting away from the salty tang of the ocean.

'Did you know they used to make paper out of trees?' Niko asks, gazing abstractedly at the litter on his table. 'It can't have smelt the same, though.'

I don't ask him what trees are. I don't want to get lost in another of his mental labyrinths: *trees and bees*. What use learning about things that are gone forever?

'They must still exist, you know,' he says, in one of those flashes of connection that make it feel as if he's reading my mind. 'Somewhere out there, on some remote storm-wracked islet. Else, where would driftwood come from?'

'Paper was made out of the same stuff as *driftwood*?' I ask, sucked in despite myself – because I can't imagine it, flimsy green sheets and smooth solid sculpture coming from the same source.

He nods. 'And the islands used to be mountains, before the rest of the world was drowned.'

'Mountains?'

'The highest parts of the land. There was a whole country here – Elláda, one of many lost beneath the ocean. Before the Rising, you could have stood at the top of the Hive and looked out across all that unflooded ground. You could have walked to the next peak along.'

'How do you know all this?'

'Down in the Honeycomb, the carders have a machine with a million books stored on it. They can print a copy of any of them, if needed.'

Reading is dull, Euphemie used to say, throwing her schoolbooks to the floor. *Who wants to learn all this boring history?* It never occurred to either of us that anything other than the approved texts existed.

'You must have spent a lot of time in the Honeycomb, then,' I say, looking around at all the books on his shelves, and he laughs.

'Yes. I get at least three new books every time I go down there. It's what I spend most of my allowance on – that and lab equipment.'

'So *that's* why you always wear the same coat,' I say, and he laughs again. Making him laugh gives me a warm feeling that I'm not familiar with.

'Most of the books are about the technology that maintains the Hive,' he says. 'Which is why the carders are allowed to keep the machine at all. But there are others as well. That's how I learnt about bees, and mountains, and an order of robed warriors who used to go around battling evil with laser swords.'

'Doesn't it make you sad, learning about things that are gone?'

'Not really. I figure learning about them keeps them alive.' He reaches behind another stack of books and pulls out a bottle of kelpin, the green liquor that's reserved for the royal family. I'm surprised he wasn't carrying it around in one of his pockets like everything else. 'So how about a drink?'

'I'm not allowed—' I begin, then catch myself and chant, under my breath, *'You're not a shield any more, Feldspar.'*

'Exactly,' he says, accepting the mimicry without any sign of offence. Grinning, he pours a measure into two cups and holds one out to me. I take a cautious sip, then another. 'Well?'

'It tastes like . . .' I try to find the words for *what* exactly it tastes like. 'Liquidized seaweed. Except burnt. And sharp. As if someone harvested it after it was struck by lightning and thought no one would notice it was all shrivelled and disgusting.'

'So you like it, then.'

'Put it this way: it makes me even happier not to be an ascendant if *this* is the delicacy you keep for yourselves.'

I take another sip, though I'm not sure why. Then he asks quietly, 'Have you never wanted to be an ascendant?'

'No.'

'Why not?'

'Because . . .' Once again, I struggle for words. 'It's all about getting people to love you.'

'You don't want to be loved?'

'I wouldn't know how to go about it. Convincing the queens and everyone else that I'm worthy. I used to watch Euphemie flirt and wonder how she did it, when it seemed so exhausting . . .' I drink again. 'And even if you become part of the Apex, it isn't as if you gain much.'

Niko raises his eyebrows. 'Except total control over the population of the Hive.'

He's right, of course. If Euphemie had been selected as a queen, she would have won the right to bear children, to pass down the royal gift. But even if she hadn't, as part of the Apex, she would have had a say in everyone else's lives and deaths. Who should be permitted to reproduce. Whether the next cutter child should be a soldier or a handmaiden. Who should be winnowed if numbers were in danger of increasing beyond capacity. She *wanted* all that.

'It sounds terrifying to me,' I admit. 'But then, it's not what I was designed for. I suppose, if you're born an ascendant, it all comes naturally.'

'You'd think so, wouldn't you?' His voice is flippant, but there's a dark undertone to it. 'Of course, it also seems that if you're born an ascendant, you may become the target of an untraceable killer. And I don't know how to—'

He breaks off. I almost touch his arm before remembering myself.

'We can still do this,' I tell him. '*You* can still do this.'

His dark eyes search my face. If it didn't seem so unlikely, I'd think he's looking for reassurance that I mean it. That I believe in him.

'All right,' he says at last, sitting back in his chair. 'What do we least understand? Whenever I'm trying to figure something out, I start from my point of greatest confusion.'

We sip our drinks while we consider it.

'I don't understand why Euphemie's death was different,' Niko says finally. 'The other two ascendants were killed by their shields, who instantly succumbed to the bond and died themselves. But with Euphemie . . .'

I open my mouth, then close it again as a thought hits me.

'I was going to say I didn't understand why Euphemie was first,' I say slowly. 'People liked her. And also . . . I didn't want to admit it before, but you were right. She wasn't the obvious choice for anyone trying to eliminate rivals. She never had a chance at the throne.' It feels awful to say that, yet it's also something of a relief. 'But maybe the reason is also the answer to a question you once asked me.'

'What question?'

'Why anyone would want to keep me alive. If someone knew killing Euphemie wouldn't kill me . . .'

'Then killing Euphemie would set you up as a scapegoat,' Niko agrees. 'Euphemie's death was different because the killer wanted someone to pin the blame on – knowing that your survival would become the focus to the exclusion of all else. Though that doesn't explain *how* you survived, or how the killer knew it would happen.'

'No, but what's the alternative? That I killed her, then went on a murder spree from my locked cell in which every dead shield only made me look more suspicious as the sole survivor?'

'True. If you were going to kill someone, you'd go about it much more competently than that.'

'Exactly!' A heartbeat late, I catch up with the full implications of what he just said. 'Wait. Then—'

'I don't believe you killed Euphemie, or anyone else. Consider yourself officially struck from the list of suspects.' One side of his mouth tilts up. 'Sorry it took me so long.'

'Oh.' I pull myself together. 'I mean, that's all right. I would have suspected me too.'

'I'm also sorry you still have to return to your cell every night,' he goes on. 'But in a way, it's safer. Once we can explain how these murders are carried out, whether by poisoning the shields or some other method, I *assume* we'll also be able to prove that they couldn't possibly have been committed by a girl behind a locked door. In the meantime . . .'

Jumping to his feet, he crosses to a cabinet that looks as if it was originally intended to house his crockery and other household bits, but is now cluttered with beakers, tubes and pipettes. After rummaging for some time in the cupboard below it, accompanied by a muffled commentary on its state of disarray, he emerges with something wrapped in a piece of cloth.

'I had them so I could test for poison on the blades,' he says, looking slightly shamefaced. 'In case the blood was really Euphemie's . . . but we both know I didn't find anything. It's only fair that you should be able to defend yourself, if it comes to it.'

Inside the cloth are my knives. I touch the nearest hilt, fighting back a surge of emotion. Euphemie gave me these knives for my sixteenth birthday, ten days before she came of age herself. I was carrying them the day she died. I always carried them. Not that it did her any good, in the end.

'Niko,' I say, when I can speak again. 'Are you sure you're allowed to—'

'It doesn't matter. I don't want you to end up dead just because you're helping me catch a murderer.'

'I'm not really helping,' I mumble.

'Yes, you are. You're the only one who is.'

'I'm sorry about Ophion. I know you thought he was your friend.'

'*Thought* is the right word. But it's like you said, about ascendants: all they care about is getting people to love them. They don't know how to return it.' He adds another measure of kelpin to his cup, then downs it in a single moody swallow. 'Still. I'm never really alone, am I? I have Astrapē.'

I bite my lip. Usually when he mentions Astrapē, I play

along, like a nurse indulging a small child. Yet Niko deserves better. He has faith in my innocence when no one else does; I ought to do him the courtesy of treating what he says with equal respect.

'Do all practitioners of the dark arts have familiars?' I ask.

'Familiars?' He looks taken aback. But then understanding dawns, and the corners of his mouth twitch as though the question has amused him. 'No. She was a gift from the storm.'

I still can't decide whether I believe in her existence, or even whether *he* believes in it. Yet the kelpin is making me feel kind of fuzzy, and I decide it doesn't matter whether Astrapē is really there or not. If he tells me he has an invisible, shape-shifting creature around his neck, that's what he has. *Reality* has nothing to do with it.

'What makes her change shape?' I ask.

'What makes anyone's mood change? She reacts to me. To our surroundings. Currently, for instance, she is—'

'A snake.' Gazing at his shoulder, eyes unfocused, I almost think I can see it: barely visible flickers of light forming the long, coiled shape. Or rather, not the shape itself. The places where the shape would catch the light. Highlights without shadows.

'Yes,' Niko says. 'She must be beginning to trust you.'

Startled, I look into his face and find that he's looking straight at me. 'You mean, there really is something there?'

'Astrapē is a creature of captured lightning,' he says, with no

164

apparent reaction to the revelation that I've been doubting her existence all this time. 'She will not be contained by so much as a glance, unless she wishes it.'

Just when I thought I understood Niko, and what the dark arts really are, my perception has shifted again. In a near whisper, I say, 'That doesn't sound much like what you call science. It sounds . . . impossible.'

'Yes,' he agrees, very seriously. 'But if something exists, we can't deny its existence because we don't understand it. That wouldn't be science at all.'

Neither of us has broken eye contact. Perhaps it should be uncomfortable. In the past, someone's gaze resting on me for this long would certainly have set me on edge – particularly if their eyes conveyed a message I didn't know how to read, as Niko's do now. Yet I'm surprised to find that I don't mind.

Very softly, he says, 'Feldspar—'

A knock makes us both jump. I study my drink, strangely embarrassed, heart racing although I haven't been exerting myself at all; perhaps that's the liquor. Meanwhile, Niko goes to unlock the door. A woman enters, leaning heavily on the arm of another. Queen Doralie, supported by her shield, Agate. I scramble to my feet, ducking my head respectfully.

I haven't set eyes on the Elder Queen for some time. She rarely appears in public these days, leaving Sirene to deal with the day-to-day running of affairs in the upper levels, although she retains the final say in any cases where the two queens disagree. It's a shock to see her so frail and thin, as if she's wasting away. Perhaps it's true, what they say: that the royal gift drains the life out of the queens. As the ascendants grow older and stronger, the queens wither and fade; once the new queens are chosen and the new Apex is formed, that's when the old queens will die – as will the old Apex, who are bonded to them. Although, as the Younger Queen, Sirene still looks strong – even the smallest age gap makes a big difference, at the end of a queen's life – she must be aware that the same fate is waiting, not far away.

'Ma'am,' Niko greets his mother, using the formal honorific as all ascendants do when addressing the queens, related or not. He must have seen her far more recently than I have, so her fragile appearance won't be a surprise; still, his voice is gentle as he bows over one of her bony hands. 'What brings you here?'

Doralie's detached gaze scans him from head to toe. She is paler-skinned than Queen Sirene, a lightish tan; her small face is framed by masses of curly hair similar to Niko's, though silvering into morning, where his is all night.

'You know perfectly well, Nikolos,' she says, without any warmth whatsoever, and he recoils as if she slapped him.

With the same dispassionate air, Doralie turns to me. I drop my chin to avoid looking her in the eye, my ingrained habits surfacing just in time. I remember hearing that while Sirene gained her place through leadership skills and prowess in weaponry – as the higher ascendants often do – for Doralie, it was strategy and shrewdness that won the previous queens' approval all those years ago. Hearing her voice, as cold as the stone that surrounds us, I can believe it. Her body might be failing, but her mind is as sharp as ever.

'My daughter Halimeda is dead,' she says. I risk a quick glance upwards, to find her staring tight-lipped at the cup in my hand. Being caught drinking kelpin clearly hasn't raised her estimation of me. 'Your execution has been scheduled for noon tomorrow.'

Without waiting for a reply, she nods at Agate and they turn towards the door. I freeze for a moment before stumbling after her, the floor swaying oddly beneath me. After what Niko told me this morning, I should have expected this, yet it's still a shock.

'I didn't do it! I was in my cell. I knew nothing of it until Niko woke me—'

Slowly, she pivots to face me again, and I can tell that she noted my use of Niko's nickname. Noted, and disapproved. Before I can protest that he told me to use it, she says icily, 'You have forgotten your place, Feldspar. You have forgotten that you should already be dead. All the more reason to rectify the situation.'

Niko steps to my side. 'Please don't do this, ma'am. Not now. I need her if I'm to solve these crimes.'

'The decision is made, Nikolos. Almost the entire Apex is in agreement. Sirene may have been lenient, but I will not make the same mistake.'

'But she didn't kill anyone!' he yells. It's the first time I've ever heard him raise his voice that way. 'What if these deaths continue after she's gone, and you realize you executed her for nothing?'

Doralie shrugs. 'It is worth the risk.'

'You're willing to execute an innocent person *just in case* it protects your children?'

'Hardly innocent. She failed. Besides, a shield without an ascendant is a waste of resources, killer or not.'

I said something very similar to Niko myself, not so long ago. Even in the moments when I felt I could get used to surviving without Euphemie, I knew this day would arrive sooner or later. Yet now, faced with it, the hot wash of realization leaves me trembling: *I don't want to die*. Slowly, I retreat until the backs of my legs hit my chair, where I sit down hard.

'That isn't fair,' Niko is saying, the lights flickering wildly around us. 'You can't—'

'Be quiet, Nikolos,' the Elder Queen says, still without emotion. 'You had your chance after Euphemie died. You swore to the whole Apex that if we let you continue evading your Winnowing duties, you could be of use in a different way. You could use your *unique* skills to find out the truth. Yet here we stand, with two more bodies and no sign of any progress.'

The lights stop flickering; Niko's shoulders slump. 'I've tried the best I can.'

'And apparently, it isn't good enough. No, you must be bonded to a new shield and take your place with the rest. Without that—'

'I'm as much of a waste of resources as she is?' he supplies bitterly. 'Is that what you were going to say?'

She doesn't reply, but her silence speaks for her.

'Whereas if I take another shield and get both of us killed hunting down surplus cutters in a Winnowing, that won't be a waste of resources *at all*.'

'There is no need for you to die,' Doralie says. 'You could use your substantial gifts to carry you through every Winnowing, even the final one – which you know very well is mandatory, despite the fact that you are no longer contending for a place in the Apex. As it is, you and Feldspar are both . . . vestigial. Parts of the system that no longer serve a purpose.'

'Then I guess the two of us belong together,' Niko says, lifting his chin. 'You can't kill her!'

Her lips tighten again. 'The sentence stands. Take her back to her cell, Nikolos. If she does not attend the sunroom at noon tomorrow, she will be fetched. And I advise you not to stand in the way.'

She casts a final dismissive glance at me, before she and Agate leave the room. The door closes behind them with a soft click that's somehow more final than a bang.

'The sunroom,' I whisper through cold lips. My hands are shaking. 'They're going to give me to the sun.' They'll lock me in and leave me there, beneath a cloudless sky and a sun too hot for anything to withstand. I'm not sure if I'll burn to death or boil from the inside out, but either way, it will be slow. A proper traitor's execution.

Maybe there will be storms at noon tomorrow, I imagine Euphemie saying – comforting me after death as she never did in life. *Maybe you won't die.* But I know that's not true. The Apex will have checked the forecast before selecting the manner of my death. The forecast is always accurate. And even if it wasn't, they would simply leave me there until the sun returned – which would be worse. Watching and waiting, as the sky brightened and the temperature crept upwards . . .

'Feldspar.'

I look up, half hoping that Niko will touch me between the shoulder blades as he did once before and let Astrapē warm me. But he's holding out a hand.

'Come with me,' he says. 'And don't worry: I'm *not* taking you back to prison.'

I don't question it. I let him pull me out of his room and along the corridor, my mind still whirring and buzzing with fear, as well as a lingering fuzziness from the kelpin. But after a while, I'm alarmed enough by Niko's set expression, his fever-bright eyes and the heightened colour in his cheeks, to ask him, 'Then where are we going?'

'To find Ixion. Get him to fix the *waste* that is the pair of us.'

'The shieldmaster? But—' I stop dead as understanding hits me. 'No. Niko, you can't.'

He stops too, turning to face me. 'Why not? This is exactly what Doralie wants of me.'

'It won't help.'

'Of course it will! For you as well. They want to kill you because you're a shield without an ascendant. So let's give you an ascendant. Maybe we'll both be taken more seriously if—'

'*Niko.*'

We stare at each other. Beside us, one of the stormglow panels flares to unbearable brightness, emits a loud bang, then fades to grey with a dying wheeze. I can see Astrapē more clearly than ever now: something large and round and spiny, like a puffer fish defending itself against a predator, glowing with the light that the panel once held. *She's* what affects the stormglow. Not Niko himself.

'The shieldmaster won't act against the queens,' I say. 'You heard what Doralie said: the whole Apex is in agreement.'

'She said *almost* all of them.'

I wonder who didn't want me dead . . . but in the end, it doesn't matter. 'We can't fight their decision by finding a loophole. Even if Ixion *did* agree to bond us today, which he wouldn't, they'd still kill me tomorrow. And you'd only be forced to take another shield.'

'Then how *do* we fight it? You can't tell me you still want to die to atone for your failure to protect Euphemie, because I won't believe you!'

'No,' I agree slowly. 'I don't want to die.'

The flutter of my frantic panic hasn't subsided. Somewhere in my mind, it's slamming itself back and forth between the walls of a tiny cell – a trapped bird, as Niko once said. Yet somehow, seeing his fear has allowed me to close mine off. And standing guard in front of it is pure determination. It acknowledges and ignores the ice-cold chill in my bones. It drives away the last traces of fuzziness, leaving clarity in its wake. And it's what allows me to look into Niko's eyes and say, quite calmly, 'That's why it's important that we don't waste time.'

'What do you mean?'

'If you're really not taking me back to my cell, then we've a whole night and half a day left between now and noon. I haven't given up on finding out the truth.' I gesture back the way we came. 'Please, Niko. There's still time to prevent my execution – and prove yourself to the queens besides. I live; you don't have to winnow; both of us escape this. We just have to work out who really did it.'

FOURTH MURDER

FIVE DAYS AFTER

'Where are we going?' Niko murmurs, when we pass the turning to his chambers without stopping. He doesn't seem to mind that I've taken charge. In fact, his expression is one of slightly surprised pride.

'I can think of two areas worth further investigation,' I say, trying to sound like I know what I'm talking about. 'First, Alexios said Euphemie could have been killed by a rat poison called aroura, which is made in the Honeycomb by the carders. If we ask them who's sent for aroura recently, we can shorten our list of suspects that way. But I imagine visiting the Honeycomb isn't a quick task?' I wait for his confirmation before concluding, 'So I'm making that number two.'

'And number one?'

'We never asked the chief advisor about what Zephrine said. You know, the secret group of ascendants. I don't believe Euphemie knew about it, but that's irrelevant if she was killed to make me a suspect. Which leaves Halimeda and Leandros, and both of them are likely to have known one way or the other. Don't you think? In which case, finding out who's in the group could give us a possible motive. Because that's what we haven't been able to pin down, and I don't see how we can solve anything without it . . .' I'm talking too much. I fall silent, anxiously awaiting Niko's verdict.

'Yes,' he says. 'And yes.'

'Then . . . ?'

'I agree with everything you just said. Let's visit Alathea.'

'Oh. Good.'

'And may I say, I'm very glad you forced me to let you help me. Even if it has turned out to be the other way around.'

I'm pretty sure that works out as a compliment, and it leaves me oddly embarrassed.

'Feldspar,' he says, slowing down to face me. 'I'll do everything I can to make sure you survive this. You know that, right?'

He's looking at me as if he sees me. Not a shield, but *me*, myself, whoever that is. I'm not sure anyone has ever looked at me that way before Niko, and it doesn't feel at all like his dark gaze is too intense. Not any more. I resist the urge to rest my head against his shoulder and cry. 'I know.'

Members of the Apex live on the second level of the Hive, below the sunroom. Between the wide doors with their gilded frames, a tessellating pattern of gold and white hexagonal tiles and similarly shaped stormglow panels covers the walls – which is why I will forever associate hexagons with loneliness. Apart from lessons, the only time that Euphemie and I were separated was when we came here. Once a week, she'd walk under the arch marked with the royal emblem at the end of the passageway and pass through one of the two sets of imposing double doors beyond: spending one-on-one time, as all female ascendants do, with the two women who would decide her future.

I was allowed as far as the arch, but no further. I'd watch her walk up to the doors, chin up, back straight – telling herself, I'm sure, that *this* would be the day she impressed the queens so much that they chose her as one of their heirs – and my heart would race just as much as when I thought she was in danger. I wanted so much to help her, but this wasn't like the Winnowings. This, she had to do on her own.

Afterwards, she'd always be quieter than usual. If I asked her about it, she'd tell me it was none of my business; if I said nothing, she'd accuse me of not caring. Perhaps it would have upset me, her lashing out no matter what I did, if I hadn't seen the fear in her eyes. She didn't have to say it for me to know what she was thinking. *It wasn't enough. I didn't prove myself worthy. I'm failing so hard that I'll never become a queen.*

'Are you all right?' Niko whispers.

'Yes . . .' Not for the first time, an unfamiliar lump of

175

emotion fills my throat. The golden grandeur of the royal quarters bears down on me with every breath I take, reminding me that the queens have all the power and I have nothing. I find myself stammering out, 'But are we allowed to be here?'

'Would you turn back if we weren't?'

I drag my gaze away from the arch to focus on his face. He's looking at me as if he can see my anxiety and understands it. Strangely, that's enough to lessen it. 'I mean . . . what's the worst they can do to me? Execute me twice?'

He smiles. 'That's the spirit.'

I turn back to the door in front of us. It's one of five with a carved title beside it, similar to the numbers on the ascendants' levels, showing where to find each member of the Apex aside from the queens. The chief advisor's rooms are right next to the arch. I wonder if Doralie came back up here after descending on Niko's chambers to announce my death. If she sees us, she'll know he's disobeyed her and call someone else to march me straight back to prison. The thought leads me to rap on Alathea's door with an unnecessary amount of vigour.

'Yes?' Her shield, Coquina, opens it. Her hair is bristle-short and purple, with a series of zigzags shaved into the sides; both ears are lined with metal rings. Like all the older shields, she's heavily muscled enough to be intimidating, but she doesn't scowl or posture at us. Instead, her lips twitch as if she were about to offer a smile before remembering herself.

'We'd like to speak to Alathea,' Niko says.

'Do you have an appointment?'

'No, but this is important.'

'Hold on.' With an apologetic grimace, she closes the door in our faces. It's an agonizing wait before we're admitted to the most welcoming room I've ever seen: walls hung with embroidered fabrics, furniture with gently rounded corners, a soft glow – like sunshine in the brief moments before it becomes too hot to bear – filling the air from an unknown source. The only indication that it belongs to the chief advisor is a shelf of ancient-looking books along one wall.

Alathea comes forward to greet us. She's a small woman, dressed plainly and neatly in a long-sleeved robe, without the jewellery or make-up affected by so many of the royal family. She doesn't look much like her sister, Queen Sirene, nor does she have the same overbearing air. Her skill is in diplomacy, I remember now. That's how she achieved the important role of chief advisor. But she's no fighter – her first shield died protecting her in a Winnowing, and Coquina was the replacement.

'Are those . . . ?' Niko begins before she can speak, gesturing at the books.

She inclines her head. 'Melissa's original texts.'

No wonder they look so old – and no wonder he's eyeing them so hungrily. Melissa founded the Hive; he and all the royal family are descended directly from her. Those books set out every law we have and every rule we follow. I don't need him to tell me that he'd love to study them in excruciating detail.

'Before you ask,' Alathea adds, amusement warm in her voice, 'I'm forbidden to let you read them. Understanding and upholding Melissa's word, as set out in those books, is my life's work. That's what the role of chief advisor entails. For everyone else, what you were taught growing up is considered to be enough.' She smiles. 'So what can I do for you both?'

'You know I'm investigating the recent deaths,' Niko says, pulling out his notebook. He's taken the lead again without us having to discuss it; we both know it would be a bad idea for me to appear too forward in front of a member of the Apex. 'In the process, I heard something rather delicate that I'd like to discuss with you.'

'Go on.'

'Apparently, you have been advising some of the ascendants about . . . shield-bonds.' It's surprisingly tactful. If the rumour is true, she'll know what he's talking about; if not, it's vague enough not to alarm her. From the arrested expression on her face, I'm going to guess it's the former.

'I'm glad you came,' she says. 'I'd have sought you out myself if not. It isn't something I could tell the queens, you understand. They wouldn't approve of the group's aims.'

'So there is a group?'

'Yes. A small number of ascendants who believe the shield-bond is immoral. They came to me a while ago now,

178

seeking advice.'

'But why did they think *you'd* know how to break the shield-bond?'

'Their aims are broader than that, Nikolos. They seek to abolish Winnowings altogether. And they wanted advice on how they might legally achieve that, once your generation is in power.'

Abolish Winnowings. I struggle to breathe. I thought doing away with shields was controversial enough, but getting rid of the Winnowings entirely . . . I don't see how that could ever be possible. Everyone knows the Hive can only support a certain number of people.

'You helped them?' Niko asks, sounding as stunned as I feel.

Alathea runs her fingers absently along the row of law books on the nearby shelf, as if touching their worn covers might somehow alleviate her guilt. By helping the group, she'd be going against her own life's work.

'You know, I suppose, that my first shield was killed,' she says. 'We had grown up together. Shared some portion of every day since the two of us were born. She died for me in a Winnowing, when a group of unarmed carders overwhelmed us through sheer force of numbers and would have beaten me to death without her intervention. After that, I was bonded to Coquina.' She pulls a contrite face at her shield. 'An ascendant who has lost their original shield is at a disadvantage. Coquina had been a soldier – she was fully trained and she'd had all the conditioning – but she hadn't been devoted to me from birth. At the age of eighteen, she was forced into the role of ultimate protector for a stranger. She kept me alive through the final Winnowing to gain a place in the Apex, but it can't have been easy.'

'And you think that wasn't fair?' Niko guesses.

Alathea frowns at the law books, deep in thought, and I watch her with my own mind racing. This is the second time today that someone has referred to the final Winnowing, and it's revived an old curiosity as to what it involves. Every ascendant participates in their generation's final Winnowing, in which the new queens are formally selected; immediately afterwards, the Apex is formed. I know that much, because Euphemie and I were both taught so, but we were never given any detail – only that it would be key to her proving herself. If it was difficult for Coquina to get Alathea through theirs, that means it must be particularly challenging or dangerous in some way. And from what Queen Doralie said to Niko, he'll have no choice but to participate, candidate for the Apex or not. Maybe I should let him bond me as his shield after all . . . That is, if I survive beyond tomorrow.

'I can understand why some of the ascendants might see it that way,' Alathea says finally. 'With an Apex chosen purely for their ability to govern, rather than their ability to cast people out and kill them if necessary, there would be no need for shields. No need for anyone to devote their lives to us, or to die for us.'

Does she *agree* with them? When I look at Niko, I see the same question in his eyes. It seems impossible. Yet she didn't tell the queens about it. That, above all else, suggests where her sympathies lie.

'Our laws should evolve as we do, don't you think?' she adds, confirming that impression. 'As chief advisor, I know better than anyone that what might have been necessary centuries ago may no longer be appropriate now. We can uphold the spirit of Melissa's word without following it to the letter.'

'Who is in the group?' Niko asks.

'I can't tell you. But two of its members were Leandros and Halimeda, and now they are both dead. You must understand, Nikolos – before Halimeda was killed, I had no reason to believe any of this relevant to your investigation. It's only with her death last night that I began to wonder.'

'*Leandros?*' The disbelieving question is out before I can stop it. Hastily, I add, 'My apologies, Chief Advisor . . . you say the Second was part of this group? But – but you were there in the sunroom, the day Euphemie died. When he was arguing that we should kill any group that's marked for winnowing, instead of giving them the chance to survive in exile.'

She looks sorrowful. 'I believe he was trying to convince Calista that, morally, killing our surplus population and forcing them out of the Hive to die slowly are one and the same. If anything, the latter is worse, because it increases their suffering.'

Strange, how the same words can be interpreted so

differently. I might find it hard, from what I saw of Leandros, to believe that he was standing up for a principle, but I suppose people have many faces. Like Niko: a master of the dark arts and the kindest person I know.

'Tell me,' Alathea adds, 'do you know what the royal emblem represents?'

I always liked to think it was a type of rock, like the one I'm named after: the stripes forming the layers, the six radiating lines showing it to be shiny and precious. *It means shields matter*, I used to tell myself. *The royal family rely on us, and their emblem shows it.*

'It's something called a bee,' she says – and once again, I look at Niko to find him looking at me, because this is the second time we've talked about bees in the space of two days. 'A tiny creature that once lived in a multi-chambered house called a hive. The queen bee was the heart of the hive, the one who could create new life. All the other bees lived and died purely to serve and protect her, because without her, their kind would be doomed to fail. If she was threatened, they would sacrifice themselves without hesitation. Indeed, they thought and acted as one, under her control: a *hive mind*. That's what people needed to survive, after the Rising: a willingness to surrender their lives to the good of the whole, instead of fighting and struggling and destroying themselves. That's why, when she founded this colony, Melissa followed the bee's example.'

It's like what Niko told me about bees, but not. I study the gold brooch gleaming at Alathea's shoulder. The six lines must be legs, then. The pointed, striped oval, the body. The only other creatures I've seen with six legs are the cockroaches that steal our scraps; bees must have been far more beautiful. And it makes sense. It's how I was brought up. We're created not to be selfish or greedy, but to put the needs of the Hive above all else.

Our lives for the Hive. The words come into my head like an echo of agreement. Yet they make me shiver, though for now I can't place why.

'All of us must live and die for the sake of the Hive as a whole,' Alathea says. 'But that doesn't mean the Winnowings are the only way to do what must be done, or that the ascendants should be the ones to do it. As long as we preserve the royal family and their unique ability to create new life, all other laws can change.'

'Right,' Niko agrees. 'The royal gift is all that matters.'

She gives him a gentle smile. She may not have noticed the sarcasm, but I did. I can't understand why he doesn't have more respect for his heritage.

Only a tiny remnant of humanity was judged worthy enough to survive the scouring of the earth by storm and sea. Even then, most were infertile, poisoned forever by the very same chemicals their ancestors had used to pollute the world: nature's way of achieving justice. But Melissa was different. Without her and her descendants – the royal family – none of us would be here. That's why we follow her laws.

'Alathea,' Niko ventures, sounding unusually hesitant. 'Do you think it's possible that the group discovered a method they thought would work for breaking the shield-bond? That they tried it and failed horribly?'

'Perhaps, if it was just one death. But they wouldn't have made the same mistake twice.'

'Then it's vital you tell us who the other members of this group are. Because if they aren't behind the murders, they may be the targets.'

'I can't tell you,' she repeats. 'And I mean, I *can't*. I don't know. Only Halimeda and Leandros came to me. As the First and the Second, they believed themselves safe from reprisal. They told me there were others, but not who.'

'Not even a hint?'

Alathea shakes her head. 'I wish I could be of more help. Convincing some of the Apex to join me in voting against Feldspar's execution would have been *something*. There simply isn't enough evidence to support putting her to death.'

So she's the one who stood up for me. I feel a glow of warmth towards her that's only slightly dimmed when she adds, 'Though I must admit, I don't see how she survived the shield-bond.'

'We haven't figured that out yet,' Niko says. He finishes scribbling in his notebook, then lowers it and says very seriously, 'Is there *anything* you can do to prevent the execution? Even if we could delay it for a few days ...'

'I'm sorry.' She glances in my direction with genuine regret. 'Doralie is adamant. Halimeda's ignoble death must be paid for, even if it's by the wrong person.'

'Yes.' Niko sighs. 'Thank you, Alathea. You've been very helpful.'

'They want to abolish *Winnowings*,' he says, once we're alone. 'Not just shields.'

'I know!' Then I see the expression on his face and realize . . . 'You agree with them.'

Niko looks at me like the shieldmaster trying to assess whether I'm strong enough to withstand a blow.

'We call the Winnowings population control,' he says finally. 'The maintenance of the Hive. But let's be honest: what we're talking about is mass murder. *Repeated* mass murder.'

'It isn't murder.'

'Why not?'

'Because the winnowed are sentenced to exile, not death. They only die if they choose to fight that sentence.'

'You've been in two Winnowings,' Niko says. 'And in both, there were some who fought back, right?'

I nod.

'The older ascendants have also never experienced a Winnowing where there was no killing. In the last generation, Alathea's original shield was lost in a Winnowing. Ascendants have shields *because* we know the Winnowings are dangerous.

Some of the population being killed in the process of being driven out is built into the whole concept. It's not an accident, Feldspar! The Apex just like to be able to say that the Hive doesn't want to kill anyone. That these deaths are down to the individual choices of the winnowed. We show mercy; they're the ones who don't take it.'

'That's true, isn't it?' I venture. 'If people choose to resist rather than leave—'

'I don't call that much of a choice. Stand, and fight, and die. Or accept your fate, and walk out of the only home you've ever known – a place you've been told your whole life is your sole protection from the dangers of the outside world – to die anyway, more slowly, out of sight. Leandros was right about that. It's no wonder some people would rather make us *see* their deaths, and carry out the killings ourselves. At least that's honest.'

'But the colony can only support so many people. And the colony comes first. Like Alathea said, we live and die for the Hive.'

'Then grow fewer people in the first place. Once someone is alive, killing them – whether directly or indirectly – is murder.'

'It doesn't count as murder if you have a chance to survive.' I'm not sure what I believe any more, but I have to at least try and uphold what I was taught my whole life. 'That's why no Winnowing removes all of one particular group. It's three-quarters or two-thirds, so that those who are judged most favourably are allowed to remain.'

'Meaning it's their own fault if they're selected for exile?'

'That's not what I—At least it's a fair process.'

'Fair?' Niko echoes. 'How is that fair? It's a choice that's not a choice, exactly like whether to walk out of the winnowing gate or fight back. It gives the illusion of fairness so that no one complains.'

I don't know what to say. I feel sick.

'That's why it's so ironic that the Apex are desperate to find the perpetrator of a handful of murders,' he adds, 'when they themselves are responsible for far more murder than that.'

'But I don't understand. I saw Leandros kill multiple people in just the two Winnowings Euphemie was in. Stab them and slice them and cut off their heads as if it were nothing—' My voice catches at the memory. 'How could he do that, when he was so against it?'

'Perhaps he too felt he had no choice. Perhaps he thought it was the only way to become part of the Apex and change things.'

I never thought I'd feel sorry for Leandros, but I do. In fact, suddenly, I feel sorry for everyone: killers and killed. I still believe we have to dedicate ourselves to the colony. Be like bees, the way Alathea explained it. But maybe Niko is right: maybe there's a better way of doing it . . .

Escape execution first, Feldspar. Think about all this later.

'It makes sense as a motive for their deaths,' I offer. 'Leandros and Halimeda, I mean. Because if you were against the abolition of the shield-bond, what would be the best way to prevent it? Kill those ascendants who were for it, in a way that made it seem as if the shields had turned on their charges. In one blow, you remove those you disagree with and make their beliefs appear foolish and dangerous.'

Niko nods. 'Then if that's the motive, who do we know that would be against the group?'

'Calista,' I reply promptly. 'She and Halimeda had an ongoing disagreement about this exact question. Now we know Halimeda was part of the group, that makes sense.'

'Perhaps. She was certainly quick to blame you for the deaths. But Pyrene gave her an alibi for last night. Besides, how would she have known you'd survive?'

'I'm not sure,' I admit. 'And there must be other ascendants who'd oppose abolishing the Winnowings. Perhaps it's more likely to be someone who's kept their views to themselves, rather than the one person who's been loud enough for everyone to hear . . .'

I have to pause to tamp down my renewed panic at the sheer number of things we don't know.

'But that's why we're heading to the Honeycomb,' I add, clinging to the original plan. 'Find the person who poisoned Euphemie, and we find the person behind all the murders. So all we have to do is discover who bought aroura. Right?'

'Right,' Niko says staunchly. 'Honeycomb, here we come.'

FIVE DAYS AFTER

I never appreciated how long it would take to walk through the entire Hive. From Alathea's chambers, we pass back down through the ascendants' levels, finishing with the royal nurseries and the schoolrooms; then several levels for the drones. All of those are familiar to me, from the golden detailing around each ascendant's door – less ostentatious than the queens' level, but still pretty – to the plain but colourful tiles of the drones' quarters. The lowest level where I've spent any significant time is the one between the drones and the cutters, where the training floor and my jail cell are located. Two guards are stationed at the top of the staircase to the next level down, and both of them give me narrow-eyed glances, but Niko's presence is enough to let us pass unquestioned.

The passageways in the cutters' quarters are narrower, with no adornment to break up the bare rock. This is where my parents must live, if they haven't been winnowed. All cutters work in service of the topmost levels somehow – whether as soldiers or medics, couriers or handmaidens, teachers or cooks – so most of their time is spent up there. But if nothing else, they come home to sleep, in these one-room chambers with barely enough space for a bed and a clothes chest. It feels like I'm seeing it all for the first time. I've only passed this way twice before, when Euphemie and I came down to the winnowing gate; then, the details of my surroundings were lost in a blur of anxiety and determination.

The winnowing gate is positioned in an outer wall of the Hive just above the high tide line, which means that when we descend the next flight of stairs, we'll be descending beneath the sea. There are more guards here, making sure that only people with legitimate reasons – couriers and soldiers – pass between the upper and lower levels. Yet once again, they let Niko pass, and me with him. Niko even greets one of them with a nod. He really has made this journey many times. His freedom, as an ascendant, to go anywhere he likes awakens a surprising envy in my chest.

Euphemie never mentioned leaving the upper levels. I'm not sure it occurred to her. Once we left the nursery and moved into our own chambers, with the number seven carved into the stone beside the door, that was it. She was in her rightful place and she only ever looked up, towards the throne. She didn't consider what was happening below her feet. And nor did I, not really. She thought of being a queen, and I thought of her.

That was how things were. Still, I must have had some concept of what the Honeycomb would be like, or I wouldn't be so surprised at what's here: nothing. No rooms and no people, just narrow, empty corridors and endless flights of stairs, like a maze out of a nightmare.

'We're not there yet,' Niko murmurs, anticipating me as he does sometimes. 'This is . . . a buffer, I suppose. A way to put off anyone, in either direction, who doesn't know where they're going.'

It becomes darker and darker. In the upper levels, there are *some* sources of daylight – the sunroom, the ventilation gaps in the thick outer walls – and besides, the stormglow in the royal quarters is bright enough that you don't miss natural light, most of the time. But down here, the panels are spaced further apart, their light dimmer, and there's no way for daylight to penetrate. I'm suddenly aware of the weight of the Hive above me: all that rock, ready to crush me. The air has closed in around us, damper and mustier than it is higher up. My muscles are so tense, they hurt.

Then the light begins to change again, and we emerge into a very different kind of place. The roof is low, held up by hundreds of stone columns, yet although that means I can't see very far ahead, I get a sense of space stretching out in all directions. There are no stormglow panels any more, but there's still light: a million tiny pinpricks of it, miniature electric lamps embedded in the rock overhead like stars. They illuminate the carvings in the pillars, ancient and intricate designs showing birds and fish and animals I have no names for. Although Euphemie and I never once came down here, it reminds me of her all the same. She loved beautiful things. She would have loved this.

'This is what I imagine a forest would be like,' Niko murmurs.

'A what?'

'I've read about them. Thousands and thousands of trees, all growing together, providing food and shelter for the living things in their care. I think it would have been like this. Somewhere to explore and get lost in.'

'Niko . . .' Throat aching, I turn to look at him. 'This is amazing. Why don't the Apex want us to come down here?'

'Because then we'd see the carders are people.' Before I can ask him to elaborate on that, he adds, 'Besides, why would my family or any of the drones bother, when they have *servants* to do it for them? Even the couriers don't stay long. They fetch what they're sent for and leave.'

As my eyes adjust, I notice a series of openings in the walls to the sides, half visible between the pillars: like open-fronted chambers or caves, with stalls set out to offer the various wares. The people behind those stalls are all carders. I've barely ever seen their kind outside a Winnowing; they're not allowed in the upper levels unless they're being taken to the winnowing gate or unless something breaks that's too large to bring down for mending, like a stormglow panel. Even then, they're always flanked by cutter soldiers, as though they can't be trusted to walk through the Hive alone. Still, I didn't forget how small they are, slighter than even the daintiest drone – almost child-sized in comparison. I could snap any one of them in half without breaking a sweat . . . as could the soldiers. Because there are soldiers here too: standing guard by the stalls, patrolling among the columns, the royal emblem adorning every uniform. They'd be hard to miss, given that they stand head and shoulders above the rest.

'They're everywhere down here,' Niko says softly, following my gaze. 'Important to keep science under tight control, right?'

'Surely the Apex don't fear it that much.'

He shrugs. 'They fear another Rising. Did you know that the carders aren't allowed to invent new methods of doing things? Everything has to be done exactly as Melissa decreed when she founded the Hive. I once saw a man beaten for figuring out a quicker way to dry mushrooms. It's as if they believe any hint of innovation could throw us right back into the chaos of the Dark Ages.'

'*Change is always a form of destruction*,' I quote from one of Euphemie's schoolbooks. '*Most of the time, what is lost is greater than what is gained*.'

'I didn't think shields had time to read.'

'Sometimes I used to help Euphemie study for tests. And it's not exactly wrong, is it? What we have now is a working system in precarious balance. Alter one part of it and the whole could collapse.'

'Which I'm sure is one of the arguments against abolishing the Winnowings,' Niko agrees. 'With everything we were taught, perhaps the real surprise is that there were enough ascendants in favour of it to form a secret group.'

'And yet I'd join, if I could,' I say half to myself. It's only once I've said it that I realize it's true. The Hive must be kept strong, yes. We have to be careful with the limited resources we possess. But there must be something better than a system that simultaneously venerates the royal bloodline for its ability to create life and yet treats most lives as disposable. I think . . .

I think my life should have mattered in itself. Not just in relation to Euphemie's.

Niko glances at me, but all he says is, 'Come and take a closer look.'

As he leads me on a winding path through the columns, past several people who are shopping for goods, I see counters of clothes, jewellery and make-up. Euphemie's favourite salt-water candies. A woman selling paper, a man selling cups and plates. Not the basics, which are taken from the Honeycomb and distributed throughout the Hive. These are the luxuries – special things crafted for the benefit of the royal family and the drones, anyone who has enough tokens to buy them. The air hums with indecipherable conversation.

'They never close,' Niko says. 'Whatever time it is, day or

night, you can always send someone to fetch whatever it is you've decided you really can't live without. Though I don't see Orfila.'

'Orfila?'

'The man in charge of poisons. He's the one we need to speak to. He must be in the lab tonight.'

I gaze around the unending rows of pillars. 'Then . . . there's more?'

'Yes. This is only a gateway. But to get any further, you need to pass the gatekeepers.'

He walks me over to the pale-skinned woman selling paper. Her expression as she watches him approach is welcoming, but when she registers my presence at his side, it shifts into something more guarded. A sort of blankness. At the sight of it, an ill-defined discomfort settles in the pit of my stomach.

'What can I get you?' she asks me, stilted and formal.

'It's all right, Koops,' Niko says. 'We're not here for paper.' Then he says something else, from which I glean nothing more than *Feldspar*. Another language. He's speaking another language. *That's* why I've been struggling to understand the buzz of conversation all around me. The carders can speak to me in the language I know, but they have a second language all their own. And Niko has learnt it. I wonder if the couriers do the same.

When I voice that thought, Koops pulls a contemptuous face. Whatever Niko told her about me seems to have relaxed her enough to reveal what she's really thinking.

'Most people from the upper levels don't bother,' she says. 'Which is fine by us.'

'Do you sell paints?' Euphemie used to send for paints regularly; it's only now that I'm thinking about where they came from. But Koops shakes her head.

'Mainly paper, and some ink. I have people down here from the treasury all the time, fetching red and green inks for the ledgers. But if you want paints, you need to speak to Vaneyck.'

'Thank you,' I say softly. All my life, I've watched couriers arrive and depart, carrying requests, bringing goods. I knew everything was sourced from the Honeycomb. I knew the carders made it. Yet it never once occurred to me to be curious about it all. I feel like someone who's been staring at a blank stone wall all her life, only to be turned round and shown an open door behind her.

Niko says something else to Koops; though I can't tell what, the word *Orfila* suggests he's asking to visit the poison-maker. In turn, Koops speaks to the younger man guillotining paper behind her, who moves forward to the front of the cave. Then, beckoning to us, she walks away, deeper into the darkness at the back. It's not just a cave. It's a passageway. All these caves must be the entrances to passageways. Heart racing, I follow.

After a few steps into the darkness, a glimmer of light appears up ahead, warmer in colour than the multitude in the cavern of pillars. The passage descends a flight of steps into what appears to be a paper storeroom, illuminated by yet another type of stormglow fixture, this one a long orange strip along the top of each wall. Koops doesn't slow down, walking straight past the stacks of paper to a door in the far wall, which she unlocks for us. She gestures to Niko, saying something, and he leads me through the door. The air on the other side smells strongly of the sea. When I hear the key turn in the lock behind us, I freeze.

'Don't worry,' Niko says. 'We'll find someone to let us out again. All the openings you saw in the market hall are connected to the Honeycomb, and I know my way back to half a dozen of them from here.'

'All right.' I still don't like the idea of being trapped down here, but I have to trust him. And while I've become more nervous, he seems to have relaxed, like a creature entering his natural habitat.

He turns to grin at me, Astrapē bright on one shoulder in the form of a mouse. Beyond him, a whole new network of passageways stretches off into the distance. The Hive is tapered in shape, meaning this level is more spacious than any of those above it, yet from here I can see the tops of staircases leading even further down into the depths of the earth. How big *is* the Honeycomb, exactly?

'Orfila's in the lab,' Niko says. 'It won't take long.'

He leads me along unfamiliar routes until I'm thoroughly

lost. He could abandon me down here and I'd probably wander around until I died of hunger. Finally, we wind up at a room labelled with words that are strange to me, not in their lettering, but in what they say.

'*Toxins laboratory*,' Niko explains. 'It means a place where people study the science of poisons.'

We're intercepted by a scowling soldier, whose frown is hastily wiped clean once she registers who he is. Turning her head, she barks an order over her shoulder, and after a moment, a second person appears next to her: an elderly man with a creased face. This must be Orfila. His abundant greying hair is tied back from his forehead with a length of fabric, and he's wearing eyeglasses.

I'm not used to seeing them. Thanks to genetic testing and selection, ascendants and drone children are born close to perfect, and the physical strength of a shield starts to be enhanced before birth. Yet they evoke a vague memory: my first-nurse tending to Euphemie and me with a similar pair of little lenses perched on her nose. Perfect eyesight isn't considered necessary for nurses. As for the carders . . . by the time this man had worked long enough to earn the medical intervention needed to fix his eyes, he was probably already too old to make it worthwhile.

'This is one of the most heavily guarded sections of the Honeycomb,' Niko murmurs to me, after dismissing the guard. I can see that for myself: beyond the old man, as well as carders working at the benches, there are three or four soldiers patrolling up and down, watching them closely. 'It's viewed as one of the vital areas, like the water-treatment plant and the generators. The soldiers make sure there's no manufacture of unapproved poisons and no theft. The only way to get hold of aroura is to buy it through the official channels.'

He and Orfila exchange half a dozen rapid sentences in the language I don't understand, complete with gestures and laughter, before Niko turns to me.

'I told him you had questions for him. This was your idea. Only fair that you get the answers.'

Tentatively, I smile at Orfila, and he nods back.

'You make and sell the poisons for the Hive?' I venture.

Another nod. As with Koops, having to speak the official language of the colony seems to render him formal and taciturn.

'My charge – my . . . friend – she was poisoned with aroura. Someone must have bought it from you, and I wondered if you might remember . . .'

Orfila spreads his hands. 'The rats in the upper levels are no better than the rats down here. Everyone needs rat poison.'

'But perhaps someone different sent for it recently?' I persist. 'Or someone came that you hadn't seen before?'

'Your Apex sends a courier every week for aroura. Sometimes the same person, sometimes not. And most days bring a request from at least one drone family. If someone intended harm with the poison, it would be easy for them to lie about its destination.' His lips twist. 'Poison is controlled down here as if one drop of it could destroy the world. But in the upper levels, there is more freedom.'

I thank him, though I feel sick with this last loss of hope.

'No need.' Abruptly, his solemn expression splinters into something soft and compassionate. 'I'm sorry.'

The discomfort in my stomach swells, but I manage another smile in return. Orfila says a few final words to Niko, then retreats into the laboratory and leaves us alone in the corridor. I draw in a long breath and release it, trying to slow my racing heart.

'That's that, then.'

'Maybe not.' Niko pulls his notebook out of his pocket and starts flicking through the pages. 'There must be another lead – something we've missed—'

'Niko.'

'Mmm?' He doesn't lift his head. Draped over his shoulder in eel form, Astrapē flickers like a faulty stormglow panel. I can see the shape of her quite consistently now. Maybe I'm too tired or too afraid for my brain to keep filtering out the impossible.

'Let's take a break,' I say, shoving my panic back into its metaphorical cell. As the night has worn on, it's become increasingly good at escaping, until it's started to feel like a physical enemy I'm fighting without success, wearing out my muscles and setting my lungs on fire. 'Show me something interesting, will you?'

'But, Feldspar—'

'I've never been here. I'd like to see everything before . . .' *Before I die.* I don't need to say the words for him to understand.

'All right.' Squaring his shoulders, he tucks the notebook away again. 'Where do you want to go first?'

After that, it's all a blur. Niko shows me the vast store of unidentifiable metal parts, relics from an earlier time, and the furnaces where they're melted down ready to make useful things. He shows me the paper mill, the bakeries, the mines where clay and sand can be harvested. He introduces me to Edison, who works on the electrical system, and Tull, who oversees the seed bank and the pollinators and all the plants being grown for food and fabric. Every kind word spoken to me makes my stomach hurt more. And every new sight emphasizes how much of what's involved in running the Hive I've always taken for granted.

When I tell Niko that last part, he says, 'I sometimes wish I'd been born among the carders.'

'But the restrictions . . .' Even setting aside the inevitability of being winnowed once they fail or get too old, he must know how much worse off the carders are than us. They're forced to labour all day, every day. They give up the best of everything they produce to serve the upper levels. Not only that, but they have to earn any significant medical intervention, including what's needed to reproduce. It would take two carders at least a decade of work each to be granted permission for a child – and that's without the tests that drones and cutters undergo in similar circumstances, to make sure the genes are a good match.

'Remember I told you I saw the body of a carder child who'd eaten rat poison?' Niko asks me. 'I was only there because I heard her parents crying. *Wailing*. As if nothing in the world would ever be right again. They struggled their whole lives to have her, and they loved her. Do you suppose my mother would cry that way for the *waste of resources* I turned out to be?'

Before I can work out how to reply with both honesty and some degree of comfort, he adds, 'They care nothing for us, down here. We're an irrelevance, like lice on a whale.'

I don't believe that's true at all. We were all taught about the uprisings of the past, when the carders tried to rebel against the Apex of the time and were slaughtered in their hundreds. With that ancestral memory carved into their bones, extinguishing any possible spark of rebellion, how could they ever view the royal family as an irrelevance? Particularly with the guards here: loitering in the shadows or looming over the workers, weapons gleaming under the stormglow to match the royal emblem gleaming on their uniforms. Even being used to the company of soldiers, I find it unsettling, so how must the carders feel? It reminds me of being in a Winnowing

– a heightened, fearful anticipation of bloodshed and death – except it's like that *all the time*.

'Ignore them,' Niko says, when I try to explain some part of that. 'It's what everyone else does down here. It's what I do.'

But surely he realizes the difference. I think the carders ignore the soldiers because if they let themselves really think about it, they'd be too scared to do anything at all. Yet they *are* scared. I can see it in the way they very carefully avoid looking in certain directions. The way they carry out their tasks, with a sort of performative openness that seems designed to prove they're following the rules. The way they walk: like shields, constantly alert for threats.

Niko, on the other hand, can ignore the guards because he's an ascendant, so of course they won't hurt or kill him. He's able to find freedom in the Honeycomb precisely because he's free to leave it. He doesn't realize how lucky he is to be able to try on another life that way, as simply as shrugging on a coat.

He's studying my expression. Remembering my theory that he can read minds, I bite my lip. But all he says is, 'Follow me. I'll show you a place with no soldiers.'

Standing in front of a closet labelled *Cleaning supplies*, I look sceptically at Niko. I might want to see everything there is to see, but mops and buckets are a step too far.

'Have a little faith, Feldspar.' With a grin, he opens the door to reveal a small room crowded with glass-walled enclosures, each of which seems to contain a living creature. A rat, a salamander, a tumble of cockroaches – even a vast container of water with fish swimming in it. I've seen fish before, but never alive. And the other creatures, the ones that live alongside us in the Hive, have always been fleetingly glimpsed nuisances rather than something to be studied and admired.

'This room shouldn't exist,' Niko says. 'The Apex aren't interested in animals, only animal *products*. As far as they're concerned, Darwin is a janitor. That's why there are no guards here. But in between cleaning jobs . . .'

He waves his hand at the cages. I lean down to peer into the nearest, where the salamander crouches. It's pure white, from its nose to its four feet and the tip of its tail, with the exception of a pinkish ruff around the neck. There are no obvious eyes, only two dark indentations.

'Niko.' The voice makes me start and straighten up. A woman with roughly cropped white hair is walking towards us from the back of the room. 'Who's your friend?'

'This is Feldspar. Feldspar, Darwin.'

She smiles a greeting, and the ache in my stomach blooms into full-blown pain.

'I found something,' she tells Niko. 'A new animal. Want to see?'

'Of course.'

She leads us over to one of the enclosures. I can't see anything obviously living in it; only a pile of earth and a dish

204

full of syrupy liquid.

'I can't think where it came from,' she says. 'I found it in one of the blocked-off tunnels, crawling over the rocks. It's very docile . . .'

She reaches into the glass cage. When she draws her hand back out, there's something crawling on it, which she passes to Niko.

'It may not last long,' she says sadly. 'I don't have much to offer it. But as far as I can tell from the identification books, it's some type of bumblebee – and in that case, if it's a young queen, I hope it may dig a tunnel in the soil to hibernate.'

Bee. Based on the royal emblem, I imagined a creature like a weapon, sleek and hard and cold. This thing is small and furry, with cheerful black and yellow stripes – and *wings*. Niko studies it with the same intense expression he gets when he's trying to work out a problem. On his wrist, Astrapē flickers as she tries to mimic its form.

'This is amazing,' he whispers, and warmth curls in my chest. I like the way he's fascinated by bees and books and ideas. The way those things matter to him.

He glances at Darwin. 'May I . . . ?'

At her nod, he reaches out to me. Our fingers touch, making a bridge for the bee to cross, and I catch my breath. I don't know if it's the strange electricity that always seems to run from Niko to me, or the light, soft crawl of the bee's feet on my skin, or the sheer wonder of it all – being here, in this one extraordinary moment, with a creature out of mythology on my hand and Niko next to me, leaning so close that a lock of his dark hair brushes my cheek as lightly and softly as the bee itself. Whatever it is, it makes me feel brand new. Alive, for the first time in my life.

'I don't want this to be the end,' I tell Niko, the truth spilling out no matter how much I might want to hide it. The bee ambles back in his direction; instinctively I curl my fingers closer over his. 'I want to learn more about the world. To see everything I've never seen. I want—'

I want to keep touching you. The thought comes out of nowhere, sending the heat rushing to my face. But I don't back away. What would be the point? I'll be dead soon. I might not want it to be the end, but that doesn't stop it being so.

Niko's dark gaze moves over my face as if he's reading something there in a language he's only just beginning to understand. Very quietly, he says, 'It doesn't have to be.'

What? I open my mouth to ask the question, but he's already turning away, passing the bee carefully back to Darwin. And with that, the connection between us is broken. I'm suddenly aware of the room around us, of the fact that we're not alone. My cheeks heat further. I avoid looking in Niko's direction, focusing on Darwin as she replaces the bee in the enclosure. It flies down from her hand with a soft humming sound, like a gentler form of electricity.

'Bees were wonderful creatures,' she says. 'Humanity relied

on them for both sustenance and beauty. To ensure a good harvest. To make flowers bloom. Without them, it wasn't long before our world collapsed around us.'

'That's why we tried to follow their example?' I ask, striving to appear completely unaffected by whatever just happened. 'Living and dying for the colony?'

She looks doubtful. 'We are all named after bees, yes. The queen and the drones. Leafcutter bees and carder bees. But we are people, not insects. I believe we were meant to work together for the common good, as equals. That's what we should have learnt from the bees. Not treating human lives as if they're worthless.'

'How do you know so much about all this?'

She darts a look at Niko, perhaps wondering whether she can trust me – a cutter girl who looks like a soldier – but then her chin lifts. She's courageous enough to keep an illicit collection of animals in a laboratory disguised as a closet. She's courageous enough to speak her mind, even if it costs her.

'If they wanted to oppress us forever, they should have taken our books,' she says. 'Knowledge is the opposite of oppression. It sets us free.'

'See?' Niko says cheerfully, ignoring the sudden tension. 'There's a good reason why I read so much.'

I extend my hand to Darwin, and after a moment, she takes it. A lump fills my throat. Earlier today, I wondered why Niko bothered learning about things that are gone forever. I think now I understand.

'Thank you,' I say. 'I won't tell anyone about any of this, and – and I hope the bee survives.'

Back outside the room, Niko shakes his head. 'Did you ever see anything like that before?'

I frown at him. I think the carders we've met are genuinely fond of Niko. Alone among all the ascendants, he's refused to participate in the Winnowings. He's made the effort to learn the carders' language and understand their work. He treats them with respect. But at the same time, if I were them, I'd also find him exasperating – because at the end of each visit, no matter how angered he might be by some of the ways in which they're treated, he returns to the comfort of his own life and does nothing at all to change their situation for the better. And now, finally, I recognize the discomfort gnawing in my belly. It's the knowledge that these people must look at me and see a killer no better than the one we came down here to hunt. The fact that neither Niko nor I have ever killed anyone doesn't matter; we're part of the system that does the killing.

'Niko,' I say cautiously. 'Don't you think . . . I mean, earlier, you called the royal family irrelevant. Lice on a whale. But a louse can't kill a whale whenever it chooses.'

'No. No, you're right. My point is that most of the concerns that consume us are meaningless. Politics and campaigning for places in the Apex. The queens selecting their heirs. None of that makes any difference to these people.'

I can't argue with that, though I want to. Because if who sits on the throne really means so little, in the grand scheme of things – if nothing will improve, no matter who is chosen as the queens – then what does that say about how my life has been spent?

Though perhaps it could be different. If the secret group were ever to come to power, their plan to do away with Winnowings would change things for the carders as well as for ascendants and shields. And perhaps they could go further still ...

But I won't be around to find out.

My expression has shifted: I can feel it on my face, the waxy mask of fear. Though I try to smile at Niko, he must be able to see it. Gently, he says, 'There's one more thing I want to show you.'

SIX DAYS AFTER

I knew the Spire was tall. That much was obvious, given that it towers above even the sunroom. But it's only now, standing at its immensely broad base, that I understand just how tall it is. My head is tipped back so far that my neck hurts, but I can't see the top from down here. The tapering metal column – not smooth as I thought, but shaped with an asymmetric spiral that runs its entire length – seems to cut the sky in half. The open space around me is loud with the whir of fans and the buzz of machinery.

A fine tremor runs through my body. This is where the hum comes from. The one I hear all the time, the one that changes when a storm is coming. And it's changed now. Tasting it on the air, I flinch. Here, more than anywhere else in the Hive, I'm close to lightning. Up there, high above me, the storm is building. When it breaks, the Spire will catch the lightning and pull it into all these ranks and ranks of machines to generate and store the electricity we need, and if I'm too close when that happens . . .

You're going to die tomorrow, I remind myself. *No, today – it's well past midnight. So what is there left to be scared of?*

Straightening my shoulders, I stand still and let the breeze ruffle across my scalp. As well as containing the Spire, the central core of the Hive is where all the air vents lead to, releasing the warm air from inside to rise up and out. When the wind is fierce, the air currents within the Hive get stronger; I've noticed that even in the upper levels. Down here, the breeze makes it feel almost like being outside.

The hum intensifies. I dig my nails into my palms. And then the lightning strikes.

It's so bright that I instinctively jump backwards. Eyes watering, I try to blink away the white streak that seems to be seared into my vision. But it isn't that. Rather, the Spire is continuing to glow in the aftermath of the strike, its light intense but more bearable than before. I want to laugh, or cry; I'm not sure which. I'm glad the queens didn't select this as my method of execution. I don't think I could have borne it.

'Why did you bring me here?' I whisper to Niko.

'Because I have a proposal to make. And before I do, I . . . You've only ever told me the truth, Feldspar. I want to do the same in return.' He hesitates, then says with a break like a sob in his voice, 'This is where Slate died.'

Startled, I turn to find that he really is crying. I can see the tears, gleaming blue in the reflected light, and Astrapē huddled on his shoulder as a tiny, drab moth. I think about taking his hand.

But a shield never touches any ascendant apart from her own.

But I am no longer a shield.

When I wrap his fingers in mine, he smiles through his tears.

'What happened?' I ask softly.

'The rumours are true, Feldspar. I killed him. Not on purpose,' he adds quickly, as my breath catches in my throat. 'But I did it all the same. Because I was selfish and arrogant and I thought myself untouchable.'

He doesn't say any more. After a while, I offer, 'You once said that people have tried before to break the shield-bond. You meant you and Slate?'

'Yes. We – he and I—'

I squeeze his hand, because he doesn't have to tell me the story. Not if he doesn't want to. But after another long pause, he starts talking.

'Slate and I started coming down to the Honeycomb when we weren't long out of the nursery. At first, it was a dare, and then it became a place to learn everything we weren't being taught in lessons. Slate was always more cautious than me, but he was fascinated by how things worked – the machines and the supercapacitors. So it was never hard to convince him to come.'

Convince him. He's making it sound as if Slate had a choice. 'You were friends?'

'Yes. For a long time, yes. But as we got older . . .' He glances at me, then quickly away. 'I started getting frustrated. Because he was always there, you know? One step behind me. Warning me away from danger. Telling me why I shouldn't do whatever silly thing I'd taken it into my head to do. And it was his life too; of course it was. If I died, he died. But I couldn't see that. All I could see was my own frustration at his constant, unavoidable presence.'

I wince. This must be how Euphemie felt about me too. Even as we give up our lives for theirs, they resent us for it.

'It wasn't just him,' Niko says. 'It was the whole system. The way we'd convinced ourselves that it was fine to throw people away once we decided they were no longer useful. Slate was like a symbol of that. A constant reminder that when we came of age, we'd become part of the whole bloody mess. That was his entire purpose: to make sure I didn't die while I was casting other people out to die themselves. So when I was fifteen, I decided that I'd find a way to break the shield-bond, then leave the Hive.'

'*Leave?* But how? Through the winnowing gate?'

'You know I don't believe anyone can survive that way. No, I was going to try and escape through the tunnels. Raiders supposedly come through them, don't they? And if there's a way in, there must be a way out. Most of the tunnels are patrolled by soldiers, but some of them are blocked and abandoned, like the one where Darwin found the bee. I knew of one tunnel where the barrier was weakening, the rubble coming loose. I was sure I could find a way through. Of course, Slate would come after me, but if I could break the bond first . . .'

He pulls his hand out of mine, folding his arms defensively. His shoulders hunch further. I can see quite clearly what he would have looked like at Zephrine's age, not wrapped around with the defensive colouring of the dark arts, but a young boy torn apart by guilt. Still in moth form, Astrapē creeps up his neck to hide beneath his hair.

'I shouldn't have done it. No one had ever succeeded in breaking the shield-bond. But I convinced myself that I would be the first. And so – and so I . . .'

'What?' I whisper. 'What did you do?'

'The shield-bond is made by electricity – did you know that? It flows through the two unborn babies and somehow their lives are connected. No one knows how. It's a scientific discovery without explanation, like anaesthetic used to be. But it seemed logical to me that if electricity could make it, electricity could break it. Which is why . . .' He turns to look me directly in the face, as if determined to make me understand the full perfidy of his crime. 'One night, when the forecast was stormy, I sneaked out of our rooms and came here. I'd seen what happens when lightning strikes the Spire, how it glows white-hot. If anything could break the shield-bond, it would be that much power. So I climbed it, all the way to the top.'

'You climbed the *Spire*? In a *storm*? But—'

'But that would be suicidally dangerous?' he finishes for me, lips twisting. 'Yes. Slate knew that too. That's why he followed me. And that's why he climbed up after me. Because it was his job to protect me.'

'So . . .'

'He begged me to come down. We could both hear the humming. We knew the storm would break soon. He was frightened. I . . .' Niko swallows. 'I said a lot of unkind things. That I'd never wanted him. That he made my life unbearable. I told him, if he was that scared, he should go away and leave me alone. Instead, as the lightning hit, he – he pushed me off. He saved my life. And he died.'

I shudder. I doubt I could have been as brave as Slate if it had been Euphemie up the Spire in that storm. He did everything a shield is meant to do. He protected his charge, even at the last extreme. Yet in all honesty, I don't understand how either of them survived. There's a reason that chaining someone to the Spire is used as an execution method.

'I should have died too,' Niko agrees with my unspoken thought. 'I felt the lightning rush through my body. Not heat, but light, in every part of me, scouring me from the inside out. I remember falling, and then – nothing. Nothing until I woke to find myself lying here at the base of the Spire, beside Slate's body . . .'

His voice dies. He wipes the tears roughly from his face.

'I've no right to grieve,' he says. 'It's my fault he's gone.'

No sensible person wants to be struck by lightning. When he said that to me, I had no idea he was speaking from personal experience. I can't even tell him that it's not his fault, because in many ways it is. Yet it's not *only* his fault. It's also the fault of a society that sets more importance on some lives than on others – and now, for the first time, I'm glad I survived Euphemie's death, however briefly. Because if I hadn't, I never would have understood how broken the Hive is, in so many ways.

'You didn't think to leave, afterwards?' I ask softly.

I'm not sure he will answer to start with. His face is remote and imperious, reminding me of his mother, Queen Doralie. But then he looks at me, and his expression softens.

'I could have,' he says. 'I was free to do it. It was only once I had that freedom that I realized I didn't want it. Not at the cost of Slate's life. Leaving would have been . . . I don't know. A betrayal. A willingness to accept his death as the price of my own satisfaction. Does that make sense?'

I nod.

'And besides,' he adds, 'there was Astrapē.'

Belatedly, I remember what he told me about Astrapē: *a creature of captured lightning*. Does that mean . . . ?

'She started to appear about a week after Slate's death,' Niko says. 'No more than flickers and glimpses at first. I

216

thought I was hallucinating. Going out of my mind with guilt. But over time, I learnt to see her. It took me a lot longer than it took you.

'I don't know where she came from. An undeserved gift from the storm. Sometimes I believe she's the last remaining part of Slate, protecting me beyond his death. But if I leave the Hive, I think she'll cease to exist. Not that I have any scientific basis for that, but it's one hypothesis I've never been willing to test.'

He's watching me closely. I remember, when I first met him, feeling defenceless beneath that bright black gaze. But now, it's different. Now, I feel better when he looks at me: strengthened by the sense that, like bees and books and ideas, I'm one of the things that matter to him.

Slowly, he adds, 'Until now.'

'What?'

'That's what I wanted to say. This doesn't have to be the end for you, Feldspar. For either of us. That tunnel with the loose rocks is still there. I could find our way through it. With some food and water and a reliable source of light, we could leave the Hive.'

'But you just said – Astrapē—'

'Saving your life would be worth it.'

I'm as close to crying as I've ever been. If I wanted any more proof that he sees me as a person and not merely as a shield, the fact that he's willing to sacrifice his companion – and possibly the last remnant of Slate – is more than enough. Strange to think that on the day of my death, I finally know what it's like to have a friend.

'I'm grateful,' I choke out. 'I really am. But I can't leave.'

'Why not? We're out of time. All that's left to do is run.'

'No, I mean I *can't* leave. There's a tracker implanted under my skin. If I leave the Hive, they'll hunt me down, and if you're with me . . .' Imagining it makes my chest ache. 'I don't want you to get hurt.'

Niko frowns. 'I'm willing to risk it. Maybe it's better to die in search of freedom than to live in captivity. Because what do I get if I stay here? A new shield, whether I want one or not. Enforced participation in the Winnowings. Pushing people out of a door to drown or die of starvation while telling myself I'm somehow better than the murderer I failed to catch.'

'*Or* you could do some good,' I insist. 'Learn the truth, whatever it takes. Make sure you bring the killer to justice. And after that . . .' All the things I've realized over the last few days that I want to do, but will never get the chance. 'You could join the secret group. Help convince the others to do away with the Winnowings. Make it so that *no one* has to lose their life for the benefit of the Hive.'

'But without you, I'm not sure I . . . Please, Feldspar. We could make it through the tunnels. We could stay ahead of the pursuit until we work out how to remove the tracker. I'd rather seize a small chance for both of us to survive than watch you go to your certain death.'

He touches my arm, and once again electricity runs between us. I want to say yes. I really do. I'm just not sure it's the right thing.

'Can I ask you something?' I venture. 'When you were at the top of the Spire, what did you see?'

'Mainly storm clouds, all rolling and boiling. And ocean, as far as I could see in all directions.' Clearly understanding why I asked the question, he adds, 'I'm not going to lie to you, Feldspar: it's as barren and unforgiving as they say it is, out there. But before the lightning hit, I thought I saw a far-off light.'

'A star?'

'Lower than that,' Niko says. 'About the same level as the top of the Hive.' Half to himself, he adds, 'It was golden. Not cold, like the stars. A tiny gleam of hope.'

'Hope for what?'

'That we aren't alone.'

'Of course we're not alone,' I say, though a shiver that could be fear and could be wonder is crawling down my spine. 'Raiders attack the Hive regularly. It's why the tunnels are blocked. It's why we have soldiers to defend us.'

'Maybe.'

'What do you mean, maybe?'

'Have you ever wondered . . . ?' He darts a glance at me. 'Never mind. Wrong time. But if there are raiders, most likely they come from another underground society. If we left, that's what I'd try to find.'

That doesn't match what we've always been told: that our own community is the only one to have risen above the lawlessness that consumed the end of the Dark Ages. When the Apex refer to raiders, it's never in terms of them being people like us. They're treated as a natural phenomenon, like storms and merciless sun: something that has to be weathered.

'You really think there are other Hives out there?' I ask.

'I think there's something. Another human colony. A craggy island inhabited entirely by gulls – we know they still exist, and they must live somewhere. A surviving grove of trees, like I said before. Something better than what we have now, or something worse. Who knows? But Darwin's bee must have come from somewhere. And if *bees* can survive out there, then so can you and I.'

We fall silent. I'm familiar with silence; for years, I only spoke when Euphemie invited conversation, or when neces-sary. Yet this silence doesn't feel like that. He's waiting for my answer. And part of me wants to agree, because I don't want to die. Because I like the way he's talking: as if the two of us are a team who can overcome any obstacle together, as if I'm his shield and he's my charge.

But we haven't yet succeeded in what we set out to do. If we leave, no one will ever know who killed Euphemie. I can't put myself before her. And, much as I might want to, I can't put

Niko before her either. He might not like what his life will be if he stays here, but it isn't as if he'll die of being forced to take a shield. Whereas Euphemie is already dead, and waiting for someone to avenge her. I still owe her that. Moreover, I owe it to the Hive not to take Niko away, when he could do so much good here. Though I've realized now that I matter, I don't matter more than an entire colony. Do I?

'You've given them your whole life,' Niko says, soft and pleading. 'Don't you think you deserve to put yourself first for a change?'

'Do you really think I could be happy, knowing that because I lived, a murderer was free to keep killing?'

A brief, sad smile touches his face. 'I hate it when people answer a question with a question.'

I want to run with you. Just looking at him makes my determination waver. Finding the balance between him and me and Euphemie and the Hive is a problem I don't know how to solve.

'At least let's keep trying until the very last moment,' I say. 'We're not quite out of time yet. We still have half a day. And – and after that, if we're no further forward, then ask me again. All right?'

'All right.' His expression is a mixture of hope and reluctance, but he accepts my decision without any further argument – for which I'm grateful. 'What do you have in mind?'

'See if we can speak to Zephrine's old nurse, assuming she hasn't been winnowed.'

'I thought you said that story was silly.'

'And you said every story contains a grain of truth. If one of the Apex really did have a forbidden child who's bonded as a shield, then maybe . . .' I try to work out something plausible. 'Maybe the secret group found out. Maybe that's their motivation for trying to break the shield-bond – because that shield would be part of their family, right? But the shield's charge wants to keep their shield, so decided to kill anyone who knows the truth . . .'

None of it sounds realistic, even to my own ears. I stop talking. But Niko nods gravely as if what I just said makes perfect sense.

'Let's do it,' he says. 'I'd like to know that we tried everything.'

SIX DAYS AFTER

Finding Zephrine's old nurse is easier said than done. She's called Daisy, and she lives somewhere in the cutters' quarters; it took climbing all the way back up to the Tenth's room to find that out. Now we're halfway down the Hive again, navigating through a maze of twisty passageways in search of a door with the right name chalked outside. I'm exhausted – the only thing worse than a sleepless night, in terms of wiping out your physical strength, is a sleepless night that involves a lot of stairs – but adrenaline is keeping me going. However unlikely this is to lead to anything, it's my last chance. If this fails, it will be die or run.

Ascendants and their shields are looked after by nurses until they reach the age of eight and move into their own chambers. Since an ascendant's nurse is expected to dedicate herself solely to the pair of children in her care, the first-nurse is usually the shield's mother. She attends the royal birth and looks after the children until they turn four. At that point, to avoid the shield remembering their mother and to prevent her from growing too attached to the child, the pair is moved on to a second-nurse – often someone who's been first-nurse to a different pair before.

Zephrine told us that after Daisy had finished being her second-nurse, there were no more young ascendants left to take care of, so she was assigned a batch of soldier children. Cutters are removed from their mothers when they're a few months old, placed in groups of ten to a single nurse. They leave the nursery aged eight, like ascendants, and head off to train for whatever role they were created to fulfil. Zephrine used to visit Daisy in the cutter nurseries sometimes, but she's no longer there. Apparently, she'd started forgetting things, and one of the children in her care had got hurt when she wasn't paying attention. So when they left her for training, she was added to the list for the upcoming Winnowing.

Zephrine couldn't tell us where Daisy's own room is located, which is why we're hunting through the cutters' quarters. Unlike the ascendants' chambers, which are always inhabited by the same people – or rather, the same titles – the occupants of these rooms change quite frequently, which is why their names aren't carved but simply written in chalk. Often the lettering is smudged or unclear, making the search a slow process. And all the while, the stormglow around us is brightening. It's past sunup. We don't have much time.

Comet. That's a courier name. And *Rocket* is another. But a few turnings further on, we start finding nurses. *Marigold. Campion.* On the other side of the passageway, Niko has *Poppy* and *Cornflower.* I've often wondered what nurse names mean. Since shields and soldiers are named after the rock we live in, strong and unchanging, I'd guess that the names given to other cutters also have significance. Yet I've no idea what *daisy* is, or why a nurse should be called after it.

'Here!' At last, Niko has spotted a doorjamb with the right name. Unlike the ascendants' chambers, these rooms can't be locked. When there's no reply to his knock, he simply pushes the door open.

'Hello?' he calls as we enter. 'Daisy?'

The room is small, dark and sparsely furnished. In one corner sits a single chair in which a woman is slumped, apparently asleep. Nothing adorns the bare walls but a single nail, from which hang two nurses' medallions – the engraved metal discs that nurses wear as identification when they're working in the royal nurseries. The top one, bright and shining, bears the name *Daisy*; the one underneath is heavily tarnished, but when I take it down and give it a vigorous polish, I can make out the word *Clover.* I hold it up to show Niko, who nods. Perhaps Clover was Daisy's friend, the one from the story.

'Daisy?' Niko says again, crossing the room towards her. Slowly, her eyelids lift. She isn't as old as I expected – her light, freckled skin only slightly lined – but her blank stare and unresponsive movements make her seem infirm.

'We wanted to talk to you,' Niko says gently. 'You were Zephrine's second-nurse?'

Her head swivels in his direction. As if dredging the name up from a great depth, she echoes, 'Zephrine.'

'She told us a story. About your best friend.'

Her eyes cloud. She looks away from him again, fingers twisting into her skirt. 'Clover.'

So the second medallion did belong to Daisy's friend. Niko and I exchange glances.

'The story was that Clover had a baby,' he persists. 'A royal baby. Bonded as a shield. Is that true?'

'I . . . I don't . . . She said she wished she hadn't done it.'

'Done what?'

Her hand shoots out, clutching his arm so tightly, the knuckles turn pale. 'She's delusional! I don't have to listen to her! Not when she's saying . . .'

'What did she tell you, Daisy?' Niko asks, ignoring her death-grip on his sleeve. But she subsides, her fingers loosening as though she's forgotten why she was holding on in the first place.

'Who are you?' she asks suspiciously. 'Why are you here?'

'I'm Niko. I came to talk to you about Clover.'

'She never shirked her duties,' Daisy mumbles. 'Even at the end, with her own babe barely a day old, she attended the royal birth. Already dying, she was. But she said she had to go.'

'When was this?' Niko asks urgently. 'Which ascendant's birth did she attend?'

'When she came back, she collapsed, and that's when she told me ...'

The door, which we left ajar, rattles suddenly in its frame; all three of us jump, turning in that direction. But no one is there. It must have been one of the random sea breezes that gust through the Hive. Niko turns back to the nurse.

'Please, Daisy. When did Clover die?'

There's a long pause. Then she blinks up at him, her cheeks wet with tears. 'Clover is dead?'

'I'm sorry,' he says. 'We didn't mean to upset you.'

He fumbles a handkerchief out of one of his pockets and offers it to her, but she shakes her head. The flare of emotion or memory fading to nothing, she closes her eyes and sinks into her chair again.

Back in the corridor, I offer with more hope than belief, 'I don't suppose that meant more to you than it did to me?'

'No.'

'Hardly surprising. I'm not sure why I thought ... Real life doesn't work like one of Zephrine's stories.'

'I think Daisy does know something,' Niko says. 'A secret of some kind. But it's well buried. Maybe, if the wind hadn't caught the door at that moment ...' He meets my gaze. 'I'm sorry, Feldspar. There's nothing left to do except run.'

I hesitate, struggling once again with this unsolvable problem. I don't want to die. Nor do I want Niko to get hurt. But I don't know where to go without him, and I can't force him to stay and solve the crime based on my principles alone . . .

'All right,' I say finally. 'Let's head for the tunnels.'

His answering smile is almost worth it. *Almost*. Yet as we head back in the direction of the Honeycomb, my heart beats out a reproachful refrain: *You're letting Euphemie down. And the whole Hive with her.*

We turn a corner into an empty corridor. Our footfalls strike a muffled echo from the rock. Then Niko says gently, 'Feldspar . . .'

And I hear a soft sound, like a sigh.

No. No no no. Not again. I can't—

Yet I'm already moving, stretching across Niko's body, one knife rising in front of his chest to shield his right shoulder. There's a metallic *ting* as the arrow ricochets off the blade. But then another arrow skims past me on the left, and Niko gasps, and when I turn, I see him clutching his *left* arm with his *right* hand, and now I can't breathe. I drop to a crouch, palms hitting the ground hard, failure drumming in my ears. She's there again, on the floor, looking up at me, begging me to save her. To save *them*. And I can't. I can't do anything.

'I'm sorry,' I whisper.

The stormglow flickers wildly around us, then goes out. The darkness is thick and absolute. All I can hear is my own frantic pulse. He's dying. Maybe he's already dead.

I cradled her in my arms.

Her eyes looked through mine.

A whimper catches at the back of my throat.

Then light flares from beside me, fierce and white. Blinking in the glare, I find myself staring up at the attacker – swathed head to toe in black, save for the eyes. The figure's gaze locks with mine before, with an indeterminate cry, I lurch to my feet. Yet I'm still slow and stumbling, and before I've done more than lift my knife in challenge, the dark figure has gone.

I turn. The light is coming from Astrapē, snakelike in form, curled on Niko's shoulder where he's slumped against the wall. Will she burn like this until she loses hope? Until someone comes to take Niko's body away? With a dry sob, I kneel beside him, seeing twitching limbs, blue lips, eyes filmed over with death – but then I blink and Euphemie's face fades, and Niko's voice says hoarsely, 'Feldspar.'

I look at him again in the fierce white light. His lips aren't blue. His limbs aren't twitching, nor are they unnaturally rigid. His right hand is still holding his left arm.

'You—' But I have to stop and swallow, moistening my dry throat. It takes me three attempts before I manage, 'You're alive.'

'The evidence would appear to point that way.'

'But the second arrow?'

'It scratched me.' He tries to sit up straighter, only to fall

229

back again. 'You should run anyway. Brave the tunnels alone. There's still time before noon.'

'That's a ridiculous thing to say,' I tell him, angry now that my panic is fading. Ignoring his rusty chuckle, I crouch down and drape his arm over my shoulders. 'There may not be enough poison in your bloodstream to kill you straight away, but that doesn't mean you're safe. You need help.'

I haul him to his feet. He staggers, leaning against me, Astrapē skittering up and down his arms – something smaller now, maybe a salamander like the one I saw in the Honeycomb – sending light and shadows swirling around us.

'Feldspar,' he chokes out, a shiver wracking his body. 'Go.'

'I'm not going to leave you to die.'

'But—'

'I never expected to survive longer than Euphemie,' I tell him. 'You know that. Nothing is being taken away from me except a gift I should never have been given in the first place.'

He doesn't argue. Probably because he's finding it hard to remain conscious, but I choose to believe it's because he agrees. As quickly as I can while supporting most of his weight, I set off in what every instinct says is the wrong direction: not towards the Honeycomb, the tunnels and possible freedom, but back towards the upper levels.

We've only gone a few steps before Astrapē's light glints off something on the floor ahead of us. The first arrow – the one I deflected. I nearly send both myself and Niko tumbling to the floor as I stoop for it, but when I straighten, it's clutched in my free hand.

Finally. Proof that I didn't invent the attacker.

I slide my hand into the correct pocket of Niko's coat to retrieve the handkerchief he offered Daisy, which I tie around the metal tip of the arrow to protect me from the poison. Then we're off again, stumbling as fast as we can. There's only one person I can think of who might be able to save Niko's life.

SIX DAYS AFTER

Supporting Niko against my shoulder, I bang on the Eighth's door, repeating the same words to myself over and over as if I can make them true through willpower alone. *Alexios is a healer. This is safe. I'm doing the right thing.*

Yet it doesn't help. Because my old knowledge means nothing now: any of the ascendants could be a threat. And if Alexios is secretly interested in murder as well as medicine, we've come straight to him. When he opens the door, rather than Flint, I find a knife in my hand without any conscious decision to reach for it.

'Nikolos!' he says, gesturing us inside. 'I was waiting to speak to you all yesterday afternoon. I sent Flint several times . . .' But the words die as he takes in Niko's shivering form. 'What's wrong?'

'Poison.' I'm breathless with exertion, my left arm shaking with the effort of bearing Niko's weight. 'The same one that killed Euphemie.'

'What happened?'

'Someone shot at him in the cutters' quarters. The arrow only grazed him, but . . .'

Alexios glances at the knife in my hand, but doesn't comment on it. He moves to Niko's other side. 'Bring him over here.'

We stagger to a door that in Euphemie's quarters would have led to the lounge room: a space for parties, complete with musicians' dais and drinks cabinet. In the Eighth's quarters, it contains a workbench and shelves full of tools and ingredients, plus a curtained-off area, behind which are a bed and a couple of chairs. Niko collapses on to the bed, not even protesting when Alexios helps him to remove his coat. He looks younger without it.

Alexios takes his pulse, his temperature, then shines a light into his eyes. When he straightens up, his expression is grave. 'It looks like aroura, as I said before. But without knowing for sure . . .'

'I brought this.' I pull the wrapped arrow out of my belt. 'The attacker fired twice, but the first one didn't hit him.'

Alexios almost snatches it out of my hand. 'Thank the Sun for the common sense of a shield! I can confirm the poison with this. Well done, Feldspar.'

He disappears to the other side of the curtain. I gaze after him suspiciously until Niko croaks, 'Feldspar.'

I return my gaze to Niko. He's ashen and trembling,

Astrapē curled up like a guttering flame in the curve between neck and shoulder; my stomach clenches as I take in the faintest tinge of blue on his lips. All the same, his expression of mild amusement is very familiar.

'You can . . . trust him,' he gasps.

'I don't trust anyone.'

'He's a . . . healer. He's dedicated . . . his life to it.'

'Learning how to keep people alive is also the perfect way to learn how to kill them.'

'And yet you . . . brought me here,' Niko points out with the hint of a smile.

'I didn't know where else to go.' I can't believe they'd have paid any heed to my claims of poison if I'd hauled him all the way up to the medical centre.

'You wouldn't've . . . thought . . . not safe.'

I don't tell him that I didn't catch half that sentence. That his shivering is getting worse. I'm sure he must already feel it. Throwing an agonized glance in the direction of the curtain, I'm relieved to see Alexios returning with a cup in his hands. He doesn't stop to speak, but moves straight to Niko's side and holds the cup to his lips. I start forward.

'What are you—'

'Giving him the antidote.'

I dig my nails into my palms. Yet it's not as if we have any choice. If Niko doesn't take something to counteract the effects of the poison, it could kill him. There's clearly less of it in his blood than there was in Euphemie's, or he'd already be dead, but his condition has worsened since we arrived here. We have to gamble on Alexios being trustworthy. So I force myself to say nothing, *do* nothing, as Niko drains the contents of the cup and falls back against the supporting pillows.

'Thank you,' he says, faint but steady; the shivers have gone. Astrapē is a mouse, still small and dim, but no longer flickering.

'You need to get some rest,' Alexios tells him. 'But you'll be fine when you wake up.'

Alarm sparks in Niko's eyes. 'I can't sleep now! Feldspar – the execution!'

I'd managed to forget about that, temporarily. My stomach plunges. Alexios looks troubled, but says only, 'I'm afraid you won't have much choice.'

He moves away again, taking the empty cup back to the main workroom. Depending on how long Niko sleeps for, this might be my last chance ever to speak to him. Yet I don't know what to say.

'Why aren't you escaping?' he asks, before I can claw the words together. 'I'm safe now. Go.'

He's already drowsy, or he'd realize that there's no way any of the guards will let me down to the lower levels without him. I'd have thought of it sooner myself, had I not been so distracted by him getting shot.

'In a little while,' I tell him. And then, because I want

everything to be right between us before I die, I admit, 'Niko, I got it wrong. I should have—'

'No, you shouldn't.'

'But I failed you.'

'You're not my shield, Feldspar. You have no obligation to protect me.'

'Not obligation,' I whisper. 'Friendship.'

'As your *friend*, I probably ought to point out that you saved my life. The first arrow would have hit me without you. I couldn't have asked for a better shield.'

'The attacker made a mistake,' I mutter. 'If they hadn't aimed in exactly the same place on you and Euphemie . . .'

Niko closes his eyes. 'One of these days, you'll let me compliment you without finding a way to explain how you were actually at fault.'

One of these days, I'll be dead. But he sounded half asleep, so I don't say it. Alexios told him he needs to rest. Instead, very softly, I say, 'It was nice knowing you, Niko.'

Taking a deep breath, I turn away. The stormglow is bright white; noon is nearly here. I don't have any way to escape by myself. So that only leaves . . .

Submit, part of my brain insists. *You can't hurt Queen Sirene or anyone else who comes after you. You are a shield without anyone to defend. You have no purpose.*

Yet I defended Niko today. And the knife is back in my hand.

'Feldspar?' Alexios returns to our side of the curtain and sits down in one of the chairs. Once again, he pays no heed to my weapon – as if the blade is simply irrelevant to him. He gestures at the second chair, and automatically I drop into it. 'Are you all right?'

'Yes, Eighth. The attacker didn't touch me.'

'That's not what I meant.'

Meeting his earnest brown eyes, I admit, 'I'm terrified.'

'Nikolos said . . . execution?'

I guess the Apex haven't told the ascendants. And why would they? I'm just a nuisance to be disposed of, an anomaly to be ironed out of existence. I'm not important enough to warrant an official announcement.

'They'll come for me at noon,' I tell Alexios dully. 'Take me to the sunroom.'

'Not if I stop it.'

'How?'

'That's what I wanted to tell Nikolos yesterday. Did he not get my note?'

'We haven't been back to his chambers since . . .' I can't remember. Probably this time yesterday, but it feels like forever. 'What did it say?'

'The water he asked me to test. He was right; there's poison in it. I identified it.'

'What?' I sit up straight in my chair. 'But Niko said it wasn't any of the common poisons . . . It's a rare one, then? Not like

237

the one that killed Euphemie?'

'Very rare,' Alexios agrees, gaze dropping to his lap. 'In fact, as far as I'm aware, I'm the only person who knows of its existence. And you're right – it's nothing like aroura. It doesn't kill at all. At least, not the person who consumes it.'

'Then . . .'

'A few years ago, I was asked to work on developing a potion that would give our soldiers an advantage in battle against the raiders. Something that would make them stronger, more aggressive, give them endurance. I had one promising candidate, which I called kratos. I was looking to test it further. But then . . .'

He swallows. The shadows of a dark memory dance in his eyes.

'Flint drank it,' he says quietly. 'I don't know how it happened. I'm always so careful. But there must have been a mix-up. Anyway, it drove him into a battle frenzy, as intended, but – but it was worse than that. He turned on me. And for a moment, I feared for my life.'

'What happened?'

'I stabbed him,' Alexios says. It's a confession, rather than a boast; the darkness is still in his eyes. 'I managed to subdue him long enough to give him the antidote. Then I nursed him back to health, and destroyed the potion and all my notes on it, and told the Apex that what they had asked for was impossible. And I never brewed the stuff again.'

'You don't think Flint could have . . . ?' I begin tentatively, but he shakes his head.

'I wouldn't believe it of him. And besides, I'm not sure he knew the ingredients. I kept my notes locked away, and the key hidden.' His fingers twine together restlessly. 'I should have mentioned it when you came before. Maybe if I had, Halimeda would have survived. Both she and Leandros must have been killed by their shields under its influence. But since I was the only one who knew anything about it, that seemed impossible. It still does.'

'Unless you're the killer,' I think aloud. 'Though I suppose if you were, you'd have kept the story to yourself and let me go to my death without ever knowing the truth . . .' Belatedly, I notice his shocked expression. 'Sorry – of course I don't believe you murdered anyone. Niko's way of thinking must be rubbing off on me. It took him five days to exonerate me as a suspect in Euphemie's death.'

'That's the trouble with the dark arts, I suppose. Even the obvious has to be proven before it can be believed.'

Obvious. Then . . . 'You never thought I killed her?'

'Oh, Feldspar.' Alexios gives me a sympathetic smile. 'The way the two of you were before she died . . . Anyone could see how much you loved her.'

It's the first time anyone's acknowledged that. Everyone else has always started by approaching me with suspicion. I surprise myself by bursting into tears.

'I see it all the time,' I sob. 'Her lips turning blue. Her limbs twitching. And nothing I could do about it . . . Earlier, when I heard that same sound, the blowpipe, I thought it would take Niko too, and I—'

'You're still in shock from Euphemie's death,' Alexios says. 'And you haven't been given time to grieve. To save his life, after all that you've been through . . . I hope you know how impressive that is.'

I shouldn't be crying. The initial burst of emotion is already being replaced with shame at the extent to which I've lost my self-control. Yet I can't seem to stop.

'I wanted to apologize to you,' Alexios adds, which is un-expected enough that it helps me to get a grip on myself. Scrubbing my face with the back of one wrist, I look up.

'What for, Eighth?'

'Leandros . . . that day in the sunroom, I could tell you were uncomfortable. I should have done more to curb his behaviour – we all should. As it was, I did nudge Euphemie to intervene, but I think . . .' He meets my gaze. 'I feared, afterwards, that may have been the wrong way to go about it.'

'She was angry with me,' I find myself admitting. 'Though I didn't understand why.'

'And do you now?'

'Niko said she liked being the centre of attention. I can't argue with that.' Suddenly, I want to confide in him. Why not? My life is in his grasp. Either I'll die or his testimony about the poison will save me, so I might as well trust him.

'The thing is,' I say, 'the longer I've survived without Euphemie, the more clearly I've seen her flaws. Niko seems to believe that will make me mourn her less. But it doesn't! I miss her just the same.' I look down at my hands twisted in my lap. 'Does that make me a fool?'

'People are complicated,' Alexios says softly. 'And seeing someone's flaws doesn't stop you loving them. Only a fool would fail to understand that.'

A loud knock comes at the external door, and I realize the stormglow has reached the brightness of noon. It's time. It's time for my execution and I haven't shown up, and now they've followed the tracker to fetch me. I stand up so fast that my chair topples over, dimly aware of Flint opening the door and Sirene's voice speaking.

'You'll support me?' I ask through the ringing in my ears.

'Of course I will, Feldspar.'

I walk into the exochamber, knife in hand. Sirene is there, four soldiers with her. When she sees the weapon, her eyebrows go up.

'Are you really going to try it?'

Fight, part of me urges. *Submit*, the other part contradicts. I'm trembling all over, and my brain is full of fog. Desperately, I try to pull my thoughts into some kind of order – because neither of the impulses I've been brought up with will help me now. What I need is some of Niko's facility with words.

241

'I'll use the knife if I have to,' I manage. 'But I shouldn't have to. Because I didn't kill anyone.'

Sirene doesn't reply, only gestures the soldiers towards me. I back away, raising the blade defensively, the suffocating fog of panic lifting in the face of a familiar threat. Yet my nervous words lag behind, tripping over themselves on my tongue.

'Nik—the Sixth and I have discovered the truth. The shields are being turned against their charges with poison.'

Sirene frowns. 'Where *is* Nikolos?'

'Asleep. The murderer tried to kill him using aroura, the same poison that killed the Seventh. But Al—the Eighth gave him the antidote.'

'There is altogether too much poison in this story,' Sirene remarks. 'And you are just wasting time, Feldspar. As always, there is nothing to prove any of your outlandish claims. If Nikolos really is injured, I have little doubt that you sought to kill him yourself.'

One of the soldiers reaches for my arm; twisting away, I say hastily, 'I can prove it!'

'How?'

'The Eighth told me about a potion he invented that drove Flint into a frenzy. He called it kratos. He was able to identify the same substance in the strengthening water that the Second's shield drank right before he attacked.'

'And where exactly did Alexios get this water from?'

'Niko and I took it from the Second's chambers.'

'At whose suggestion?'

'Mine . . .' My voice dies beneath her contemptuous stare. I can see where this is going. I was the one to point out the difference in the strengthening water. In the Younger Queen's eyes, I could have added something to it myself before Niko took the sample. My proof isn't enough.

'Is that all?' Sirene asks. Fuzzy panic threatens to overwhelm me again, but I push it back.

'No, ma'am. If you don't believe that, then take a sample of the strengthening water from the First's chambers – where no one has been since she died – and you'll see I'm telling the truth.'

If Halimeda's shield didn't drink all the water, the voice of doubt nags. *If there's enough left to test. If Sirene permits us to break the seven-day rule and disturb Halimeda's possessions . . .*

She allowed it for Leandros, but that was at Niko's request. I wish he was awake. Practising the dark arts gives a person licence to demand all kinds of outlandish things. I wait, barely daring to hope, until Sirene's expression sours and she turns to Alexios.

'You support this?' she demands.

'Yes, ma'am. In fact, with your permission, I will send Flint to fetch a sample of the strengthening water right away, so that we can settle this question once and for all.'

She gives a grudging nod. 'If you insist.'

While Flint is gone – which feels like an age – the silence

in the room is absolute. I look at the queen; she glares at me. I look at the soldiers; they glare at me. I look at Alexios; he smiles, and that's almost harder to bear than the rest, because what if we're wrong? What if he tests the water and finds nothing?

It's not as if they can do anything worse to you, I remind myself. *They were already going to burn you to death.*

Finally, Flint returns with a tube full of liquid. Then I have to wait some more, without even the Eighth's smile to cling to for encouragement. When Alexios re-emerges from his work-room, his expression is grave.

'Feldspar is right,' he says. 'The strengthening water from Halimeda's chambers contains the same version of my failed potion that was used on Basalt. Someone is killing ascendants by using this – this *poison* to turn their shields against them.'

A murmur goes round the waiting soldiers, but ceases as soon as Sirene raises her hand.

'What can we do to stop it, Alexios?'

'We should warn everyone not to eat or drink anything that hasn't been tested first. Kratos smells sweet, but depending on what it's been added to, that might not be noticeable. I can supply a simple test to detect its presence.'

'Very well.'

'I don't know who did this,' Alexios adds. 'I don't know who could possibly have used a poison that no one knew about. But it does prove one thing. Feldspar can't have killed Leandros or

Halimeda, since she has had no opportunity to administer it.'

Sirene says nothing.

'And Nikolos saw his own attacker,' Alexios persists – as serenely as ever, but with an implacable edge to his voice. 'Not only that, but I have one of the aroura-tipped arrows in my possession. So that lends credence to Feldspar's account of Euphemie's death as well.'

The queen sighs. 'All right. I suppose her execution must be suspended until such time as this matter is resolved. Have Nikolos send me a report as soon as he wakes up, Alexios.'

'Yes, ma'am.'

The soldiers troop out again, one by one, and I release a long breath, weak with relief and the aftermath of fear. Yet before Sirene turns to leave, she gestures to me; reluctantly, I go to her side, lowering my gaze to her boots.

'For some reason that I cannot fathom, you do seem to acquire your champions,' she says in an undertone. 'But none of this explains how you survived Euphemie. And until I understand the manner of *that*, you remain alive only on sufferance.' Her voice drops further. 'Remember: if you and Nikolos hadn't left the Honeycomb in good time, the soldiers down there would have arrested you. If the two of you had tried to return there, the guards would have blocked your way down. There are always eyes on you, Feldspar. As for Nikolos, you can tell him that he's forbidden to waste time in the lower levels in future.'

I say nothing. Then she's gone, and I can no longer hold myself upright. I slide down the door until I'm sitting on the floor, tip my head back, and close my eyes.

Alexios leaves me alone, but Flint comes to sit next to me.

'You all right?' he asks.

'I don't know.'

'I'm sorry about the Seventh.'

'Thanks, Flint.' Better late than never.

We sit in silence for a bit. Then, in the voice of someone trying to present an entertaining distraction, he says, 'You were returning from the cutters' quarters when the Sixth was shot?'

'Yes.'

'You're lucky you missed the fuss down there. I heard two handmaidens talking about it on my way back from the First's chambers just now: lady found dead in her chair. Her neighbours got all upset about it, though she was due to be winnowed anyway. Can't recall who they said it was – one of the old nurses . . .'

A chill passes through me, as if I've been consumed by a ghost. 'Daisy?'

'Right. Died in her sleep. How did you know?'

But the chill has settled deep in my bones, and I don't reply.

FIFTH MURDER

SIX DAYS AFTER

I must have fallen asleep on the floor, because when I open my eyes, Alexios is crouched beside me with a bowl in his hands, and the stormglow has yellowed considerably from the bright white of noon.

'I thought you might be hungry,' he says.

I struggle upright. 'Is Niko—'

'Still sleeping. If you want, you can take your soup to his bedside.'

'Food in the workroom?' Flint remarks, somewhere beyond him. 'He must like you. I usually get a lecture about hygiene.'

Groggy but willing, I follow Alexios back through to the workroom. As he said, Niko is asleep, looking washed out and vulnerable enough to reawaken my anxiety. I take the nearest chair, scrutinizing his face.

'Is he all right?'

'Fine. Sleep is a much better healer than I am. But I expect he'll come round soon.'

'Thank you,' I say, belatedly realizing how much I owe him. 'If you hadn't told me about kratos . . . You saved my life.'

Alexios smiles at me. 'I think you'll find you saved your own.'

He leaves, and I hear him talking to Flint in the exochamber. I realize he was right: I am hungry. I eat the whole bowl of soup, then try to doze a bit more, but I'm too alert for that now. So I sit, and wait, and think.

The first hint that Niko is waking up comes from Astrapē, who stirs from her position coiled along one arm and slides sleepily up towards his shoulder. A moment later, his eyes open and he smiles at the ceiling in a bemused sort of way.

'Feldspar . . .' His gaze drifts to the warm, dimming light of the stormglow panel beside his bed; he sits up abruptly, setting Astrapē swirling around his neck as she dissolves from a snake into a barracuda. 'You're here! But the execution – it must be nearly sundown!'

'Oh, they let me off. Seeing as I solved the mystery while you were sleeping like a baby.'

His wild eyes focus on my face. 'You *what*?'

Laughter bubbles in my stomach. I'm not sure I've ever felt this particular emotion before, so I'm not sure what to call it. Giddiness, maybe. It reminds me of the way Euphemie used to dance, twirling in the centre of the room with her arms flung out to either side. 'All right. That was an exaggeration. But Alexios and I figured out how the shields are being turned, which was enough to finally convince Queen Sirene that I didn't do it.'

'Clearly, I should pass out more often,' Niko mumbles. Rubbing a hand over his face, he darts a sidelong glance at me and says, a touch acerbically, 'Are you going to enlighten me?'

I explain. By the time I've finished, his irritation has melted away.

'I'm impressed. Also annoyed with myself – because if I'd been at home to receive Alexios's message yesterday, you wouldn't have come anything like as close to being executed – but mostly impressed.'

He gives me a little bow – which, since I've never been the recipient of a bow before, I don't know what to do with.

'Queen Sirene barred you from the Honeycomb,' I blurt out, self-consciousness and guilt combining to force the confession from me, but Niko only shrugs.

'Their threats are stacking up, aren't they? Take a shield, winnow, stay on my own level like a good little ascendant. But we've won a reprieve now. That's what matters. You don't have to choose between your survival and what you feel is right.'

I hadn't realized he understood my dilemma that well. Hastily, I say, 'There's still a lot to work out. Almost all of it, in fact. Who did the poisoning, for one thing. But also, how they were able to use a poison that Alexios kept secret, and destroyed.'

'That's a good question,' Alexios says from behind the curtain. He pops his head round, smiling at Niko. 'I thought I heard your voice. How are you feeling?'

'Fine,' Niko says, so absently that I can't tell if it's true. 'Thanks for de-poisoning me, but do you mind if I ask you a few questions?'

'I imagine I can't stop you.' Alexios takes the second seat, handing him a cup of some murky beige liquid. 'But I'll only answer if you drink this. You need to regain your strength. Though I warn you, it tastes disgusting.'

'Deal.' Niko takes a sip, grimaces, then forces down a longer gulp. 'So, who knew about your original research? For someone to have stolen and copied your notes, they must have known there was something there to look for.'

'It's a long list, I'm afraid. The whole Apex knew, since they were the ones who asked me to work on it in the first place. The eldest five ascendants, those who had already come of age at the time. I don't know about anyone else.'

'And do you remember anyone in particular hanging around your chambers during the time you were working on it? Someone who could have slipped into your workroom, maybe, while you were talking to someone else? I know you were careful, but before you realized kratos was quite so dangerous, perhaps you wouldn't have thought anything of leaving your materials out while you paused to greet a visitor.'

'It's possible,' Alexios says. 'But I can't narrow that down much either. People are in and out all the time. Not so much the Apex, who are more likely to visit the *real* medics, but the ascendants . . . I guess they trust me more. The older ones are frequently in here with minor wounds. The younger ones bring me the concerns they're too embarrassed to raise with a medic. I never turn anyone away.'

Niko looks at me, and I know we're thinking the same thing: it's the older ascendants, First to Fifth, who are on both of those lists. Who had the knowledge and the opportunity. Yet of those five, two are already dead, and the other three have an alibi for at least one of the murders.

'Whoever is doing this must be *making* kratos, right?' I ask Alexios. 'It's not as if they can buy it ready-brewed from the market hall. So would they need any special equipment? Have you noticed any ingredients going missing?'

'Most of the ingredients are the sort of stuff you can get hold of easily. The key one, though, is crimson algae. Buying a lot of that would be harder to hide, because it's not as if it's edible.'

'Then why do we farm it?'

'For red and purple dyes, mainly. The carders extract the colour and use it to make clothes, ink, that sort of thing. As for equipment . . .' Alexios shrugs. 'Formulating the recipe in the first place was hard, but following it wouldn't require any specialist techniques. Anyone could do it, with a bit of concentration and some basic kitchen tools.'

'And the other poison, the aroura on the arrows – we found that anyone could have sent a courier to fetch that from the Honeycomb, so that's no help either.' Anger rises in my throat, thick enough to choke me. 'We have to find this killer. We *have* to. What kind of person would – would *dispose* of others as if they were no more than vermin?'

Maybe they don't see any difference between that and stabbing people to death if they refuse to leave the Hive in a Winnowing, part of me answers. It's the same part that began to awaken when we visited the Honeycomb: the part that supports the secret group, that sees a need for change. Maybe the first part of me that ever learnt to form an opinion of its own. *If you're brought up to believe that killing is necessary under certain circumstances, then what does the manner of it matter?*

Yet there is a difference. And it isn't that some of the deaths are acceptable and the rest are wrong, as I once thought; by now, I'm convinced that no one should have to die for the Hive. It's that the poisoner is compelling shields to turn against the people they love, the people they've been brought up to believe matter more than themselves, and forfeit their own lives in the process. That's cruel, and it has to stop.

'I wouldn't have thought it of any of my family,' Alexios agrees, looking troubled. 'But whoever it is, they've done a remarkable job of concealing themselves from the rest of us.'

'Whoever it is, they're a coward. Forcing other people to do their dirty work for them—'

'You say coward,' Niko puts in. 'I say cautious and clever. The killer didn't want anyone to realize the deaths had anything to do with poison. They wanted everyone to think it was something going wrong with the shields, like your failed bond. We haven't figured out how your survival fits into the rest of it, but I'm pretty sure it fits somewhere.' He frowns, deep in thought. 'Alexios, will you make us the antidotes to both poisons?'

'Yes, but only if you finish your medicine. You haven't touched it since we started this conversation.'

He moves off to the other side of the curtain. Niko scowls at the beige liquid with such ferocity that I can't help but laugh. He turns his scowl on me.

'What?'

'You are *older* than Alexios, right?'

'Shocking, isn't it?' Alexios says through the curtain.

Niko swallows the rest of the medicine in three large gulps. 'There. Happy?'

'Very.'

It strikes me, sitting here, that Niko isn't quite as isolated as he thinks he is. Alexios, at least, doesn't treat him with fear or suspicion. But then, Alexios seems to be a naturally kind person. He has certainly been kind to me ... and, I understand now, he was kind to Euphemie. I always thought he took an interest in her because no one could help but do so, but the fact is, he took an interest in everyone.

'Here we are,' he says, returning to our side of the curtain with two glass tubes. 'I labelled them so you'll know which is which.'

'Thank you.' Niko goes to put them in his coat, then realizes he isn't wearing it. A look of sheer panic crosses his face in the moment before he sees it draped neatly at the end of his bed. Suppressing a grin, I pass it to him.

'Alexios?' I ask, while Niko is busy tucking his antidotes away in different pockets. 'Do you know anything about—' I stop, suddenly unsure if it's safe to ask. But Alexios saved both of us. He hates the way that death is part of life in the Hive. He's a healer and a good person. Whether he's aware of this secret or not, he wouldn't use it to harm us. 'About a group of ascendants who want to free the shields and abolish all Winnowings?'

His face closes, much as it did when we asked him about poisons that first time. But then he lets out a long breath.

'I won't keep any more secrets,' he says quietly. 'Yes. I'm part of it. Though I'd rather you didn't tell the queens about its existence, unless you have to.'

'And Halimeda and Leandros were both part of it too?' Niko asks.

'Yes.' Alexios looks alarmed. 'You don't think—'

'I don't know. But we're still looking for a motive. This secret group is one thing that linked them.'

'What about Euphemie, though? She wasn't part of the group. I approached her, but . . .' Alexios falls silent, shooting me a worried glance. Though it's no surprise that she wasn't interested, I have to swallow the sadness in my throat before I can ask the next question.

'Can you tell us who *is* part of it?'

'It was only the four of us: Halimeda, Leandros, Pyrene and myself. We all despised what we were made to do in the Winnowings. Perhaps you wouldn't have thought it, seeing the others fight, but being good at such things isn't the same as enjoying them. We wanted to make it so that future ascendants didn't have to grow up as killers; so that the Hive didn't have to be *governed* by killers.' Reflectively, he adds, 'Pyrene and I will have to start recruiting more members if we're to stand any chance of getting the law changed when our generation comes to power.'

'Perhaps you'd also consider allowing ascendants without shields to take a role in your new Apex,' Niko says, rather acidly. 'That would gain you another vote.'

Alexios looks startled. 'I didn't—Of course, Nikolos. If you're interested.'

'And the ascendants who aren't in the group?' I ask, refusing to be distracted. 'Why aren't they?'

'Let's see . . . Calista refused outright. Said the shields would turn on us if we freed them. Ophion said he'd consider it, but we never pinned him down to anything. Euphemie thought it was a silly idea –' once again, his glance is worried – 'and so far, the younger ones know nothing about it. We only formed a few months ago, and we've moved very cautiously.'

'So you haven't asked Karissa? Or Zephrine?'

He shakes his head.

'Or me,' Niko puts in. 'Was that because I was no use to you without a shield, Alexios? Or because, having murdered my own, I couldn't possibly be interested in shields and their rights?'

'Neither.' Alexios's brows draw together. 'Nikolos, you've held yourself apart since Slate died. Raised the dark arts as a barrier between yourself and the world. Ascendants are meant to trust each other, but when you act as if you don't *want* to be trusted . . .'

'All I did was embrace what all of you were already saying about me. The barrier started on your side, not mine.' Niko folds his arms. 'Just like everyone else, you abandoned me after Slate died. Which means I can only assume that just like everyone else, you believed I killed him on purpose.'

'That's what I'm saying. You never denied it.'

'I shouldn't have had to!'

They glare at each other. I'm frozen, caught between conflicting impulses: my heart tells me to dive in and mend the situation between two people who obviously care about each other, while my training instincts are trying to force me to leap automatically to Niko's defence.

Before I can overcome it and make a rational decision using my actual brain, Niko swings his legs off the bed to stand, slightly wobbly, on the floor. 'I should get back to my own quarters.'

He puts his coat on, then manages a few steps before staggering sideways into the wall.

'Please, Nikolos,' Alexios says. 'I didn't mean to—You should stay. You need rest.'

'You mean, like the rest I've been having all day?'

'You were *poisoned*. It's not the sort of thing you can brush off. Tell him, Feldspar.'

I look at Niko. His expression is as vague as it can possibly be. Anyone would think he didn't feel strongly about this at all – that he wasn't, in fact, desperate to be back in the safety of his own solitary rooms.

'I'll make sure he gets home,' I say.

Our cups from yesterday are still sitting on Niko's table. Surely it wasn't that recently that I drank kelpin for the first time and saw Astrapē for the first time and was threatened with execution for the ... well, I've lost count on that one. But I feel so much older. I saw a real bee last night. I walked through a new world and learnt so much in the process. I'm not the same person.

Manoeuvring Niko into one of his chairs takes far longer than it rightfully should because his legs don't seem to be able to move in a straight line. Once it's done, I linger, looking down at him. Both of us could have died today. Neither of us did. Maybe that's why I'm feeling soft and sort of *tender* towards him, in a way I've never felt towards anyone before, not even Euphemie.

Cheeks heating, I lower my gaze. 'I'll see you tomorrow.'

'You can stay, if you want,' Niko says.

'I thought—You want to be alone, right? Alone is safe.'

'Yes. But you don't count. I mean . . . you're part of the safeness.'

I don't know what to say. I almost think I'm going to cry again.

'And anyway,' Niko goes on, 'what are you going to do? Return to the cells and lock yourself in? I don't see why you should be in prison any more. You . . .' He hesitates, then nods to himself. 'You can sleep in Slate's old bed. I have spare blankets. And spare clothes. And it'll save me bringing you breakfast in the morning.'

'Queen Sirene won't like it. She might have suspended my sentence, but that doesn't mean she wants me roaming free.'

His chin lifts. 'To be honest, Feldspar, at this point I don't care what the queens or any of the Apex think. I want you to stay. And if they don't like it, they can take it up with me.'

It feels like the best kind of compliment: his willingness to brave Sirene's anger for my sake. As a result, I find myself equally willing to endure whatever punishments might be thrown my way.

'All right, all right,' I say. 'I'm convinced.'

I shouldn't be surprised to discover that Niko's particular approach to home decorating extends to his bedchamber, with books crammed into another set of shelves and spilling on to the dressing table and the second bed. Nor should I be surprised that the latter is raised, so that it's almost on a level with Niko's own. Slate was never a servant to Niko like some of the other shields are to their ascendants.

At Niko's direction, I bundle the books on to the floor, then grab some blankets from a chest. Once I'm lying down, I discover two things. One, this bed is far comfier than the prison cot I've slept on for the past week, and even than my old bed in Euphemie's chambers. Two, if I turn my head on the pillow, I can see Niko and he can see me. It's comforting in a way that I didn't know I'd been missing, to lie here and listen to someone else breathe.

'Good night, Niko,' I say.

'Feldspar . . .' He props himself up on one elbow to get a better view of my face. 'I heard you crying earlier.'

He must mean when I was talking to Alexios. I thought he was asleep. Rather peevishly, I say, 'Yes, well, as you like to point out, I'm no longer required to maintain a shield's stoic demeanour.'

'I didn't mean—That's not why I brought it up. I was . . . I wanted to apologize.'

'What for?'

'When we first met, I assumed the worst of you. Like everyone did to me when Slate died. And even when my opinion began to change, it never occurred to me to think about your grief. About what it must be like for you now, without her. I'm sorry.'

It's the single best thing he could have said to me. I feel utterly *seen*, as if the two of us are in perfect harmony and he understands me completely. Then he ruins it by adding, 'I suppose what exists between ascendant and shield is a kind of love.'

'Not just *a kind*. I loved Euphemie.'

'Of course you did.'

The words appear neutral, on the surface, but something in his tone makes me look narrowly at him. 'What's that supposed to mean?'

'I'm sure Slate loved me too. It was *encouraged*. How else would they make sure that our shields were willing to die for us?'

'No one forced me to love her!'

He says nothing. I sit bolt upright in bed, turning to face him. 'I mean it, Niko. You don't get to tell me that what I felt was a lie. You can't just . . . If none of it was real, then—'

My eyes are stinging. Furiously, I blink back the tears. I am *not* going to cry again. Once in my life is enough.

'I'm not saying it wasn't real,' Niko says. 'No doubt you loved Euphemie. I know I loved Slate. I'm saying you had no *choice*.'

I glare at him. 'You're always doing this. Pointing out all the ways my life as a shield was constrained. All the ways I was controlled. But that doesn't mean I had a bad life, or that Euphemie was . . . I mean, a person in a cage can still . . .'

Ugh. I should leave the metaphors to Niko. Mine appear to be working against me. I barely know what I'm arguing for any more, except that every time he criticizes the system I grew up in, it feels like a criticism of *me* – because I put up with it for so long. Because I'm only now starting to question it.

Hugging myself, I lie back down and stare at the ceiling. 'I don't understand why you're so obsessed with choice.'

'What else is there?'

I turn my head sharply, suspecting him of flippancy, but his expression is serious.

'I think choice is all we have,' he says. 'It's what gives life meaning. What gives *love* meaning. But I didn't intend . . . I wasn't trying to get at you, Feldspar. I like you a lot.' He sounds very matter-of-fact, as if it should be obvious. 'I think you're smart and brave and loyal, and – and I respect you more than anyone else I know. It's what's around us I don't like.'

I want to stay angry with him. Yet no one has ever given me anything like his list of compliments before, and it's left me warm and floaty inside, as if I've swallowed a draught of pure happiness. So, trying and failing to keep the corners of my lips from turning up, I say, 'For future reference, Niko, you can apologize to someone without immediately turning it into an ideological debate.'

'I'm sorry.'

I wait for the follow-up argument, but there isn't one. He smiles at me, and I can't keep my own smile from widening in response.

'I like you too,' I say. 'Just so you know.'

SEVEN DAYS AFTER

When I wake, I can tell by the light that it's well past sunup. I don't think I've slept this late since . . . ever. Confused, I sit up. This isn't my cell. This is an ascendant's bedchamber . . . *Euphemie*—

The surge of pure and total relief recedes as I wake up properly and take in my surroundings. This is Niko's room. The events of the past week weren't a nightmare after all. And I wonder how it's possible to know that, and grieve that, and still feel like everything is going to be all right.

Niko is asleep, so I creep out into the exochamber and find myself some food from his store cupboard. I think about trying to tidy up the clutter on the table, but for all I know, he has a system that only looks like complete chaos from the outside. So, with a strange, guilty feeling of freedom, I pick up a book called *The Uninhabitable Earth* – which seems to be an ancient Dark Ages text predicting the Rising – and sit down to read.

It's nearly noon when a knock comes at the door. I open it without thinking – as if I'm still a shield, admitting the morning's business for my charge. Alexios is there, with Flint at his shoulder. Though the Eighth smiles at me, his heart isn't in it.

'Is Nikolos awake?' he asks.

'Not yet.'

He nods. 'It's to be expected. He needs rest. He may sleep for most of the day.'

'Do you want to come in?'

'No. No, I came here because . . .' His shoulders slump. 'Because Pyrene is dead.'

'What? But I thought Queen Sirene was to—'

'She sent the word round. Not to eat or drink anything that hadn't been tested. How to test it. But this death was . . . different.'

'Different how?'

'It wasn't my poison that did it.' He looks as if he wants to be relieved about that, but thinks it would be inappropriate. 'Breccia – Pyrene's shield – didn't kill her.'

'How do you know?'

'Because Pyrene had locked Breccia in the bedchamber overnight, to ensure both their safety. Breccia was found dead, still locked away. And Pyrene . . .' His throat dips as he swallows. 'She was garrotted. Someone crept up on her to do it. And whoever it was, she must have let them in.'

I shiver. Did Breccia know what was happening? Was she

forced to listen, trapped behind a locked door, as her charge was murdered? Or did she die peacefully, never knowing that the act of separation intended to save them both may have been the very act that doomed them?

'I think we have to assume it's the same killer, despite the differences. And another of your secret group is gone.' Impulsively, I touch Alexios's arm, looking at Flint to include him in my words. 'Be careful. Both of you. If that's really the reason behind all this . . .'

'Then I'm the only one left,' Alexios says. 'I know. I'm carrying the same antidotes that I gave you and Niko.'

'And I won't let anyone into our chambers,' Flint adds.

Suddenly, I'm desperate to be rid of them – not because I want them to leave, but because it doesn't feel safe for them to be out there in the corridor where anyone could get at them. 'Thank you for taking the risk of coming to tell us. I'll let Niko know.'

'If you don't mind,' Alexios says. 'And, Feldspar . . . tell him I heard that the queens have called an emergency meeting of the Apex for this afternoon. They're thinking about holding the final Winnowing early, younger ascendants included – even though they're not yet sixteen – to give them a fair chance. With the heirs chosen, and the rest of us bonded to them, surely the carnage would cease.'

Closing the door, I slump against it and let out a long breath. I thought we'd bought ourselves some time. Instead, the killer has switched straight to another method without even slowing down.

Could it be Zephrine? I noted, before, that her build matched that of Euphemie's attacker, but I'd more or less dismissed the idea. It seemed so unlikely that a girl not yet out of school would set herself against grown ascendants. Yet with Pyrene gone, there aren't many potential queens left: Calista, Karissa, Zephrine and one younger girl. Bearing in mind Karissa's long-standing intention to be treasurer, that gives Zephrine a far better shot at the throne than she had before all this started. On the other hand, Pyrene was garrotted. That takes physical strength. Knowledge of weapons and how to use them. I've never heard that Zephrine excels in that area. She'd rather trade in words than blows.

I poke my head round the door to Niko's bedchamber, but he's still asleep. So I sneak a piece of paper from the jumble on his table and start making lists.

Victims: Euphemie, Leandros, Halimeda, Pyrene. Three of them part of a group that wanted to free the shields and do away with Winnowings altogether. As for Euphemie, when Niko and I talked about why she died first, we decided it was to throw the blame on me – make me a scapegoat. In which case, she doesn't need to fit the pattern alongside the rest. The only unexplained part of it is how I survived.

After a moment, I add Niko and Daisy to the list. I haven't forgotten what Flint told me yesterday: the old nurse was found dead not long after our visit. I don't believe that's a coincidence. And if she didn't pass naturally, but was murdered . . . well. It implies that of all the odd things we did yesterday, from midnight to sunup to noon – wandering around the Honeycomb, standing too close to the Spire in a storm, visiting Zephrine's old nurse – it was the last encounter that most threatened the killer. We might not have got it out of her, but Daisy knew something important. A secret that scared the killer into going after her straight away, even though her exile in the next Winnowing was imminent – because I can't believe she would have been one of the few who were judged valuable enough to remain in the Hive. And if the killer had succeeded in murdering Niko as well as Daisy, no doubt I would have been blamed for his death and executed, thereby eradicating any remnant of the secret's existence.

Suspects. This list has to include all the surviving ascendants who are of age: Calista, Ophion, Alexios, Karissa. Zephrine as well, given my earlier thoughts. I strike Alexios from the list straight away – helping us the way he did would have been thoroughly counterproductive if he were the killer – but any of the others seem possible. Calista is vehemently against freeing the shields, and also benefits from the deaths because she, Halimeda and Pyrene were the main contenders to become Elder Queen. Though she and Pyrene gave each other alibis for Halimeda's death, maybe that was a lie. Based on my limited interactions with him, I'd say Ophion would do anything that suits his own self-interest; although Niko was with him the night of Leandros's murder, perhaps he could have sent his shield, Gabbro, to slip the poison into Basalt's cup. I've already noted what Zephrine gains from the current situation, and Karissa ...

I stop, tapping the pen next to Karissa's name. On the face of it, she's the least likely suspect. She doesn't seem like a murderer. She doesn't want a throne. But I have the strong sense that I'm missing something important when it comes to Karissa.

Setting that aside, I start a third list: *Evidence*. We know the murderer has a secret, which we assume they killed Daisy to protect. They turned two shields against their charges using kratos, a poison that Alexios believed he'd kept secret and that requires a supply of crimson algae to make. They used a different poison, aroura, on the darts they shot at Euphemie and Niko. They're strong enough to strangle someone, yet they were trustworthy enough to be admitted to Pyrene's chambers at a time when all the ascendants are suspicious of each other, and the figure I saw was slender and short ...

How can any one person be capable of all this? I stare at the list of contradictory points and try not to wish that Niko would wake up. Even though I know he'd do some science or whip some handy device out of one of his multitude of pockets, and figure out exactly what we should do next.

'Come on, Feldspar,' I mutter. 'You can do this. Science is

just common sense, remember?'

Yet I can't make it fit together. I've already noted that Calista's skill with the bow would have come in handy when firing poison arrows at people, but I can't imagine her sneaking around with poison. Conversely, Ophion is exactly the type to use poison, but he's too broad in the shoulders to be the shadowy figure I've seen twice now. The two of them are the only ones I'd assess as having the ability to strangle someone – and in Calista's case, a bow string would make a decent garrotte – but with her shield separated from her, Pyrene would have been very cautious about who she admitted into her chambers. It seems more likely she'd have trusted Zephrine, or Karissa . . .

'Crimson algae,' I say aloud. Because that's what I've been missing. Crimson algae is used to make ink. And Karissa – as apprentice treasurer – can access red ink in unlimited quantities. That means she's the only person we know to have a source of the poison's key ingredient.

Heart racing, I look through the evidence again. Poison – yes. Darts – maybe. She claims to have no skill with weaponry, but maybe her aim is better than we know. Slender and short – yes. Trusted by Pyrene – perhaps, if she made the same assumption as me, that Karissa was no threat. Harbours a secret – maybe. The only part that doesn't fit is the garrotting. Unless . . .

I wondered, just now, how anyone could be capable of everything on the list. But what if they're not? What if two or more of my suspects are working together? If a group can form to fight against the Winnowings, another group can form to stop them . . .

'Feldspar?' I jump at the sound of Niko's voice. He's standing in the doorway to his bedchamber, hair all mussed up, blinking. One hand gestures in the direction of the nearest stormglow panel. 'Is it really after noon?'

I hadn't noticed the slowly increasing orange tint to the light. I open my mouth to say so, but find myself pouring out everything: the news of Pyrene's death, the possibility that the new queens will be chosen early, all my thoughts since. I hand him the sheet of paper containing my notes, which he takes without a word, gazing down at it as I talk. When I stop, it's more because my mouth is dry than because I've run out of words. It's been a long time since I last had a drink.

'I'm beginning to think I should spend my entire life asleep,' Niko murmurs. 'It certainly seems to do *you* a world of good, at any rate.'

'Then you agree with my science?'

He smiles slightly at that. 'The science is sound. Two or more people working together would certainly explain some of the discrepancies. And I think you're right that Karissa's red ink is the best hypothesis we have for how someone might have got hold of enough crimson algae to make kratos. But you didn't say much about *this*.'

He's indicating the name *Daisy* on my list of victims.

Right . . . He was asleep yesterday when I found out about that. 'She's dead. Flint told me.'

'And you think she was killed.'

'Yes. Which must mean she gave us useful information, or at least the murderer thought she *might* have. I can't see why else they should suddenly be afraid enough of you to want to kill you.'

'Thanks.'

I almost think he's offended. Then I remember my similar response to something he said to me – *I can't fathom why anyone would want to keep you alive* – and grin.

'The silly thing is, if the murderer hadn't panicked and tried to kill both you and Daisy, I wouldn't have thought that visit was significant. It's really only her death that made me realize how important it might be.'

'But the little she told us was so confusing,' Niko says. 'Isn't it possible that the killer had wanted to be rid of me for days, and seized the first opportunity they could? And that Daisy was already ill, and there's nothing sinister about her death at all? It's not as if she seemed in the best of health when we visited her.'

I watch Astrapē snake up and down his arms, sinuous and agitated.

'You don't believe that,' I say finally. 'You think what Daisy said meant something.'

His chin dips. 'I know I've missed it. The one piece that

would make the incoherent story of a forbidden royal baby fit into the same picture as all these deaths. I just can't decipher what it is.'

'It's what we need to work out, though, isn't it? Maybe Calista and Karissa are working together. Calista has the motive, and Karissa has the means. That little scene on the training floor the other day could have been no more than an act. But until we know why they wanted Daisy dead, we have no real facts to use against them.'

Niko snaps his fingers. 'The archive. It holds records of the royal family going back to the founding. If we find out whose nurse Clover was—'

'Then we find out who might have been willing to kill Daisy in order to keep a secret,' I agree. 'And that's the first step to finding out what the secret actually is.'

SEVEN DAYS AFTER

'Are you sure you know how to do this?' I ask, scanning the corridor to either side of us as Niko crouches beside the door to the archive.

'I am a master of the dark arts. No barrier can stand in my way.'

'Yes, but—'

'I told you, I once spent three days with a locksmith in the Honeycomb . . . Ah. There we go.' With a soft click, the door swings open, and Niko straightens up with a smug expression. Astrapē lurks in a fold of his sleeve, shaped like a cockroach, which apparently is her contribution to being stealthy.

'All right,' I say. 'Count me impressed. Now let's get inside before anyone comes past and sees us.'

We're on the communal level here – above the ascendants' quarters, but below the Apex – so being seen is a genuine risk. No one is meant to enter the archive without permission from

Trystan, the keeper of the records, since he's the one who maintains it alongside full accounts of all matters relating to governance. But the Apex are currently gathered in their emergency meeting, so at least none of them will catch us in the act.

I expected the archive to be a vast room full of shelves and shelves of musty papers – something like Niko's chambers, but on a larger scale. Instead, the room is small and almost completely bare, save for a rectangular object in the centre. It looks like a stormglow panel, flat and matte grey. Yet when Niko presses the side, it lights up. Four coloured squares float across the surface. I touch one, but feel only smoothness.

After a bit of whirring, the panel makes a chiming noise and a set of simple little pictures pops up. There are similar panels in the medical centre, where the medics can access all your details when they're treating you with growth medicine or bone repair or whatever. But the illuminated side of the panel always faces them, so I've never seen what it looks like before. I imagined it would show something complicated, with unfamiliar terminology and diagrams of the human body. Not this.

'What now?' I ask.

'Not sure. I've never used it before.'

'You're telling me there are things in the Hive you *don't* know about?'

'Perhaps one or two,' Niko says with great dignity. 'Now, which of these pictures looks like something you'd use to search for a record?'

'Try that one.' I point to a circle with a line attached to it. When he touches it, an empty box appears on the panel with letters and numbers underneath. Niko's eyebrows lift.

'How did you know?'

'It looks like a fishing net. You know, a child's net on a stick. And we're trying to catch something, aren't we?'

One at a time, Niko taps the letters that spell out CLOVER. When he touches the fishing-net picture again, a spinning circle appears on the panel, then is replaced by a list. Each item consists of two names, grey and underlined: ascendant–shield pairs. Yet none of them are people I recognize. Names are reused all the time among the cutters, so it isn't surprising that multiple former ascendants might have had a nurse called Clover, but none of the current royal family from either generation are listed here.

'She never existed,' I say. 'Not in our lifetime. Daisy was just a confused old woman.'

Niko shakes his head. 'We know she existed. We saw her nurse's medallion.'

'Right. Then maybe ... We know Clover was *intended* to be a first-nurse. She'd given birth to her own child, the shield, then attended the birth of that child's charge, the ascendant. But Daisy said she collapsed as soon as she came back from that, so maybe she didn't live long enough to be listed as a nurse.'

'She'd be listed as a mother, though. These records give full parentage of ascendant and shield.'

'Then you think—'

'Someone must have altered the records. And that means we're on the right track.'

'We know that according to her story, Daisy was living in the royal nurseries when Clover died,' I volunteer, 'because Clover would have moved there herself once her baby was bonded, in preparation for the birth. Daisy wouldn't have seen what happened unless she was living there too. So maybe, if we look for *Daisy's* records . . .'

'Good plan.' Niko taps in DAISY. This time, the spinning circle spits out a list in which the topmost three pairs – presumably the most recent – are green instead of grey, and consist of familiar ascendants and shields. Daisy started as first-nurse for Calista and Porphyry, because she was Porphyry's mother. Later she was second-nurse to Pyrene and Breccia, and after them, Zephrine. When Niko and I add it up, we find that her time in the nurseries covers the births of all the surviving ascendants of all ages, which doesn't reveal anything.

'Find Karissa's record,' I suggest. 'The crimson algae is the closest thing we have to solid proof. See if there's anything in her record that doesn't add up.'

He searches for Karissa's name, then touches the top result: *Karissa & Quartz*. The panel fills with flickering text that's divided vertically into two halves: ascendant on the left, and shield on the right. Each column contains key information for the person in question, including birth date, parents, first- and second-nurses, dates for completion of different stages of training, Winnowings participated in, and cause and date of death – though that final row is currently blank, of course.

'What's this?' Niko asks, pointing to the string of letters and numbers below Karissa's name.

'Her blood-code.'

'Her what?'

'You know. So that every time they inject something into you, they can get the dosage exactly right.' I take in his blank, slightly horrified expression. 'I guess you haven't had as many injections as I have. But you'll have a blood-code too – entered into the system by a medic as soon as you were born and they were able to take samples from you, and impossible to change. It's used to make sure anything the medics give you matches your blood, your genetics. Otherwise, you could get ill, or even die.'

'I had no idea.' He frowns at the display. 'And this is the one piece of information that the medics use to treat us? What if there was an error in the records?'

He really hasn't spent much time in the medical centre. 'They take a blood sample every time you visit. Match it to your blood-code in the records. If there was an error, it would be in the records, not in the blood-code. But so far, they've always known that I'm Feldspar, so I guess the records are fine.'

'I can't understand this code at all,' Niko says, sounding genuinely offended by the inability. 'Even the first bit makes no sense. It looks like it's a sequential number, which would be logical – putting the blood-codes in order of birth. But even though Quartz was born the day before Karissa, her code is one digit higher.'

I shrug. 'I don't know which bits of the code mean what. I've only ever seen my own before today.'

'Well, I can't see anything that stands out as strange in this record. Can you?'

I shake my head. Niko hesitates, then taps the single date listed under Winnowings participated in, which is underlined like the original results. Different text appears: a record of that Winnowing. All the ascendants who took part are listed in order of age, along with how many people they individually killed and whether their shields survived. There's also a vast amount of other information, including the number of soldiers involved, how many carders, cutters and drones died altogether and how many were sent into exile, and whether the targets were met.

'I'm notable by my absence,' Niko murmurs, gesturing at the part of the list where *Ophion, Fifth Ascendant* sits directly above *Euphemie, Seventh Ascendant*. 'But I couldn't, Feldspar. I just couldn't.'

'No.'

'Anyway, that's it. I can't think of any other way to try and track Clover down. If someone removed her from the records, there's nothing we can do.'

He rifles through the pages of his notebook, while I consider the glowing panel. Now we've declared the archive a dead end for the purposes of the investigation, curiosity is beginning to gnaw at me. No one seems to have noticed we're here, where we're not supposed to be. And I'm never going to get another opportunity . . .

It feels like my fingers make the decision for me, moving to Euphemie's underlined name without any instruction from my brain. Touching it gives me an almost physical shock; my heart thuds against my ribcage. Yet there it is. *Euphemie & Feldspar*. The record of our lives.

I scan down the left-hand side, drinking in Euphemie's details. Her mother, Queen Sirene. Her father, a man from a medium-sized drone family. She always wondered about him, but she knew they would probably never meet – or if they did, she wouldn't know it. Only once the new queens and Apex have been selected can ascendants learn about the lesser half of their parentage, if they want to, by which time the man will most likely have been winnowed anyway.

Of course, shields don't get to know who their parents are either – not just until the new Apex is formed, but ever. It would prevent us from being dedicated solely to our charges. But I could look, now. Couldn't I? My instincts are saying no . . . but then, those are the same instincts that told me to go straight to the identity of Euphemie's father without even thinking about the identities of my own parents. If I've learnt anything from these days with Niko, it's that my instincts are not my own.

Bracing myself, I move my gaze across to the right-hand side of the panel. To the bare facts of my existence, two lines of flickering letters.

My father was a soldier. Though I don't recognize his name, I may have met him once or twice – I've exchanged greetings with plenty of soldiers during my years of training.

My mother was our first-nurse, mine and Euphemie's, as she should have been. But she died before we turned one, and was replaced by someone else.

'Are you all right?' Niko asks. I turn my head; he's looked up from his notebook and is watching me with concern.

'Yes. I . . . My mother's name was Larkspur.'

He grasps the implication of the past tense immediately. 'I'm sorry.'

'What do you think it means? Larkspur?'

'I don't know. But it has *spur* in it. I expect she was as strong as you.'

'They sound a little the same. Feldspar and Larkspur.'

'Yes.' He scans the panel, taking in the details for himself. Then he says quietly, 'At least she would have loved you while she had you.'

His face bears the same expression as it did when he talked about being better off living among the carders: a kind of intense wistfulness. And although I still think he doesn't realize how lucky he is, in a lot of ways, I'm willing to concede that this is one way in which both carder children and shields are luckier than ascendants. My own mother might not have survived, but most shields get a mother to love them for the first four years of their life. Though they don't remember it when they're older, that foundation of security is there. Whereas the queens' interest in their offspring – particularly their sons, who can't inherit their position – is detached and cold. I only have to think of the way Queen Doralie speaks to Niko to know that.

'Do you want to see your record?' I offer, though I'm not entirely convinced it will help. He hesitates, before returning to the fishing-net page and spelling out NIKOLOS.

Nikolos & Slate. Their record marks Slate's death, followed by Niko's refusal of another shield and his disqualification as an eligible candidate for the Apex. Niko runs his fingertips down Slate's side of the display as if he can conjure a memory from the touch.

'At least the blood-codes are in chronological order for us,' he says, a little hoarsely. 'Slate was born after me; his code falls after mine. I wish I knew how they assigned those.'

By now, I can tell when Niko is distracting himself with an academic question to avoid a personal one. I let the silence stretch, giving him space, until he speaks again.

'I recognize my father's name. Member of a prominent drone family. He died before I ever lost Slate, but all the same ... I must be a terrible disappointment to my relatives.'

'Of course you're not a disappointment,' I say hotly.

'Oh, but I am. They'll have hoped for social advancement. A connection to the Apex. And instead, they got someone who refuses to take part in the contest.'

'But you're clever, and interesting, and kind—'

'I'm sure that's a great consolation to them.'

'It should be! Kind is important! But if not, what about the dark arts? Surely they're impressive enough for any drone family.'

'The dark arts,' Niko echoes miserably. 'Right.'

Eyes glazed, he stares at the glowing panel. I think he's about to say we should leave. Then, slowly – in the tone of voice that tells me he's figured something out – he says, 'Go back to the results for Daisy, would you?'

I do it. His finger moves down from the first three results to a lower item on the list.

'I thought I'd remembered correctly. There's another pair in green: *Doralie & Agate*. That's my— Queen Doralie and her shield. I expect they were nursed by a previous Daisy, one who died before ours was born. But above them, which we think means more recent, there's a pair in grey. *Rhea & Onyx*. I've never heard of a Rhea.'

'A sister of one of the current queens who was killed in a Winnowing?' I suggest.

'Perhaps . . .'

He pulls up the details for Rhea and Onyx. Sure enough, they died before the queens formed their current Apex. The cause of death is listed simply as *Final Winnowing*. Niko and I exchange glances. Here, at last, is a chance to learn something about the mysterious last test that all ascendants must undergo when the new queens are selected.

Yet when he displays the information about that Winnowing, it doesn't make sense. Unlike the Winnowing we viewed for Karissa and Quartz, with its multitude of details, it lists only ascendants and their shields. Twelve pairs took part in total; seven of them survived. The exact number needed to form an Apex. There were no soldiers or drones or carders involved. Because . . .

With agonizing slowness, my brain slots the pieces of what I'm seeing into place. The participating ascendants made five kills between them, and five of them died. No one else was there except them and their shields; no one needed to be.

Because in the final Winnowing, the ascendants were winnowing each other.

And this time, there was no banishment. The only option was death.

Astrapē creeps up Niko's sleeve to press herself against the side of his neck, changing from a cockroach to a moth as she does so. Niko's fingers move frantically across the panel, returning to the fishing net, entering FINAL WINNOWING. He views Winnowing after Winnowing, digging further and further back in the history of the Hive. But it was the same for every single generation of ascendants. Every time, they underwent one final Winnowing in which they cut themselves down to the exact number needed to rule.

'We've been in here long enough,' he says finally. 'Better leave before someone notices.' He presses on the side of the panel again, and the stark summary of all those deaths vanishes into flat grey.

Once Niko has relocked the door behind us, we head back down towards the ascendants' quarters. Neither of us speaks to start with, though I don't know why Niko is quiet. I can't imagine it's shock; he may look at the world through an idealistic lens when he's imagining a different life for himself, but his view of his own family has always been clear-eyed to the point of cynical. For myself, I'm struggling to accept what we just found out. Not because I can't believe it of the Apex – I can – but because it's such a vast betrayal that I don't want to.

'So,' he says eventually. 'At least we found out what's so special about the final Winnowing.'

I can't quite form words, but I make a sound of agreement.

'You can see how it works, can't you? By that point in each generation, all the ascendants would have been through several

Winnowings, and the older ones far more. Every Winnowing detaches them further from committing murder, until it isn't so much of a stretch to be told that the final Winnowing is just a continuation of that. A last test of their ruthlessness and fitness to rule.'

'But killing each other,' I whisper. 'By *design*. When we're told the ascendants are meant to work together for the good of the Hive . . .'

'If carders and cutters and drones can die *for the good of the Hive*, why can't ascendants?' His lips twist in a bitter smile. 'Though the Apex are even more hypocritical than I thought. What troubles them now isn't that ascendants are dying. It's that they are dying *too soon*.'

'How can the queens want their own children to die?'

'If you think about it, only two of them need to survive,' Niko says. 'The daughters who will reproduce and pass on the royal gift to the next generation. The rest are as disposable as everyone else.'

I shiver. My imagination is throwing up scene after scene: the older ascendants turning on Euphemie, hunting her down just as they hunted the helpless carders, running her through and leaving her to bleed out on the floor. *Protect your ascendant. Protect all other members of the royal family, unless that conflicts with the first rule.* I used to wonder why they'd added the last bit, when there was no conceivable situation in which it could apply; now I know. There was always going to come a time when I had to protect Euphemie by hurting the other ascendants I'd spent my life respecting.

And I'd have done it, no doubt about that – or I'd have tried. I'd have stood between her and them. Yet although I was trained to do whatever it took to keep Euphemie alive, I wasn't ever trained to defend her against her own family, fierce and intent and lethal; they'd have killed me, and they'd have killed her. No use pretending otherwise. When she set herself up as a rival for the throne, she was setting herself up for death, and she didn't even know it. And Niko . . . I swallow painfully as another piece of the puzzle slots into place.

'The other ascendants will eliminate you,' I blurt out. 'Without a shield, you're disqualified from a role in the Apex. So if only seven can survive the final Winnowing, there's no point in keeping you alive.'

Vestigial, Queen Doralie – his own mother – called him. And what else was it she said? *There is no need for you to die.* Not *would be*, in some hypothetical situation, but *is*. That's why she was trying to force him to take a shield: she knows the truth. The whole Apex know it. They know, and they keep it a secret.

'The emergency meeting,' Niko whispers, his face pale. 'If the queens decide to bring forward the choosing of their heirs, our final Winnowing could be as soon as tomorrow.'

'But we're so close. If we can just find the murderer before anything is announced . . . surely the queens would rather allow the younger ascendants time to come of age before the heirs are chosen.'

'But I—'

I take his hand, squeezing it tightly. 'It'll be all right, Niko. No matter what, before the final Winnowing begins, we'll ask Ixion to bond me as your shield after all. I'll get you through it. I promise.'

'Or we run.' Some of the colour creeping back into his cheeks, he returns my grip. 'After we find the truth, after we stop the murderer, we run. Leave the Hive and find the place where real bees still live.'

'Or we run,' I agree.

SEVEN DAYS AFTER

We don't speak as we hurry back towards Niko's chambers. I can feel him shaking; he's always been opposed to what the Apex stands for, but a fight to the death that could happen any day now is a lot to take in, even for him. After a while, I realize we're still holding hands, and release my grasp just as he does the same.

'Niko?' I venture, trying to cover my confusion as much as anything. 'What were you going to say about raiders, the night we went to the Spire? Remember, you started to ask me something . . . ?'

'Are you sure you want to know? After everything we've discovered?'

'If it's about the Apex, I'd rather have the full picture of what we're dealing with.'

'All right,' he says. 'Then . . . did it ever occur to you that there might not be any raiders?'

'*What?*'

'I mean, have you seen one? Has anyone?'

'There's no reason why we would. The soldiers drive them back, every time. The dead are incinerated. I was always told that not so much as a single carder has ever been harmed in a raid because the attackers never break through.'

Niko's eyebrows lift. 'And that doesn't strike you as unlikely?'

'Maybe,' I mutter. 'Or maybe spending too much time with you has taught me to doubt everything. I don't trust the Apex, not any more, but why would they lie about this?'

'Hear me out. The population of the Hive must remain constant, to match the space and resources we have available. Right?'

I nod.

'So when there's war, we winnow some drones or carders and grow more soldiers in their place. Only that doesn't make sense, because some of the soldiers also die. So in reality, over time, the population must be decreasing. Not only that, but although everyone gets less food in wartime and more when the fighting is over, the rations never quite go back to where they started . . .'

'What are you saying?'

'That by all the evidence, the number of people who can be supported by the Hive is slowly diminishing. Not constant. The raids give the Apex an excuse to limit rations without sending everyone into a panic.' He glances at me as if to check my own panic level; from his shoulder, Astrapē eyes me in gull form. 'And if I'm right, our only hope of long-term survival is to head out through the tunnels ourselves. Find new places to live. Because rather than shutting everyone else out, we may have shut ourselves in.'

As usual, I can't argue with his logic. Particularly not when we've just discovered what the Apex have in store for the ascendants. Like I said, I no longer trust them – I can't. Yet I'm hesitant.

'Think about it,' he urges me. 'There has to be a lie some-where. We've been told that Mclissa had this unique gift: the ability to create life. That she used it to save our ancestors while the rest of the survivors of the Rising were doomed to age and die without ever having children of their own. But in that case, it's impossible for anyone to be alive outside the Hive. Not after all this time.'

I can't believe I didn't see the contradiction. Either there are no raiders, as Niko said, or the royal gift isn't as special as the Apex claim.

'I sometimes wonder if *that's* the real reason for our involve-ment in the Winnowings,' he adds. 'Ascendants are taught that everyone else in the Hive has to be kept under control. The carders by constant hard work. The cutters by the conditioning you all undergo to perform your different roles. The drones with luxury and the promise of potentially seeing their offspring take the throne one day . . .'

I shiver to hear it set out that starkly. I was always taught to be grateful – to be a shield, to be bonded to Euphemie, to be alive at all. It's only now I realize that gratitude is another form of control: if you can be made to feel grateful for the little you're given, you never think to ask for more.

'One way or another, everyone is too distracted to ask questions,' Niko says. 'And maybe that goes for us too. Maybe the Winnowings keep us focused on driving out and killing other people not only so that it becomes second nature to us, but so we don't have the chance to think about anything else.'

'If you're right about the raiders, the Apex must know.'

'Yes. And I imagine my generation will be told the truth too – those of us who survive the final Winnowing. But by then, we'll be in charge ourselves. And if there's one group of people who have no motivation to change the system, it's those who have just fought their way through it to power.'

By now, we're back on our own level. I'm about to reply when a shrill scream echoes from the direction of the Third's chambers. Instantly, I break into a run. The door is ajar; I burst straight through, Niko hard on my heels, to find Calista backed into a corner. Though she looks almost as poised and deadly as usual, her knife wavers in her hand, blood dripping to the floor from a crimson-soaked sleeve. She's wounded. Her shield, Porphyry, is approaching her with a similar weapon, poised to strike.

'Porphyry!' I yell.

She turns, eyes wild, and lunges for me, faster than I would have thought possible. The air displaced by her blade brushes my skin as I pivot out of the way. Taking advantage of the near miss, I grab her arm with my left hand and yank her past me, trying to throw her off balance. My right fist connects hard with her abdomen. It should at least have driven her backwards, if not temporarily put her out of action. Yet she doesn't so much as falter. She spins round and barrels into me, knocking me to the floor. My head bounces off the stone, jarring my teeth and sending sparks of light flashing across my vision. This isn't good. I've never sparred with Porphyry before – we're too far apart in age to have been together in training – but I know she's skilled and strong.

'Porphyry!' I pant. I still have a weakening grip on her arm, but the knife is inching towards my throat. 'I'm no threat to you. To Calista. Stop it!' But she's looking right through me, the scar on her cheek burning a fierce white against her skin. I don't think she even knows who I am.

I suck in a deep breath, gathering my strength. Then I push up with my hips and hook her other arm inward, rolling her over. She bucks and writhes, snarling at me, trying to throw me off. I hold her down and slam her knife hand against the floor until her fingers open. The weapon skitters away from us.

'Niko,' I say through gritted teeth. 'The antidote.'

He drops down beside us, one of the tubes from Alexios in

291

his hand. Porphyry thrashes wildly, but I keep her pinned and Niko pinches her nose closed, forcing her to open her mouth while he pours in the antidote. She splutters, then gradually subsides. Her eyes struggle to focus on my face.

'Feldspar?' she mumbles. 'What's going on?'

I release my death-grip on her wrists. 'Nothing. It's all right.'

'I'm really tired.'

'Probably best if you sleep for a bit.'

Her eyes close. Niko grabs a cushion from a nearby chair and tucks it under her head, while I sit on the floor beside her and wait for my pulse to slow to something approaching a normal level. Perhaps we really are getting closer to the truth. The murderer must be panicking or they wouldn't have attempted a daytime kill – the others were done at night, when there was much less chance of anyone being around to intervene.

'Are you all right?' Niko asks Calista.

'I'll live.' She emerges from the corner, wincing as she drops her knife. Her gaze moves from Niko to me, and her lip curls; but what she says is, 'I owe you. Both of you.'

'You should see a medic. Or Alexios.'

Her head tilts in the direction of a nearby cupboard. 'Pass me a bandage and I'll be fine.'

He does it.

'Weren't you told about the poison?' he asks as she wraps

the bandage around her arm. 'Not to allow your shield to drink anything unless you were sure it was safe?'

'Don't blame me,' Calista says. 'I knew it, and Porphyry did too. She's the one who recklessly endangered both our lives.' Yet despite the irritable tone, her eyes are soft as she looks at her shield.

'Then what happened?'

'I don't know. After I heard about Pyrene's death this morning, I was . . . upset.' Her tone suggests she will answer any questions on that subject with violence. 'And I hadn't slept, either, so I suppose in the end I dozed off. Only to be woken by Porphyry attacking me.'

'She attacked you in your sleep and you *still* survived?' I blurt out.

'Yes. And?'

'It's impressive, that's all.'

For a moment, she looks both surprised and pleased: two emotions I've never seen on her face before. Then the sneer returns. 'Guess you're easily impressed.'

So, being attacked by her own shield hasn't changed her all that much. But she's answering our questions, which would present me with a good opportunity if I could only think what to ask. We have to assume that her own near death rules her out as a suspect – *Unless*, a sceptical inner voice that sounds very like Niko says, *she and Karissa were working together right up until Karissa turned on her* – but I'm sure she must know something useful.

'Daisy is dead,' I say slowly. 'Did you know?'

Calista shrugs. 'Should I know who that is?'

'She was your first-nurse.' I don't hammer home what that means for Porphyry, but Calista knows as well as I do that an ascendant's first-nurse is usually the shield's mother. Her expression softens, ever so slightly. Taking that as an encouraging sign, I press on. 'Did she ever tell you anything about a friend she had? Another nurse, called Clover?'

'If this Daisy was my first-nurse, then I left her when I turned four. Who remembers being that age?' She frowns. 'Though her name does sound familiar . . . She was Pyrene's second-nurse, right?'

I nod.

'Pyrene once told me that her second-nurse made her promise to look after Karissa and Quartz. That's why she used to stand up for them, when I . . .' For the first time ever, Calista fails to look arrogant; she ducks her head, picking at a non-existent thread on her sleeve. 'I'm going to miss her.'

'You and Pyrene were friends?' Niko asks softly.

'No, Nikolos.' Her chin tilts up, the usual look of amused condescension returning to her face. 'We hated each other. But that was what made it fun.'

'If it's any consolation, she might not have survived much longer anyway,' I confess. What Niko and I discovered in the archive is still sitting like a weight in my stomach, too heavy to ignore. Calista turns on me with something close to a snarl.

'What's that supposed to mean?'

'The final Winnowing . . . we found out that it's always the ascendants alone. No drones or cutters or carders needing to be forced out of the Hive. Just you, killing each other, until you're whittled down to the exact number needed to form an Apex.'

She shakes her head dismissively, but I can see doubt behind it. 'They wouldn't.'

'They would, and you know it,' Niko says. 'Didn't it ever occur to you that there are more of us than places in the Apex? Think of the older generation: seven of them living, yet twelve were born. Feldspar and I have seen the records. And those same people are meeting at this exact moment, talking about bringing forward the final Winnowing for us. This time tomorrow, you could be stabbing your family to death.'

'I don't believe you.'

'A week ago, I wouldn't have believed it either,' I say quietly. 'But it's true.'

'We've told you what we learnt, Calista.' Niko is already heading for the door. 'Do what you like with it. In the meantime, we have a murderer to catch.'

SEVEN DAYS AFTER

As soon as we've left Calista's chambers, Niko turns to me in excitement. 'Why would Daisy ask Pyrene to look after Karissa and Quartz – a pair she'd never nursed, and had no reason to care about – unless . . . ?'

'Unless she did have a reason,' I agree. 'Unless Quartz was her best friend Clover's child.'

'Which, if Zephrine's story is true, makes Quartz's father a member of the Apex. But why would Karissa be willing to kill Daisy to keep that secret?'

Slowly, trying to unpick it, I say, 'What if Quartz is different from the other shields?'

'What do you mean?'

'Everyone overlooks the shields.' Now my thoughts are running too fast for me to keep up; I do my best, stumbling over my words. 'I overlooked the shields, even though I was one . . . When I saw that the evidence didn't fit one ascendant,

I jumped to two or more working together . . . but what if it's an ascendant and a shield? What if Karissa and *Quartz* worked together to commit the murders? Pyrene would have trusted Karissa. And Quartz could have strangled her. She's a shield. She's strong enough—'

'Slow down,' Niko says, his gaze intent on my face. 'How would Quartz have broken her conditioning?'

'Maybe she didn't need to. Maybe she never had it. In which case, there's only one member of the Apex who could possibly be responsible . . .' I take a deep breath. 'Niko, what if *Ixion* is Quartz's father?'

He sees what I'm getting at straight away. 'Then he wouldn't have applied shield conditioning to his own daughter. He'd have wanted to make sure she could defend herself, no matter the situation.'

'And he might have warned Quartz about the final Winnowing,' I say. 'That would have given her and Karissa a clear motive to get all the most dangerous ascendants out of the way before the time came. They're trying to protect themselves. Nothing to do with the secret group at all.'

'We can assume that Quartz has the ability to use a blowpipe and a garrotte. Meanwhile, Karissa has access to crimson algae, so she could have made kratos and had Quartz slip it into the other shields' strengthening water—'

'And Flint and Quartz are in love!' I conclude triumphantly. 'Which explains how Karissa learnt how to make kratos. Flint

297

knew more about it than Alexios realized, and he passed it on to Quartz. Which makes him partly responsible for all this, but of course he couldn't have known what would happen.'

Niko hugs me. I think it surprises him as much as it surprises me; he lets go almost straight away, looking embarrassed, though he's also smiling. It's a good thing I'd already finished setting out my theory, because my thoughts seem to have completely disintegrated. All I can focus on is the way my entire body is glowing with warmth where he touched me. My gaze locks with his, and he moves a half-step forward as if he's going to hug me again. I *want* him to hug me again, although I'm not sure what I'll do if he does. But then he looks away, leaving my heart pounding as if I've been running.

'You may very well be right,' he says, rather hoarsely. 'But although this is amazingly *good* conjecture, it's still conjecture. Without evidence, I doubt the queens will take us seriously.'

'Whoever killed Euphemie, I cut their arm deeply enough that the mark will still be there,' I remind him. 'Finding that would be something, at least.'

'All right. Then it's time to pay Karissa a visit.'

Predictably, Karissa is in the treasury, where she spends much of her time. Euphemie and I came here once a month, to collect her allowance from the treasurer, but we never went inside. Although the work that's done here is important – keeping track of all the resources of the Hive and how they flow back and forth between the upper levels and the Honey-comb, including food and goods as well as the tokens that can be exchanged for those things – Euphemie had no interest in it.

The room is quiet. With the treasurer – Gregor – still in the same meeting that kept Trystan out of our way earlier this afternoon, only Karissa and two cutter scribes are here, each of them bent industriously over their desk. Their surroundings are tidy and polished, with shelves of perfectly aligned ledgers, as well as a neat metal rack containing paper, ink and pens. Quartz stands behind Karissa, watching the door and looking bored; although her arms are folded, I can see the fingers of one hand plucking out a rhythm on her sleeve. It must be dull for her, trapped within these four walls day after day, seeing the same handful of people and forced to remain alert for a threat that will never come. But then, perhaps she prefers that to a situation like the one on the training floor the other day. Better to be bored than in fear for her charge's life.

Or perhaps, I remind myself, *Karissa and Quartz's mundane routine is just camouflage for their true nature.*

When we enter, Quartz says something urgent under her breath to Karissa, but it isn't until Niko orders the scribes out of the room and closes the door behind them that Karissa looks up.

'Nikolos?' She sounds just as pleased and shy as she did when he talked to her before. 'What are you doing here?'

'I have some further questions for Quartz,' he replies, at his most dark-eyed and inscrutable. 'And I brought something along to make sure she answers them properly.'

We agreed before we arrived that instead of jumping straight in with accusations, it would be a good idea to try and force Quartz into revealing her faulty conditioning. That would give us the proof we need. But since even a fully conditioned shield can hurt another ascendant in defence of her own charge, first we need to create a situation in which a threat to Quartz can in no way be interpreted as a threat to Karissa.

From a pocket, Niko retrieves a long, slender piece of metal with a rounded ball at one end and a series of teeth at the other. It looks suspiciously like a torture device; Quartz takes a step back, glancing at her charge as if preparing to defend her.

'I want you to hold this,' Niko tells her. 'If you give me the truth, you'll be fine. If you lie, you'll be dead before you've finished speaking.'

'Please, don't—' Karissa scrambles up out of her chair. Niko pins her with a glance.

'Queens' orders,' he says. 'Unless you want me to tell them your shield refused to answer my questions.' Then, to Quartz, 'Take it.'

'Yes, Sixth.' Quartz extends a tentative hand towards the device, only to snatch it back when a spark stings her skin. Again she looks nervously at Karissa, and I wince in sympathetic memory. I remember how terrifying it is to face interrogation with the dark arts when you don't know what the dark arts actually are.

'Relax,' Niko says. 'I don't intend to hurt Karissa. You're the one I'm interested in.'

'But—'

'There's nothing to be afraid of, as long as you're honest.'

She hesitates. 'What if I can't be?'

'Then you die.'

'But you don't understand. Karissa can't—'

Niko presses the metal device into her hand. 'Can't what?'

'Survive without me.' Quartz closes her eyes. 'All right. I'll give you whatever truth you want. Just . . . please don't kill us.'

By now, I'm thoroughly confused. If she were keeping the secrets we think she's keeping, surely she would have fought back against Niko by now and revealed her broken conditioning. She believes that answering his questions will condemn her anyway, so why wouldn't she take the risk of trying to silence us, given the amount of blood already on her hands?

'Very good,' Niko says. 'But the thing is, Quartz, we already *know* the truth. We know about you and Karissa. About Ixion.'

I'm watching Karissa carefully, but there's no need for any perspicacity. The horror on her face confirms our suspicions straight away.

'Please don't tell anyone,' she begs. 'Quartz and I are both happy with the way things are. We don't want to get Ixion in trouble . . .'

She dissolves into tears. Quartz looks at us defiantly.

'Flint and I are happy,' she says. 'I won't be an ascendant. I *won't*.'

What? I'm completely lost. But Niko says to Quartz, in a wondering tone of voice, 'Karissa was born before you.'

She shrugs, clutching his bit of metal as if it's a weapon.

'The blood-codes in their record,' he says, turning to me. 'Remember? The order of the codes didn't match the birthdays. According to what's written in the archive, Quartz was born the day before Karissa. That matches what Daisy told us – that Clover attended a royal birth just after her own baby was born. But the numbers in the blood-codes were the other way round. The *correct* way round.' He looks back at Karissa. '*You're* Ixion's forbidden child. It's Quartz, not you, who is the Elder Queen's daughter and a potential heir to the throne.'

She bows her head, still sobbing.

'He swapped the two of you when you were babies. So that his child would be an ascendant and have a chance at a better life. That's what Daisy meant, when she said Clover *wished she hadn't done it*. Though why he didn't swap the blood-codes too ...'

'He couldn't.' I'm reeling from the shock of this revelation – *Quartz* should be the ascendant, and *Karissa* the shield? – but I can answer that point, at least. 'I told you, the medics set the code at birth, and they take a blood sample every time someone visits the medical centre. Not only would it be too

302

dangerous for someone to have the wrong blood-code, but it would soon be discovered.'

'Right. It's as you said. The error is in the records, not in the blood-codes. They have the codes they were given when they were born; Ixion couldn't change that. All he could do was swap the information associated with each code, and hope that no one ever noticed the anomaly in the numbering.'

'Which was a reasonable hope,' I say dryly. 'Given that you're the only person in the Hive who would even have thought about it.'

He shoots me a swift grin, before turning to Karissa. 'How did you find out?'

'Ixion told me when I was quite young. He wanted to make sure I never let Quartz do anything that would put her life at risk. Because if she died, I'd die too.'

Of course. Their shield-bond was formed in the womb; putting Karissa and Quartz in each other's places doesn't change the fact that it's the child born a shield whose life depends on the child born an ascendant. When Quartz said that Karissa couldn't survive without her, she meant it literally.

'And that's why you killed so many ascendants?' Niko asks. 'To try and keep yourself safe? Because Quartz is conditioned to protect you, yet you can never let her do it.'

'You killed the very people who were working to free the shields,' I burst out. 'They could have helped you, if you'd given them a chance.'

Karissa shakes her head. 'I don't know anything about that.'

'And she didn't kill anyone,' Quartz puts in. 'Neither of us did. Karissa told me the truth straight after she found out, and all we've done since is stay out of trouble.'

'You were never tempted to tell anyone?' Niko asks. 'To claim your rightful place?'

But I know the answer to that without needing to see Quartz shake her head. By the time she found out, she'd already learnt to view Karissa as the centre of her world. Even if she'd wanted the position of ascendant for herself, she wouldn't have risked Karissa getting hurt as a result of the truth being revealed.

'What about Alexios's poison? Are you going to tell us you didn't get the details of it from Flint? And Karissa has access to red ink as a source of crimson algae—'

'Anyone can buy red ink,' Quartz says. Then, shifting uncomfortably, she adds, 'Although you're right. Flint did tell me about kratos.'

'Quartz!' Karissa hisses, but the shield holds up the metal device.

'I have to tell the truth, don't I?'

'You do,' Niko says gently, taking it from her. 'But I'd rather you did it willingly.'

Quartz hesitates, then nods. 'You know the worst of our secrets already. And you stood up for us against Calista . . .' She meets my gaze. 'Flint knew how to make kratos. He told me about it – he was distraught after what happened, after he attacked the Eighth. And I told the shieldmaster.'

My nails dig into my palms. Ixion knew how to make the poison. Ixion, who has a secret daughter, against everything that's written in Melissa's law books. No doubt he'd do anything to protect her, and to prevent anyone from learning the truth. Yet I can't believe it. Not of him.

'Will you both show us your left arm?' Niko asks Karissa and Quartz.

The two of them look bemused, but obediently roll up their sleeves. Neither Quartz's muscled arm nor Karissa's slender one bears any trace of a healing wound.

'Well, then,' Niko says grimly. 'We'd better talk to Ixion.'

'No,' Karissa breathes. 'You don't think . . . No. He wouldn't have.'

'Not even to make sure you survived the final Winnowing?' He takes in the lack of surprise on her face. 'So you did know about that. Well, then. By removing the older ascendants, Ixion makes sure you won't be a target.'

Having children can do strange things to a person: that's what Daisy told Zephrine. I can understand why Ixion might have wanted to keep his daughter safe, but surely he couldn't justify such a cruel way of going about it.

'He was kind to me,' Karissa says, starting to cry again. 'Quartz and I used to go to the training floor all the time so she could practise, but really it was so Ixion and I could talk. It was nice, having a father – being loved . . .' She sniffs. 'He wanted me to be safe and happy. He told me that himself. And you're right: he did tell me about the final Winnowing. But that's why I've always been so set on becoming treasurer! It gave the others a reason to keep me alive, to do the job they didn't want. So why would Ixion have killed for me?'

'We already know he wasn't the figure I saw with the blow-pipe,' I add. 'It doesn't fit.'

'But that's the only part that doesn't,' Niko says. 'He had a motive. He knew about kratos, and was in a better position than anyone to slip it into the shields' strengthening water. Pyrene wouldn't have believed him a threat, so he easily could have strangled her. As far as I'm concerned, he's now our prime suspect.' His gaze moves over all three of us. 'I'm sorry.'

I don't know how to feel. I realize, now, that I've never just wanted to uncover the truth. All along, I've wanted revenge. A chance to look Euphemie's killer in the eye and make them pay. But we're talking about *Ixion*. The person who taught me everything I know. Without him, I wouldn't have saved Niko's life or Calista's. And I can't reconcile the man who helped me understand what it really meant to be a shield, who encouraged me to stay alive so I could keep my charge alive, with the idea of a murderer who forced his own students to turn on the same people he'd taught them how to protect.

Your task is not to sacrifice yourself, his voice comes back to me. *By dying for your ascendant, you would condemn her to death.*

Of course he said that to us. To me, and Flint, and Quartz. Because he knew that if Quartz died, his daughter would die too. Did everything else he told me have an ulterior motive? Did he really train all those shields, knowing that one day he would set out to destroy them?

The idea makes me feel shivery and weak, as if I have a fever, but I can't reject it. Not in the face of the evidence. Dismissing the most probable theory because I don't like it wouldn't be science at all.

'We should go and find him,' I say numbly. 'Last period of the day before sundown . . . Assuming the Apex's meeting ends in time, he'll be on the training floor.'

'Please,' Karissa whispers. 'Try not to hurt him.'

'If he wiped out four ascendants and three shields for your sake, he's much more likely to hurt us.'

She swallows. 'I hope you stay safe. I hope this is all a misunderstanding.'

I wonder what she'll do if we don't come back. Nothing, probably. Telling the truth about what happened to us would condemn her father, as well as reveal her own identity – and I can't believe the Apex would treat her kindly for masquerading as an ascendant all this time. Maybe she'd be executed. Since we can't expect her to risk her life for us, we're on our own.

'Whatever happens,' I say, 'we won't tell anyone about you and Quartz. I promise.'

Before she can answer, Gregor enters the room, the scribes

scurrying behind him. He gives Niko a glance that's hard to interpret – somewhere on the scale from disappointment to outright contempt – but doesn't speak to either of us. Rather, he addresses Karissa.

'Go back to your chambers. You have an important day ahead of you tomorrow. Unless the murderer is found beforehand, that's when our queens will be choosing their heirs.'

SIXTH MURDER

SEVEN DAYS AFTER

'What was that thing you made Quartz hold?' I ask numbly, as Niko and I make our way to the training floor.

'No idea. I took it from the metal parts store in the Honey-comb because I liked the shape of it.'

'Oh.'

We keep walking. Then Niko says, 'Feldspar.'

He's stopped, so I do too. We're alone in the corridor. A stormglow panel blinks gently behind him.

'I'm relying on you,' he says.

'What?'

'We're going to talk to Ixion now. Right?'

I nod.

'Even though, as soon as he finds out what we know, he'll probably try to kill us. Right?'

I hesitate, then nod again.

'Then I think you're the only chance we have of getting out alive.'

'But—'

He meets my gaze. His expression is serious, uneasy, as if he's about to make a terrible confession.

'You think we have the dark arts on our side,' he says. 'But I'm a fraud, Feldspar. All I really have is Astrapē. The rest of it is just stories.' His lips twist wryly. 'The dark arts . . . they're my shield, if you like. I wasn't willing to risk another boy dying for me, or to take people's lives in the Winnowings. But that doesn't mean I wanted the other ascendants to bully me the way they did Karissa for not playing her part. I needed *something*.'

I can't help smiling. 'Do you think I don't know that?'

He stares at me.

'All the mystery, and the rumours, and the coat . . .' I wave my hand to encompass the whole of him. 'I know you used it as a form of protection. Maybe forced on you, to begin with, until you saw how you could use it. Do you think I've spent all this time with you without figuring that out? But, Niko . . . as far as I can see, the dark arts mean science, and logic, and refusing to believe something just because everyone else does. They mean being curious and empathetic and – and *wildly* untidy. And, no, none of that is what people *think* the dark arts are, but it isn't nothing!'

'No,' he says, after a long pause. 'It isn't nothing.' A smile flickers on his face, then dies again. 'But I can't defeat Ixion with science. If he's the one who killed all those people, directly or indirectly, then he's what I only pretend to be: dangerous. And that's why I'm relying on you to protect me.'

'I can't,' I say automatically. 'You know that. I'm forbidden to hurt any member of the royal family except in defence of my own charge.'

'You heard what Ixion himself said. That's only conditioning. It might be hard to break, but it can be broken.'

'What Ixion said,' I repeat. 'The man we're about to accuse of murdering multiple ascendants and shields. You think we can believe anything he's told us?'

Niko freezes, his eyes locked on mine. Then, calmly, he says, 'Punch me.'

My stomach clenches. 'What?'

'Punch me.'

I can't. I'm not allowed. Something terrible will happen. Faintly, I say, 'I'm not going to—'

'Euphemie is dead, and it's his fault.' He leans forward, speaking through the sickening twist in my stomach and the ringing in my ears. '*Punch me.*'

I do it. Even as my fist flies forward, I can't believe it's really happening. But then it connects with his upper arm, and he staggers backwards, and an instant later I feel the impact of it ringing in my knuckles.

'Ow,' he says mildly.

'You did tell me to.'

He prods the spot, then winces. 'You didn't have to do it that hard.'

'I didn't think I was going to do it at all!'

'At least now we know you can defend yourself.'

'But how—'

'*You're not a shield any more*, Feldspar. I know you hate me saying that, but this time it matters. No one's ever been in your position before. Which means you can do *anything*.'

This time, the concept of infinite possibility doesn't terrify me. Instead, it gives me a light, buoyant sensation.

'You're capable enough for both of us,' he says, cementing the feeling. 'Just keep us alive. I'll do the rest.'

When we reach the training floor, we find Ixion teaching a group of young soldiers: barely out of the nursery, by the look of them, aged eight or nine. They're in pairs, practising some basic forms of duelling, while Ixion and his shield – Rhyolite – move round and correct them. Perhaps some of them are the last children that Daisy looked after before she died. The idea makes my chest ache.

Niko heads straight for Ixion, his coat billowing behind him. The stormglow flickers overhead. He doesn't stop for anything. And the young soldiers part for him, falling back and falling silent as he crosses the floor. I follow, equal parts impressed and unsettled. Even knowing the truth about the dark arts, I can't deny the power he has over the room. Part of it is rumour – has always been rumour – but it helps that Niko is very good at projecting an aura of utter confidence. If it weren't for our last conversation, I'd almost believe it myself.

By the time we reach Ixion, though, my own confidence has dwindled to nothing. Niko thinks I can protect him, but this is the *shieldmaster*. He trained me. Not only does he know more than I know, he's also aware of every single fear and weakness I possess. How can I possibly expect to defend us against him?

'We know the truth,' Niko says, just as Rhyolite arrives beside Ixion. He'd started crossing the room as soon as we entered, sensing a possible threat to his charge. It's no more than I would have expected, but all the same, I have to dig my nails deep into my palms in order to stand my ground. Ixion alone is dangerous. The two of them together are deadly.

'What are you talking about?' Ixion demands. 'What truth?'

'That you murdered Euphemie and Pyrene. That you poisoned the shields of Leandros and Halimeda to turn against them. That you killed a nurse, Daisy, to prevent her from revealing your secret.'

Rhyolite's stance shifts, his hand hovering near his belt. I can't tell if he knows the accusations to be true or if they're an utter surprise; like me, he's trained not to reveal any emotion. And to be honest, it makes no difference. He's been with Ixion for decades. He'll defend him no matter what.

Ixion nods at his shield, which could mean *Be ready* or *Don't worry, I'll handle this* or anything in between. To us, he says, 'I did nothing of the kind. Now get out before I—'

'We know about Karissa,' Niko says. 'She told us herself.'

Ixion's gaze flicks to me. His angry expression has shifted to a blank mask. Yet behind it, I sense the furious whirring of his thoughts.

'Told you what?' he asks finally.

'What you are to her. Do you really want me to be more specific with all these young ones in the room?'

Ixion turns to the new soldiers, most of them watching us curiously.

'Training is over for today,' he says. 'Go back to your quarters.'

Then it's true. A cold stone settles in my stomach as they file out. Once the four of us are alone in the cavernous room, Niko keeps pushing.

'Then you admit it? You had a daughter, against the laws of the Hive. She was bonded as a shield. But you swapped her with her charge at birth.'

'Yes.'

Rhyolite's expression is still impassive. He must have known, surely. However well trained he is, he couldn't have heard that confession for the first time without some kind of reaction. Which means, whatever Ixion has done, Rhyolite must be in on it too. It's like being kicked when I've already been stabbed.

'You believe being an ascendant who'll die if her shield dies is better than being a shield?' Niko asks Ixion.

'Karissa is free. Her life isn't bound up in servitude. She isn't conditioned to value another's life before her own. That's all I wanted for her.'

'Then you agree the shield-bond is wrong,' I whisper. 'Conditioning too. Yet you let the rest of us suffer it.'

'You didn't suffer,' Ixion says. 'Because you didn't know any better.'

I shake my head. That doesn't make it right.

'If you wanted your daughter to be safe, then why did you kill the ascendants who could have made that happen?' Niko demands. 'Halimeda, Leandros, Pyrene . . . all of them wanted to free the shields and abolish the Winnowings.'

'I've no idea what you're referring to. I didn't kill anyone, and you have no evidence to show otherwise. Else you'd have presented me with it already, instead of trying to tangle me up with your endless talk.'

'The evidence is circumstantial,' Niko agrees. 'But if you don't confess, I'll be forced to take it to the Apex, and then the truth about Karissa will come out. I think we'd both like to avoid that.'

Ixion's mask remains in place, but once again I get the impression that he's thinking hard. Finally, he says, 'All right. Leave Karissa alone and I'll admit to everything. What difference does it make now?' He pauses, seeming to brace himself. Around us, the room is absolutely silent. Then he says, 'You're correct, Nikolos. I killed them.'

I try to stay alert, ready for any sign of attack, but my hands are shaking. How could he do this? How could he betray everything he ever taught us?

'Like you, they were full of talk,' he adds. 'But I knew it would never come to anything. And even if it did, it would be too late for Karissa. They'd only achieve what they wanted when they came to power.'

'By which time, Karissa could already have been killed in the final Winnowing,' Niko agrees.

'Exactly.' Ixion doesn't show any surprise that we know about this. 'The more ascendants I got out of the way, the fewer would have to die at the end, and the greater Karissa's chances of survival.'

'Still, was it really worth murdering so many of your own family? So many shields you trained yourself? I can under-stand you wanting to protect Karissa, but she's practically guaranteed to become treasurer. What made you think she'd be at risk in the final Winnowing?'

'To stay safe, Karissa has had to hold herself and Quartz back from joining in the other Winnowings,' Ixion says. 'And that has made her ill-liked among the older ascendants. It was better to be safe.'

'Only she's not, is she?' Niko shoots back. 'Because we saved Calista's life, earlier. And now Karissa is facing the final Winnowing early.'

For the first time, uncertainty crosses Ixion's face, but all he says is, 'It will be enough.'

'And Euphemie?' I can't restrain myself any longer. 'I saw the figure of the person who killed her, and it wasn't you. So how—'

He shrugs. 'One of my soldiers did it. But after she failed to silence Nikolos, she threatened to tell others, so I was forced to put an end to her.'

Something about that doesn't ring true to me, but I can't work out what. In the face of his horrifying indifference, I'm finding it hard to achieve coherent thought.

'Will you confess all this to the queens?' Niko presses.

The old scathing smile returns to Ixion's face. 'And what possible motive could I have for that? No. If somehow you managed to haul me in front of them, I'd contradict every word that came out of your mouth. I'd tell them I'd tested Feldspar more thoroughly and proven her conditioning broken. Who do you think they'd believe?'

'We're willing to take that chance,' Niko says stoutly.

'Luckily for you, I have no interest in wasting my time on it.'

Ixion pivots on his heel and heads for the door, Rhyolite at his shoulder. I shake off my frozen dismay and run after him, overtaking him near the edge of the room – where I draw my knives and turn so that I'm between him and the way out. 'I won't let you leave.'

'You?' His lip curls. 'You didn't even manage to keep

317

Euphemie alive. What makes you think you can beat us?'

I look from Ixion to Rhyolite, two of the most competent warriors in the Hive. 'I don't, but I'm willing to try. Because I might not have saved Euphemie, but you're the one who's responsible for her death.'

Rhyolite tenses. His spiky strip of hair is pure black today, I notice with the heightened attention to detail that comes with fear. 'Are you threatening the shieldmaster?'

'Yes. Yes, I—'

He punches me. I block it, but the impact knocks the knife from my hand. I try to stab him with the other one, but Ixion is there, wrenching my arm back, and now I've lost that weapon as well. As fast as that. I've sparred with these men before, for practice, but it's only now I understand how much they were holding back.

Ixion spins me round, pinning both my wrists behind me. This time, Rhyolite's punch lands, snapping my head back against Ixion's chest. Blood fills my mouth, the sickening taste of defeat, as Rhyolite raises his fist to hit me again—

'Stop it.' Suddenly, Niko is there between us, and Rhyolite freezes, uncertainty in his eyes. He can't hurt Niko without a direct threat to the shieldmaster.

'Where will you go, Ixion?' Niko asks a little breathlessly. 'Even if you get past us, you can't leave the Hive.'

'You think I'm not aware of your secret escape tunnel?' Ixion snaps. 'I run the patrols in the Honeycomb, Nikolos. I know exactly where you were planning to go, before Slate died.'

'We'll send people after you. You won't have time to get away.'

'You can't do that if you're dead.'

He yanks me to one side, throwing me off balance, and goes for Niko. Maximum efficiency, minimum fuss. A punch below the ribcage, doubling him over. A second blow to the kidneys. And now Niko is on the floor, and I'm screaming and hitting and kicking Ixion with every scrap of fighting technique erased from my head except the desire to inflict pain. My nails claw his face, deep enough to draw blood. My knee connects with his groin. But then there's a knife in his hand, and he's forcing me backwards. My back hits the door. He traps my wrists above my head with one hand. And then—

I feel the impact, followed an instant later by white-hot pain. My forearm is on fire. I try to struggle, but the heat flares higher, until every nerve ending seems concentrated in that single limb. Fighting for breath, I attempt to blink away the fuzzy spots in front of my eyes, but nothing happens. So I walk the fingers of my right hand up my left arm until they encounter the hot slipperiness of blood. Then the hilt of a knife. He's pinned me to the door.

I wait for the killing stroke, but it doesn't come. I don't know why. One of the most basic principles of battle the shieldmaster taught me is that when your opponent is incapacitated, you end her. Maybe Ixion can't bring himself to do it. Not face to face. Not to one of his students . . .

But he's already killed a soldier in cold blood. Not to mention the shields he's forced to act against every impulse he himself drummed into them, killing their charges, and themselves in the process.

'Shieldmaster,' Rhyolite says urgently. 'The Sixth—'

Niko. Did he make a break for it? There's another door, on the far side of this vast chamber. If he can fetch help—

'*You* finish her off,' Ixion says, and his footsteps sprint away. He's gone after Niko. At my flinch, another wave of agonizing heat radiates from my pinned arm. *Breathe through it, Feldspar.* I'm only going to have one shot at this.

I can see a little by now. Shapes and colours, enough to provide a basic sense of my surroundings. As the dark man-shaped blur that is Rhyolite looms over me, I yank the knife out of my flesh and lunge. The blade meets resistance, then breaks through it. He bellows, wrenching at my injured arm, and dizzy pain floods me again. Gritting my teeth, I push my weapon deeper. Then the two of us are falling, darkness swimming in my head.

When I open my eyes, I'm sprawled across Rhyolite's body. Both of us are drenched in blood, but I think most of it is his. He's dead, or if not, he soon will be. I must have blacked out for a moment. And Niko—

I struggle to my feet, lurching sideways, then righting

myself. The impact of the fall drove the knife partway back out of Rhyolite's body; it comes free easily. I pause only to bind my bleeding arm with the fabric belt from my trousers, so that I don't pass out. Then I hurtle across the training floor after Niko and the shieldmaster, wiping my bloody blade on my bloody clothes as I go.

Ixion must have caught Niko just before he reached the door. He's holding him tight against his own body, one hand with a knife to his throat. He looks up as I sprint across the floor towards him, and I slow to a halt.

'Let me leave,' he says. 'Or I kill him.'

You can't hurt the shieldmaster – but I ignore that residual flinch of reluctance. My gaze locks with Niko's, and it's as if he really can read my mind. He swings one heel sharply backwards, connecting with Ixion's shin. I use the distraction to hurl myself forward, driving my blade into the back of Ixion's wrist. His weapon scores Niko's skin, not deep enough to be lethal, before falling to the floor. I kick it away, pulling Niko out of his loosened grip. Ixion backs up a step and watches us calmly.

'Go ahead, Feldspar. The queens are waiting for an excuse to execute you. Killing me would hand it to them on a plate.'

'I don't care.' My voice wobbles. 'You had Euphemie killed. You let me take the blame. You acted like you despised me for something you'd done yourself—'

I stop. If I keep talking, I *will* cry again, and I'm not going to let that happen. Not in front of the man who taught me that tears were a source of shame. He looks at me, and I'm sure he knows everything I'm thinking. If he yelled an order at me right now, there's a good chance I'd obey it. Instead, he spreads his arms to his sides.

'Then finish it, if you can.'

The knife in my hand trembles violently. My conditioning can't stop me. This is a final defence of Euphemie, a way to protect her even in death. And yet he knows I can't do it. Not when he isn't trying to defend himself. Punching Niko when he asked me to was one thing, but *this*—

'She doesn't have to,' Niko says, tense but in control. 'If you won't give yourself up, then I'll stop you.'

'You?' Ixion swings to face him. 'You're incapable of wielding a blade, boy. You wouldn't have the stomach for it.'

'Ah, but you forget: the secrets of the dark arts are mine to command.'

Ixion snorts. 'You're clever, Nikolos. You know how to make that cleverness seem arcane. But you and I both know there is no such thing as *the dark arts*.'

'Nevertheless, I can stop you with a single word.'

'And that is?'

Niko hesitates. His vague gaze skims past my face, and my stomach sinks. What can he do? Ixion is right: cleverness is his weapon, and he's reached the end of it. But then—

'Astrapē,' he whispers.

A flicker flows down off his shoulder and through the air, coalescing into a shape larger and deadlier than any I've seen before: moonlight catching a shark's skin, glints of silver. It lunges at Ixion's throat, sinking into his flesh. For a heartbeat, nothing happens, and Ixion begins to smile—

Then the flickering is back, all over his body, like invisible flames. The smell of charred flesh fills the air. And Ixion screams.

Screams.

When Astrapē leaves him again, she's smaller: a dolphin, playful and innocent. She flows back to Niko, dancing sunlight on a summer's day. Behind her, the lifeless husk of Ixion's body topples to the floor. *Struck by lightning*.

'I guess the dark arts are real after all,' I mumble. And the world tilts around me as I keel over.

EIGHT DAYS AFTER

I thought I'd feel something, when I woke up this morning. And I do, physically: my arm is sore, my face is sore, pretty much my entire body is sore. But where my response to Ixion's death should be – the relief that we finally stopped a killer, or gratitude that Niko and I both survived – there's nothing. Just emptiness, tinged with guilt. In light of what we discovered, the queens have called off the early final Winnowing; that's something, at least. It gives us time to work out how to prevent it altogether. But that doesn't make me feel any less numb.

'Feldspar?' Niko enters his bedchamber, carrying a breakfast tray. After I collapsed yesterday, he grabbed a passing courier and sent her to fetch Alexios. The two of them brought me back here, where Alexios provided a sling for my arm and some medicine for the pain. Apparently, I came round a couple of times, asking for Euphemie, asking for Niko. I don't remember any of it. But once I woke up properly and started stringing together coherent sentences, Niko decided that must mean I needed feeding.

'Thank you,' I say, taking the tray. 'How are you feeling?' I know I'm the one who was wounded, but he killed a man too. More than that – his own uncle. That's a lot to deal with, for a boy who has always tried to avoid violence.

He sits on the edge of my bed. 'To be honest, I don't know how to feel. I mean . . . I was too late. Too many people died. I wish I'd been quicker. And I also think . . . perhaps I shouldn't have killed him. Perhaps he would have stopped anyway, after Calista. If we hadn't saved her, it would have left Karissa the eldest surviving female ascendant.'

'Or maybe he wouldn't,' I retort. 'Under the pressure of the early final Winnowing, maybe he would have gone after Zephrine as well. That would have made Karissa safer than anything – with only two female ascendants left alive, she would have become a queen by default. And really, from his point of view, what's the difference? More than that number of ascendants would have died anyway, in the end.'

'True.'

'Anyway,' I go on, trying to convince myself as much as Niko, 'it's what he'd already done that matters, not what he was going to do. We couldn't let him escape justice.'

'Then you think we did the right thing.'

'Yes.'

'Even if it doesn't necessarily feel like it.'

I wish I could express all my jumbled thoughts: how I admired Ixion and Rhyolite for years, how I still can't believe one was a murderer and the other his accomplice, how it makes me fear that you can't ever truly know anyone. How my guilt is partly for the fact that I killed Rhyolite and partly for the fact that I *didn't* kill Ixion, and partly for being alive at all when so many are dead. How I wish I could cry, because that would be far better than numbness. But Niko is dealing with his own confusion, so all I say is, 'You gave him a quicker death than he would have received from the Apex. That's the best he could have hoped for.'

We lapse into silence. I pick at my food. After a while, Niko says, 'Speaking of the Apex, we've been called to give evidence at noon. They want to understand exactly what happened.'

I tense. Every time I've seen either of the queens since Euphemie died, they've made no secret of wanting me dead. But surely it will be different now. I've helped Niko to stop the killer who's been decimating their children. That must count in my favour. Mustn't it?

'I'll be ready,' I say.

'And before we go, there's something I need to tell you.'

'All right.'

Rather than speaking, he scans my face as though searching for the tiniest of clues. His eyes are worried and not at all powerful. Astrapē flutters mothlike on his shoulder.

'My offer still stands,' he says finally. 'The tunnels.'

I gape at him. 'You think we should run *now*? Before we explain ourselves to the Apex? But why? Surely they'll take it as an admission of guilt and hunt us down – assuming we get further than the cutters' quarters. Queen Sirene banned you from the Honeycomb, remember?'

'We might be able to sneak out while they're waiting for us in the audience chamber. Even if we were killed in the attempt, it would be better than what awaits you up there.'

'I haven't done anything wrong.'

'No. I know. But, Feldspar . . .' He hands me a piece of paper. It's a copy of Euphemie's and my birth record.

'I don't understand,' I tell him.

'Look at the blood-codes.'

And that's when it hits me. I was born before Euphemie, yet the number at the start of my blood-code is one higher than hers. Just like Karissa and Quartz. Which means . . .

'No,' I whisper.

'It makes sense. The one thing we've never been able to solve is how you survived Euphemie's death, but when we learnt that Karissa and Quartz were swapped at birth . . . well. I realized that the simplest explanation for one of an ascendant–shield pair dying and the other surviving is that it was the *shield* who died.'

'But Niko, why . . . ?' Again I can't find the words, yet he seems to understand.

'When Ixion and Clover decided to cheat the system and

have a baby together, they must also have decided that they wouldn't allow their child to grow up as a disposable weapon – hence the swap. But they had to be sure that it would go undiscovered. So I think Ixion opted to try it out on a different pair first, and when he looked for suitable candidates . . .' Niko's hand covers mine. 'There you were. You and Euphemie. Still babies, and more to the point, babies who looked enough like each other for the swap to remain unnoticed.'

'But – but surely someone would have realized. My mother, Larkspur – she was our first-nurse—'

'Not *your* mother,' he reminds me gently. 'But, yes. Though people always said how alike you and Euphemie looked when you were little, your nurse could never have been fooled. Not the woman who gave birth to one of you, who had looked after you every day since.' His fingers tighten on mine. 'And that's why I think Ixion must have killed her too.'

I nod, drowning in a wave of that same unexpected sorrow that came over me when I first read my record and learnt that she'd died before I turned one. Niko's grip on my hand is like a lifeline, and I cling to it. Yet as the wave subsides, I feel my guilt over Ixion's death washing away with it. Almost since I was born, he's been murdering innocent people because they were in his way. He deserved what he got.

And I . . .

I am in Euphemie's place. She was in mine.

Like Quartz, I have been living a lie all this time.

I should have been an ascendant.

And if Euphemie had known, as Karissa did? Would she have confessed the truth and insisted on reinstating me? Or would she have clung to power, as everyone in the upper levels of the Hive clings to power, allowing it to consume their lives, allowing it to become more important than truth or justice or what is right?

I think I know the answer to that.

Niko's fingers and mine are still intertwined, but I flinch at the realization that we're now . . . what? Part of the same family, at least. Different sides – his mother is Queen Doralie and mine, apparently, is Queen Sirene – but all of a sudden, everything I feel when I touch him seems too complicated. I pull my hand away from his.

'*This* was what you meant when you said running would be better than what awaits me in the audience chamber?' I ask.

He doesn't look at me. 'It makes perfect sense, if you don't assume that death is worse than being an ascendant.'

It takes me a moment to parse that. When I get there, unexpected anger flares in me. 'Really? Being an ascendant is worse than death? You should try being a shield!'

'Feldspar—'

'I'm not going to run, Niko. And if you knew me at all, you'd understand why.'

'Fine,' he snaps. 'Take your place as the Seventh. There are few enough girls left that you'll have a good chance of becoming a queen.' He gives me a mocking bow. 'For what it's worth, you'll have my wholehearted support.'

Now I want to punch him. 'You're forgetting that to compete for the throne, I'd have to take a shield. And if you really believe I'd be willing to let another girl sacrifice her life for mine—'

'Of course I'm not forgetting that!' he yells at me. 'But what other option do you have? It's that or remain ineligible for the Apex and be wiped out in the final Winnowing. Which is what will happen to me, if I stay here. Or had *you* forgotten *that*?'

'Obviously not!' I yell back. 'Just because I can't become your shield any more, doesn't mean I'm going to let you die!' And then, softer – because my stomach is hurting the way it used to when Euphemie was cross with me, only worse – 'Niko, do you honestly think I'd try to become a queen at the expense of your life?'

He glares at me, not backing down, Astrapē all claws and snapping teeth. 'Why not? You've always seemed so sure of everything. How the world works. The rightful place we all have within it. So now that it turns out your rightful place is different from what you thought, why not make the most of it?'

I can't stay here. Flinging aside the covers, I clamber out of bed. The room spins, but I grit my teeth until it stops. I'm still wearing yesterday's bloodstained vest and trousers; that will have to be enough. When I reach the door, I turn to look at Niko.

'If this is true,' I say, 'then I have a chance to change things, for us *and* for the Hive. To do what Halimeda and Leandros and Pyrene wanted, and stop the Winnowings. Prevent any more children from being brought up to believe their lives only matter in relation to someone else's. You can do that too, Niko. The difference is, you always could have.'

Then I walk straight out of his chambers, without looking back.

After a blur of placing one foot in front of the other, trying not to feel or notice or think very much, I lift my head to find myself in the sunroom. I don't see any of the Apex, but Calista and Ophion are here with some of their followers. Word must have got around concerning Ixion's culpability and subsequent demise: they and their shields no longer look through me as if I'm already dead, instead regarding me with wary curiosity and – in Calista's case – a brief nod that's as close as she'll come to respect. I meet their collective gaze without flinching, wondering if they're happy to be the pre-eminent survivors. Wondering what they'd do if they knew that I'm technically their sister.

It's a strange feeling, after so long with no family at all. I am Queen Sirene's child; should I choose to accept that, I'll inherit a whole set of blood relatives. Leandros, dead and gone, who delighted in inspiring discomfort in those who were forbidden to defend themselves against him. Calista, beautiful and lethal. Ophion, the serpent, always ready to stab people in the back. I'm not convinced I want to be one of them. But then

331

there's Zephrine, whose kinship I would gladly claim . . .

I wish I knew what I should do. I wish I knew what *Euphemie* would have wanted me to do. I wish I knew whether her opinion still matters to me.

What I said to Niko is true: as an ascendant, I could make a difference. That on its own should be enough to sway me. Yet I'm not the only one to be affected by this decision. When I go before the Apex, they'll want to know the whole of it, including how I survived. That's what Niko was asked to investigate in the first place, after all. But the full and true explanation that instates me as the Seventh would also break my promise to Karissa and Quartz – because their story is intertwined beyond unravelling with mine. And then what? Quartz would be separated from Flint. Karissa might be executed for knowingly taking an ascendant's place. Even if we claimed they didn't know the truth, their lives would be torn apart. I don't think I have the right to do that.

Come on, I tell myself, looking up through the glass roof at the grey sky. *This is solvable. Use logic on it, like Niko would . . .*

But thinking about Niko makes me angry again. I can't believe he thought I'd take a shield and aim straight for the throne, leaving him to run or die alone. Not after everything. Was I really that unshakeably convinced of how life should work, back when we first met? If I'm honest . . . maybe. But you'd think he could see how much I've changed. How much I've *learnt*. His solution to all the problems of the Hive is to run from them, but surely there must be a better path forward. Not sacrificing myself for the colony, as I was always taught, but not abandoning it either. Both of those options accept that the way things are is the only way they can be, but change is possible. Niko himself taught me that.

The brightness of the light around me catches my eye. It's nearly noon. I have to go. Whether I'm ready or not, I have to find my way through the maze ahead of me.

SEVENTH MURDER

EIGHT DAYS AFTER

As I wait outside the audience chamber, tension swirls in my stomach. I'm not being accused of anything – not this time – but I still have to get this right. As far as I can see, there's only one path through it that protects everyone who needs protecting.

'Feldspar?' Niko has come up beside me. I turn to face him, but say nothing.

'I'm sorry,' he says.

I wait for the *but*. It doesn't arrive. Looking down at his feet, he goes on, 'After Slate died, I convinced myself that no one understood, but really, I didn't want them to. I liked believing I was different from them. Better. The only person to see the world's defects. Yet I never once tried to improve it. And I should have.'

'You were right about one thing,' I tell him. 'For seventeen years, I was convinced that the way the system worked was the only way it should work. Because that's what they did to me. That's what they do to all of us. But *you*—'

He lifts his head to meet my gaze. His expression is wary, as if he isn't sure quite where I'm going with this.

'You're the one who made me see things differently,' I say. 'You always treated me as a person, Niko, even before you knew I was . . .' I bite my lip. 'Part of your family.'

'Only in name. We're not related.'

Maybe this doesn't have to be complicated after all. Smiling, I say, '*Equal*, then. You always treated me as an equal.'

'That's because you always were.'

We look at each other, properly, as if for the first time. Little by little, my lingering hurt eases. Niko is supercilious and infuriatingly logic-driven and too smart for his own good, but he's also a genuinely kind person. He scoffed when I told him that before, but it's true. Like Euphemie, he isn't perfect, yet I can still choose to love him. Not the same way I loved her, but that doesn't make it better or worse – only different. I never realized before that there's more than one way to love someone. Perhaps as many ways as there are people.

'All right,' I say. 'In that case, I need you to do something for me. Two things, I suppose.'

'Go on.'

'I need you to trust me—'

'Done.'

'And I need you to let me take the lead in there. This is . . .

335

It's my life that was changed with the swap. My story. So it's up to me to decide how to tell it.'

'You don't need to explain,' Niko says. 'The first thing means it goes without saying that I'll do the second thing, if you ask me. Even though,' he adds with a virtuous expression, 'I would have taken great pleasure in walking the Apex through every step of our impressive deductive process.'

'And *that's* why I want to do the talking.'

'Rude, but ultimately fair.' He glances at the nearest storm-glow panel. 'We'd better get in there before they take offence at our lateness.'

Two guards search us for weapons, before ushering us through into the audience chamber. I know this is where the Apex meet to discuss the running of the Honeycomb, to hear requests and hold trials, but I've never seen it. I'm immediately daunted by its grandeur.

Behind us, at one end of the room, is an oval table with seven sturdy chairs, two of which are larger than the rest and marked with the royal emblem. That must be where meetings are held. But in front of us . . . We've definitely been called to a hearing, rather than a meeting. A single enormous golden throne sits in the middle of the far wall, its back stretching right up to the ceiling in an intricately carved design of hexagons interspersed with winged creatures, which I recognize, from my time in the Honeycomb, as bees. The two queens sit together on the throne, their shields standing at either side. To their left and right are five further seats, each with a tracery of golden lines. Four of those are occupied: chief advisor and treasurer on one side, head medic and keeper of the records on the other. The fifth seat is empty.

'Nikolos. Feldspar.' Queen Doralie takes the lead, rising to her feet with her shield's aid and fixing each of us with a hard stare. 'You have been called before us to account for the death of the shieldmaster. What have you to say for yourselves?'

It's a more aggressive start than I expected. Niko sent the Apex a message immediately after Ixion's death, outlining what had happened. They already know we identified him as the murderer. All the same, I begin politely, 'He is dead because he tried to kill us, ma'am. And he did *that* in an attempt to escape justice. He was the one behind all the ascendants' deaths.'

'Be careful what you say,' she snaps. 'Easy enough to brand my brother a murderer, now that he is gone.'

While here you stand, still alive, is the unspoken implication. *As much of a waste of resources as ever*. My guilt over Ixion's death undergoes a surprising resurgence.

'Ma'am,' Alathea says softly. 'We should hear their full testimony, as we intended.'

The Elder Queen hesitates, before sitting back down.

'Fine,' she snaps. 'Start with the events of yesterday.'

So, avoiding any mention of Karissa or Quartz, I explain how we accused Ixion of murder. How he admitted it. How he died.

'I killed him,' Niko says. 'With the dark arts.'

337

'We both did it,' I correct him firmly. 'But since the shield-master had just confessed, and was doing his best to kill us at the time, we had reason.'

Queen Sirene smiles. It seems she's been waiting for this. 'The reason doesn't matter. You are a shield who helped to kill a member of the royal family without the justification of defending your own charge, and therefore – whatever that person's crimes – your own life is forfeit.'

And there I was, thinking that at least I wasn't being accused of anything this time. How naive. Still, I retain my composure.

'Perhaps, ma'am, you would be willing to listen to the entire report before making a judgement on that. You haven't yet heard how we knew Ixion was guilty, and how I survived Euphemie's death – and, as it happens, they were one and the same.'

Though she gives almost nothing away, I catch the light of interest in her eyes – because she's wanted the answer to the second question since I was first arrested. 'Go on.'

I pause, making sure I have my story straight.

'Ixion killed Euphemie first,' I say, 'because he knew I would survive it. And he knew that because he swapped us when we were babies.'

Sirene opens her mouth to speak, but Alathea gets in first. 'Why would he have done that, Feldspar?'

'It was an accident,' I say, hoping this will be enough. Hoping I won't have to implicate Karissa and Quartz. 'By the time he discovered his error, my conditioning had already begun – so he never told anyone. But when he began to resent the endless work of protecting the royal family without ever being allowed children of his own – when he began to consider how he could take his revenge for that – his mistake became a weapon. He knew that once a shield was seen to survive her charge's death, no one would look elsewhere for a suspect when other ascendants began to die.'

With a face like a storm cloud, Sirene shakes her head. 'This fantasy will get you nowhere.'

'It's true. And Niko has the proof.'

Taking his cue, Niko steps forward and explains the blood-codes, before handing over his copy of my birth record. In turn, each of the Apex studies the sheet of paper. I can't begin to predict what they'll do. The whole thing must be a huge embarrassment to them. Maybe they'll simply kill me and Niko so that the secret never gets out ...

'All right,' Sirene says at last. 'With Xavierre's expertise to draw on, we'll soon settle this.' Then, to the head medic herself, 'Will a blood sample be enough?'

'Yes, ma'am,' Xavierre says. 'Allow me to fetch a kit and I'll find an answer for you.'

There are no more questions while we wait. Sirene watches me narrowly; the rest of the Apex murmur among themselves. When the head medic returns, I extend my arm for the blood sample to be taken, and Sirene does the same. We wait some more while Xavierre compares our blood, then speaks to

Sirene in a low voice. Once she's finished, the queen stands up, her expression unreadable. The entire room falls silent to hear the verdict.

'I cannot deny it,' Sirene says. 'You are my daughter, and a true ascendant. And you have defended yourself well.'

She moves towards me, hands outstretched, but I step back. Moments ago, she was desperate to execute me. Yet now, upon discovery of my bloodline, how quickly her verdict has shifted from murder to self-defence. Is that really how the world should work? With the morality of killing wholly dependent on who I'm related to?

At my retreat, her hands drop. She inclines her head, sadly, as if she understands my reluctance.

'I am sorry, Feldspar,' she says. 'For everything you have suffered. But this is your chance, now, to step into the light. To take your rightful place as a royal daughter and a possible future queen. Will you accept it?'

I don't reply straight away. I think of what my life was as a shield, and what it could be as an ascendant. I think of the tracker under my skin. I wonder if Sirene truly believes it to be that *simple*: that the sole flaw in the world was the swapping of babies, and if they are restored to their starting positions, then all will be made right. I reflect that once, not so long ago, I would have believed the same.

But I've chosen the only path that makes sense, and I have to see it through.

'Yes,' I say. 'Yes, I will.'

'Excellent.' Sirene seems excited by my capitulation. I suppose, to her, I represent another chance to see her line continue. One more daughter than she thought she had left this morning. And this woman is my mother . . . My stomach lurches with revulsion.

'As such, I would like to claim a reward,' I push on. *Follow the path.* 'Not for myself, but for Niko. Without him, I never would have been reinstated. In fact –' and here I let my voice sharpen – 'I would have been executed.'

Doralie has the grace to look somewhat abashed, but Sirene is unaffected. 'Indeed. I think we all agree that we have reason to be grateful to Nikolos. What is it that you wish to claim on his behalf?'

'After his first shield died, Niko refused another. As a result, despite the many skills he has to offer, he is currently not permitted to play any part in the future of the Hive – and that seems wrong.' I take a deep breath. This is an important step for both of us. 'Therefore, I would like to request that the rules be amended so that not only are ascendants allowed to remain without shields, if that is their preference, but such ascendants are still permitted to take a role in the Apex.'

'Is this what you want, Nikolos?' his mother asks softly.

He hesitates. No doubt this isn't the reward he would have chosen for himself; no doubt he would have asked for his own laboratory or a coat with even *more* pockets. Yet he must see the sense in it, given that he'll no longer be hounded to take another shield or be considered disposable in the final Winnowing – and so he keeps his word, in his own way. 'Apparently, yes.'

'Then I see no reason to reject the request,' Doralie says, and Sirene shrugs agreement. 'Unless, Alathea, there is anything in the law that precludes it?'

'I don't believe so,' the chief advisor says. 'But I will double-check the texts to make sure. The request can be ratified next time we meet.' She glances at me, and there's a smile in her eyes. *We can uphold the spirit of Melissa's word without following it to the letter*, she told us before. I doubt she'll bring forward any evidence that would prevent the change.

Following her lead, the other members of the Apex murmur agreement. An official vote confirms it.

'Very well,' Sirene says. 'Add it to the record as a royal decree. And then, Euphemie, we must see about reinstating you.'

My stomach heaves so violently that I'm sure I'm going to be sick. It really is as simple as that, for her. I was named Euphemie at birth, so I'm still Euphemie. It's only *Feldspar*, a mere shield, who died. Our names can be taken from us and swapped around, because as far as she's concerned, we're inter-changeable as people. What matters is that the one who bears her blood survived.

'First,' she goes on, oblivious to my inner turmoil, 'we'll have to bond you to a new shield. A few of the best soldiers are around your age. And at least you don't look *completely* wrong for your status . . .'

Her gaze touches the fuzz of hair on my scalp. Shame I didn't find time to shave this morning, just to spite her.

'Ordinarily, I would say it was too late to aspire to become my heir,' she adds, 'given your lack of proper schooling and our unfamiliarity with you as a candidate. However, you have shown great capability over the past week – and, of course, recent events mean that the field is wide open . . .'

I shudder.

'With the greatest of respect, ma'am,' I force out, 'I think *first* should be removing the tracker from my hand.'

'Really? But it will take some time to extract without dislodging it into your bloodstream. I wouldn't want to see *that* kill you, after you have survived so much.'

'I have lived long enough as a shield. I want to be who I was born to be.'

She considers that, then nods. 'Very well. I understand.'

The rest of the Apex plus Niko clear the room, leaving me in relative privacy: only Sirene, Xavierre and their shields to deal with. While my hand is being probed with the needle, I close my eyes to avoid anyone trying to speak to me, and I repeat the same mantra to myself. *Follow the path. Follow the path.* I might not like any of this, but it's the only way forward.

Once the head medic has finished her work, she speaks to the Younger Queen quickly again before leaving. I feel the webbing on my left hand. The tiny lump has gone. I may feel sick to my very core, but I got what I wanted.

'Now then,' Sirene says. 'Your new shield. It's a shame that Ixion is gone, but he had a cutter assistant who I daresay is capable of carrying out the bonding process . . .'

'No.'

She frowns at me. 'You appear to be letting ascendancy go to your head, Euphemie. You may not be a shield any longer, but as my child, you still owe me respect.'

'I don't mean to be disrespectful,' I say, though I do mean it. I mean it very much. 'But I don't want a shield.'

'All ascendants have shields, you silly girl!'

'Niko doesn't.'

'Yes, and it was a source of great grief for me and his mother. Everyone must play their proper role in the Hive. But at least he could never have been a queen! You, on the other hand . . . It would be a great waste of potential if you were to reject a chance at the throne.'

I want to scream at her. I want to declare my defiance as loudly and as angrily as I can. *No shield. No throne. But I will be part of the new Apex, in accordance with your latest decree. And when that happens, you can be sure that I'll see an end to Winnowings and shields alike. Our generation will be the last to suffer those things, and there will be nothing you can do about it.* But that would gain me no more than a target on my back, so I bow my head.

'I'm sorry, ma'am. But I'm sure you understand, I only want

to do what's right for the Hive.'

'That does you great credit, but—'

'I hope to gain a place in the Apex,' I go on hastily. 'But as someone who has been trained as a shield, not taught as an ascendant, I wouldn't presume to aim for the throne.'

'Euphemie—'

'*I'm not Euphemie.*'

A horrible sort of silence falls. I try to tell myself to follow the path, but I'm too furious to remember what that means. I just want Sirene to stop pretending that none of this mattered. That *Euphemie* didn't matter.

'I see,' she says finally, her voice cold. 'Perhaps you have, after all, been a shield too long. You may go.'

I stalk to the door. When I get there, I turn – and now I can't help but let a little of my anger and disgust spill out into the room.

'Euphemie was your daughter. She laughed and danced and flirted. She was angry and lonely, and sometimes terribly sad. She lived, and then she died, and I loved her.'

Sirene stands calmly, waiting for me to finish. Her beautiful, arrogant face might as well be carved from stone. But for the first time in my life, I look her straight in the eye.

'You don't get to erase her existence,' I say. 'And you don't get to erase my history. We may have been born one thing, but we became another. And whether you like it or not, my name is Feldspar.'

NINE DAYS AFTER

I suppose I could have slept in Euphemie's quarters last night. *My* quarters, as I'll have to start thinking of them. Yet after I left the audience chamber yesterday, all I wanted to do was find Niko. Once I'd told him what happened with Sirene, he brought me large quantities of food and talked in great detail about how the carders make biscuits, which I recognized as his way of trying to make everything feel normal. But nothing is normal. We might have found the murderer, but there's a far bigger problem left to solve: the Winnowings.

Ever since we woke up this morning, we've been attempting to work out how to approach them. The next one is in two days' time . . . *The day after Euphemie's party*, I think with a distant pang. Although we could do as Niko has always done and simply refuse to participate, at this point, doing nothing to stop it feels no better than taking part. And then there's the final Winnowing. That might have been postponed again, but the queens are on edge now. They could bring it forward at the slightest hint of trouble. Which means we're in a one-sided race: before the Apex realize what we're doing, we have to convince the other ascendants to change everything about the world we live in. Because it's only together that we have any hope of achieving it.

All that is a lot for someone who's only been an ascendant for a day. So when a knock comes at the door, I welcome it as a distraction from my growing panic. To my surprise, it's the chief advisor, with a bottle of kelpin in her hand and her purple-haired shield, Coquina, behind her.

'Seventh,' she says, with a smile that removes any possible sting from the title. 'May I come in?'

'I . . . Of course. Are you here for Niko?'

'No.' Her gaze touches my sling. 'I wanted to see how *you* are. You are my niece, after all. A niece I thought was lost.'

'Oh.' I gape at her, before regaining my scattered wits. Backing away, I gesture her into the room, saying quickly over my shoulder, 'Alathea is here for a visit.'

Niko puts down his pen, Astrapē swirling up his arm to hide beneath his hair. A smear of ink that wasn't there when I got up to answer the door stripes his left cheek with a dark purple shadow. I can't help smiling, knowing how it will have happened: shoving his unruly hair back from his forehead in deep concentration or fascinated discovery – with Niko, they're basically the same state anyway – and quite forgetting the exposed nib of the pen in his hand. Now I think about it, ink stains are another good reason for wearing all that black.

'Hello,' he says amiably to the chief advisor. 'Take a seat.'

Alathea looks doubtfully at the chair next to him, which appears to contain three shirts with the sleeves knotted together to make a rope. I don't know what that was about. Hastily, I move them off. Everything looks different, seen through a stranger's eyes. I've grown to like Niko's academic clutter: the books keeping his place in other books, the trails of indecipherable notes that follow in the wake of one of his random trains of thought. Yet now we have a visitor, suddenly the logic has collapsed and all I can see is mess.

'It's very kind of you to come,' I say, using my uninjured arm to shove everything on the table into a couple of semi-ordered piles. And it *is* – it *is* kind. She didn't have to acknowledge me as a relative or make the effort to visit me. Yet at the same time, Niko's exochamber feels somehow crowded with two additional people in it.

Alathea takes a seat, placing the kelpin in front of her.

'Do you have any clean cups?' she asks Niko, with a faint emphasis on the word *clean*.

'Probably not.'

I roll my eyes. 'I'll get them.'

I'm halfway back before I notice that I'm only carrying two cups. Part of me was planning to deliver them before going to stand behind Niko, as Coquina is standing behind Alathea. A lifetime of conditioning can't be fully broken in a handful of days. I have to force myself to fetch a third cup, then sit down at the table as if I belong. I confronted the whole Apex. I declared my defiance to the Younger Queen. So why does this feel so awkward?

'Here.' Alathea pours a generous measure into each cup, before handing one to Niko and another to me.

'Thank you.' I raise it to my lips, trying not to pull a face at the smell of the kelpin. I suppose, if I'm going to be an ascendant, I have to get used to the horrible stuff.

'So what will you do, my dear?' she asks, interlocking her hands around her own cup and gazing across it as if she finds me fascinating. 'Now that you're in your rightful place?'

I suppress a wince. Everyone seems to think I should be happy to be reinstated to a position I never had any reason to believe was mine – as if my bloodline matters far more than my life up to this point. Perhaps that's true, to them. And that's why it needs to change.

'It's too early to be sure,' I say diplomatically. 'There's a lot for me to get used to.'

'But you claimed a particular reward. For ascendants without shields – in other words, you and Nikolos – to be permitted to join their generation's Apex.' Her smile is both warm and knowing. 'I assume there was a purpose behind that.'

I hesitate. It would be no more sensible to tell Alathea of my plans than it would have been to tell the queens. Yet I know she's on my side. She's the one who advised Halimeda and Leandros about the secret group originally. She's the one who stood up for me against the rest of the Apex. And she agreed, yesterday, that there was no lawful reason why my requested reward shouldn't be granted. So I return her smile.

'Let's just say, we have to be able to influence the laws of the Hive if they are to evolve as we do.'

I'm quoting her words of a few days ago back to her, but she frowns. 'You're referring to the abolishment of Winnowings and shields? Surely all those who supported that idea are dead.'

'Alexios still lives,' I say. 'And—'

I stop, but she finishes for me. 'You and Nikolos.'

She doesn't seem annoyed about it. On the contrary, her frown has smoothed away, as if I've confirmed exactly what she thought.

'Clever of you,' she says. 'Though perhaps still a risky move, so soon after everything that's happened. To those who disagree with your intentions, it will be obvious who to target next.'

'But the murders didn't have anything to do with preventing the abolishment of the shield-bond, in the end. Ixion was trying to protect his daughter.'

'Of course.'

Even as she says it, my mistake hits me: I wasn't supposed to mention anything about Ixion having a daughter. I managed to hold it back all through my questioning by the Apex, yet now I've blurted it out. Though Alathea is by far the most sympathetic of the older generation, I shouldn't have done it.

Then, with the force of a blow, *her* mistake hits me. Because she just acknowledged that she knew about it. And if that's the case . . .

'More kelpin?' she offers, reaching for the bottle. The sleeve falls away from her left forearm, and I glimpse something. A mark on her skin.

Wait.

Is that—

I threw the knife. It hit the attacker's arm.

Clearly, this cut was deep. It's healing, but rather jaggedly, as if it were inexpertly stitched by someone who didn't want official medical attention. I grip the table, trying to stay calm, but I can't stop the sickening realization that's sweeping over me. *The royal brooch.* That's what didn't make sense about Ixion's story of sending a soldier to kill Euphemie. There's no reason for a random soldier to have dropped a royal brooch. But Alathea . . .

In the silence, she glances down to see what's seized my attention. Fleeting annoyance crosses her face before she shrugs and sits back.

'You . . .' I can barely get the words out. '*You* killed Euphemie.'

Niko starts coughing, but I can't look at him. My gaze is fixed on Alathea's. On those familiar eyes, the same ones that stared into mine when Niko was attacked.

'But why?' I whisper.

'It's unfortunate,' she says. 'I was so close to having the two youngest girls chosen as queens: a pair of scared, impressionable children, easy to mould and guide in the correct direction. But then you had to go and save Calista's life, before identifying Ixion as the killer! Without that, the final Winnowing would have gone ahead, Nikolos and the other unruly elements would have been eliminated, and I'd have been rid of the lot of you without having to lift another finger. As it is, you've brought this on yourself.'

My mind is spinning. If she *wanted* the final Winnowing to happen early, that means . . .

'It wasn't just Euphemie's death,' I say slowly. 'You were involved in all of it. Working with Ixion to destroy the ascendants and shields – even the nurse, Daisy—'

Her laugh is harsh. 'That one was your fault. I'd no idea Ixion's precious Clover had a friend who knew her secret until I followed you that day. Otherwise I'd have disposed of her before I started on this course. As for Ixion, he was a weakling. Unwilling to sacrifice the shields he'd trained for the sake of a greater good. But I knew his secret, and that meant I was able to convince him to help me.'

'A greater good? What good could there possibly be in murdering so many people?'

'The Winnowings are necessary,' she spits. 'And the final one most necessary of all. It separates the strong from the weak. It ensures that only the best endure. Your generation, with your obsessive focus on *fairness* – what do you know of what it takes to keep the Hive running? *Fairness* would make us all carders, grubbing deep underground to survive. No, the royal family's strength is built on blood, and has been for centuries. Yet a handful of children who barely understand the world around them think they can change that?'

I can't find the words to reply. She goes on, sneering as though my silence is no more than she expected.

'Even the best of you were infected by it. Leandros, Halimeda – I was horrified when they approached me with their plans. They were warriors, the pair of them! They could have governed the Hive as it should be governed! But they told me they didn't believe it was right to winnow the surplus population, or to raise the royal family to carry out the task, or to force others to protect them with their own lives. As if the lives of shields have ever mattered.'

'So you pretended to be on their side,' I say hoarsely. 'And you killed them.'

'The whole Apex was behind me. I can't count the times our meetings devolved into complaints about the foolish opinions of the younger generation. They just didn't have the guts to act on it themselves.' Alathea shrugs. 'So I acted for them. I forced Ixion to tell me about kratos, and to slip it into my targets' strengthening water once it was brewed. Gregor supplied me with as much red ink as I wanted, never asking what it was for. And I did the rest.'

I scrabble to think it all through. She must have known about me: Ixion's test swap. So she killed Euphemie to make me a suspect, then used a different method on the ascendants she truly wanted to be rid of so that no one would give any credence to my claim that Euphemie was poisoned. She tried to kill Niko after we visited Daisy because Ixion would no longer have any reason to keep silent about her secret if his own were uncovered. And after that . . . who knows? Maybe she knew more about the membership of the secret group than she told us. Maybe she couldn't be sure who else was in it, so she kept going after the older ascendants just in case, knowing that it would bring on the final Winnowing – a way to cut us down to size before we got too out of hand. Either way, Pyrene died, and Calista nearly did too. And for what?

'What about our laws evolving as we do?' I choke out. 'Upholding the spirit of Melissa's word, not the letter? You *supported* me yesterday!'

'Of course I did. I had to buy myself time. Once the pair of you are gone, I will return to the Apex and inform them that, in fact, your request cannot be ratified under the law.'

The pair of you. Gone. She's going to kill us. That should have been obvious since I saw the mark on her arm. I glance desperately at Niko, but he's in the grip of another coughing fit.

'As for Melissa's word,' Alathea says, 'I fought my way to becoming chief advisor with a single purpose: to read Melissa's law for myself, so I could prove it was all worth it. Losing my shield, watching my family kill each other in the final Winnowing, nearly dying myself – none of it would matter, once I studied our founder's original texts and understood the absolute necessity of our rules. Yet when I got there, do you know what I found?'

I shake my head.

'Melissa's word is *nothing*. Just the frightened thoughts of an ordinary woman who found herself leading an underground colony armed with no more than a little medical knowledge and a rare gene that allowed her to escape the infertility crisis. She was a naturalist, so she decided that for humanity to survive, everyone would have to work together for the common good in the same way that bees do. All harmony and equality, with no one's life mattering more than anyone else's.' Alathea's lip curls. 'It was only after she was gone, as the people of the Hive understood the true reality of their situation, that they began to apply some of the more useful features of bee colonies. There's no room for *thought*, in a beehive. No room for *individuality*. The queen has ultimate control, and the rest do what they must to protect her – until she's too old to produce more children, at which point they kill her. Then the young queens fight each other until only one remains alive to take over the hive.'

I shudder. Her words make bees sound like they really were as cold and cruel as the royal emblem would suggest.

'*That's* the ruthlessness we need,' Alathea adds. 'If anything, our current system is too soft. Seven ascendants allowed to survive the final Winnowing! It wouldn't matter if we strangled all the boys at birth. If we forced the girls to keep killing each other until only two were left. The *only* thing that matters is preserving enough queens to pass down the royal gift to the next generation. So you may think me evil for what I've done, but I've simply accepted the truth: individual deaths mean nothing, as long as the colony survives.'

Perhaps she's right. Perhaps all of this is necessary. But then I think of the real bee, Darwin's bee: how soft it was, how fragile its wings. *Humanity relied on them for both sustenance and beauty.* We might have turned it into a symbol of brutality, but that isn't what Melissa intended. As Darwin said, people aren't insects. We have to be guided by more than the blind will to keep our species alive.

'I always thought so too,' I say. 'Until I was given the chance to *be* an individual for the first time. If what you say is true, our laws have changed before. Why can't they again?'

'Because we'd lose far more than we gained!' I hear the echo of Euphemie's lessons in her words. 'As our resources lessen, as the balance of the Hive becomes more precarious, weakening the royal family would only lead to disaster. Already, a queen can't have as many children before she withers. That's why we have two queens now, instead of the one powerful monarch there would have been in the early days of the colony. Even the royal gift itself is not what it was.'

'Then Niko is right,' I whisper. 'The Hive is failing. Are there really no raiders?'

'Oh, people come through the tunnels sometimes,' she says dismissively. 'To steal our resources, to seek refuge, to make contact or offer trade . . . What difference does it make? They all get the same welcome: we kill them. We can't allow anyone out there to believe the Hive is open to new inhabitants. We're struggling to support our own population, let alone anyone else.' She spreads her hands. 'So, you see, we can't afford change. The strong must survive, and the weak must die. Just as it's always been.'

'And then what? We kill more and more people to keep ourselves alive, until we become so few that it's impossible to sustain the Hive anyway?' As I talk, my logic solidifies into unshakeable conviction. 'You're wrong. We *have* to change. Our current system won't work in the long term. If we're to have any hope at all, we need new ideas. Clinging to power at the expense of the future would – would make us no better than the people of the Dark Ages.'

All this time, Niko has been silent except for his fitful coughing. I've been too intent on the horror unfolding in Alathea's words, and my own defence against it, to wonder why he hasn't spoken up. Yet now he reaches for his cup only to knock it over, sending the last trickle of kelpin across the table. His other hand goes to his throat. Astrapē swirls frantically around his shoulders, changing from one form to another without ever settling.

'Feldspar,' he croaks. 'I can't breathe.'

I stand up so fast that my chair falls over. 'What have you done to him?'

'The same poison that killed Euphemie.' Alathea doesn't move. 'It's slower to act through the stomach than in the blood, but it will get there in the end. You'll see.'

She poisoned the kelpin. The very thought awakens a tickle in my throat. 'Someone will try to solve it, if you kill us.'

'Oh, I don't intend for the two of you ever to be found. They'll assume you ran away, as Nikolos always planned.'

'And what about the rest of the ascendants who support us? You can't murder everyone.'

She shrugs. 'With the two of you gone, this unnatural drive for change will collapse. Perhaps the final Winnowing will be brought forward again, but it doesn't matter either way. Calista and Ophion will always put themselves first, I can use Karissa's secret to coerce her if necessary, and Alexios . . . It would be a shame if I had to kill Alexios, but one dissenting voice should make no difference. And if he starts to cause too much trouble, I won't hesitate to be rid of him. After all, there will still be three too many ascendants to form an Apex.'

The tickle in my throat turns into a cough, and Alathea smiles. I dart a look at Niko, wishing he really could read my thoughts. *We need the antidote. The one that Alexios gave us. Where is it?*

Maybe he can, because his head tilts ever so slightly in the direction of his coat, hanging on the back of the door. Of course. Where else would it be?

I start to edge in that direction. Alathea watches me with apparent unconcern.

'The key isn't in the lock, Feldspar. Don't you think I took care of that when I came in?'

Even as she speaks, I see the twitch of her hand. I see the subtle change in her stance. And when she lunges for me, I'm in time to deflect the blow. I force her backwards until she regains her footing and brings her knife up defensively. Beside her, Coquina draws her own blade, ready to protect her charge. A shield's duty ends only with death.

'You won't last long,' Alathea snaps. 'Not after drinking a whole cup of my kelpin.'

Behind me, Niko's laugh is a weak wheeze. 'I'm willing to bet she didn't.'

'He's right,' I say, gesturing at my untouched liquor. 'I hate kelpin. Guess my upbringing means I don't have the refined tastes of an ascendant.'

Alathea glares at me. 'Then I'll tell everyone that you were the killer all along. That you poisoned Nikolos, and tried to poison me. Only your behaviour made me suspicious, so when your back was turned, I swapped the cups and avoided the poison, giving me the chance to stab you.'

'It's a fun story,' Niko gasps. 'But no one will believe it.'

She shoots him a glance. 'And why not?'

'Because if Feldspar were going to poison someone, she would *never* be so careless as to turn her back on the cups.'

I have to swallow an unexpected burst of agonized laughter. Niko is one hundred per cent correct. He's also trying to distract her so I can reach the antidote. Yet Alathea and I both know that it would be a bad idea for her to get distracted, because it would give me a chance to take out Coquina. She'd be unable to protect herself, as long as I was attacking her and not Alathea – because I'm an ascendant now, and she knows it. Her conditioning keeps me safe. Whereas if Alathea leaves Niko to die on his own and concentrates on goading me into a fight, she'll put her own life in danger, allowing Coquina to fight at her side.

Sure enough, Alathea lunges at me again. I stumble backwards, mind racing. Two against one, not to mention my useless left arm. It's hard to see how I can win. Maybe if I focus on defence rather than attack, Coquina won't get involved . . .

But every moment I prolong this fight is a moment closer to Niko's death.

I raise my knife, and immediately Coquina steps in. Tall and broad-shouldered, a fully grown adult warrior. I remember how easily Ixion and Rhyolite bested me, and a shiver runs down my spine.

'Please,' I say. 'I don't mean Alathea any harm – I only want to save Niko—'

But I know it's no use. I know it from how I felt, as little as nine days ago. What chance does Coquina have of breaking her conditioning while her charge lives?

We circle each other, searching for weaknesses. She feints, but I see the knife change hands and twist out of the way, pivoting.

'Did you know what she was doing?' I ask.

No answer.

'Did you know she was turning shields against their own charges? Shields who would have done anything to protect their ascendants, forced instead to kill them?'

No answer.

'Do you think they knew what was happening to them? Do you think they felt the agony of it, taking their charges' lives and their own against every fibre of their being—'

'Stop talking!' Abandoning caution, Coquina hurls herself at me. I catch her wrist, wrenching it aside. The tip of my blade glances off her chest and scrapes upwards, trapped between us. It must have hurt, but she doesn't so much as flinch. Locked together, we stagger back and forth, each striving to free our own knife while keeping the other's at bay.

'I knew what she was doing,' she says through gritted teeth. 'I'm her shield. She keeps no secrets from me.'

'And did you approve?'

'It's not my place to—'

'You're a person, aren't you?' I fling at her, ignoring the fact that I sounded the same, not so long ago. 'You're entitled to an opinion. Do you think what she did was right, killing so many ascendants and shields solely to ensure that more people would die in the future?'

'The Winnowings have to continue,' she says. 'It's the way things are.'

We break apart again, panting. My palm is as sweaty as the rest of me; I renew my grip on my knife. Blood stains Coquina's shirt. We circle each other again, more warily than before.

'I could understand it if you'd been her shield since birth,' I say. 'But you've only been with her since you were both eighteen. You didn't grow up believing your life was hers.'

'No,' she agrees. 'Soldiers aren't conditioned to devote themselves to one ascendant, but to *all* of them. The entire royal family. My life had no other purpose than to serve their will. But Alathea chose me. She raised me out of the ranks to become something more. I would never disobey her.'

'Despite the fact that her actions led to all those royal deaths?'

'Maybe I didn't like it.' Coquina's voice is fierce and low; her eyes are sad. 'But I can't let you hurt her.'

'I know. I was a shield for seventeen years, until your charge killed mine. But the way things are doesn't have to stay the same.'

'Yes. It does. Or what does that make me?'

On the last word, she lunges again. Though I dodge the blow, this time she follows me round, aiming for my unprotected left side. I try to block her jab, but I'm not used to the sling on my arm, and her blade scores down from shoulder to elbow.

'It makes you someone who was used as a tool, like I was,' I gasp, through the stinging pain. 'And if you let me and Niko die, many more people will go through the same. You heard what she said. *As if the lives of shields have ever mattered*.'

For an instant, she falters – and I move in, fast, feinting high before driving the knife low. She tries to block my blade, but too late. It slides into her belly and she staggers back, then drops to her knees, eyes wide.

'Coquina!' Alathea pushes past me, letting her own knife fall as she crouches beside the other woman, hands desperately trying to stem the tide of blood. It's clear that what she said never applied to her own shield. Not at all. 'You're going to be fine – Coquina, please—'

'I'm sorry,' her shield mumbles. Then her head drops, and her body goes limp. And I, bracing myself to commit what in any other situation would seem an entirely shameful action, step up behind the grieving chief advisor and hit her over the head with one of Niko's bookmark rocks.

'Niko!' As Alathea slumps over Coquina's body, I'm already running to the coat and rummaging through the pockets. 'Niko, tell me you're alive . . .'

He doesn't answer, but I hear a faint rattle. Hands shaking, I keep searching, cursing the sheer number of pockets and the even greater number of random objects he's crammed into them, until finally my hand closes around the second glass tube that Alexios gave us. The antidote to aroura: the poison that killed Euphemie, and that's now almost killed Niko twice. I stumble to his side and, without much finesse, wrench his head back so that I can pour the liquid down his throat. He coughs and splutters, but gradually the blue tinge fades from his lips and his eyes focus on my face.

'Feldspar . . .'

Trembling all over, I sink down on the floor next to his chair and, for the second time in my life, burst into tears.

BEGINNING

TEN DAYS AFTER

I stand in the doorway of the chambers I used to share with Euphemie, trying to make myself step inside. More than seven days have passed since she died, which means this space is no longer off limits. Not only that, but now I've been confirmed as the Seventh, it officially belongs to me. Once I take one step, I'll be able to take another. But I can't seem to move.

'It looks exactly the same,' I murmur. Which is a silly thing to say, because of course it does. No one's been in here since her death. But it's so *real*. Her paints are still scattered over the table. Her scarves are still draped across the furniture. If I walk into the room, it will be like stepping back in time. And I'd do it, if I could bring her back. But I can't.

'Objects are cruel,' Niko says behind me. 'They don't have the decency to change when someone dies. They lie in wait, ready to make your throat ache with memories.' He ducks under my arm, walking backwards into the exochamber with hands outstretched, Astrapē a salamander curled round his wrist. 'But at least you don't have to do it alone.'

I take his hands, let him draw me into the room. And it does help, him being here – because he was never here before. There's no way I can fool myself into believing that Euphemie is in the bedchamber, that at any moment she'll walk in and ask me what I think of her new hairstyle. If Euphemie were here, Niko wouldn't be. Yet at the same time, I feel like a thief. In every possible respect, I have stolen her life.

'You know,' Niko says diffidently, 'you don't have to move in here straight away, if you're not ready.'

'I'm not going back to sleeping in a jail cell.'

'That's not what I meant . . . You could keep staying with me, for a while.'

Intense relief floods me, prickling in all my limbs. Until now, I hadn't realized quite how much I was dreading this.

'Thank you,' I say. 'I'd prefer that. If you're sure you don't mind.'

'To be honest, at this point I'd kind of miss you if you weren't there.'

He's still holding my hands. Astrapē creeps down his arm and up mine, on to my shoulder. She's in the form of a bee – a proper bee, fluffy and winged, like the one we saw in the Honeycomb – and her feet on my skin feel like the taste of the air before a storm.

'Niko,' I whisper. 'How—'

'She'd miss you too.' He gives me a smile that's as bright and clear as music. 'Is there anything you want to take with you?'

I move quickly from room to room, packing up my clothes and a few other bits. They fill a single small bag. By the time I've finished, I'm weighed down by a hard lump of guilt: as if I'm erasing every trace of myself and leaving Euphemie behind, alone, to gather dust. It would have been her party today. She intended to wear her blue dress with the embroidery around the hem . . .

My breath catches. I linger by her dressing table, running my fingers over the pots and tubes, snagging on the single long hair that's tangled in her brush. Then I look up, risking a glimpse in the mirror; but the only reflection in the glass is my own.

I touch the fuzz of hair on my scalp. It's been a few days since I last shaved, despite Niko's continued offering of the razor. I don't think I'll do it again. As everyone knows by now, I'm not a shield any more. But nor will I let it grow long, as Euphemie did – because despite my new status, I'm not really an ascendant either, and that's fine. Perhaps it's time to stop defining myself as a role, and start defining myself as a person.

Swallowing hard, I leave the bedroom.

'I have everything I need,' I say. 'Let's go.'

*

Breathing cold, unfiltered air fresh off the ocean is the best sensation I've ever felt. I pace back and forth at the threshold of the winnowing gate, sucking the wild, salty breeze as deep into my lungs as it will go, until it feels like I'm bursting. This is it. Either I'm about to change the Hive forever, or I'm going to learn exactly where the limits of possibility lie.

'Do you think any of them will come?' I ask Niko.

'I don't know. But it won't help if you drown.'

I stop pacing long enough to cast a glance down into the churning waters. High tide. He's right: if I slipped and fell into the ocean now, I wouldn't stand any chance of survival.

It feels strange to be here without all the blood and screaming. Euphemie would never have thought to come here voluntarily, despite the fresh air and the accessible sky; this place was the subject of too many of her nightmares for that. But today, it seemed . . . well. Niko said *thematically appropriate*, and I wasn't going to argue with him.

'I heard Alathea is going to be executed,' he says.

I wince.

'She's responsible for six murders, if you include Ixion,' Niko goes on. 'Some of which had more than one victim: ascendant *and* shield. Don't you think she deserves to die?'

'Seven,' I correct him dully. 'Seven murders. I might have killed Coquina, but Alathea is the one who murdered her. And yes, but . . .'

'But what?'

'But I don't see how yet another death helps anyone. We're trying to *reduce* the amount of murder. Isn't that why we're here today?'

'Yes. You're right. But all the same, could you ever really forgive her for what she did? She killed Euphemie.'

'No,' I whisper. 'I can't forgive her.'

Wrapping my arms around myself, I keep pacing. Before Euphemie died, everything seemed so simple. My life consisted of doing as I was told, acting as I'd been raised since birth to act, and thinking the thoughts I'd been trained to think. It's only now that I realize how complicated life is, and how difficult it is to ever make the right decisions. Maybe that's the price of freedom.

'Feldspar,' Niko says softly.

I look up. The other ascendants and their shields have arrived – all of those we spoke to during our investigation. I expected Alexios, since he's the only surviving member of the secret group, and Zephrine, because she likes to keep up with what's happening. Karissa seemed likely too, given that we know her secret. But I hadn't expected Ophion to show up, and certainly not—

'Well?' When she catches me looking at her, Calista's lip curls. 'What's this about?'

'The final Winnowing,' I say.

'There are twelve of us left,' Niko adds. 'Once the youngest comes of age, or maybe before, we'll be required to reduce that to the seven needed to form an Apex. Five of us will be winnowed.'

'But not driven out of the Hive, as we do to the cutters and carders,' I finish. 'They expect us to *murder* each other, right here, and give the bodies to the sea.'

The silence is uneasy. None of them seem to know where to look. I wonder how many of them are thinking, as I am, about the Winnowings they've taken part in before. Do they feel it serves them right to face the same fate to which they've condemned countless other people? Or are they outraged, having for so long believed themselves special among the inhabitants of the Hive?

'If that's true,' Ophion says finally, 'what are we supposed to do about it?'

'Refuse.' It comes out more fiercely than I intended. 'Not just the final Winnowing, but *all* Winnowings. You don't have to do their dirty work any more.'

'What's the point? If we don't do it, the soldiers will.'

'Only until the new queens are chosen,' Niko points out. 'After that, if we all agree, then it doesn't matter who the heirs are. We can put an end to winnowing for good.'

'There's one scheduled for tomorrow,' I say. 'If none of us take part, there'll be nothing the current queens can do about it.'

'Except disqualify us all from roles in the new Apex,' Ophion shoots back.

'But other than Zephrine, there are only five ascendants left to come of age, and four of them are male. That's not enough to provide both our current queens with heirs, let alone form an Apex. At least one of us here, now, will be a queen. They *need* us. That gives us the power to change things.'

'But we'd all have to agree,' Niko concludes. 'Finish what Halimeda and Leandros and Pyrene started, and work together to achieve it. Get the younger ones on our side as well, and we'll be unstoppable.'

No one replies straight away – but then, I didn't expect them to. I scan each face in turn, trying to work out what they'll say. A lot depends on this. My future and Niko's. The royal family's. The entire Hive's.

Then Calista says, 'I'm in.'

I pivot to face her so fast, it feels like I strained a muscle. I'm sure the expression on my face must be ridiculous. But of all the people who might have agreed to the plan, I never thought she'd be first. And we need her – there's no doubt about that. If she didn't join us, she'd be the obvious choice for the next Elder Queen: ready to wipe out all the most trouble-some ascendants in the final Winnowing and perpetuate the system as it is now.

'Halimeda and Pyrene tried to convince me,' she says. 'They wanted me to be part of a plan like this. But I refused. And thanks to Alathea, they will never have the chance to see it happen. Thanks to Alathea, I no longer have any credible rival.' Her gaze locks with mine, daring me to comment. 'There's no honour in that. No honour in killing any of you in order to take the throne. Knowing what the Apex have always intended for us, I will no longer fight for them.'

She dips her head briefly to me, and I understand: she's discharged the debt she owes me. Now she can go back to hating me – a condition that isn't nearly as daunting as it sounds. Because as far as I can tell, Calista's main way of caring about people is to hate them.

'I agree,' Zephrine says. 'Because now I understand why we have shields. I would have refused the group too, if they'd asked me before all this. But that was because I didn't realize . . .' She directs an apologetic smile at Marl. 'Ascendants are given shields because of the final Winnowing. That's the only reason, really. To make sure we have a chance to survive even if we're younger. But how is that fair on them? Niko said it puts us in a more equal position at the expense of their lives, and I think he's right.'

'I'll happily refuse the Winnowings,' Karissa agrees, her face fiery with embarrassment. 'I've only ever wanted to stay quiet and keep out of the way, so this suits me just fine.'

She tilts her head to rest against Quartz's shoulder, and Quartz mirrors the gesture. They're standing next to Alexios and Flint, and I notice that Quartz's hand is locked tightly in Flint's. Maybe those two have a chance to be happy now. Maybe, as part of what could be the last ever group of shields, they *can* have room in their lives for something other than their charges.

Alexios may be thinking something similar; he certainly gives Flint a contented glance before turning to us. 'I'm in too. I've no interest in murder. You all know that already.'

By now, several people are looking at Ophion, who in turn is very deliberately not looking at anyone at all.

'Ophi,' Niko murmurs, and the Fifth shrugs.

'Fine. I won't do it – the final Winnowing or any of the rest. It's not as if it would be worth my while to kill any of you anyway.'

Gabbro gives him the gentlest of nudges. That's all – the shield doesn't say anything, at least that I can hear – but Ophion flushes.

'To be honest, I've never liked it,' he mumbles. 'The way we cast people out and kill anyone who won't go quietly. It would be a relief not to have to do it any more.'

'Well, then,' Alexios says, grinning round at everyone. 'Sounds like that's settled. No more Winnowings. Now, who wants to come back to my chambers for drinks?'

Once the others are out of earshot, Niko releases a long breath. 'Well.'

'Well,' I echo.

We look at each other. I should be happy, I know that, and yet the future is still a daunting prospect.

'You've achieved a lot in the past ten days,' he says, as able as ever to tell what I'm thinking.

'I suppose so.'

'But?'

'But there's so much more that needs improving! The carders' lives, for a start. The cutters' too. Everyone in the Hive—'

'Feldspar,' he says. 'I get it. But you can't solve *all* the world's problems in less than a fortnight. Give yourself some credit.'

His dark eyes shine with an affectionate pride that makes the heat rise in my cheeks, but I don't look away. Once, Niko struck me as sinister and aloof: a boy constructed entirely from the stuff of nightmares. Yet now, somehow, just seeing his face makes the future far less daunting and happiness much less remote.

'Do you think it will work?' I ask him.

'I hope so. If not, there's always the tunnels.' He turns to gaze out across the ocean, where the tips of the jagged rocks are beginning to appear above the surface as the tide recedes. Very quietly, as if he isn't sure whether he's speaking to me or himself, he adds, 'And with or without the tunnels, there's always us.'

The words awaken a sensation in my stomach that's become increasingly familiar since I met him: something that's not fear and not excitement, but not dissimilar to either. It isn't something I felt, or *allowed* myself to feel, when Euphemie was

374

alive. I can't tell exactly what it means or where it leads. But, after a moment, I step closer to him and tuck my hand into his.

'There's always us,' I agree.

Niko glances at me. The hint of a smile touches his lips. When I go to release him, his fingers grip mine tighter.

Together, we stand at the winnowing gate. The gulls wheel and cry overhead. And a ray of soft sunlight breaks through the clouds, just for an instant, to touch our faces.

ACKNOWLEDGEMENTS

There are so many people involved in seeing a book through from conception to final physical form, all of whom deserve recognition, that I really think we should start including movie-style credits at the ends of books. As it is, I suspect that the short list below is almost certain to be missing someone. (If that's you, I'm really sorry.)

Let's start with the true heroes of publishing, without whom every book would be a hundred times poorer: the editorial team. (And no, I'm not just saying that because I work as an editor myself.) Endless thanks go to Rachel Leyshon, the greatest developmental editor of all time, who helped me shape the world of the Hive into something much better and more cohesive, whilst always preserving the story's heart. (I'd mention the *Hot Fuzz* jokes, but they probably wouldn't make sense to anyone but the two of us.) To Laura Myers, whose attention to detail carried the book from manuscript to beautiful finished state, and who didn't mind too much that I dug my fingernails into the dark arts and refused to let go. To Veronica Lyons, copy-editor extraordinaire, who not only made a ton of helpful suggestions but also gave me the loveliest feedback. (Vron, I know you didn't copy-edit these acknowledgements, so apologies if I've been ungrammatical anywhere.) And to proofreader Sara Magness, who knew all those tricky things like where, exactly, the hyphen goes if you are breaking a word across two lines.

Many thanks also to Barry Cunningham, Rachel Hickman, Elinor Bagenal, Jazz Bartlett Love, Ruth Hoey, Emily Groom-Collis and everyone else at Chicken House, for everything you've done to champion *The Hive* in various ways . . . and, in Barry's case, for being wonderfully welcoming on our initial video call, even though I'd had about two hours of nervous sleep and probably made no sense at all.

Of course, that video call would never have happened without Lydia Silver, my fabulous agent at Darley Anderson Children's, who first saw potential in *The Hive* when it was called something completely different. Thank you, Lydia, for taking a chance on me.

A special and glorious acknowledgement goes to Micaela Alcaino, who created the beautiful cover. Seriously, all of Micaela's covers are the most gorgeous things I've ever seen. If you want the best-looking bookshelf in the known universe, make a TBR list consisting solely of books with her designs wrapped around them.

And finally, as always, my thanks to you for reading.